# *ROMANTIC TIMES* RAVES ABOUT *NEW YORK TIMES* BESTSELLING AUTHOR CONNIE MASON!

### *A PROMISE OF THUNDER*
"Once you pick up *A Promise of Thunder*
you won't want to put it down!"

### *THE OUTLAWS: RAFE*
"Ms. Mason begins this new trilogy with wonderful
characters . . . steamy romance . . . excellent dialogue . . .
[and an] exciting plot!"

### *THE OUTLAWS: JESS*
"*Jess* . . . is a delight. Typical of Ms. Mason's style, *Jess* is
filled with adventure and passion. Ms. Mason delivers."

### *THE BLACK KNIGHT*
"Ms. Mason has written a rich medieval romance filled
with tournaments, chivalry, lust and love."

### *GUNSLINGER*
"Ms. Mason has created memorable characters and a plot
that made this reader rush to turn the pages .... 
*Gunslinger* is an enduring story."

# MORE *ROMANTIC TIMES* PRAISE
# FOR CONNIE MASON!

### *PIRATE*
"Ms. Mason has written interesting characters into a twisting plot filled with humor and pathos. If you enjoy pirates and romance, you'll enjoy *Pirate*."

### *BEYOND THE HORIZON*
"Connie Mason at her best! She draws readers into this fast-paced, tender and emotional historical romance that proves that love really does conquer all!"

### *BRAVE LAND, BRAVE LOVE*
"*Brave Land, Brave Love* is an utter delight from first page to last—funny, tender, adventurous, and highly romantic!"

### *WILD LAND, WILD LOVE*
"Connie Mason has done it again!"

### *BOLD LAND, BOLD LOVE*
"A lovely romance and a fine historical!"

# A PROMISE OF THUNDER

"I want to kiss you until your lips are swollen from my kisses and your knees grow weak." Adroitly Storm stepped out of Thunder's reach, fearing his next words. "I want to make love to you, Storm Kennedy."

Storm's mouth gaped open, unable to give voice to all the despicable names she wanted to call him. Swallowing convulsively, she managed to say, "Get—get out of here! How dare you say such terrible things to me."

"Among the Lakota it isn't terrible to want a woman. It is right and natural. You are a widow, not unaccustomed to a man's desires. And you want me, I can tell."

"You can tell no such thing! That's evil."

Thunder laughed as if sincerely amused. "We'll see, Storm Kennedy, we'll see. Just remember, lady, one day Thunder and Storm will come together in a brilliant display of passion. The confrontation should prove a spectacular one."

Other *Leisure* and *Love Spell* books by Connie Mason:
THE OUTLAWS: JESS
THE OUTLAWS: RAFE
THE BLACK KNIGHT
GUNSLINGER
BEYOND THE HORIZON
PIRATE
BRAVE LAND, BRAVE LOVE
WILD LAND, WILD LOVE
BOLD LAND, BOLD LOVE
VIKING!
SURRENDER TO THE FURY
FOR HONOR'S SAKE
LORD OF THE NIGHT
TEMPT THE DEVIL
PROMISE ME FOREVER
SHEIK
ICE & RAPTURE
LOVE ME WITH FURY
SHADOW WALKER
FLAME
TENDER FURY
DESERT ECSTASY
PURE TEMPATION
WIND RIDER
TEARS LIKE RAIN
THE LION'S BRIDE
SIERRA
TREASURES OF THE HEART
CARESS & CONQUER
PROMISED SPLENDOR
WILD IS MY HEART
MY LADY VIXEN

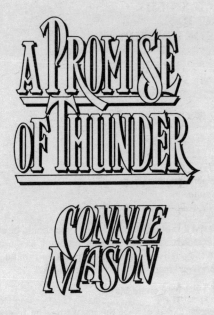

# A PROMISE OF THUNDER

## CONNIE MASON

**LEISURE BOOKS**     **NEW YORK CITY**

A LEISURE BOOK®

April 2001

Published by

Dorchester Publishing Co., Inc.
276 Fifth Avenue
New York, NY 10001

If you purchased this book without a cover you should be aware that this book is stolen property. It was reported as "unsold and destroyed" to the publisher and neither the author nor the publisher has received any payment for this "stripped book."

Copyright © 1993 by Connie Mason

All rights reserved. No part of this book may be reproduced or transmitted in any form or by any electronic or mechanical means, including photocopying, recording or by any information storage and retrieval system, without the written permission of the publisher, except where permitted by law.

ISBN 0-8439-4860-4

The name "Leisure Books" and the stylized "L" with design are trademarks of Dorchester Publishing Co., Inc.

Printed in the United States of America.

Visit us on the web at www.dorchesterpub.com.

*To Alicia Condon and her new daughter Zoe*

# *Prologue*

The People called him Thunder because of the
restless fury trapped in his tormented soul.
His family had named him Grady. Grady
Farrell Stryker, son of Shannon Branigan and
half-breed Swift Blade Stryker. He was three-
quarters white; yet except for the pure deep
blue of his eyes he looked all Indian. His father
was the son of a princess of the mighty Lakota
Nation. His grandmother was daughter to a
chief.

He stood tall and proud on a high bluff, his
magnificent body silhouetted against the stark
beauty of the territory called the Black Hills. A
violent storm raged around him, illuminating
the sky with an awesome display of nature's
most powerful destructive force. Rain lashed
his massive sun-bronzed body, ill protected

against the elements in brief breechclout and moccasins. But Thunder neither noticed nor responded to the biting sting of pelting rain.

His arms were raised in open defiance, challenging the heavens, defying death, daring Wakantanka, the Grandfather Spirit, to shoot a lightning bolt through his tormented heart. He feared nothing, called no man master.

Grady Farrell Stryker had been an idealistic young man before he fled from his home near Cheyenne, Wyoming. But heartsick and bitter over the tragic death of his young wife, Summer Sky, he had joined his father's tribe looking for revenge. There, among the People, he had gained maturity and strength, if not peace of mind. He had participated in the sacred Sun Dance and had the scars on his chest to prove it. He had ridden with renegades and taken the lives of men like those who were responsible for Summer Sky's death.

Most White Eyes called him "Renegade," but the People thought him brave and majestic. He was despised by the whites for the havoc he wrought in their lives. He knew no peace; he knew only the thunder of discontent in his heart. He worshiped no White God but rather the Earth, the Sun, the Sky, the Moon, and the elements that provided him sustenance. He believed in the Grandfather Spirit because He was the mighty provider who nourished the People.

A wild cry of protest and outrage flew past Thunder's mouth as he raged against the whites who stole Indian reservation land and opened it up to settlers despite treaties. The People were forced to exist on smaller and smaller tracts of inferior land where food was scarce or nonexistent. Food promised by Indian agents never arrived, and Thunder had stolen many a shipment of beeves and grain destined for white consumption to give to the People.

Jagged streaks of lightning struck the ground around him, but Thunder neither flinched nor moved, standing as if carved in granite. His face was set in stone, his tawny muscles sculpted from sturdy oak. Yet he survived the storm to live another day, though it mattered little to him if Wakantanka called him to join his ancestors.

"Why, Grandfather?" he called out in a mighty roar that rivaled the very name he was given. "Why have you spared me? Of what use am I to the People? Little by little our culture is dying and the People scatter like leaves before the wind. The day of the mighty Lakota is long past."

Suddenly the heavens parted and a glimmer of sun shone through the dark clouds. And for the first time in all the years since he had joined the People, Grandfather spoke to him.

"Go forth, Thunder, your destiny lies not with the People. The time has come to seek the future for which you were destined. You have learned and prospered, but your greatest challenge lies in another direction."

"You would have me leave, Grandfather? What of my son, Summer Sky's child?"

"Little Buffalo will be safe with the People until you return for him."

"Why must I leave, Grandfather? My spirit will not rest until I have avenged Summer Sky's death."

"Riding with renegades brings no honor to your name, Thunder. There is no peace in your heart; it craves vengeance and thrives on violence."

"How will I find peace, Grandfather?"

"The peace you seek will come with the Storm. Until you meet and conquer the Storm your spirit will know no rest. Always remember that Thunder is the harbinger of Storm, but Thunder can only exist in the bosom of Storm's soul."

Puzzled, Thunder mulled over Grandfather's words, awed by the wisdom that went beyond mortal comprehension.

"Grandfather, I do not understand."

The heavens were silent; Wakantanka spoke no more.

# *Chapter One*

*Guthrie, Oklahoma*
*September 12, 1893*

Grady Stryker viewed the territorial capital of Oklahoma with a jaundiced eye. He had arrived the day before purely out of curiosity, and now he pushed and shoved his way through the crowded streets and wondered what in the hell he was doing in Guthrie four days before the biggest land rush in the country's history. He'd heard that six million acres had been purchased from the Cherokee tribes and that 100,000 people were expected in Guthrie to participate in the run. If the crowded streets were any indication, Grady suspected most of those 100,000 souls were already in town.

Pausing a moment to get his bearings, Grady was jostled from behind as someone plowed into his broad back. Gaining his balance, he turned to scowl at the man. It took only one look at Grady's dark visage to make the man turn and flee. Grady gazed after him, a lopsided grin hanging on one corner of his mouth. He wondered what the man would have done if he'd seen him six months earlier, wearing only breechclout and moccasins, his muscles rippling beneath his smooth, sun-bronzed skin.

In deference to civilization, he was wearing buckskin trousers now, made especially for him by Laughing Brook, and a butter-soft shirt of the same material. But he stubbornly clung to the moccasins and adamantly refused to cut his shoulder-length hair, which he wore tied back with a leather thong. His features were proud and intrepid, his Indian ancestry evident in the bold slash of his cheekbones, finely chiseled nose, and sun-bronzed skin. Only the deep blue of his eyes, inherited from Shannon, his Irish-American mother, marked him as having white blood.

There was no denying that Grady Farrell Stryker was handsome, as handsome as his father, Swift Blade. And dangerous. There was a dark, brooding sensuality about him that most women found irresistible. As for his heart, Grady had none. From the moment his pregnant wife, Summer Sky, had been killed by irresponsible white men looking for a good time, he had erected a shell of bitterness around

himself and disavowed his white heritage. Then
he had fled to the People with his small son,
where Jumping Buffalo, Summer Sky's father,
had welcomed him. From that day until the day
on the mountaintop when Grandfather spoke
to him, advising him to leave the reservation,
he had been known as Thunder, most feared
of all the renegades roaming the plains.

Snorting in disgust, Grady wondered again
what he was doing in Guthrie. It wasn't as if
he intended to take part in the rush for land.
Had he wanted land he could have gotten it
from his own father, who owned countless
acres in Wyoming. Thinking about his family
gave Grady an empty feeling in the pit of his
stomach. He hadn't seen his father or mother in over three years and assumed that they
had heard of his lawless existence by now and
disowned him. Until the day Summer Sky was
killed he had been a most dutiful son.

He had been but twenty-two years old that
fateful day and had grown up instantly as he
held his dying wife in his arms. Before then
his life had been idyllic, with nothing to over-
tax him but the changes in the weather. He had
married his childhood playmate at age nineteen
and by twenty-two had one child with another
on the way. He knew no hardships, encountered no difficulties, faced no challenges. Until
his wife had been taken from him in a single
act of violence.

Grady ambled down the street, his mind a
thousand miles away, to a place where only

happiness existed. Fortunately he had grown older and wiser since then and had learned that happiness was only a myth. Distracted by his thoughts but ever aware and watchful for potential danger, his attention was captured by an errant ray of sunlight as it caught a reflection and sent it back to him, nearly blinding him.

If it wasn't such a clear, sunny day, Grady would have sworn a flash of lightning had descended from the sky. But there wasn't a storm cloud in sight. When his vision cleared he saw that the brilliant light was the result of sunshine reflecting off a woman's long shiny hair. And what hair it was! The color of molten gold, it cascaded down her shoulders to her waist, hampered only by a length of ribbon to keep it from flying around her face. He couldn't see her features, for her back was turned as she peered down the street as if waiting for someone, but instinctively Grady knew she would be beautiful.

He watched her, arrested, unable to turn away from the spectacle of her glorious mane of hair, brushing her waist in so provocative a manner. Grady's own mother's hair was a deep, rich chestnut, but somehow this particular shade of blond was much more titillating. Suddenly the woman turned, and Grady saw that the rest of her was just as enticing as he supposed. He hadn't looked at another woman with desire since Summer Sky had been taken from him. His brief encounters with the opposite sex had taken place merely to appease his healthy body and lustful urges, usually with widows of the tribe who made themselves available to unmarried males.

Storm Kennedy tapped her foot impatiently. Where was Buddy? she wondered as she peered anxiously down the street for the wagon they had driven all the way from Missouri. Married less than a month, Storm and Buddy had decided to take advantage of the free land offered by the government. They had left their home in Missouri to take part in the land run in Oklahoma the moment they learned the Cherokee Strip had been opened to settlement. It seemed the only way they would ever be able to own land, and since neither were fainthearted, they had bid their families good-bye, pulled up stakes, and set out for Guthrie. They had arrived just this morning, and Buddy was out now trying to find them a place to sleep until the actual day of the land rush. While she was waiting, Storm had mailed a letter to their parents, informing them that they had arrived safely.

Jostled by passersby, Storm found it increasingly difficult to maintain her stance at the edge of the wooden sidewalk. The sun was hot and she had forgotten her bonnet in the back of the wagon. Even now she could feel the heat penetrating the thick strands of her hair and beads of sweat collecting on her neck and dampening her collar.

Suddenly she felt a prickling sensation at her nape and her flesh tingled, warning her of danger. Her warm sherry eyes narrowed as she raised them to seek out the cause of her distress. She saw nothing but people. People everywhere, coming, going, milling in front of stores and queuing in long lines at the train station to purchase tickets to take them to the Cherokee Outlet.

Then she saw him.

He was staring at her, his stark face intense with concentration. His midnight black hair hung beneath his shabby broad-brimmed hat to brush his massive shoulders, clubbed at the back with a leather thong. His dusty buckskins molded to the thick muscles of his torso and thighs. Instead of boots his feet were encased in comfortable moccasins. He wore his gun low on his narrow hips, tied down at the thigh in the manner of gunslingers. A wicked-looking knife was tucked into his belt. Storm thought she had never seen a more dangerous-looking man. At first his inscrutable expression and torrid scrutiny frightened her, then it made her mad. Obviously he was an Indian. Or even worse, a half-breed. One of those despicable men scorned by both cultures.

She returned his look, lifting her stubborn little chin at a defiant angle. She held his blistering gaze for all of five seconds before dragging her eyes away and deliberately turning her head in another direction. How dare the brazen creature stare at her in such a bold manner! she fumed in impotent rage. She was a married woman, for heaven's sake. She had loved Buddy since they were both five years old.

Grady was so amused by the frosty blonde's efforts to ignore him that he allowed the tiniest of grins to soften his hard features. Briefly he wondered who she was and what she was doing in Guthrie. But his rapt attention diminished when he recalled that the woman was white, and her scathing perusal made it perfectly clear that she felt nothing but contempt for him. Which was fine with him. He had no use for whites, male or female. He had abandoned his mother's people when he left Peaceful Valley to seek a life among the renegade tribes of the once mighty Lakota, called Sioux by the White Eyes.

Grady shrugged off the unaccountable need to bound across the street and confront the woman and continued on his way. Remaining in Guthrie held little appeal for him, and he decided to retrieve his horse from the livery and be on his way. He wasn't exactly unknown in these parts, due mostly to his association with renegades and later as a gunman spoiling for a fight. No matter what town he had drifted to since he left the reservation months ago, he had managed to cause enough trouble to earn him the title of "Renegade."

His reputation usually preceded him, and there were always men anxious to challenge him in those nameless towns along the Western Frontier. In the past six months he had drawn against more men than he could count on his two hands. Though he had rarely been the challenger, he was never reluctant to practice his amazing skills with a gun. Many of those men ended up dead by his hand, and more often than not the sheriff had escorted him out of town. Since he hadn't been the one to offer the challenge, he had never been arrested, but Grady knew that one day his luck would change. Either he'd fail to outdraw his opponent and end up pushing up daisies in Boot Hill or find himself behind bars. Either way made little difference to him. His life had become a succession of violent acts for which his soul was forever damned. He didn't even have the courage to go back home, despite the fact that his parents would probably forgive him if he mended his ways.

Violence begets violence. Hadn't those words been drummed into him as a child? Now it was too late to change his ways; too late for Summer Sky, whose life had been taken when she had had so much to live for. It would take a miracle to make him whole again, Grady decided as he hastened his steps toward the livery. His son, Little Buffalo, would be better off without him. Laughing Brook, Summer Sky's younger sister, loved Little Buffalo dearly and would see to his raising. As for him, Grady wished that Grandfather hadn't advised him to leave the People. His own restless spirit demanded satisfaction for the brutal death of Summer Sky, and even though he hadn't yet reached his twenty-sixth year he felt his life's cycle drawing to an end.

A miracle, that's what he needed.

Grady knew miracles didn't exist.

Suddenly, without warning, Grady's keen perception sensed danger. He could smell it. Grady tensed, his hand hovering inches above his gun, every muscle in his body taut; his years of living precariously had taught him self-preservation and survival of the fittest. Every one of his instincts were intact when he sensed someone stalking him, someone whose revolver was already clearing his holster. Fortunately Grady was accustomed to performing at a disadvantage and had learned to work with it in ways that only Indians could comprehend.

"Draw, Renegade! You killed my brother in Dodge City and now you're gonna pay."

The roar of thunder sounded in his ears. The People had named him well. In that instant Grady Stryker ceased to exist and Thunder was reborn, swift, keen, perceptive—deadly.

Sensing trouble, people on the streets scattered like leaves before the wind. Women screamed, clutching their children as they hustled them out of harm's way, and men, placing themselves behind protection, watched with perverse fascination as the two men prepared to outdraw one another.

Across the street, Storm Kennedy noticed nothing but Buddy approaching in the wagon.

Expelling a sigh of relief, she stepped out into the street. Buddy stopped the wagon beside her, preparing to jump down and boost Storm into the seat beside him.

"I found us a place to stay!" Buddy shouted, excited that he had obtained lodging in a city so obviously overcrowded. "We can sleep in a real bed tonight. Mrs. Luke over at the boarding house just threw out a guest because he couldn't pay, so she let us have his room. I knew luck was with us."

"How wonderful," Storm cried. Buddy's boyish enthusiasm for this venture had fired her own, and she was as eager as he to claim their 160 acres of land and become landowners.

Grady knew the odds were against him, but giving up wasn't his style. He'd faced tougher competition than this during the past months. If he'd killed the man's brother, it was because the brother had recklessly challenged him. He recalled that day in Dodge City, even remembered what the brother looked like. And as had happened so many times in the past, that face took on the characteristics of the men who had killed Summer Sky. The man had accused him of cheating at cards, drew, and lost. Grady felt no remorse over the death of another nameless white drifter.

Gathering his wits, Grady turned and dropped to one knee, at the same time drawing and aiming. He knew from the sound of his voice exactly where the man stood—it was an uncanny ability, knowing where the enemy was—and fired off a shot, all in the space of a heartbeat. The man squeezed the trigger an instant later. Already wounded by Grady's bullet, his arm flew up and the shot went wild. It found its mark in the body of Buddy Kennedy.

A high-pitched screech was the first indication to Grady that something was amiss, something that had nothing to do with the man lying wounded in the dusty street. Once the danger was past, people began streaming into the open, seeming to converge on one place. Before the crowd cut off his view, Grady had a brief glimpse of a golden head bent over a still figure lying in the street beside a wagon.

Noting that his friends were already helping the wounded gunman to his feet, Grady gave him no more than a passing glance, holstered his gun, and rose to his full six feet three inches. He had no idea what dire mishap had taken place across the street, but something compelled him to investigate. Stretching his long legs, he strode briskly across the teeming thoroughfare and plowed into the crowd milling around the two figures who appeared to be the center of attention. When people saw who it was they opened up a path for him, allowing Grady a clear view of the scene.

A young man, younger even than Grady, lay stretched out on the ground. He was so white Grady knew instinctively that he was dead. Blood seeped from a neat round hole in his head, staining the ground beneath him. The blond beauty Grady had noticed earlier was bent over him, her shoulders shaking uncontrollably, her heartrending sobs piercing the air.

Shock and disbelief nearly paralyzed Storm. One minute she was talking to Buddy and the next he lay dead on the ground. Even in her grief she didn't need a doctor to tell her that her childhood friend and companion was dead. It was all so senseless, so utterly wrong, that Buddy should die because two vicious men carried their grudge into the streets where innocent passersby could be hurt. Why Buddy? she raged in silent protest. He had so much to live for—so much enthusiasm for life and this new venture they had undertaken.

She felt a hand on her shoulder, burning through the material of her dress. Turning her head, she peered at Grady through eyes misty with tears—and the breath slammed out of her chest. It was *him*! The half-breed Indian who was the cause of Buddy's death. Her warm sherry eyes turned glacial, her face hardened, and she deliberately shrugged off his hand where it gripped her shoulder.

"You!" The word exploded from her mouth like a vile curse. "Murderer!"

For a moment Grady looked stunned. Then his face cleared as he realized what had happened. He had heard the other gunman fire his weapon, but had given it little thought since the bullet had gone astray. It appeared now that the bullet had struck down an innocent bystander—the woman's brother? husband?

"I'm sorry," Grady muttered. He had difficulty working his tongue around the words. Apologizing was something he rarely did. And when he did, it was never a graceful admission. "I fired only once and my aim was true. It wasn't my bullet that struck down your . . ."

" . . . Husband. Buddy was my husband. And he would be alive right now if you and your friend hadn't aired your differences on a public thoroughfare." Her voice had risen steadily until she was screaming at him.

"Calm down, lady," Grady urged. He wished desperately that he had never set foot in Guthrie, Oklahoma, this day.

"How can I calm down when my husband lies dead? How dare you! What does a savage know about grief?"

"More than you give him credit for," Grady bit out as he sought to soothe the distraught young woman.

"Just go away! Can't you see you're making matters worse by just being here?"

Frowning, Grady stepped aside, allowing a woman to help Storm to her feet. Two men quickly stepped forward to lift Buddy into the wagon and drive him to the undertaker.

"What are you going to do now, dear?" Grady heard the woman ask as she led Storm away.

Grady wanted to follow, to ask the blonde's name, but by then the sheriff was pushing his way through the crowd, and Grady spent the next hour answering questions. By the time the sheriff had interviewed witnesses and satisfied himself that the attack upon Grady had been unprovoked, the beautiful widow was gone.

On September 13, 1893, absolute chaos reigned in the town of Guthrie. The line to buy train tickets to the new towns of Enid and Perry, where settlers hoped to claim land, was even longer than the day before. But for reasons he himself did not understand, Grady lingered in town, sleeping in the livery when he found no other suitable lodging. For a man without a conscience, he had lost a lot of sleep thinking about the provocative blonde and her dead husband. He wondered what she planned to do now that her husband was dead. Did she have family back East somewhere?

Try as he might, Grady could not deny the fact that it was his conscience that brought him to the undertaker that bright September morning. A somber man dressed in black greeted him at the door.

"How may I help you?"

Grady cleared his throat and glanced around the room filled with wooden boxes.

"There was a man brought in here yesterday. Young, gunshot. Do you know his name?"

"Ah, you must mean Mr. Kennedy. The funeral is this afternoon. Are you a member of the family?"

"No," Grady said harshly, unwilling to admit he was the indirect cause of the young man's death. "Has the burying been paid for?"

"Why, no, it hasn't," the undertaker said. His suspicions fully aroused now, the undertaker took a good look at Grady, put two and two together and came up with the right answer. "Why, you're the man who shot Mr. Kennedy."

Grady's mouth stretched into a grimace. "I don't shoot unarmed men. Kennedy was killed by a stray bullet. But I'm not here to defend myself, I want to pay for the burying."

"Why? The man has a widow."

"Just tell me how much," Grady said tightly. A man of few words, he saw no reason to offer explanations when he couldn't even explain his reasons to himself.

The undertaker named a figure. Grady nodded, took the appropriate sum from his money pouch, and placed it in the man's hand. "Are you sure that's enough? I want him to have a decent burial."

There was a rustle of calico, and then an angry feminine voice asked, "Why should you care what kind of burial my husband has?"

While Grady and the undertaker were talking, Storm had entered the establishment in time to hear their words.

Startled, the undertaker sent Storm a sheepish look. "Mr.—er—Mr. . . . ." He slanted Grady a quizzical glance and waited for him to supply a name.

"Stryker. Grady Stryker."

"Yes, well, Mr. Stryker has just paid for your husband's burying."

"What! The man's a savage; why should he offer to pay for Buddy's funeral?"

"Why don't you ask him?" the undertaker suggested. It mattered little who paid for the burial as long as someone did.

"All right, I will." She turned to Grady, her eyes dark with fury. "I don't want your charity, Mr. Stryker."

"It's not charity. I'd—" he began.

"Just take your money back. I don't want it. Buddy and I weren't rich, but I have enough to pay for his burial."

"Now, Mrs. Kennedy, perhaps you should reconsider," the undertaker offered kindly. "You will need the money to return to your family. Mr. Stryker said he didn't kill your husband. Can't you accept his offer as a gift of kindness?"

"Kindness?" Storm fumed. "Look at the man! Does he look the sort who is accustomed to doing good deeds? He looks like a gunslinger to me. And heaven only knows what he'd want in return for his 'kindness.' Give him back his money, Mr. Lucas."

Silas Lucas shrugged and handed the money back to Grady. "You heard the lady, Mr. Stryker." Then, sensing a confrontation, he turned and walked away rather than be privy to the clashing of two explosive tempers.

"I only wanted to do what was right, Mrs. Kennedy," Grady said tightly. Truth to tell, he felt sorry for the young widow. Her expressive sherry eyes were red-rimmed from crying, and she looked as if she hadn't slept a wink the night before. He wondered if she even had a place to stay in this crowded town.

"Your sympathy isn't appreciated. Save it for someone who needs it," Storm said. "You hardly look the type to feel regret. If it wasn't for you, Buddy would still be alive."

"I had no idea a man would come gunning for me here in Guthrie," Grady returned. "Had I known, I would have been more cautious."

"A man like you must face death every day," Storm said disparagingly. "But Buddy wasn't a violent man. He loved life, he—" Suddenly the burden of Buddy's death became too much for Storm to bear. Her shoulders shook uncontrollably and she broke into tears.

If he lived to be a hundred, Grady would never understand what made him pull Storm into his arms and offer the comfort of his strength. She felt so small, so warm and soft, that he groaned in response to the unaccustomed surge of compassion he felt for this small, helpless female. The last woman he'd felt that kind of protectiveness toward was Summer Sky. And this woman was nothing like Summer Sky.

At first Storm allowed the small intimacy as Grady clumsily patted her shoulder, forgetting for a moment everything but the need to vent her grief over Buddy's death. Then, slowly, she became aware of the carefully controlled power of the arms holding her and of the hard strength of the body pressing against hers. This man felt nothing like Buddy. The feeling of

Grady's huge body enveloping her was so foreign that for a moment she could neither move or speak.

"Are you all right?" Grady asked quietly.

The sound of that low, intense voice was the catalyst that brought Storm abruptly back to sanity. Realizing she was accepting comfort from a man she should despise, she dragged herself from his arms, standing back and staring at him as if he were the devil himself.

"Don't touch me!"

A dull red stained Grady's neck. "I'm sorry." It startled him to hear himself apologizing again.

"Good-bye, Mr. Stryker." Deliberately she turned her back on him.

But Grady was not ready to leave. "What will you do now?"

"That's none of your business."

"I'm making it my business. You've accused me of causing your husband's death so I'm accepting responsibility for your welfare. Do you need money to return to your family?"

Storm whirled to face him, and Grady was mesmerized by the swirling mass of blond hair that settled around her like a gleaming veil of gold. She was the most provocative woman he had ever encountered, and the most contrary. Summer Sky had never offered a harsh word or argument of any kind in all the years they had known one another.

"Very well, since you asked I'll tell you exactly what I'm going to do. I intend to participate in the land rush. I'm going to be right there at the starting line when the signal is given, racing with the rest of the homesteaders to claim a piece of land for myself."

Her voice was fervent, passionate, intense with defiant determination. Vaguely, Grady wondered what it would be like to be the recipient of all that passion and intensity. Then, abruptly, the meaning of her words sunk in.

"You're what!"

"You heard me, I'm going to claim the land Buddy and I had staked out for ourselves."

"You're a woman." His voice was incredulous. "A woman clings to her man. She doesn't set out to accomplish things women have no business attempting."

"In case you hadn't noticed, I have no man. No one, do you hear me, no one, will stop Storm Kennedy from taking part in the land rush three days from now. Certainly not some half-breed gunslinger."

Grady heard nothing past the name Storm had inadvertently supplied him.

Storm.

It was as if a sign had been given to him by Wakantanka. His vivid blue eyes grew distant as he recalled that fateful day atop the mountain, when he had sought his vision and Grandfather spoke to him.

"The peace you seek will come with the Storm. Until you meet and conquer the Storm your spirit will know no rest. Always remember that Thunder is the harbinger of Storm, but Thunder can only exist in the bosom of Storm's soul."

Grady's face turned white beneath the bronze of his tan, and he stared at Storm as if his life had just been blown to hell.

# Chapter Two

"What are you staring at?"

It was a struggle to drag his thoughts away from the prophecy and concentrate on what Storm was saying. "Don't you know how dangerous it is for a woman to participate in a land rush? In town you're treated with respect because of your fair sex, but once you join the men at the starting line it will be every man, woman, and child for himself. With one hundred thousand participants, there can't possibly be enough land to go around."

"Why should it matter to you? I'm willing to take the risk and that's all that counts. It's what Buddy wanted, and now it's what I want. When the shot announces the start of the run I'll be in line, Mr. Stryker."

"And should you succeed, you won't be able

to hold on to your land," Grady snorted derisively. "You're only a woman."

"And you're a pigheaded, opinionated, half-breed savage," Storm returned indignantly. "I'm no meek Indian squaw. Too bad you won't be around for me to prove you wrong."

"Perhaps I will, Mrs. Kennedy, perhaps I will," Grady said tightly. "But don't expect me to pick you up when you fall flat on your face."

"I expect nothing from you. Just leave me alone! If not for you, Buddy would still be alive. Good day, Mr. Stryker."

*September 16, 1893*

The run was going to be even more unruly than Grady had imagined. Troops of the Third Cavalry were stationed all along the line between Kansas and the Cherokee Strip to try to maintain order, but it would not be easy.

One of the biggest problems would be the "Sooners"—men who were sneaking into the Cherokee Strip before the starting time. Their claims would not be legal, and there promised to be many a confrontation over land claimed by more than one man.

At fifteen minutes before noon, the lines at the train station were enormous. The slow movement of tickets had tempers soaring— only 20,000 an hour could be sold. Once the signal was given, trains would leave the station at two- or three-minute intervals. At the other end of the line, in the newly designated towns of Perry, Enid, and Kildare, quarter-acre town sites would be allotted to the first arrivals.

Grady guided his sturdy Indian pony, Lightning, along the starting line. The horsemen and bicycle riders were at the front, while the buggies and lighter wagons were in the second row, with heavy teams bringing up the rear. It amused him to see a gaily decorated surrey in the second row loaded with four flamboyantly dressed prostitutes, who flirted outrageously with the men around them.

Exactly when Grady had decided to join in the rush for free land was unclear in his mind. All he knew was that after the confrontation with Storm Kennedy in the funeral parlor, he had done a considerable amount of thinking. And after much soul-searching he had come to the conclusion that he was tired of violence and bloodshed. Perhaps this was his opportunity to forge a new life for himself and his son.

Grady grew pensive when he recalled his last words with Storm Kennedy, when he had urged her to abandon her reckless plan to run for land. He had seen her only once after their argument, and then only briefly. Though she had maintained a stubborn silence during their encounter, he hoped he had made an impression on her.

Wheeling his mount into place, Grady knew exactly which piece of land he wanted. He had ridden through the area many times in the past, before it had been purchased from the Indians.

About ten miles from Guthrie, the prime piece of acreage Grady had in mind had everything a homesteader could want. Water, rich grasslands, and abundant trees. He had no interest in claiming one of the town sites, but instead pictured Little Buffalo running free and wild on farmland tilled and cultivated by his own hands. It would be a fit legacy to leave his son, something Grady had accomplished on his own.

Storm Kennedy steadied the team of horses with a firm hand. Her light wagon was in the second row of racers behind the horsemen and bicycles, but she had every confidence in her ability to beat the competition. As it turned out, she wasn't the only woman racing for land today. Here and there she could see other females, some on horseback, some driving wagons.

Glancing ahead to the front of the line, Storm saw that the horsemen were bent low over their mounts in anticipation of the signal. Reacting to the tension, she grasped the reins tighter. Suddenly her face drained of all color as she stared incredulously at a particular rider. He sat his horse with the grace of a man born to the saddle. Tall and supple, dressed in buckskins that molded to his body, his lean, lithe frame seemed an extension of his mount.

The half-breed, Grady Stryker!

What was he doing here? Storm wondered, stunned by the notion that a drifter and gunslinger would attempt to claim land that by right should go to decent homesteaders.

Grady spoke softly in the Lakota language to his mount as the tension grew. He knew only seconds remained before the sergeant of the Third Cavalry would fire the shot that would signal the maddest rush ever made in the country's history. He glanced behind him, searching the faces of his fellow racers, trying to judge his chances of beating the competition.

Then he saw her and spat out a curse that made those beside him turn and stare. Had nothing he said gotten through to the little witch? Her husband had been buried but one day before and she should be home mourning him instead of trying to compete with men twice her size. He compared her to gentle, submissive Summer Sky and found her lacking. Storm Kennedy was too forward, too brash for Grady's liking, too independent and reckless. Her stubbornness appalled him.

The crack of the carbine scattered his thoughts. Reacting instinctively, he dug his heels into Lightning's flanks. The sturdy pony lived up to his name as he sprinted into the lead. Behind him horses were bucking and pitching, throwing one of the riders almost immediately, before the line had fairly been broken. But the unfortunate man was equal to the occasion, and immediately stuck his stake into the ground, staking his claim to a quarter section of the finest farming land in the strip.

Behind Grady the ground shook with the reverberation of hooves and heavier equip-

ment as buggies and wagons thundered over
the hundred-mile-wide racetrack. Along the
Santa Fe tracks trains kept pace, crammed
with humans as never before. The platforms
and roofs were black with homesteaders, and
so many hung out of the window they were in
danger of spilling out.

Storm cracked her whip above the team's
head, appalled when she saw wagon after wagon overturning, strewing disappointed settlers
across the prairie. Sheer grit and fierce determination kept her hands steady on the reins
despite the fact that her arms felt as if they
were being pulled out of their sockets. She
had no idea which land would be best to
claim, but decided that any land along the
Santa Fe would be considered desirable. But
each time she found a likely looking spot she
was disappointed to find others ahead of her,
already hammering in their stakes and setting
up makeshift tents until more permanent dwell-
ings could be raised.

Unwilling to accept defeat, Storm left the
tracks, turning slightly north toward the river,
where she knew from gossip that prime tracts
existed. She had no interest in town sites, only
in farmland. That was a decision she and Buddy had made before they started the trip to
Oklahoma.

Swirling, choking dust rose up to sting her
eyes and clog her throat, but Storm gritted her
teeth and held on for dear life as the wagon
bounced and bumped over terrain so rough the

wagon was in danger of breaking up. After ten grueling miles she spotted the river up ahead. She noted the thick, lush grasslands surrounding it, the stand of trees lining the bank, and immediately fell in love with the spot. It was everything she and Buddy had hoped for, and it looked as if no one had arrived before her. But as she drew closer she saw that she was wrong, and groaned in despair. Already a makeshift tent had been set in place, and rope and stakes marked the boundaries.

Reining in the team, Storm stared in disbelief at the man who was bending over one of the stakes. Grady Stryker! Would he always be around to make her life miserable?

Grady raised his eyes to study the newcomer, struck dumb when he realized it was Storm. He had expected her to give up long before now, yet he couldn't help but admire her fortitude and endurance. Evidently she was stronger than he gave her credit for.

"I should have known you'd get here ahead of me," Storm bit out furiously.

"And I should have known you'd ignore my advice and not give up this foolishness," Grady replied. "If you had your eye on this particular spot, then you're too late. I've already staked my claim. And in case you're interested, all available land bordering the river has already been claimed."

Gazing past Grady, Storm took careful note of the stakes already in the ground. If her eyes weren't deceiving her, there were two sets of stakes. "Looks like someone got here before you. Is that your tent?"

"No, but I'm not worried. Only a 'Sooner' could have gotten here before me, and his claim doesn't count. There are laws against those who jumped the gun. You'd be wise to return to town, Mrs. Kennedy. You don't belong here."

Storm glared at him furiously. How dare the despicable half-breed tell her where she belonged or didn't belong? She had as much right to this land as he did. Casting her gaze farther afield, Storm saw that no stakes were set out on the land adjacent to that which Grady had claimed. It was inferior to the grassy knoll bordering the river, but still offered good potential. And better yet, no one had arrived to claim it. Jumping down from the wagon, she fished in the wagonbed for a stake and mallet, walked a short distance past the boundaries marked by Grady, and pounded in her own stake. Then, savoring her triumph, she turned and sent him a saucy grin.

Grady threw up his hands in defeat. There was nothing more he could do to convince Storm of the danger existing for a woman trying to eke out a living on her own in a new land, where men had to claw and fight for survival. But when she failed, and fail she must, he'd be there to buy up her land. His blue eyes were troubled as he watched Storm ride away to lay stakes along the borders surrounding her quarter section. Then he turned away to mark off his own boundaries, carefully pulling out the stakes he'd found already in place when he'd arrived.

"Turn around real slow, mister, if ya wanna live to see tomorrow."

Grady froze, turning slowly to face the speaker. The man, mounted atop a skinny gelding, was in his middle years, poorly dressed in threadbare denims and flannel shirt, wearing boots that had seen better days. His hat was battered beyond redemption and a growth of whiskers covered his pock-marked face. The shotgun he held was pointed at Grady's middle.

"Who in the hell are you?"

"I'm the man what owns this claim. Name's Fork. Lew Fork. Them are my stakes yer pullin' up, Injun."

The dull red of anger crept up Grady's neck as he let the insult slip by. "There's only one way you could have arrived here before me, Fork, and that's by jumping the gun. If you're one of those 'Sooners' you'll find yourself in a heap of trouble. I suggest you get out of here while the getting's good. I can draw and shoot faster than you can pull the trigger on that shotgun."

Fork snorted derisively, but the sound ended abruptly when he noted the calm confidence in Grady's chilling gaze, the steadiness of his hand poised mere inches above his gun, and the stance that marked him as an experienced gunman. Sweat broke out on his forehead and his hand was suddenly no longer steady. Never had he seen a man more poised or sure of himself, a man whose expression conveyed utter contempt and disdain—a man not afraid to defend himself or his property. Fork backed down in the face of such overwhelming odds, but being a sneaky man, he had already decided how best to deal with the situation.

"Yer bluffin'."

A muscle twitched at the corner of Grady's eye. "Try me."

Slowly Fork lowered the shotgun. "All right, mister, you win. But I ain't forgettin' this or the fact that you done me outta my land." Backing down left a bitter taste in his mouth.

"The land was claimed illegally; it was never yours. Now throw down your weapon. I'll give you five minutes to pull up your tent and hightail it out of here."

Sliding from his horse, Fork tossed his shotgun at Grady's feet. Then he quickly and efficiently dismantled the rough tent composed of two stakes and a canvas and stowed it behind his saddle, glaring murderously at Grady all the while. When he mounted and rode away, Grady made the fatal mistake of turning his back. It was something he never did under normal circumstances, but Fork had appeared so intimidated, Grady hadn't thought he had the guts to try to outwit him. But he should have known the man was a coward, and cowards were unpredictable. What saved Grady from certain death was his superb sense of hearing.

Attuned to danger and trained to listen for the slightest change in the air around him, he recognized the distinctive click of metal against cold metal. He should have known that a man like Fork would have another gun stashed away somewhere.

Reacting instinctively, Grady ducked. Thus it was that the bullet meant for vital organs slammed into his shoulder. But Fork assumed the shot was fatal and didn't stick around long enough to find out. Once the shot left his gun he spurred his mount and rode hell for leather back to town. Since the land was already staked he could claim it any time. He just didn't want to be around when the body was found.

Storm heard the shot and lifted her head from her back-breaking task, recognizing the sound immediately. She shaded her eyes with her hand as she scanned the surrounding land. She saw nothing suspicious, only other racers flying by to claim what was left of the land. Nor was there another shot. Still, she couldn't shake off the premonition that something was amiss.

Unable to pinpoint the cause of her distress, Storm took another stake from the wagon and drove it into the ground. She'd been at it for quite a while and still had a ways to go before she'd reach the place from which she started. When she finished she'd have the full 160 allotted acres staked out. Then all she had to do was erect a crude shelter and file her claim in Guthrie.

Who said a woman wasn't as capable as a man! She couldn't wait to prove to that opinionated half-breed that she had done exactly what he said she couldn't.

It was dusk when Storm arrived back at the place where she had started and prepared to erect her crude dwelling according to the rules. It didn't need to be fancy, just something to prove the land was occupied. She glanced over at the adjacent land, noting that Grady hadn't yet erected his tent. Then she saw something that froze the blood in her veins.

Through the settling dusk she saw the figure of a man rise unsteadily from the ground, stagger clumsily, then fall. Common sense told her not to interfere with something that was none of her business, but her conscience demanded that she take a closer look. What if the "Sooner" had arrived on the scene and Grady Stryker had shot him? What if the man she saw was Grady himself? What if—There was no sense speculating, Storm decided as she climbed aboard the wagon, picked up the reins, and set the horses into motion. Placing her shotgun—the one Buddy had insisted she always keep nearby—beside her on the seat, she crossed the short distance to Grady's land.

She heard him groan before she stopped the wagon. She knew instantly that it was Grady by the size of the long, lean frame sprawled on the ground. She was out of the wagon in a flash, stepping over the boundary markers and falling to her knees beside him. There was blood everywhere. On his clothes and soaking the ground beneath him. Panic-stricken, Storm felt as if she had leaped backward four days to the nightmarish moment when she had knelt beside a dying Buddy.

"Can you stop the bleeding?"

Grady's voice brought her abruptly back to reality. She couldn't think of one reason why she should help a man like Grady Stryker. He had brought her more pain than she had ever known and disrupted her life from the first moment she set eyes on him in Guthrie. He might not have pulled the trigger of the gun that had killed Buddy, but she held him fully responsible for the accident.

"Storm, snap out of it. I asked if you can stop the bleeding." His voice was harsh with pain.

"I—I don't know. How serious is it?"

"How in the hell do I know! You tell me."

Gingerly Storm turned him over, looking for the point of entry. She spotted it immediately, high on his left shoulder. The bullet appeared to have cut cleanly through the flesh, exiting on the opposite side.

"It doesn't look too bad, if we can stop the bleeding. The bullet went clear through." When she continued to stare at him, as if mesmerized by the sight of blood, Grady lost his temper.

"Dammit, lady, I'm apt to bleed to death before you make up your mind to help me. You are going to help me, aren't you?"

Lost in the vivid blue of his eyes, Storm nodded and began tearing strips from her petticoat.

"Who did this to you? How many are there out there waiting their turn to prove themselves a faster draw?"

Stifling a groan, Grady said, "That damn 'Sooner' showed up. I figured I'd scared him off, but he was smarter than I gave him credit for. The minute I turned my back on him he fired."

"You're not as smart as you thought if you didn't disarm him first," Storm said with a hint of censure.

Grady didn't answer. It took all his concentration to keep from crying out as Storm stripped off his shirt and pressed folded strips of torn petticoat against his wound to staunch the bleeding.

For some unexplained reason she found the sight of his bare chest strangely unsettling, and her hands shook clumsily as they touched his taut flesh.

"Don't you know how to be gentle?" Grady chided when she pressed harder than he thought necessary.

"Only when it pleases me," Storm said sweetly. "I have no reason to treat you gently, or even to help you at all. Not after what you did to Buddy. He—" She paused to steady her voice. "He was my best friend."

"I thought you said he was your husband."

Storm flushed. "Yes, of course he was my husband. But he was also my friend."

Grady grew quiet as Storm worked over him, affording her a few moments of private recollection. It was true, Buddy had been her friend long before he had become her husband. She had loved him like a brother, and when it came time to marry, she could think of no one she'd prefer for a husband. But even though she had shared his bed for over a month, she still couldn't think of him as anything but her dearest friend. She accepted his timid lovemaking, enjoyed it up to a point, but never could discover what all the fuss was about. Making love was nothing special, certainly not the earthshaking experience she had been led to believe. It was a duty she had performed more for Buddy's sake than her own.

Yet their marriage would have been a happy one, blessed with children, laughter, and a warm regard for one another. What more could a woman ask for? She missed Buddy fiercely, for he had been her companion and friend most of her life.

Storm eased Grady into a sitting position and wound the last strip of material around his chest to hold the compress in place. Only a small amount of blood stained the bandage, and Storm hoped the worst of the bleeding had been staunched. Fortunately for the half-breed, the bullet hadn't hit anything vital, and he should recover with no ill effects.

"Can you sit a horse?" Storm asked as she helped him to his feet. "Or should I take you back to town in the wagon?"

"I'm not going back to town tonight."

"Are you crazy? What if infection sets in? Are

you prepared to handle a fever?"

"Did anyone ever tell you that you live up to your name?" His face wore the faintest of smiles.

"All the time, but that doesn't change things. You should be seen by a doctor and report the 'Sooner' to the authorities."

"Tomorrow is soon enough. If I were you, I'd see to erecting a tent. I'm sure there are claim jumpers about, and if there is no dwelling on your claim you're liable to find it taken from you."

"What about you? Will you be all right tonight?"

"Do you care?"

His question startled her. By rights she should feel no compassion for the half-breed gunslinger. All her conscience required was that she discharge her Christian duty, which she had already done, and leave him to his own devices. Intuition told her he was a hard, bitter man who had built a protective shell around his heart. Something had made him the kind of man he was today. Did being a half-breed have anything to do with it? she wondered curiously. Yet Storm sensed a brooding sadness in him that begged for compassion and understanding. She might hate what the man had become, but she felt a strong, compelling attraction for the kind of man he could be once he mended his wicked ways.

"You didn't answer my question," Grady repeated softly. "Do you care what happens to me?" Why was he pursuing this line of thought when he knew damn well Storm had good reason to despise him?

Her skin looked so soft and velvety, he longed to reach out and stroke her cheek. She was so close he could smell violets wafting from the thick blond strands of her hair. Grady had thought all feelings of tenderness long buried, but somehow this young widow had stirred memories that suddenly emerged from the ashes to disturb and titillate him.

Drawn into the electric blue of his eyes, Storm had to shake herself to escape his spell. She heard his question and found it offensive.

"I don't care a fig about you, Mr. Stryker. I helped you because my Christian upbringing demanded it. I still think you're a violent man who courts danger."

The brief softening of Grady's features abruptly hardened into an inscrutable mask. He must have been crazy to think Storm Kennedy would consider him anything but an uncivilized savage. Next time he'd know better than to deal civilly with the woman. Over three years ago he had chosen the kind of life he wanted to lead. What made him think he could or should change now?

*Because of your son*, his conscience whispered. Certainly not because of a golden-haired witch with the face of an angel.

"Perhaps you should return to your claim, Mrs. Kennedy," Grady said dully. "According to the rules you must erect a shelter." His shoulder hurt like hell and he felt weak as a kitten from loss of blood, but he'd be damned if he'd ask Storm for any more than she was willing to give.

Storm shot him a quelling look. "You're right, there's still much to be done." She started walking back to the wagon, turned suddenly, and asked, "What about your tent? Can you manage on your own?"

"I can manage. It's only a flesh wound. I've had worse."

Storm nodded and continued on her way. The provocative sway of her hips and a flash of shapely ankles held Grady mesmerized, and he forced himself to look away. He had no damn business desiring Storm Kennedy, no business at all. She was a part of the white society he held in contempt. And she was so different from Summer Sky, he wondered why he was drawn to her.

Thunder and Storm.

The names implied power, wrought by the tremendous forces of nature, uncontrollable, wild, unpredictable. Combined they made men cower and the earth shake.

Thunder and Storm.

The fury they unleashed created havoc in both the heavens above and the earth below.

Grinning crookedly, Grady decided Storm needed Thunder to bring forth the fire. Perhaps Wakantanka was right. Thunder could only exist in the bosom of Storm's soul. But everyone knew Storm would be weak and ineffective without Thunder. Taming a Storm might be more rewarding, certainly more entertaining, than allowing it to pass by in the night.

# *Chapter Three*

Storm had her makeshift shelter erected before the inky blackness of night descended over the prairie. She and Buddy had prepared well, having purchased stakes, canvas, and supplies to last them several months, or until the land started producing. Buddy had used an inheritance from his grandmother to finance their trip, and there were still sufficient funds left in the bank in Guthrie to build a snug cabin on her new land.

Using some of the extra stakes, Storm built a fire and started coffee boiling. She was famished, having eaten nothing since early that morning. Rummaging in the back of the wagon, she found a tin of beans, another of fruit, and some hardtack. The next day, when she went to Guthrie to file her claim, she'd buy bacon, eggs, flour, sugar, and the other supplies necessary for her survival.

In a very short time she was seated before the fire, shoveling beans into her mouth and thinking how lonely it was without Buddy. He had been her constant companion for so long, the loss sent a sharp pang through her innards. She hadn't really cried or had a chance to mourn Buddy since his death, and when tears appeared suddenly she didn't try to stop them. She let them course down her cheeks, finding solace in the healing flood. When it was over she knew she could continue, with or without Buddy. She would always mourn her husband, but she had never been one to dwell overlong on the injustices of life. Life simply went on.

When she and Buddy had struck out for Oklahoma, she had eagerly welcomed the challenge of pioneer life, and not even Buddy's death would make her give up the dream of owning one of the last tracts of free land in the country. Abruptly, Storm's thoughts wandered in another direction. She wondered if the half-breed had managed a fire and a meal. When she glanced over toward his claim she saw nothing but dark stretches of land for as far as the eye could see. The moon and the stars provided the only light, except for that projected by her meager campfire.

Storm didn't want to worry about the half-breed, didn't even want to think about him, but somehow his image intruded upon her thoughts. It was difficult to hate a man who was wounded and helpless. Although helpless hardly described Grady Stryker, Storm realized that he couldn't have entered the race as fully prepared as she and Buddy had been, for to her knowledge his decision to homestead had been one made on the spur of the moment. He probably had no food or even a spare blanket to keep him warm during the coolness of the night.

Suddenly Storm came to a decision. She filled a tin plate with the remainder of the food she had prepared, picked up the coffeepot, and started walking the short distance to Grady's claim. Since it was full dark and she had to pick her way carefully, it took fifteen minutes to reach his roped-off claim. Stepping over the barrier, she saw that Grady had indeed erected a shelter. Upon closer inspection she saw that his tent consisted of a shotgun stuck into the ground as a tent pole and a blanket stretched over it and staked down on all four sides. There was absolutely no way he could stuff his tall, lean frame into the small enclosure. Setting the plate and coffeepot on the ground before the tent, she called his name.

She heard his tethered horse snort softly in response, but Grady was nowhere in sight. She was ready to return to her own claim when the sound of rippling water caught her attention. Since she had wanted to wash up before she retired, she headed in the direction of the river, wishing she had been one of the lucky ones to claim land bordering the water. As things stood now, she'd be forced to negotiate with the half-breed for her water until a well could be dug.

The moon lit her way as Storm walked across the lush prairie, happily aware of the fact that she had claimed a piece of prime farmland. Though she didn't know a great deal about farming or raising animals, she was determined to learn. Surely she wasn't the only woman to claim a piece of Oklahoma for herself, nor was she the first woman pioneer whose man was killed before he could realize his dream.

Storm stumbled upon Grady quite suddenly. He was poised at the edge of the water, his back to her, nude except for a breechclout covering his loins. He looked like an ancient heathen god, standing as tall and straight as a towering spruce. His stance emphasized the strength of his thighs and the slimness of his hips. Moonlight danced along the ropy muscles of his biceps, highlighting his shoulders, a yard wide and molded bronze. In fact, he was gilded bronze all over, even the taut mounds of his buttocks. His midnight hair shone with glistening pearls of water, as if he had just emerged from the river. Storm's breath lodged in her throat as she stared at him, fascinated by the pagan splendor of his powerful body.

He was the closest thing to an unclothed man Storm had ever seen. She and Buddy had never undressed before one another. They had discreetly shed their clothes in private, and when they made love, Buddy, in order to protect her sensibilities, had raised her voluminous nightdress without looking. Though Storm had never seen her husband without his clothes, she knew he had looked nothing like Grady Stryker. Was there a man anywhere on earth the equal of him?

Grady tensed, sensing that he wasn't alone. In the past his keen senses had served him well, but this time he detected no menace, felt no danger from the intruder. He had bathed in the river to cool his feverish body. Then he silently communed with the moon and river, both of which the People worshiped as givers of life. He had heard the nearly silent footsteps and stood ready to spring, until the sweet scent of violets wafted to him on the breeze.

"Have you come to bathe, Mrs. Kennedy, or merely to watch me?"

A startled squeak escaped from Storm's lips. "How—how did you know I was here?"

"My reflexes have been honed to recognize danger no matter what its guise," Grady said, turning to face her. "Had I not recognized the scent that lingers on your skin and on your hair, I would have attacked you. Next time announce yourself."

"I—came upon you suddenly and—and—" Her tongue seemed glued to the roof of her mouth as she stumbled over the words. "I wasn't spying," she finally spat out.

"What *are* you doing here?"

"I brought you something to eat, and when I didn't find you, I decided to wash up before I returned to my claim."

"You brought me food?" Grady asked, incredulous.

She was grateful the darkness hid her flushed face. "If you want it," she said, shrugging. "You couldn't have carried many supplies on your horse."

"You're a strange woman, Mrs. Kennedy—Storm." He grew pensive, then asked, "Why do you have an Indian name?" He left the water's edge, and her eyes fell unbidden to the bulging muscles of his thighs and the intriguing way they flexed with each step he took. He didn't stop until he stood close enough to feel her soft breath against his cheek.

Her lips went suddenly dry and she had to lick them before she could speak. "It's not an Indian name, not really. I was born during a violent storm and my parents thought it appropriate to name me Storm."

"It is the same with the People."

"Why do you have blue eyes?" Storm asked before she realized what she was saying.

Grady's features turned grim, as if recalling something painful from his past. But to Storm's surprise, he answered readily enough. "They come from my mother. She is a white woman."

"You look like a savage."

Grady's eyes turned flinty. "Looks are often deceiving."

"Was your mother a captive?"

"Captive?" Grady's laughter vibrated the air around them. "Those who know my parents say my father is the one held captive by my mother."

"But how—"

"You ask too many questions, Storm Kennedy."

*And look much too lovely in the moonlight*, he thought, but did not say aloud.

"Thank you for the food, but I think you should leave. Aren't you afraid of being here alone with me? I'm a renegade. If you aren't afraid, you should be."

"I'm not afraid of you," Storm retorted, "but I'll be all too happy to go. If you'd kindly leave me alone for a few moments, I'll clean up and be on my way."

"If I recall, your land does not border on the river."

"That's why I'm asking permission to cross your property to reach the water." She hated being beholden to the half-breed, but there was no help for it.

"I'll have to think about it."

"Are you always so disagreeable?" Storm asked, stomping her foot furiously.

"I am when dealing with White Eyes. For the most part they are untrustworthy, prejudiced, and dishonest."

"Your mother is white," Storm shot back.

"My mother lives far away on a ranch in Wyoming. Leave her out of this," Grady said tightly. "Most whites are evil."

"And most Indians are dirty savages. You don't even have a proper Indian name."

"I am called Thunder by the People."

"Thunder," Storm repeated softly. The name conjured up visions of violence, mayhem, and destruction—it fit him perfectly.

"My parents named me Grady. When I left the People to live among the White Eyes I assumed that name."

"You left the—I don't understand."

"There is nothing for you to understand," Grady said tersely. "You may cross my land to the river whenever it pleases you." He turned to leave with an abruptness that startled Storm, as if he couldn't wait to be rid of her. The bandage she had tied around his chest shone stark against his bronzed flesh, yet she hadn't thought to ask him about his wound.

Let him suffer, she thought; it would serve him right for being so darn ornery. Had he learned no manners at his mother's knee?

Kneeling at the river's edge, Storm plunged her hands into the cool water and proceeded to wash her hands, face, and neck, unaware that Grady had turned to watch her as she unfastened the top buttons of her blouse and dribbled water between her breasts. Moonlight beamed down benevolently upon her, turning her hair into a halo of pure gold as she bent forward. Grady couldn't recall when he had seen a more entrancing sight or witnessed anything quite as sexually arousing as Storm, raising her face to the stars, splashing water on her face, neck, and breasts. And what made it even more provocative was the fact that she wasn't even aware of what it was doing to him.

Grady smiled in spite of himself, envisioning what it would be like to quench his lust in the cradle of Storm's loins. He wondered if she would be as tempestuous, wild and untamed, as her name implied. Those forbidden thoughts made his flesh rise and harden with a need he had thought subdued long ago. He had wanted no woman in his heart but Summer Sky; now, suddenly, he was overwhelmed with desire for a white woman named Storm who had whirled into his life with all the fury of a tornado.

Shaking his dark head in denial of what his flesh was demanding, Grady spun on his heel and stomped away. When Storm passed by his crude tent a short time later, Grady was just finishing the plate of beans and bacon she had left for him.

"If you're finished, I'll take the plate." Her voice was cool.

Grady handed her the plate and coffeepot. "Thank you, it was very good." He hadn't realized just how hungry he had been until he had picked up the fork. Tomorrow he'd have to see about getting some supplies out there and building some sort of shanty to serve as a dwelling. Getting them out to his claim was going to be a problem unless. . . .

Storm took the plate and coffeepot from Grady's hands and started the trek back to her own claim. "Storm, wait."

Storm paused, uncomfortable with the idea of the half-breed using her first name. "Was there something you wanted to say to me?"

"I told you earlier that you could cross my land to use the river whenever you liked. Perhaps in return you could accommodate me?"

Storm stiffened, her face twisted into a mask of shock and dismay. "Accommodate you, Mr. Stryker? In what way?"

"We both need to go to Guthrie tomorrow to file our claims and we both need supplies. Perhaps you'd be good enough to carry some of my supplies back in your wagon since we are going to be neighbors."

Immediately Storm relaxed, realizing she had jumped to the wrong conclusion. But she'd be a fool to trust the half-breed renegade. Obviously he hated whites, and his hatred extended to women as well as men. He seemed to hold white women in as much contempt as he did white men. Curiously, she wondered what had happened in his past to turn him against the white race. He was intelligent and well educated, and he spoke English as well as she did, better even. Yet something had turned him against all white men and their ways.

Grady Stryker was secretive concerning his past. All she knew about him was that he was born in Wyoming on a ranch, hated whites, and could handle a gun like a pro. And he was heart-stoppingly handsome in a rugged way that brought shivers to her flesh.

"It's a deal," Storm agreed. "Though it boggles my mind to think of a man like you settling down on a farm, we *are* going to be neighbors, and it would behoove us to help one another. But don't get the wrong idea, Mr. Stryker. I still hate you for what you are and the way my life has changed because of you. If Buddy were alive today, we would have been here first to claim land on the river. Good night, Mr. Stryker. I'll be by for you in the morning."

Grady was waiting for Storm early the next morning when she drove the wagon past his claim. Dressed in skintight buckskins and moccasins, he had his long ebony hair tied back with a leather thong. He must have been wearing his spare shirt, for there were no telltale holes where the bullet had entered or exited his flesh. In fact, he gave little sign that he had been wounded at all. Was the man not human? Did he not feel pain like other mortals? Though the wound hadn't been life threatening, it surely was serious enough to cause him distress. Yet there he was, looking as hale and hardy as he had the first time she saw him in Guthrie.

"I'll tie Lightning to the back of the wagon and ride beside you," Grady said as he led his saddled horse over to the wagon.

Lightning and Thunder, they made a good pair, Storm thought, fascinated by the blatant play of muscles beneath Grady's buckskins as he moved gracefully to the rear of the wagon. And where did Storm come into the scheme of things? Had their meeting been preordained? Thunder and Storm. She shook her head at such a silly notion. Their meeting had been purely coincidental, and unhappily for her, an unforeseen tragedy. When Grady leaped into the wagon beside her, the brief pressure of his leg pressing against hers sent a shudder through her body.

"Are you cold? Perhaps you should have worn a jacket."

She was dressed in a split skirt and blouse, and if it weren't for the half-breed sitting beside her, she would have been perfectly comfortable. His presence confused her, made what she had felt for Buddy seem tame.

It made her angry.

"I'm fine," Storm snapped as she slapped the reins against the horses' rumps. "I just don't want you to think our being neighborly is anything but a mutual need for survival. Until I can get my well dug I'll need to use the river that flows through your land. And you'll need—"

"You may not be willing to provide what I need," Grady said with slow relish. His blue eyes, so incongruous in his dark face, blazed with an unholy light.

Storm gasped, stunned at the sexual innuendo inherent in his words. "You, Mr. Stryker, are an unprincipled rogue. How dare you speak to me in such a suggestive manner. If Buddy were alive you wouldn't dare—"

"I said nothing to offend you," Grady said, quickly defending himself. His innocent stare made her want to give him a thorough tongue-lashing. "Don't you think we should be on a first-name basis after all we've shared?"

"What we shared is the tragic death of my husband, Mr. Stryker. If you don't stop badgering me, we can forget all about the cooperation between us. I'll bargain with another homesteader for water until my well is dug."

"Don't get your dander up, Storm," Grady said, trying not to smile, but failing miserably.

Why was he feeling more lighthearted than he had in years? He couldn't recall when he'd smiled last or bantered with a woman as lovely and provocative as Storm Kennedy. It felt good, damn good. Perhaps abandoning his renegade life, settling on his own land and making a home for his son was the wisest decision he had ever made. If he could accomplish that much, there was hope of reconciling with his parents, he reasoned. And he had Storm Kennedy to thank for it.

Storm's mouth snapped shut, swallowing the angry retort on the tip of her tongue. Arguing with the half-breed was like swimming against the tide. Though she got in a few good strokes, she seemed to get nowhere with him. Until several days ago she had never even known men like Grady Stryker existed.

It was ten miles to Guthrie, but to Storm they seemed like a hundred. Grady appeared not to notice her sullen silence as he kept up a lively conversation extolling the many qualities of the land they had claimed and the endless possibilities of farming such fertile land. Finally, it got to be too much for Storm to bear.

"What does an Indian know about planting and raising animals?" she snorted in disgust. "Your life is filled with violence and killing and wreaking vengeance on white settlers."

He turned from his contemplation of the landscape to stare at her. "I wasn't always a renegade. There was a time," his eyes lost their sparkle, his face hardened and his voice grew taut, "when the land meant everything to me. A time . . . But all that is in the past. I no longer have a home, unless I can make a go of this land I have claimed. I don't even have the peace of mind I crave. One day another drifter will arrive to challenge me and there will be another gun battle. And after that another, and another, until . . ." His shoulders lifted in grim reminder that his life was precarious at best.

"I'm sorry for you, Mr. Stryker," Storm whispered softly.

After that their conversation suffered a natural death. Grady's mood had changed abruptly from most pleasant to melancholy as he stared moodily at the passing landscape. It wasn't until they reached Guthrie that either attempted speech again, and then it was only to remark on the state of affairs in the territorial capital.

Proof that the land offered for homesteading was wholly inadequate to the demand was evidenced by the vast numbers of disappointed would-be settlers, literally thousands, who were now rushing out of Guthrie to northern destinations. Every northbound train was almost as heavily loaded as when it had come in the day before, and thousands of people who returned from the land run empty-handed brought tales of as many more persons wandering around aimlessly all over the Cherokee Strip, looking for unclaimed land that was nonexistent.

Station platforms all along the line were crowded with people who had rushed in and were now looking for a way to get out. The opening of land by the government was over, the Indian land was given away, and still there were thousands of men and women without homes.

"I suppose we're the lucky ones," Storm said thoughtfully as she carefully dodged clumps of people milling in the streets.

"I'll feel better once I file my claim," Grady said.

The claims office was a madhouse as men rushed to file their claims so they could return to their land and build their obligatory shanties. Officials were so swamped they had to set up makeshift desks outside the main office in order to handle the overflow. It was to one of these that both Storm and Grady headed once they found a place to park the wagon.

The line moved slowly, too slowly to suit Grady, who had a natural aversion to idleness. Even Storm began to chafe restlessly as the sun grew high overhead and the lines grew longer. Several spats broke out in line, most caused by quarrelsome men anxious to get back to protect their land.

Suddenly Grady felt the hackles rise at the back of his neck and he turned slowly, having the distinct feeling that someone was staring at him. Had he been recognized again as one of the renegade Indians who brought terror to the hearts of settlers? Would he always be haunted by the things he had done in retaliation for Summer Sky's death? Even though his anger and gun had been directed only against those men whose hatred for the Indians made them enemies, his reputation had grown by leaps and bounds until every man, woman, and child had feared Thunder, the Sioux renegade.

He turned slowly, his right hand hanging limply at his side, his fingers flexed. Grady's eyes narrowed as he immediately identified the man who was staring at him as if he had seen a ghost. It was Lew Fork, the "Sooner" who had shot him when his back was turned. He was standing in line to file a claim.

Storm had no idea what was happening. She saw Fork and Grady facing one another, but since she had never seen the "Sooner" she had no idea who he was.

"I thought you were dead, Injun," Fork said in a loud voice. "What are ya doing in line? Did ya jump another man's claim like ya did mine?"

"Get your facts straight, Fork," Grady said tightly. "Men who jump the gun have no right to claim land."

"What makes ya think I jumped the gun?" Fork asked belligerently. "Who do ya think people will believe, me or some half-breed Injun?

You got more lives than a cat."

Goaded beyond endurance, Grady started to reach for his gun, but Storm stopped him. Though her touch was light as a feather he felt the heavy weight of her disapproval.

"Don't," Storm said softly. "Killing that man will prove nothing except your superiority with a gun. Let the authorities handle it."

"Dammit, Storm, that man is the cowardly yellowbelly who shot me when my back was turned." Never before had he allowed a woman to dictate caution to him. Not even Summer Sky had tried to quell his sudden bursts of temper.

"Let the law handle it, Grady."

"Go ahead, Redskin, draw," Fork taunted, realizing he had an ally in Storm. Immediately people began backing away.

"What's going on here?" The voice held a ring of authority, and Grady recognized the distinctive blue uniform of the military. Guthrie was teeming with soldiers, most dispatched to the territorial capital to keep peace during the land rush. They also had the thankless task of proving or disproving the claims of Sooners.

"The Injun here is tryin' to claim my land, Captain," Fork said in an ingratiating tone of voice.

The Captain studied Grady closely, missing nothing about him. Not the dangerous glint in his blue eyes, his swarthy complexion, or the way he carried his gun, strapped to his thigh like a gunslinger.

"Is that true, Mr.—Mr.—?"

"Stryker. Grady Stryker. And no, it's not true. This man claimed land he had no right to. He couldn't possibly have reached that particular quarter section before me, set out his stakes, and put up a tent unless he jumped the gun."

"I'll attest to that, Captain," Storm concurred. "I was right behind Mr. Stryker and there was no one ahead of us. When we arrived at the land Mr. Stryker claimed, it was already staked. I left to stake my own claim and when I returned I found Mr. Stryker had been shot in the back."

"Wounded?" the Captain asked skeptically. He saw no evidence of Grady being wounded as recently as yesterday. "Are you certain, young lady?"

"I dressed the wound myself," Storm said with asperity. "It should be very easy to prove."

"I'll take your word for it, miss."

"It's Missus. Mrs. Kennedy."

"Kennedy. Is your husband the man who was killed in the street recently by a stray bullet?" He slanted Grady a pointed look. "And wasn't this man involved in the incident?"

"Yes."

"I'm sorry. I'm Captain Stark. Please accept my condolences." He turned to Grady, trying to recall where he'd heard the name "Stryker" before. "If Mrs. Kennedy is telling the truth, then you have a right to file charges against the man for shooting you, Mr. Stryker."

"Ain't my word as good as the Injun's?" Fork complained bitterly.

"Are you any relation to Blade Stryker of Wyoming?" Captain Stark asked, ignoring Fork as he suddenly made the connection.

"Blade Stryker is my father."

"I thought so; you have the same look about you. Of course, your mother's blue eyes are what gave you away."

"You know my parents?"

"Your father has provided the army with some fine horses over the years. I had the pleasure of visiting Cheyenne and Peaceful Valley just last year. There are few military men who haven't heard about the secret mission Captain Stryker performed for President Johnson many years ago. It's quite a story."

Storm was stunned. It seemed unlikely that this untamed savage came from such upstanding parents. What had happened to turn him into an undisciplined renegade?

"My father is quite a man," Grady admitted. A pang of regret for the pain his parents had suffered on his account turned his features grim. He was seized by a longing so intense, he turned away to prevent embarrassment.

"Is everything Mrs. Kennedy said true?" Captain Stark asked.

"Now wait a damn minute," Fork growled. "What about me and my claim? Can't ya see the man and his whore are lyin' through their teeth? He probably killed her husband on purpose so's they could be together."

With the speed of lightning Grady reached out, wrapping his long fingers around Fork's throat. "I ought to kill you for that remark, Fork. I didn't even know Mrs. Kennedy until that gunman's bullet killed her husband." His fingers tightened, slowly squeezing the breath from Fork.

Captain Stark's quick thinking was the only thing that saved Fork. His arm flew up, abruptly breaking Grady's hold on the 'Sooner.' "None of that, Stryker. I'd hate to have to write your father that you were hanged for murder. Do you want to press charges against this man for shooting you?"

Grady shook his head. "No, let the scum go. Being left without land to claim is punishment enough. But I warn you, Fork, don't ever show your face anywhere near my land. Next time you'll not be so lucky."

Rubbing his throat, Fork glanced at Captain Stark, and when the captain made no move to stop him, he slunk away.

A man at the edge of the crowd stopped him. "Do you know who that half-breed is?" His voice was pitched so low Fork had to strain to hear him. When Fork shook his head, the man continued in a hushed voice. "His Sioux name is Thunder. Most whites know him as Renegade. He's the fastest gun this side of the Rockies and he carries a grudge against all white men."

"Why?" Fork croaked.

"Don't rightly know, stranger, but some believe it involves a woman. The man who draws against him and wins will earn the respect and gratitude of men like my friend, who challenged him yesterday and lost."

"What happened?" Fork asked, intrigued.

"It was incredible. I never saw a man draw and shoot so fast. Stryker shot my friend without blinking an eye. If you'd like to get even for what just happened, I'll take you to my friend. He could use a man like you—one with a grudge against Stryker, or Thunder, or whatever you want to call him."

Glancing back to where Grady stood talking to Captain Stark, Fork smile evilly. "Take me to your friend. I reckon we got some talkin' to do."

# *Chapter Four*

While Grady spoke to Captain Stark, a man sidled up beside Storm, tipped his immaculate new hat, and asked, "Are you all right, ma'am? I saw the confrontation between your—er—friend and the 'Sooner' and hope you weren't offended by the man's rough language."

Storm stared at the stranger, impressed by his refined speech and manners. He appeared to be in his mid-thirties, with sandy hair and hazel eyes, dressed in the latest fashion. The slim mustache gracing his upper lip twitched when he smiled at Storm. He looked like a prosperous businessman.

Taken in by the stranger's suave manner, Storm's answer came immediately. "Mr. Stryker hardly qualifies as a friend. I've only just met him. And the circumstance of our meeting was deplorable."

"Ah, yes, the tragic accident involving your husband. How sad for you, my dear. Let me introduce myself. I am Nat Turner, newly arrived in Guthrie to conduct business." He didn't mention what kind of business he was involved in, and Storm didn't bother to ask.

Storm eyed Turner warily, leery of his intentions. "I'm Storm Kennedy."

"I don't blame you for being cautious, Mrs. Kennedy. Guthrie abounds with all types of scoundrels. But I took you for a lady immediately and wished only to offer my services. In whatever capacity," he added, sliding a glance in Grady's direction. "Has the half-breed been bothering you?"

"Thank you for your concern, Mr. Turner, but I'm perfectly capable of taking care of myself."

"Of course you are, but just in case, I can be reached at the Guthrie Hotel. I see you are in line," he remarked conversationally. "Have you by chance claimed a piece of Oklahoma?"

Storm smiled radiantly, eager and willing to relate how she had claimed her quarter section of prime land. "Yes. Isn't it wonderful?"

"Remarkable, I'd say, though I can't help but wonder how you'll manage on your own. Farming is difficult enough for a man, but a woman—?"

Storm's bottom lip jutted out belligerently. "Perhaps I won't farm the land. There are other possibilities, you know. Besides, I'm quite capable of surviving on my own."

"Very commendable, yes indeed, but not very practical. I predict that once you have time to consider the tremendous responsibility you're assuming you'll have second thoughts. If you do—"

"I won't."

"But if you do, I'd be more than happy to buy your land from you at a reasonable price. Just think, you can go back home with money in your pocket and find yourself a husband to support you."

"I appreciate your advice, Mr. Turner, but Oklahoma is my home now. Come what may, I'm here to stay."

"Who is that man talking to Mrs. Kennedy?" Grady asked Captain Stark when he noticed Storm wasn't alone.

"A speculator by the name of Nat Turner," Stark said, glancing in Storm's direction. "Don't know much about him. He just arrived in town."

Grady didn't like the way the man was cozying up to Storm. "If you'll excuse me, Captain, I think I'll see what he wants with Storm."

"Very well, Stryker. Just remember, stay out of trouble. In deference to your father, I'm going to ignore the rumors concerning your past. But at the first sign of trouble, I'll be all over you like hot tar."

"I'll remember that, Captain," Grady said as he focused his attention back to Storm and the man with whom she was conversing.

"Nevertheless, please don't hesitate to call on me for anything—anything at all," Grady heard the stranger say to Storm.

"Is there a problem?" Grady asked, scowling at Turner in a manner that bespoke his displeasure.

"I'm merely offering my services to Mrs. Kennedy," Turner replied quickly.

Turner thought the half-breed looked like the kind of man he usually avoided, a man with a hot temper who acted first and asked questions later. Turner's philosophy in life was never to tangle personally with dangerous men. There were other, more subtle ways to gain the upper hand with men like that without exposing oneself to violence. He paid good money to avoid violence and keep his reputation unsullied.

"Mrs. Kennedy doesn't need your services, Turner." For some reason Grady felt an instant dislike for Nat Turner.

"I can speak for myself," Storm said, her temper flaring. What made Grady Stryker think he was responsible for her? He had no business speaking in her behalf. As soon as they were alone she intended to give him a piece of her mind. "Thank you very much, Mr. Turner, for your kind offer, but I don't anticipate any problems."

"Then I'll be on my way," Turner said, tipping his hat. "It was a pleasure meeting you, Mrs. Kennedy." He gave Grady a quick nod before continuing on his way.

"Do you always speak to strangers?" Grady

asked with unreasonable anger. "Did your parents teach you nothing?"

"How dare you suggest I'd invite a man's attentions," Storm bit out. "Mr. Turner noticed the confrontation between you and Fork and kindly offered assistance. I thought he was a real gentleman."

"Some men prefer widows for their obvious experience," Grady said crudely, "while others prey on any comely woman too naive to see through them. You're young, beautiful, and too damn desirable for your own good. You'd be wise to discourage men like Turner. You're not adept enough to handle them."

Grady noted the surprised look on Storm's face and was puzzled by it. Didn't she know men would find her beautiful and desirable? Was she so naive that she had no earthly idea she was breathtakingly lovely, with an innate sensuousness that made men itch to possess her? Nothing about her was ordinary. From the top of her shining blonde head to the tip of her dainty feet she was sensual, provocative, and fascinating. Grady thought her lips the most tempting he had ever seen. Full and lush, they seemed made expressly for kissing.

"I have no intention of listening to you or any other man, Mr. Stryker. I'll do as I see fit."

The slightest of smiles curved Grady's lips. "Seeing as how we're neighbors, why don't you call me Grady?"

"Because I have no intention of becoming too friendly with you," Storm said. Her scathing reply drew a chuckle from him. "Do you think I could forget so soon that you're responsible for Buddy's death?"

Grady's face darkened and he turned away. Storm had wanted to put him in his place and she felt a thrill of accomplishment at having done it so handily. He really is a detestable man, she thought.

*Then why does sparring with Grady Stryker make you feel so alive?* a voice inside her dared to ask.

*Because Grady Stryker is like no other man,* that same voice replied.

Storm chose to ignore those voices. All she knew was that Grady Stryker was a danger to her. If just being near him could make her forget Buddy, what would a friendship lead to? Trouble, she decided. More trouble than she could even imagine. Men like Grady Stryker didn't settle down in one place for long. Sooner or later their violent ways caught up with them.

Once their claims were filed, Storm and Grady went their own ways, agreeing to meet back at the wagon later in the day. First Storm visited the bank, receiving assurance that she had sufficient funds with which to buy lumber and hire men to build her shanty. Only she wasn't going to build a shanty. It was going to be a real cabin, small out of necessity, but comfortable enough for her immediate needs. No soddy built of turf for her. Many settlers built them for economy's sake despite the fact that they were damp and nearly impossible to keep clean.

From the bank, Storm went to the lumberyard to order wood and roofing for her cabin. The owner assured her the material would be delivered to her claim the next day. Construction could be started immediately.

Storm and Grady met by chance at the lumberyard when he stopped there to order his own lumber. Since his funds were limited, he planned to build his own dwelling.

A visit to the grocery store for provisions was her last stop before Storm headed back to the wagon. She had already arranged for a well to be dug and bought items she and Buddy had neglected earlier. She placed her purchases in the wagon beside Grady's packages. Because he had been less prepared than Storm, his goods nearly filled the wagon. Foremost was the roomy tent he intended to use until his cabin was erected.

When Grady leaped into the driver's seat, Storm offered no resistance. She was too tired to argue. The hectic events of the past few days had taken their toll, and losing Buddy had been a shock to her system. Before they reached the outskirts of Guthrie, Storm was already asleep, using Grady's broad shoulder as a cushion for her head.

Storm never stirred when Grady placed an arm around her, drawing her tightly against him. The evening had grown cool and she snuggled closer against him to absorb his comforting warmth. She didn't even awaken when they reached her claim and he carried her into her tent, placing her gently on the bedroll that served as her bed and covering her with another blanket he found nearby. After unloading her provisions and stacking them against the tent, he drove the wagon to his own claim, unloading his supplies before unhitching the horses and hobbling them nearby. He'd return the wagon the next day, he decided, giving him another excuse to see Storm.

Workers arrived with Storm's lumber the next morning, and within days the cabin took shape. Meanwhile, Grady began work on his own dwelling, which was rising much more slowly since he was working alone. Storm had decided to move her cabin site more than a half mile away from the place where she had originally erected her tent; it now stood on a grassy knoll beneath a stand of trees that would shade her home in the blistering heat of summer. The site also gave her a good view of her land. And better yet, it was farther away from Grady's cabin site, which was nestled on the bank of the river.

The digging of the well was going more slowly than the raising of the cabin, Storm thought as she trekked across Grady's land with a pail in each hand. She had driven the wagon to a section of his roped-off claim, then walked the rest of the way to the river to draw water for the day. It was a daily chore, one she had come to loathe. Each time she crossed the half-breed's land she felt more and more indebted to him, and she didn't like the feeling. Sometimes she saw him working on his cabin and she nodded in greeting, and other times he was nowhere in sight. Inspecting his land, she supposed. She had to admit it was a much better piece of land than her own quarter section and she envied him his claim.

This morning the absence of hammering sounds told Storm that Grady wasn't working on his cabin. Her relief was profound when she realized she wouldn't have to see him with his splendid torso bared to the sun as he worked on his cabin. The sight of a half-naked Grady, his bronze muscles taut and slick with sweat, nearly always sent her pulses spinning out of control.

"How is your cabin coming along?"

Storm spun around, dropping the buckets she had just filled at the river's edge and spilling the water onto the ground. "Must you sneak up behind me like that?"

"I didn't mean to frighten you. I always move quietly; comes naturally, I suppose."

"Look what you've made me do," Storm said crossly.

Scowling up at him, she nudged an empty bucket with her booted toe. Only then did she get a good look at him, and she gasped in dismay. He was shirtless, as usual, and pantless as well. The brief breechclout he wore left little to the imagination. Storm's eyes settled briefly on the taut piece of deerhide stretched across his loins before flying back up to his face.

"I can remedy that easily enough," Grady said, picking up the buckets and walking down to the river bank.

Storm gulped and tried to look away when he bent over to draw water. A goodly portion of his taut buttocks was exposed, and the sight thoroughly unsettled her. When Grady completed his task and turned around, her face had turned a dull red. When comprehension dawned, he gave a soft, mocking laugh.

"Does my body disturb you?"

"I—no, should it?"

"You make a terrible liar, Storm Kennedy. If I didn't know better, I'd think you were an untouched maiden. Did you never admire your husband's body? Or explore his flesh in ways that made you both burn with desire?"

Storm was appalled. "Why—I—how dare you suggest that I—I—participated in such depraved activities!"

Grady cocked a dark eyebrow. "Depraved? You were a married woman, Storm. What is depraved about desiring your husband? Or pleasing him and being pleased in return?"

"I—I don't know what you're talking about." His explicit questions were flustering her. She had no idea what he meant.

Aghast, Grady stared at her. The notion that Storm's husband hadn't taught her the meaning of passion was inconceivable. Was Buddy Kennedy too young and inexperienced to appreciate her woman's body and what it was capable of?

"How can that be? Did you find no enjoyment in the marriage bed?" He stared at her lips, mesmerized by the soft, pink flesh, parted slightly in shock. They begged for his kisses, and Grady's need to taste their lush contours was so pressing it obliterated every moral instinct he possessed.

Reeling in shock, Storm sensed his intention too late to turn and run. Actually, she wasn't sure she would have fled had she known what was coming. Instead, her eyes widened as his arms slid around her, letting her feel his need as he pulled her close. When the look in her eyes changed from shock to confusion, Grady asked, "Can you feel how much I desire you?"

Storm nearly fainted from pleasure. The feel of his hard body against her much softer one was a new experience. Of course she and Buddy had embraced, but never had she felt the pressure of his need branding her through the layers of her clothing. Buddy had been a gentle, thoughtful lover, ever mindful of her delicate sensibilities. Lovemaking took place only at night, under the cover of darkness, not during the day when emotions were laid bare in the daylight. Wasn't that the normal way of things?

Suddenly Grady was kissing her, his tongue tracing the soft fullness of her lips before covering them completely. She was shocked at her own eager response to his kiss, and her mouth parted in protest. It was all the encouragement Grady needed as he pressed her closer and slid his tongue between her parted lips. Abruptly his lips grew hard and searching, seeking, demanding, leaving no room for protest as his tongue explored ruthlessly, leaving Storm gasping for breath. Never in her eighteen years had she experienced a kiss quite like the one bestowed on her by Grady Stryker.

Storm tried valiantly to escape the confines of Grady's arms, but to no avail. The gurgling sounds she made deep in her throat seemed to increase his arousal as his kiss deepened, until she thought she would die of pleasure.

She hated the feeling.

She loved it.

She wished he would stop.

She wanted it to go on forever.

It wasn't Buddy.

It was the thought of her dead husband and the knowledge that Grady was giving her more pleasure than she'd ever experienced with Buddy that finally moved her to act. And when she felt his hands slide over her ribs to fondle her breasts, she knew she had to do something or burn in hell forever. Twisting from his grasp, she stepped back, breathing heavily, and not just from exertion. What she felt— what Grady made her feel—was something her meager experience hadn't prepared her for. It was something so astounding, so earthshaking, it frightened her.

Storm wasn't the only one stunned by the kiss. The tumult Grady experienced was equally shattering. What had started out as an amusing experiment had quickly turned into raw lust. His violent reaction to a woman he had no business kissing stunned him. Thus he wasn't prepared when Storm doubled her fist and rammed it into his face. The blow caught him in the eye, sending him stumbling backward. Unable to stop his descent, he sat down heavily on his bottom. What sounded suspiciously like a grunt left his lungs in a great expulsion of air. The surprised look on his face gave Storm enormous satisfaction. So did the swelling already visible around his right eye.

"Don't ever touch me like that again!"

Still stunned, Grady remained on the ground, staring up at Storm with new respect. He could feel his flesh swelling and wondered if her fist was as sore as his eye. He was amazed at the strength behind the wallop and hoped she hadn't broken anything.

"You could have warned me you were going to do that," Grady complained.

Storm bit back a smile. Though her hand hurt dreadfully, it was worth it to see the arrogant half-breed laid low. "Keep your hands to yourself, Grady Stryker, and I'll not be forced to defend myself again."

"I think you protest too much, lady," Grady said, picking himself up off the ground. "You thoroughly enjoyed everything I did to you. Are all white women so damn contrary?"

"I don't know about anyone else, but I'm not the kind of woman who allows just any man to kiss her."

"Is it because I'm a half-breed?" His flinty blue eyes probed her relentlessly, demanding an answer.

"It's because I didn't like the way you kissed me, or touched me. My own husband didn't kiss or touch me like that."

Grady looked incredulous. "More's the pity. It's about time someone did."

"What do you know about marriage?" she snorted, incensed. Obviously the half-breed knew nothing about the holy state of matrimony.

"I was married before I was twenty-one." His statement took the wind out of her sails.

"M—Married? You have a wife?" Why should that information give her a sinking feeling in the pit of her stomach? Storm wondered curiously.

"I *had* a wife."

Storm thought he was being exceptionally bullheaded and asked, "What happened to her? Did you abandon her?"

"Summer Sky is no longer alive. She left the earth over three years ago."

The hollowness of his voice gave Storm a glimpse of the agony Grady suffered over the death of his wife. Storm thought that he must have loved her deeply to still suffer the loss after so long a time.

"I'm sorry." She could think of no other words

that would express her sympathy.

"It was a long time ago. It is no longer as painful as it once was," Grady said, staring off into the distance. "In time you will feel the same about your husband. Life continues. One day you will find a new mate to share your life."

"Have you? Found a new mate, I mean."

His eyes were sharp and assessing as he said, "Perhaps."

Storm grew restive under his sizzling scrutiny. Sometimes he looked at her as if he were a cat and she his saucer of milk.

"Then I wish you luck. It will take an unusual woman to keep a man like you under control."

"Yes, very unusual."

"I must return," Storm said as she grabbed the buckets Grady had filled with water and started to move off. The conversation was becoming far too intimate for her liking. And after the kiss he just gave her, she feared he might take advantage of her again. Another kiss like that and she'd be babbling like an idiot.

"Let me carry them to your wagon," Grady said, taking the buckets from her hands. Finding no reason to object, Storm hurried away, leaving Grady to follow behind her.

Storm's cabin was ready for occupancy early in November. It was crudely finished but tight and cozy enough to keep out the winter winds when they came. She had purchased a few pieces of furniture in Guthrie and had the workers set them in place before they left. The well still wasn't completed, but work was continuing. Meanwhile, she made the daily trip for water, crossing Grady's land to reach the river.

Storm's pride and joy was the iron stove she had purchased in Guthrie. It sat like a fat black Buddha in the kitchen area of the small cabin. Later, she reckoned she could add a bedroom and maybe a separate kitchen. But for now the one large room would serve her needs quite adequately.

Her bed, consisting of a brass frame with rope supports and a thick feather mattress, occupied one corner of the cabin, separated from the work area by a blanket hung from the ceiling. A table, two chairs, and several kerosene lamps were the only other furnishings in the room. The cabin still looked bare in comparison to her parents' home in Missouri, but given time Storm knew she could make it into a home she could be proud of.

The first visitor to Storm's new house was Nat Turner. He arrived one brisk day with a small bouquet of fall flowers. Storm was more than a little startled to see him ride up to the house bearing a gift.

"I heard in town that your cabin was built and I wanted to be the first to bring you a housewarming gift," he said, smiling obsequiously. "It isn't much, but I know how lonely you must be out here by yourself."

"Why, thank you, Mr. Turner," Storm said,

touched by his thoughtfulness. "Won't you come in? I'm just about to sit down to lunch. There's plenty if you'd care to join me."

"I'd be right pleased," Nat replied, taking off his hat and entering behind her. Once inside, he looked around curiously, wondering what a woman like Storm Kennedy was doing living in a scantly furnished one-room cabin with few amenities to make life bearable. "You've fixed the cabin up right nice, Mrs. Kennedy." Lies came easily to his lips. He could lie and practice deceit with ease, as long as it benefited Nat Turner. "May I call you Storm?"

"Why, I—I suppose," Storm stammered. She could think of no reason why he shouldn't use her first name.

"You must call me Nat. I feel like we're old friends. Have you decided yet how you're going to farm your land on your own, Storm?"

Actually, Storm had given it a great deal of thought lately. She didn't have a lot of money left to hire help, yet she had to put the land to use in some way. "I'm still considering several options, Mr.—Nat. Please sit down," she said, gesturing to one of the kitchen chairs. "I hope you're hungry. I shot a rabbit early this morning and made it into a delicious stew. There's also biscuits and honey for desert."

"A veritable feast, Storm. Thank you, I'm famished. Are you proficient with a gun? Do you do a lot of hunting?"

"Just for small game," Storm said as she ladled out the stew. "Buddy—my late husband—taught me how to shoot when we were just children. I'm no expert, but I know how to handle a firearm."

"As well you should, you being out here alone and all. Has the half-breed on the neighboring spread given you any problems? It's a shame his kind are allowed to settle amongst civilized people."

Storm's spoon stopped half-way to her mouth. "Are you talking about Grady Stryker? Did you know his father owns one of the largest and most prosperous ranches in Wyoming?" She didn't know that for a fact, but the opportunity to point out that Grady wasn't the savage people thought was just too tempting to resist. Well, she amended silently, perhaps he *was* a savage, but in ways that had nothing to do with his Indian blood. It had to do with some violent act that had changed him. She had no knowledge of what had changed him, but she fully intended to learn the truth one day.

Turner's mouth dropped open. "I had no idea. Rumor has it he's an Indian renegade called Thunder who terrorized white settlers and raided indiscriminately."

"I wouldn't know about that," Storm said. Her shoulders lifted in a careless shrug.

"Look here, Storm, don't trust the half-breed. I don't care who his parents are, the man is a killer. I really think you ought to reconsider your decision to homestead."

"I'll not give up my land."

"I'll give you a good price if you sell to me.

94

Let me deal with the half-breed. I know how to handle men like him."

"If I need help dealing with Grady I'll let you know," Storm said tightly. She didn't like being pressured. "As for my claim, Nat, I'm keeping it. I know farming all my acres will prove a difficult task so I'm thinking of running cattle instead."

"Cattle! What do you know about ranching?"

"About as much as I know about farming, but that isn't going to stop me. I've already talked to someone in town about running cattle, and he's promised to sell me a small herd come spring."

"You are one determined woman, Storm," Nat said, shoving back his chair. "The lunch was delicious, but I really must be going. If you change your mind, you know where to reach me."

"I won't change my mind. The flowers are lovely. It was thoughtful of you to bring them out."

Jamming his hat back on his head, Nat left the cabin. The disgruntled look on his face showed that he was far from pleased with the result of his visit. He had hoped that Widow Kennedy would be thoroughly disgusted by now with the hardships of pioneer life and eager to sell her claim. It was a good piece of land, ideal for grazing, and if he could get his hands on it he could turn a tidy profit. The grass was so lush that if she decided to run cattle instead of growing wheat, as so many of the farmers planned to do, she would stand to make a fortune.

"What are you doing here, Turner?"

Turner was so engrossed in his devious plotting that he didn't hear Grady ride up on Lightning.

"I might ask you the same, Stryker. Or would you prefer I call you Thunder?"

A half smile crossed Grady's face, a smile that did not reach his eyes. "Stryker will do. You haven't answered my question."

"Not that it concerns you, but I heard Storm's cabin was finished and I brought her a housewarming gift."

"Storm?" he said with a significant lifting of his brows. "Since when have you been on a first-name basis with Mrs. Kennedy?"

"Since we became friends."

"Keep away from her. She is better off without your kind."

"And leave her to yours?" Turner laughed nastily. "Not likely. Besides, I doubt Storm will want to stay here once she finds out how lonely the prairie can be for a woman without a man to protect her. When she's ready to sell I'll be here with money in my hand. I'll make you the same offer, Stryker. Men like you don't settle in one place for very long. Your land is even more desirable than Storm's. Whenever you're ready to move on, I'll take it off your hands."

"I'll sell my land, Turner . . ." Turner's eyes grew round and his lips stretched into a triumphant smile, " . . . when hell freezes over."

# *Chapter Five*

"What was that all about?" Storm asked as she watched Nat ride off hell for leather. "What did you say to him?"

Grady whipped around, unaware that Storm had stepped out the door to investigate. He paused for a moment in silent appreciation before answering. He hadn't seen Storm in several days, and each time he saw her he was struck anew by her radiant beauty. Storm's golden hair and fair complexion were a vivid contrast to the dark beauty Summer Sky had possessed. But where Summer Sky had been slim as a boy, Storm could be called voluptuous, with her high-pointed breasts, narrow waist, and gently curved hips.

Storm fumed in mute affront while Grady's eyes made a slow journey over her face and form. Why did he look at her like that? she wondered. He made her uncomfortable, staring at her as if he could gobble her up. Then, unaccountably, her own eyes made a quick tour over his tall, buckskin-clad form. Did he never wear clothes like normal men? The soft, supple deerhide clung to his frame like a second skin, leaving nothing to the imagination. He looked tough, lean, and sinewy; his well-muscled body moved with easy grace. He looked powerful and intimidating—and too tempting for her peace of mind.

Suddenly she heard Grady chuckle. "See anything you like?"

Annoyed at being caught blatantly admiring the half-breed scoundrel, Storm bristled indignantly. "I might ask you the same thing."

"I like everything I see." His answer caught her by surprise.

"Well I don't," she declared haughtily as she turned her eyes to stare past him. "Mr. Turner seemed in an all-fired hurry to leave."

"He didn't take kindly to being told to keep away from you. When he offered for my land he went too damn far."

"Who appointed you my keeper? I told you before, I can take care of myself."

"For some damn reason I feel responsible for you," Grady complained. "The least you could do is show some gratitude."

"Gratitude isn't exactly what I would call my feelings for you, Mr. Stryker."

"I can think of at least a half dozen things I'd

rather you felt for me," Grady answered, surprising himself with his reply. "And a half dozen more pleasant things we could do besides fight."

His voice was a raspy growl, sending chills up and down Storm's spine. Never before had a man's words or tone of voice affected her the way Grady's did now. She felt all tingly inside, like her innards were melting. She was no virgin, for heaven's sake; why should she act like an innocent schoolgirl who didn't know what went on between men and women? And why hadn't she felt like this with Buddy? Her longstanding relationship with Buddy had been comfortable, almost like that of brother and sister. It wasn't right that this man—this arrogant, dangerous man—should make her feel as if there were so much more to life than she'd ever dreamed. His words made a sudden mockery of life as she once knew it, and it frightened her.

"Keep your opinions to yourself, Grady Stryker! When I want your help I'll ask for it, but don't hold your breath. I suppose you came here for some reason, so you might as well spit it out before I close the door in your face."

"You're a hard woman for one so young, Storm Kennedy," Grady said with a hint of amusement. "I've tried my damnedest to be helpful, feeling responsible for you and all, but you won't let me help you. I just stopped by to see if you need anything from town. I'm going to Guthrie for more nails to put the finishing touches on my cabin. I've already moved in, but it lacks a few amenities."

A dull red crept up Storm's neck. Perhaps Grady *was* trying to be neighborly, but he had no call to be rude to her visitors. Nat Turner was merely being thoughtful by bringing her a gift of flowers for her new cabin. She couldn't fault him for wanting to buy her land, and she thought it commendable that he didn't persist or become angry when she refused.

"I—I appreciate your offer, but I don't need a thing. And I'll no longer need to draw water from the river," she added. "My well was finished yesterday."

"I'm going to start digging my own well once my cabin is built," Grady said. "I hope it's finished before the ground freezes."

"Feel free to draw water from mine if you aren't able to complete the task before winter," Storm heard herself saying. "It's the least I could do since you allowed me to cross your land to reach the river. I'll show it to you."

While she spoke, Grady's eyes were strangely drawn to Storm's mouth. She had the sweetest mouth—succulent, soft, made for kissing, he thought as he stared at the lush contours and imagined himself sipping from the heady nectar of her lips. He couldn't recall when he'd seen lips so pink and inviting. He took an unconscious step forward, and at the same time, unaware of his intention, Storm started forward, intending to show him the well. They collided, their bodies coming together with a soft thud.

"Oh." Her eyes flew open as his arms came around her.

"Oh, lady." There was no way Grady could keep from kissing her since his arms were already around her and their bodies were pasted together from breast to thigh. "I don't even care if you did that by accident or merely to taunt me." His eyes narrowed to a hard glitter.

"I didn't—"

The words died in her throat as Grady's mouth covered hers and the tip of his tongue traced the soft fullness of her lips. A warm, heady sensation spread through her body as he suddenly forced her mouth open with the thrust of his tongue, claiming her in a way Buddy never had. She was just recovering from the hunger of his kiss when abruptly his lips turned hard and searching, demanding a response she wanted desperately to withhold. Then, just as abruptly, he broke off the kiss and stared into her eyes, leaving her mouth burning and her knees weak.

"Kiss me back." The plea left his mouth in a throaty growl.

"No, I—"

"If you don't, I'll kiss you until you grow too weary to resist."

"Grady, why are you doing this to me?" She licked her lips, tasting him on her tongue.

"Damned if I know."

Then his lips recaptured hers, even more demanding this time. When Storm tried to pull

101

away his hands flew up to tunnel into her hair, holding her head in place as he continued to ravage her mouth in sweet, wild torment.

"Kiss me back, damn you!"

She opened her mouth, knowing instinctively it was what he wanted. She felt him searching, searching, until he drew her tongue into his mouth and she had no choice but to kiss him in return. With a passion she didn't know existed, she gave herself freely to the fire of his kiss. Then, without warning, his mouth left hers to nibble a scorching path down her neck while his hands dropped to press her hips against the hardness of his loins. When he finally released her, her eyes were glazed and her face wore a look of stunned disbelief.

What was happening to her?

Thick, hot blood surged through Grady's veins, and he knew without a doubt that he wanted this woman. Wanted her more than he'd ever wanted another woman. And that included Summer Sky. Making love to Summer Sky had been sweetly rewarding and gentle, as natural as breathing and sleeping. But instinctively he knew that when he and Storm came together there would be nothing sweet or gentle about their mating. It would be an earth-shaking experience as wild and tumultuous as their names implied, and would change their lives forever.

Was he ready for that kind of upheaval?

Abruptly he looked away, his expression drained of all emotion. His harsh whisper came from the very depths of his soul. "What have you done to me?" His words sent a thrill of apprehension racing down Storm's spine.

"I—I've done nothing. I can't help it if you keep pawing and kissing me."

He eyed her narrowly. "Something about you makes me forget that I am a Lakota warrior. Lakota warriors are taught to restrain their lust and keep emotions under tight rein. Yet I can't seem to keep away from you. I want to touch your flesh without the barrier of your clothing." He reached out to stroke her breasts. Her nipples hardened into tight little buds against his palms and she gasped in horror. "I want to kiss you until your lips are swollen from my kisses and your knees grow weak." Adroitly she stepped out of his reach, fearing his next words.

"I want to make love to you, Storm Kennedy."

Storm's mouth gaped open, unable to give voice to all the despicable names she wanted to call him. Swallowing convulsively, she managed to say, "Get—get out of here! How dare you say such terrible things to me."

"Among the Lakota it isn't terrible to want a woman; it is natural and right. You are a widow, not unaccustomed to a man's desires. And you want me, I can tell."

"You can tell no such thing! That's evil."

He laughed as if sincerely amused. "We'll see, Storm Kennedy, we'll see. Meanwhile, if there is nothing you need from town, I'll rid you of my obnoxious company. Just remember, lady, one day Thunder and Storm will come together in a brilliant display of passion. Grandfather has spoken; Thunder can only exist in the bosom of Storm. The confrontation should prove a spectacular one."

Turning abruptly, he leaped astride Lightning and thundered off in a flurry of dust.

Thunder and Storm? Grandfather? What in the world was Grady talking about? Storm wondered curiously. He spoke in riddles, making no sense at all. Yet she knew instinctively that Grady Stryker presented a danger to her very existence. The sheer magnitude of his desire frightened her.

Grady smiled all the way to town. It had been years since anything had pleased him as much as Storm Kennedy. And whether she liked it or not, she *would* yield to him.

Grady entered the busy town and went directly to the hardware store to purchase his nails. From there he visited the mercantile. He was in desperate need of warm clothes and boots. The dependable buckskins and moccasins had served him well, but if he wanted to conform to white dictates he must dress the part. He left the store a scant half hour later clad in twill pants and flannel shirt and wearing a pair of brown leather boots that reminded him of those he owned when he helped his father on the ranch. In a bundle beneath his arm he carried a heavy sheepskin jacket and the buckskins he had just discarded.

After stuffing his parcels into his saddlebags, he headed to the bank. He still carried money on him that should be deposited in an account in his name. Thunder had no use for banks, but for Grady Stryker the bank was a practical way of preserving his remaining assets. The one thing Grady didn't get was a haircut. He couldn't bring himself to shed everything about him that was Indian. He clung to his long hair with a tenacity that displayed his utter contempt for those who called him half-breed. Grady Stryker was proud of his Lakota blood and his Indian heritage.

As Grady made his way to the bank he was unaware of the two men who followed his progress from the safety of a hotel room that overlooked the street.

"That's the bastard, Purdy. If not for him, I'd own a prime piece of land on the river."

Purdy nodded in commiseration. "Because of him my shootin' arm is outta commission. I heard the renegade was fast with a gun, but I had no idea he'd be *that* fast. I ain't through with him yet, not by a long shot."

"Me neither," Lew Fork mumbled as he watched Grady enter the bank.

"Break it off, you two," Nat Turner advised. "I hired you for a purpose, and killing the half-breed isn't what I'm paying you for. Later, maybe, if he don't pull up stakes on his own, then we can face that obstacle. Right now you're to concentrate on Widow Kennedy. She's vulnerable at this time and more inclined to sell her land than any of the other settlers who have yet to face their first winter on the prairie."

"You want us to kill a woman?" Purdy asked. He'd never killed a woman before and didn't know if he'd want to now.

"Hell no, not kill her, just frighten her so she'll come begging me to buy her land."

"What's so damn valuable about her claim?" Fork wanted to know.

"There's a rich buyer from Texas interested in buying as much of the Cherokee Strip as he can lay his hands on. The closer to the river, the better. It's my understanding he plans on running cattle into Oklahoma and Kansas."

"And you think the Kennedy woman will sell to you?" Fork asked.

"If she does, I stand to make a tidy profit," Turner revealed. "You two could share in it if you succeed in scaring her into selling. Once she leaves I don't think the half-breed will want to stay and work his land. He's hardly the kind to settle down. Instinct tells me he's more interested in the young widow than he is in his land. If Storm Kennedy sells out, the half-breed will pull up stakes and sell me his land."

"I wouldn't try to second guess the renegade if I were you," Purdy advised. "Look what it got me. He coulda killed me."

"But he didn't and now you're working for me."

"Yeah, but it's the Injun we really want," Fork grumbled.

"Tell you what," Turner said in a conciliatory

tone. "You boys do this job and I'll help you in any way I can to bring down the breed. Plus you'll be paid damn good wages for frightening Storm Kennedy off her claim."

Purdy and Fork exchanged pleased glances. "You got it, boss. You hired the right men for the job. In another week this damn arm will be as good as new."

"Another week it is," Turner agreed, clasping each man's hand to seal the bargain. "I don't care what you have to do, just don't kill the woman before she signs the bill of sale and turns the deed over to me."

"Do you care if we rough her up a bit?" Fork asked, nudging Purdy's shoulder and grinning slyly. "The widow is a damn fine lookin' woman. And young."

"Whatever it takes," Turner said, grimacing with distaste. "Just don't tell me about it once you've done your work."

Storm didn't see Grady for a full week after the day he kissed her so thoroughly outside her cabin. She groaned mentally when she recalled the devastating eagerness with which she had responded to him, and how the liquid heat of his mouth had seared her very soul. The thought of his kisses sent a bolt of pure rebellion through her. How dare he look at her with his bold blue eyes and touch her with his searing lips. And his hands! Good Lord, his hands were everywhere. Wooing her with the strength of his caresses and making her forget everything but the need to press her body against his in a most carnal way. For her own peace of mind she hoped he'd never set foot on her land again.

Unfortunately Storm's wishes weren't granted. Grady showed up at her door one brisk morning grinning from ear to ear. When he told her his cabin was finished she offered tentative congratulations.

"You wouldn't have any coffee on the stove, would you?" Grady asked as he glanced past her into the inviting interior of her cabin. His own place wasn't furnished nearly as cozily, containing only functional pieces of furniture that served their purpose and little else.

Inviting Grady Stryker inside her house was the last thing she wanted to do, Storm thought as she heard herself asking him to come inside and warm himself. She hadn't needed to use the new fireplace yet, for the stove provided sufficient heat for the cool, sunny days of fall. Grady sat down at the table while she poured him a cup of coffee.

"Have you seen your friend Turner recently?" Grady asked.

"No, should I have?"

"He's a speculator. He wants land and seems determined to have yours. Since you're alone out here with no husband and virtually no protection, he feels quite certain you'll sell out to him if he waits long enough."

"He's wrong," Storm insisted with quiet determination.

"It's going to be a long winter, Storm. Have you cut wood for the fireplace yet? There are dozens of things that must be done to prepare for those days when you won't be able to leave your cabin."

"I—no, I haven't gotten around to cutting wood yet. I suppose I shall have to one day soon."

"There's no need," Grady said gruffly. "I've done it for you. It's the least I could do for— for everything that's happened. If you loan me your wagon, I'll load it up and bring the wood to you tomorrow."

"You've cut wood for me?" Storm asked, startled. "There was no need, I—"

"Your land has few trees, while they grow abundantly on mine. I'd do the same for any neighbor. Besides, I'm accustomed to hard labor while you—well, let's just say there are other tasks you're better suited for." The intense look in his blue eyes left small doubt in Storm's mind to what he was referring.

Hanging on the frayed threads of restraint, Storm smiled obliquely and said, "And I can't think of one thing you're suited for besides hard work. From the size of those biceps I'd say you have more muscle than brains."

Storm seethed as his insufferable laughter filled the cabin. "I'm surprised you noticed."

Storm groaned in frustration. She'd never met a more exasperating man. How in the world did his wife ever deal with him?

"If you're finished with your coffee there are

chores I must do outside. Thank you for cutting wood for me. You may use the wagon whenever you like. I must confess, though, I would never have taken you for a thoughtful man."

Setting the cup down, Grady uncoiled his lean length from the chair. "You have no idea what I'm capable of, Storm Kennedy." His voice was low and strident, sending chills down her spine. "But one day you'll find out."

He turned abruptly and strode out the door, leaving Storm standing with her mouth open, ready to fling back a tart retort but unable to form the words. All she could do was stare at his broad shoulders, narrow waist, and the smooth tautness of his buttocks encased in tight twill pants.

Though Storm tried to keep her mind occupied with work, Grady's face kept appearing out of nowhere to haunt her. She couldn't deny that he was appealing. His features were handsomely sculpted. His skin was bronzed from the sun, and his black hair, though a bit too long for her liking, contrasted vividly with his striking blue eyes. And his mouth . . . boldly chiseled lips, wide but gracefully arched, generously curved, indolent . . . tempting. Goodness, just thinking about the man gave her goosebumps. But what really set her to trembling was his sultry gaze. She couldn't ever recall Buddy looking at her in quite the same way.

That evening Storm prepared herself a lonely meal, wondering if she should have invited Grady to share it with her. Or perhaps she should invite Nat Turner out one night to sup with her. Though she'd never admit it to Grady, the life she led was indeed a lonely one. The last time she was in town she'd heard there was to be a big dance next Saturday night; perhaps she should go. She quickly discarded that notion, aware that widows didn't attend dances and such doings during their time of mourning.

The mourning period seemed interminable, she thought bleakly. She and Buddy had been so young, no thought was ever given to the possibility that one of them might die any time soon. She knew Buddy wouldn't want her to grieve a long time, that he'd want her to be happy and enjoy life. Yet no matter how lonely Storm was, she knew that her land was her salvation, that come what may she'd hang on to it and survive. If only that damn Grady Stryker would stop badgering her.

Storm glanced out the window, surprised at how dark it had grown while she ate dinner and cleaned up. Not a star was visible in the inky sky, and the pale sliver of moon was obscured by thick clouds rolling in from the west. The low rumble of thunder echoed over the prairie and distant streaks of lightning lit the moonless sky. Storm hoped the approaching storm wasn't a severe one, for storms had always made her nervous. Chiding herself for being a sissy, she prepared for bed.

The fine lawn nightdress had just fallen in place over her head when the sound of advancing horsemen echoed through the darkness. She flew to the window and threw aside the curtain. It was too dark out to see a thing, but the thunder of hooves grew louder with each passing minute. A shiver of apprehension passed over Storm's body. Instinctively she knew that this was no friendly visit from neighbors. She had the light doused and the fully loaded shotgun in her hands when the shooting and yelling started.

Crouching beneath the window, Storm searched her mind for a valid reason behind this senseless attack. With bullets flying at the house at a furious speed, she tried to think of someone who would wish her ill and came up blank. She had no idea how many men were shooting at her, or why, but the rapid firing indicated that more than one man was in the raiding party. They were circling the cabin, shooting at random and shouting, when a bullet shattered the glass window pane Storm was so proud of. Cautiously raising her head, she balanced the shotgun on the window ledge and fired a few rounds at the dark shadows as they rode past. It was far better to retaliate than let the raiders think she was a helpless woman cowering in a corner, Storm thought as she squeezed off another round. She had plenty of ammunition and could protect her property as well as any man. She would feel much better though, if she knew what this was all about.

*And what would happen to her if she failed to chase the men away?*

Her answer came sooner than she had anticipated. A sudden quiet put a new fear into her as she raised her head to peer through the shattered window. She knew a moment of wild jubilation when she thought she had successfully chased the men off. But a moment later the locked door gave way beneath a pair of booted feet, crashing open with a loud bang. A scream left Storm's throat as the two men who had barged through the door saw her crouching beneath the window and started in her direction. They were upon her before she had time to raise the gun and squeeze the trigger.

Grady paced the narrow confines of his cabin in long, restless strides. Something had disturbed him, and his instincts were usually right on target. He had made the rounds of his yard twice but found nothing amiss. Glancing toward Storm's homestead, he saw nothing threatening there. He shook his head, disgusted at himself for being so damn fanciful. But usually his senses were so keen, he did not dismiss his intuition without careful investigation. Tonight had been the exception. Though his intuition told him otherwise, he had found nothing to even remotely suggest danger.

Stripping to his breechclout, Grady prepared to curl up in the bedroll that served as his bed. The air was cold and crisp; outside a storm was brewing. He'd worn much less in colder weather than this and thought nothing of walking around the cabin barefoot and nearly naked. Dismissing his fears, he stretched out on the bedroll, his mind suddenly filled with arousing visions of Storm, her honey brown eyes flashing with defiance and her body soft and warm in his arms. He closed his eyes and imagined her spread beneath him, her body moist and welcoming as he slid full and deep inside her. He could feel her tighten around him and . . .

Suddenly he bolted upright. All his erotic thoughts skidded to a halt as the explosive sound of gunfire drifted across the prairie. Who could be firing guns at this time of night? he wondered as his mind worked furiously to sort out the ominous night sounds. His body tensed with painful awareness as his acute hearing told him the shots were coming from the direction of Storm's homestead. His body reacted before his mind gave the order.

Disdaining his clothing, lying neatly folded beside the bed, Grady grabbed his rifle and knife and flew out the door. A blood-curdling war cry left his throat as he leaped atop Lightning's bare back and kneed him viciously in the ribs. He had ridden without a saddle so often in the past, it seemed second nature to him. Neither icy wind nor sharp needles of sleet driving into his bare flesh slowed him as he raced across the prairie toward Storm's cabin. His thick black brows were drawn together in a fierce scowl, his mouth clamped tight, his eyes glazed as he imagined all the potentially life-threatening situations threatening Storm in the middle of the night.

A tremendous clap of thunder unleashed the full fury of the impending storm, and Lightning reared in fright. But Grady's strong hands soon brought him under control. The blackness of the night was relieved only by the brilliant display of lightning as the dim outline of Storm's darkened cabin came into view. The shooting had ceased, but Grady knew a new fear when a piercing scream rose above the rumble of thunder.

Reining Lightning to a skidding halt before the cabin, Grady jumped to the ground, noting with growing alarm that the door was open and hanging askew from one hinge. He burst through the portal just as Storm let loose another scream.

"Hold still, ya little wildcat. Ya won't get hurt if ya relax and loosen up a little. All me and my buddy want is to have us a little fun with ya. You're a ripe little piece." He reached out to squeeze Storm's breast. "I ain't felt titties like that in a month of Sundays."

His voice was muffled, and Storm realized that the lower half of his face was covered with a bandana to avoid recognition.

"Hurry up, man, I'm so hard I'm about to bust my britches."

"What's the hurry? We got all night. I aim to do this up right."

"Bastard!" Storm bit out from between clenched teeth. Her nightdress was yanked up to her waist and she screamed again as rough fingers prodded ruthlessly between her legs. Though she knew it would do her no good, she opened her mouth and screamed again.

Then, suddenly, all hell broke loose. A huge body came hurtling through the partially open door, and both Storm's tormentors went flying across the room. Squinting into the darkness, Storm tried to discover the identity of her rescuer, but it wasn't until a brilliant flash of lightning illuminated the cabin that she recognized Grady. He was crouched on the balls of his bare feet, his lips drawn back in a vicious snarl, his bronzed skin slick with rain. The bulging muscles of his thighs and biceps flexed as he leaped forward, knife poised tightly in hand.

"Sonuvabitch! Let's get the hell outta here before the renegade kills us!"

Taking advantage of the darkness, both men streaked past Grady and out the door. Acting reflexively, Grady sent his knife flying through the air. An agonized shriek told him that his aim had been true. But unfortunately the man had only been wounded, and he and his partner were soon riding hell for leather across the prairie. Grady started to follow, but Storm's soft plea stopped him in his tracks.

"Don't leave me, Grady. Please don't leave me."

# *Chapter Six*

A flash of lightning sent jagged fingers of light arcing into the room, sculpting Grady's coppery skin in bold angles and hollows. It transformed him from mortal man to pagan deity, remote, savage, splendid in his nakedness. Storm couldn't take her eyes off him. Her arrested expression must have conveyed a message to him for he reached her in a bounding stride and picked her up. Cradling her securely in his arms, he sat down on the bed, placing her on his lap.

"It's all right, Storm, the bastards are gone. They can no longer hurt you."

Her tremulous voice conveyed her confusion. "What did they want with me?"

"I don't know, but I'm going to find out. They didn't harm you, did they?"

She shook her head in vigorous denial. "You arrived in time. How—how did you know?"

"I heard gunfire. I sensed danger long before that but could find no reason for it. I wish you had let me go after the bastards."

Her arms tightened around his neck. "I couldn't bear to be alone after—after those men tried to—tried to . . ."

"Don't think about it, sweetheart. I promise it won't happen again. Next time I'll listen to my instincts. I wouldn't be surprised if Turner was behind the attack."

Stunned, Storm insisted, "No, Nat wouldn't become involved in such nasty business."

She was still trembling, and Grady began stroking her back in slow, lazy circles, soothing her as he would a child who needed comforting. Grady didn't press the issue, but deep in his heart he knew Nat Turner was capable of much more than Storm gave him credit for.

Another streak of lightning blazed a path across the inky sky and a roar of thunder rattled the windows, bringing a new fear to Storm. She clutched at him frantically and buried her head against the solid warmth of his chest.

"What is it? Are you afraid the men will return?"

Once again her head moved back and forth in a negative motion as she offered a muffled explanation. "I never did like storms. When I was a small child one of my playmates was struck down by lightning. I couldn't understand why she didn't get up. Through the years, my fear of storms has never abated."

Grady tried to concentrate on her words, but by now the raw pleasure of having Storm warm and willing in his arms eclipsed all else. The single garment she wore offered little hindrance as his stroking hands tested the suppleness of her flesh beneath the linen nightdress. He felt the softness of her breasts against his chest and knew instinctively that he could never leave the cabin without attaining a glimpse of Paradise. And if he was any judge of emotions, it was what Storm wanted too.

"Perhaps I should leave," Grady suggested. "I'm only human, Storm. I can take only so much. Are you willing to test my endurance?"

Grady's stroking hands were so soothing, it took considerable effort for Storm to sort through his words. And when she did, she didn't care that he was asking her to send him away before it was too late. Under no circumstances did she want to be alone. The comfort she found in Grady's arms was far too pleasurable to abandon. She looked up at him with an astonishingly level gaze, and Grady had to look away, knowing that he intended to make love to her this night yet unable to stop the tide of passion that surged through his loins.

He wanted Storm Kennedy. Wanted her with an urgency that transcended all reason and thought.

"I don't know what you want from me, Grady." Her voice was shaky and unsure. "Can't you accept the fact that I don't want to be alone and let it go at that?"

"You're amazingly innocent for all your bravado, love," Grady said softly. "I understand your fear perfectly. You're the one who doesn't understand what *I* want from *you*. Look at me, Storm."

Reluctantly, she raised her head, staring into the incredible blue depths of his eyes.

"I want to make love to you, Storm Kennedy." There, he'd said it. She could order him out now before it was too late or . . .

Grady's words were like a caress against her skin. They seeped inside her, bringing a languor that prevented coherent speech. His breath was warm against her cheek, his naked chest and legs hard and unyielding. She felt the ponderous weight and substance of his hunger, so alive and palpable she could almost taste it, and something new and profound opened up inside her. It was almost as if a mystery was about to be revealed to her.

"Don't leave me, Grady." The words tumbled from her lips before her mind released them.

"Oh, lady."

His arms closed around her like steel bands; his hands grew boldly insistent as they made short work of the buttons at her throat. Then she felt his warm lips nuzzling her neck as he pushed her nightdress down her arms to her waist. She gasped as the cool night air puckered the crushed rose velvet tips of her breasts. Another flash of lightning turned darkness into daylight, and Grady raised his head to stare at her bared flesh, his blue eyes startlingly intense. He let his eyes feast on the firm, lush breasts with their impudent nipples until his heart was beating so fast he could scarcely breathe.

"Oh, lady," Grady repeated in a strangled voice. "Sweet, so sweet. I knew you'd look like this."

He tugged at the hem of her nightdress, eager to rid her of the last remaining obstacle between him and all that he desired, but Storm resisted.

"Oh, God, I don't know what I'm doing. This isn't right. I can't."

Grady groaned, all restraint fleeing in a surge of passion so profound it made a mockery of his Indian training. "I suspect you've never been loved like I'm going to love you," he managed to say. "Don't stop me now. I think I've waited for this moment my whole life." He tilted her chin up, forcing her to meet his lips. "Kiss me, Storm."

She was still murmuring no and shaking her head when she raised her lips to his mouth. A thousand thoughts flew across her mind, but all she could think to say was, "You're wicked, Grady Stryker."

"I try to be," he replied, only seconds before his mouth covered hers hungrily. The thrust of his tongue into her mouth sent shock waves through her body, and Storm felt herself floundering in a strange world where only feelings existed. Grady had kissed her before, but this time his kisses promised more, much more. More than she wanted to know. He kissed her thoroughly, ravenously, claiming the length of her tongue with bold ferocity.

When his lips finally left her trembling mouth the torment did not cease. It merely intensified as they slid down the slim column of her throat to capture the tightly curled tip of her breast. He spent long, torturous minutes nipping first one then the other tender bud with strong white teeth, then laving them with the rough warmth of his tongue to take the pleasure/pain away. Did all men enjoy doing such things? Storm wondered dazedly. Buddy had never attempted so brazen an act.

Pausing, Grady gazed into Storm's passion-glazed eyes and smiled at the arrested expression on her face. "Did you like that, sweet? It's only the beginning."

The beginning of what? Storm wondered distractedly. Curiosity overrode caution. Her reply was to sink her fingers into his long hair and pull him back to her breasts. This time he kissed tantalizing circles around the firm mounds before drawing each nipple in turn into his mouth and suckling.

"Oh." She arched against him, pressing herself more fully into the warmth of his mouth. His suckling and nuzzling continued until suddenly Storm realized that another dimension to her torment had been added. His hand had found its way beneath the hem of her nightdress!

Grady was lost in a world of sensual pleasure, thrilled by Storm's innocent response to his loving. Her flesh was the color of cream and felt as soft and velvety as a baby's. He wanted to taste and touch every inch of her succulent flesh, wanted to thrust his hardness into her softness again and again, until she cried out in rapture. He wanted her to feel more pleasure with him than she had with her husband. He wanted *his* name on her lips when she reached her peak, not the name of a dead man.

Storm moaned as Grady's hand stroked along the inside of her thigh, sliding upward, finally coming to rest on the nest of blonde curls between her legs. She felt his fingers tense as they quested upward and found the moistness she had never been aware of before. He toyed for a moment in that downy softness before gently spiraling inward with one finger. Each sensation was new and unique, and Storm grasped Grady's shoulders to keep herself from falling into a dark abyss of sensual awareness such as she had never experienced before. Then he touched that place around which her passion stemmed, and Storm nearly flew off his lap.

"Grady, oh God!"

"Relax, sweetheart. Take it slow and easy. Scream, cry, do whatever you want, I won't leave you."

Carefully he inserted another finger inside her, thrusting gently as his thumb rotated the tiny nub of flesh at the entrance, intensifying her pleasure a thousandfold. Vivid flashes of

123

lightning—or did the light come from within her?—set her body aflame as his fingers stirred her flesh to raw, aching response. Storm knew that what Grady was doing to her was sinful, that the reason Buddy never made her feel like this was because it was too shameful to enjoy something so carnally satisfying. Only a devil would know just how and where to touch her to make her cry out and writhe and act like a wanton.

"Please, I don't . . ." The words ended in a groan and shriek as the sweet ecstasy of climax took her by surprise. Thunder shook the earth, lightning charged her body from the inside out and she felt herself spinning—spinning . . . She rode the crest of sensation, hovering between sanity and madness for long, pleasure-filled minutes.

"What's happening to me?" Her cry reached out to touch Grady's heart in a way it had never been touched before.

"Have you never attained climax before?" Grady asked, stunned. He could tell by the glazed look in her eyes that she didn't know what he was talking about. Then the look faded, replaced by an incredulous expression of disbelief as she lost her hold on reality.

When she returned to awareness moments later—or was it hours—Storm was lying on the bed, naked as the day she was born, and Grady was standing over her, grinning down at her with the aggressive leer of a savage aware of his power. He had lit a lantern, and soft light filled the room with dancing shadows. With growing apprehension she watched him release the string holding his breechclout in place. Her eyes followed it as it dropped to the floor.

"Look at me." Her eyes widened hugely as they slid upward to his groin. For the first time in her life Storm saw a fully aroused male organ. It protruded like a rigid shaft—strong, bold, sure, from a thick nest of coarse ebony at the juncture of his thighs. He displayed no modesty as she stared at him, only pride in his body and the knowledge that he could give her pleasure.

"Storm." Embarrassed by her burning perusal, her eyes returned to his face. "Touch me."

Her mouth dropped open in astonishment. "Touch you?"

He knelt on the bed, the size and strength of him frightening, yet oddly stirring. She couldn't be absolutely certain, for she had never seen Buddy nude, but she was almost positive her husband hadn't been as generously endowed. Her tongue flicked out to moisten her lips in a gesture that sent Grady's senses reeling.

His eyes focused on the way her tongue probed provocatively at the corners of her mouth and licked across the soft pads of her lush lips. Every nerve and sinew came alive with the pleasure that he knew would soon be his.

"Touch me," he repeated. "Don't be afraid. I'm not much different from any other man."

*Not different?* Storm thought mentally. She wanted to disagree, to tell him he was unique, that no other man could compare with him. His strong, angular face, proud bearing, and dark coppery skin proclaimed him as different from other men as night from day.

When she resisted his plea, he reached out and grasped her hand, placing it on his distended member. Her eyes grew enormous, but curiosity overrode reluctance as her nerveless fingers stroked up and down his shaft and over its velvety tip. He groaned and lurched against her hand. When she looked up at him his eyes were closed and his face strained, as if caught in the throes of agony. Then his hand closed around hers, wrapping it more tightly around his hardness, thrusting into the soft warmth of her palm.

"Enough!" he gasped, flinging her hand away and dropping onto the bed beside her. "Now, sweet lady, we shall see if Thunder can tame the Storm."

Rising to his knees and elbows, he lay full length atop her, wedging himself snugly between her thighs. Then he was kissing her, everywhere his lips could reach, teasing, nipping, tantalizing her with the hot moistness of his mouth. His hands moved restlessly over her flesh, stroking, caressing, seeking—bold—arousing, making her feel things she had never felt before. When one hand inserted itself between their bodies and probed between her legs, Storm jerked in violent response.

"Don't, please! I don't understand what you're doing to me."

"I'm making you happy, lady," Grady replied as he flexed his hips and placed his swollen shaft into position at the cleft of her womanhood. His hands sank beneath her to cup her buttocks, holding her tightly as he flexed again, parting, penetrating, sliding into the liquid heat of her. Deep, deeper . . . When he was fully embedded in her, Storm sucked in a ragged breath as she felt herself stretching to accommodate him. Nothing in her limited experience had prepared her for the shock of total possession by a man as magnificent as Grady Stryker. Never had she felt such fullness or pleasure with Buddy, she thought wonderingly.

"Oh, lady, I've never felt anything so good," Grady groaned against her lips.

He stroked her slowly, knowledgeably, both inside and out, with his hands and lips and shaft. She tilted her hips against him, unconsciously seeking more, and he dutifully obliged. Suddenly the slow rise and fall of his buttocks grew wildly frantic as he strained toward climax, and Storm's senses erupted into wild, swirling pleasure. Thrusting, withdrawing, thrusting, she surrendered fully to his breathtaking ferocity, meeting his thrusts in staccato bursts of brilliant response that left Grady breathless with wonder.

Thunder's fury has tamed the Storm, he thought triumphantly. Nothing nature created could compare to the fierce, wild pleasure he found in Storm Kennedy's arms.

Storm soared, lifted on the wings of Grady's passion. The dazzling promise of climax dangled before her eyes like a ripe plum and she reached for it, giving herself up to the heat of Grady's loving. The second climax of her life, when it came moments later, exploded inside her in wave after wave of lush, sensual rapture, and she cried out in unrestrained awe. Through a gathering mist she felt his body's forces straining, focusing on release. His muscles tensed, his body surged and withdrew, his thrusts grew furious and uncontrolled.

The white-hot splendor that washed over Grady was like nothing he'd ever experienced before. His body was racked by spasms, his face a mask of agony and ecstasy as his seed spurted into the receptive heat of her womb.

When at last his breathing slowed to dull thunder, Grady slid from Storm's tight sheath and lay beside her. Fitting her into the curve of his body, he continued to stroke and caress her. He felt strong and invincible, stronger than he ever felt in his life, strong enough to want her again . . . now.

"Storm." His voice was soft. "Are you all right?"

Her muffled reply was a bit shaky. "Yes."

"Is it true, what you said earlier? About never having reached a climax with your husband, I mean."

Storm buried her face in the pillow, too embarrassed to allow him to see her confusion. She never even knew women *could* feel pleasure in the marriage bed. Or wanted to.

"I—why must we speak of such things?"

"Because I want to know. Tell me, sweetheart."

"Dammit, why must you know what transpired in my marriage bed?" Her anger was brilliant. "Will it make you feel any more manly to know that I never felt anything remotely like that with Buddy? Must you destroy every aspect of a marriage I thought perfect until you showed up in my life?"

Grady felt ten feet tall. Storm's reluctant disclosure brought Grandfather's words instantly to mind. Did Storm Kennedy really hold the key to his peace of mind and happiness? Only time would tell, he thought as his arms tightened possessively around her. As tired as he was, he knew he wouldn't sleep this night. There was too much to think about. And he wanted to be fully alert in the unlikely event that the two men who had attacked Storm in the dead of night returned.

"Go to sleep, Storm. It's late and you've been through a great deal tonight."

Storm preferred not to think right now. She was tired, so tired. Yet she knew when her good sense returned there would be issues to be resolved, recriminations to be confronted—and a conscience that must be placated. But it was difficult to think, let alone make decisions with her body still tingling from Grady's hands and mouth and her insides churning with lingering pleasure. Tomorrow, she thought sleepily, tomorrow I'll confront the shame and embarrassment of the terrible sin I have committed.

Storm came awake slowly. She could hear the wind howling through the shattered window, but she felt cozy and comfortable, wrapped in a warm nest of blankets. Blankets? She knew of no blanket with the feel of silky strength like that which surrounded her. Shattered window? Suddenly the events of last night came to her with devastating clarity.

She must have been out of her mind to allow a half-breed savage into her bed! And if she remembered correctly, she had responded to his loving with a dazzling display of shameful abandon. Because her response was completely at odds with what she had experienced with her husband, Storm knew that it was evil and sinful.

Dragging in a shuddering sigh, Storm slowly turned her head and found Grady awake and regarding her with an indecipherable look on his face. "You're awake," he said. "Did you sleep well?"

Memories of the pleasure they had shared during the night softened the harsh lines of his face. Though there were purple smudges of exhaustion around his eyes, he gave no indication that he had spent the night watching Storm sleep, marveling at the pure lines of her face and form and curling long strands of her lustrous blonde hair around his fingers. When she stirred and opened her eyes, Grady hardened in instant arousal. Just thinking about making love to her again gave him strength.

Storm couldn't bring herself to look Grady in the eye so she stared at his chest. It was smooth, well-developed, and bronze, with a very light sprinkling of black hair. The outlines of his muscles seemed to stretch his skin to magnificent proportions. Was there nowhere she could look without imagining his proud, regal length stretched atop hers, the exquisite fullness of him filling her . . .

"Stop!" The word burst past her lips in a loud explosion of denial before she realized she had spoken aloud.

Grady grinned with wry amusement. "Have I done something wrong?" He hadn't done anything—yet—but he was seriously considering it.

"You did everything wrong," Storm said, finally finding the courage to raise her eyes to face him squarely.

"Was it wrong to save you from those two men, who would have done God knows what to you?"

"No, not that, I—oh, stop confusing me. You know what you did last night."

An enigmatic smile lifted the corners of his mouth, and his eyes glowed with fierce possession. "We made love, Storm Kennedy, and it was magnificent. Every bit as good as I knew it would be. Don't tell me you didn't enjoy it; I know better."

She groaned and dropped her face into her hands, giving in to her despair. If she lived to be one hundred, she'd never survive the horror of waking up in bed with the man responsible for Buddy's death. The fact that she had responded to the savage's loving in a way she'd never responded to Buddy intensified that horror.

"Dammit, Storm, what is wrong with you? Those men didn't hurt you. And your cabin is unscathed save for a shattered window, a broken hinge, and a few bullet holes."

She pried her hands away from her face and whispered savagely, "Why? What kind of man are you to take advantage of a woman in distress? What kind a woman am I to—to—oh, God, I can't even talk about it. I've shamed Buddy's memory."

Grady was truly perplexed. To his way of thinking there was no shame in a man and woman wanting one another, fulfilling their mutual need in a natural way. "Buddy is dead, but you're alive, more alive than you've ever been in your life. If what I suspect is true, your dead husband never pleased you as well as I did last night. Can you deny the passion you experienced in my arms?"

"No!" she spat fiercely. Her honey-brown eyes narrowed with anger. "But it was wrong to feel like that with a—a—savage!"

The word exploded in Grady's brain like a blast from a gun. "Savage! Is that what you think of me? Am I less than human because of my Indian blood? You're a damn hypocrite, Storm Kennedy. I may be a savage, but you're a liar who's afraid to voice your true feelings. You told me last night that I was the first man to bring you to climax."

Storm gulped in fear, realizing she had trapped herself with her own words. "I—I *am* a liar. I didn't mean what I said. Of course you weren't the first man to—to—make me feel like that. Buddy and I had a very satisfying marriage."

"Are you telling me you're always such a hot little piece?"

His crude language brought a flush of color to her cheeks. "You're the expert; think what you like."

Suddenly he swept back the blanket, exposing her to his lascivious gaze. Bold blue eyes raked the length of her naked body before coming to rest on her outraged face. "Something tells me, Storm Kennedy, that you protest too much. Tell me again that I didn't please you."

"You're an arrogant bastard, Grady Stryker. Buddy was a much better lover than you." Her lie was more for her benefit than his.

Grady's eyes blazed with unholy light as he pulled her upright into his arms. She knew what he intended before his hard mouth came down on hers. His kiss was angry, his tongue a rapacious sword that stabbed past her lips in a fierce demonstration of total domination. His hands, oh, God, his hands—they stroked, caressed, and probed relentlessly, leaving no part of her free of his possession. He was every bit the savage she had called him, and more. She fought against total subjugation and lost.

With the agility and strength that was second nature to him, he lifted her atop him and impaled her fully, penetrating deeply, his hardened staff throbbing against the tight walls of her sheath. Storm gasped as he filled and stretched her, touching her so deeply and thoroughly, she felt magnificently possessed by the scent and essence of him.

She expected savagery. He gave her tenderness.

His lips softened. His mouth nuzzled her breasts with exquisite gentleness and thrilling passion. His fingers stroked and molded the soft mounds of her buttocks as he slid her up and down the engorged pillar of velvet and steel. Her climax came abruptly, shattering her into a million pieces then flinging her to the stars. She was barely aware of Grady's shout of raw pleasure as he attained man's highest reward.

"How do I compare with your dead husband now?" Grady panted into her ear.

"There's no comparison. You can't hold a candle to Buddy."

Red dots of rage exploded in Grady's brain. "You're a sorry excuse for a woman, Storm Kennedy!" The lie nearly strangled him, but it was too late to take it back now. "You are nothing like my sweet, gentle Summer Sky. At least she knew how to make me feel like a man.

There's much you need to learn about pleasing a man."

"Oh!"

Flinging himself out of bed, Grady stalked to the door, forgetting that he was stark naked, forgetting everything but the need to remove himself from the presence of a woman who wasn't honest enough to admit she felt passion with him. He flung open the partially ruined door with a bang and a curse, nearly breaking it off the remaining hinge. The raw bite of the wind stole his breath away. But he was too proud to ask for a blanket to cover his nakedness, too incensed to return for the scant protection of his discarded breechclout. He stalked out the door, pure savage and every bit as ferocious as the fearless Lakota warrior who out of bitterness and hate had vowed vengeance against the white race. He turned once to send Storm a look of utter contempt before slamming the door behind him.

Storm stared at the door long after Grady left. Long after she heard the thunder of hooves on the hard-packed earth. Sweet Lord, what had she done? What kind of woman was she to forget all she and Buddy had shared through the years? One moment of exquisite passion had made Buddy a dim memory from her past. Obviously the half-breed had cast a spell on her that turned her into a wanton hussy with the morals of an alley cat. How could Grady have found a place inside her that Buddy, her dearest friend, had never discovered?

*What made Grady different from any other man?* she asked herself.

The simplicity of the answer stunned her. *No other man had the power to move her as Grady did.*

She hated the way he manipulated her. She despised the way her body responded to the touch of his hands and mouth. And she definitely didn't appreciate the knowledge that he was the first man to reach some magical place in her that no other man had ever touched.

*Even if it was true.*

# Chapter Seven

"You bungling idiots!" Nat Turner raved as he fixed Fork and Purdy with a malevolent glare. "Can't you do anything right?"

Purdy shifted in restless agitation while Fork, wearing a bandage where Grady's knife had gauged a nasty groove, grimaced in painful recollection. He preferred not being reminded of their disastrous encounter with the half-breed. But Turner was relentless in his fury.

"What in the hell are you being paid for? You were supposed to convince the Kennedy woman that she isn't capable of homesteading or defending her property. You were ordered to scare the living hell out of her so she'd accept my offer to buy her land. But no, manhandling one frail woman was too much for you. My client in Texas is badgering me for land."

"How were we supposed to know that blasted renegade would barge in just when we had the woman where we wanted her?" Purdy complained bitterly. "Look what he did to Fork. An inch lower and the renegade's knife woulda put a quick end to him."

"Stop sniveling. I can't stand whiners," Turner returned crossly. "What you're telling me is that the two of you are no match for the breed."

"Now see here, Turner," Purdy protested, "you got no call talkin' to me and Fork like that. Soon as I heal we'll try again, only this time we'll know what to expect. Maybe we'll even hire another man to act as lookout while we rough up the woman. That damn renegade's got eyes in the back of his head. How in the hell did he know what we were up to?"

"Seeing as how I can't trust you two to do the job for me, I reckon I'll have to do it myself," Turner said. "If my methods don't work by the time Purdy is healed, I'll let you have another go at her."

"I didn't think you liked dirtyin' your hands with rough stuff," Fork said with sly innuendo. "The Kennedy woman might be young and beautiful, but she's damn feisty. Ya ain't gonna handle her with kid gloves." His snicker set Turner's teeth on edge.

"Perhaps you're wrong," Turner said thoughtfully. "Perhaps kid gloves are exactly what's needed to convince the Widow Kennedy to move on to other parts. Or . . ." an arrested look came over his face, "I could rely on that old adage about honey catching more flies than vinegar. Boys," he said, grinning wickedly, "I'm going acourtin'. Wish me luck."

Storm hadn't seen Grady since the day he stormed out of her cabin. Nor did she expect to see him anytime soon after the angry words they'd exchanged. The weather had turned blustery, and each time she carried wood into the house for her stove she was reminded that if not for Grady she would be out cutting wood right now. Truth to tell, the guilt she felt was not due entirely to the firewood he had provided. A good share of it came from their lustful coupling that night a week ago.

"Damn womanizer!" Storm muttered beneath her breath as she grabbed her jacket from the hook and stomped out the door. She had no business thinking about a no-good half-breed whose mysterious hatred for the white race left him bitter and distrustful when she had chores to do. Plucking a bucket from the doorstep, she headed for the well to draw water for the day. She was just lowering the bucket down the shaft when she saw a rider approaching in the distance.

Leaving the bucket dangling at the end of the rope, Storm rushed back inside the cabin and grabbed her shotgun. She had been so immersed in arousing thoughts of Grady Stryker that she had neglected to bring her gun along. Since the attack the other night, she had made a point to carry it wherever she went. When she opened the door Nat Turner had already dismounted and was approaching the cabin.

"Storm, my dear girl, I just heard the news in town. Are you all right? What kind of monsters would attack an unprotected woman?"

"News gets around fast," Storm replied. "I was just in town yesterday to order another pane for my shattered window and mentioned to Mr. Clark that I had unwelcome visitors in the night. Of course I also reported it to the sheriff."

"Dreadful news like that doesn't take long to spread. What do you suppose they wanted?" he asked innocently.

"I—don't know." Storm stammered. A dull red crept up her neck. She was too embarrassed to reveal that both men had attempted to rape her before Grady intervened.

"Hmmm, could be robbery. Then again, you are a beautiful woman." From what he left unsaid Storm realized he had guessed what the masked men had attempted. "How in the world did you manage to chase them away without being hurt?"

"Come inside, Nat, and I'll explain," Storm invited. It was too cold to stand outside talking. "There's hot coffee sitting on the back of the stove and apple pie left from yesterday."

Once they were seated across from one another sipping coffee and eating pie, Nat waited politely for Storm to continue her explanation of the attack.

"I had help," she revealed tersely. "Grady Stryker saved me from—from—an unpleasant experience."

Turner feigned surprise. "The half-breed? What in the hell was he doing here at that time of night?"

"It's not what you think, Nat," Storm was quick to add. "Grady's arrival was as much a surprise to me as it was to the two masked men. I owe my life to his excellent hearing and keen senses. He sensed danger even before he heard shots echoing across the prairie."

"How—fortunate," Nat said. His smile, while outwardly sincere, never reached his eyes. "I hope the sheriff finds the men responsible."

"Yes, indeed, very fortunate," Storm concurred brightly. Though she tried to subdue the memory, her eyes turned dreamy when she recalled what had transpired after the intruders left her property. Her cheeks reddened and she shook her head to rid it of every delicious detail of their passionate encounter.

Nat cleared his throat, bringing Storm back to the present. "I tried to tell you, my dear, that it isn't safe for you out here alone. What if it happens again and Stryker isn't as perceptive as he was the other night?"

"I'll be prepared next time," Storm declared stoutly.

Turner frowned. "This unprovoked attack should convince you that you're not capable of protecting your land. You need a husband, my dear. Especially if you expect to remain on your homestead."

"Contrary to your belief, I'm quite capable, Nat. I'll manage just fine on my own."

Turner knew when to retreat. The last thing he wanted was to incur Storm's anger. "I'm sure you will, Storm. Meanwhile, do you have enough money to get by until your land starts producing?"

Storm thought back to her recent conversation with the banker. Building her cabin and digging the well had cost far more than she had originally anticipated. After purchasing provisions to last the winter, she barely had enough cash left to purchase the cattle she'd ordered. The news had shocked her, but she remained undaunted. Somehow she would persevere.

"I'll get by." Her grim expression gave Turner the distinct impression that Storm *would* succeed, unless he took matters into his own hands.

"Enough of this talk, Storm. What I really came for is to invite you to a barn dance Saturday night. How long has it been since you've enjoyed yourself at a social affair?"

"A barn dance?" Storm's face flushed with pleasure. She recalled how much she and Buddy used to enjoy dancing. "It sounds won—" Her words ground to a halt. "Oh, I don't think I should."

"Of course you should," Turner contradicted smoothly. "You're still a young woman. You deserve a little pleasure in your life."

"What will people say? My husband has been dead less than two months."

"Who cares what they say? No one can take his memory away from you. I'm sure your young husband would be the first to urge you to accept my invitation."

His arguments made sense to Storm. Buddy would have hated to see her sitting home and grieving. He'd want her to enjoy herself. "You've convinced me, Nat. I'll be happy to attend the barn dance with you."

Turner grinned delightedly. "I knew you were too sensible to remain a recluse when life beckons. I'll pick you up at five o'clock Saturday evening. Don't disappoint me."

"I won't," Storm promised, already looking forward to a pleasant evening in Nat's company.

Nat left soon afterward. Storm stood in the doorway, waving good-bye as he rode away.

"That wasn't very smart, lady."

"Oh!" Whirling on her heel, Storm glared murderously at Grady. He had emerged like a wraith from the shadowy side of the cabin and stood just a few feet behind her. "Why are you spying on me? Do you always sneak around like that? I've never known anyone who can move as stealthily as you."

"I told you before I was trained to move without being heard or seen. As for spying, I was merely keeping an eye on you."

"How did you know Nat was here? I'm beginning to believe you actually do possess some mystical power no one is aware of."

He gave her a smile that completely disarmed her. "There is nothing mystical about using one's eyes and ears. I was removing a stump from my land when I saw Turner riding by. It didn't take long to guess where he was going. I thought I'd follow and see what he was up to."

"Since you obviously overheard our conversation, you know that Nat was 'up' to nothing more dangerous than inviting me to a barn dance."

"It was unwise of you to accept," Grady repeated with cool authority. "Nat Turner is a scoundrel who will stop at nothing to get what he wants. Obviously he wants your land."

"Are you saying Nat isn't interested in me as a woman? That he finds nothing desirable about me but my land?" Storm asked in a voice as reasonable as she could manage under the circumstances.

"No, lady, I'd be a fool to say that," he replied in an odd yet gentle tone.

Unable to withstand the intense heat of his gaze, Storm turned to enter the house, fully intending to slam the door in Grady's face. "Good day, Mr. Stryker."

"Storm, wait."

"I have nothing more to say to you."

"You could quit lying to yourself and admit you felt something special when we made love the other night."

"I'd be lying if I admitted you moved me in any way except to fill me with contempt." Abruptly she turned and slammed the door in his face. His curses left a trail of blue as he stormed around to the back of the cabin, where he had left his horse. She watched from the window as he rode away, wondering if she'd ever see him again and asking herself why she even cared.

Nat arrived promptly at five o'clock Saturday night, driving a horse and buggy rented especially for the occasion. Urging Storm to dress warmly, he bundled her into the buggy and took off at a smart clip. Lanterns mounted on either side of the buggy lit their way, aided by a full moon. Storm was full of excitement when they arrived at the barn, located at the south edge of Guthrie. She could hear the lively music echoing across the plains long before they reached their destination.

"You look beautiful tonight," Turner complimented smoothly. It surprised him to realize he meant every word. Dressed in her best gown of midnight blue velvet—the closest thing to mourning attire she owned—Storm looked both demure and sensual at the same time. Fashioned with a high neckline and long sleeves, the form-hugging gown was the epitome of simplicity. Its simple lines and elegant cut

145

hugged her curves like a second skin while the vibrant blue complemented her blonde coloring. There were no frills or furbelows to detract from the natural beauty of the woman wearing the gown.

Storm dimpled prettily. She hadn't felt so carefree since Buddy's death.

"Shall we dance? I'll bet you're a marvelous dancer." Nat slid an arm around her waist and whirled her into the lively group of dancers.

Later, they ate from the buffet table and drank cup after cup of the delicious punch to quench the enormous thirst caused by the lively dance steps. Nat seemed to know everyone, and in the course of the evening introduced Storm to so many people her head was awhirl with names she'd never remember. But what pleased Storm most was that no one seemed to care that she was appearing at a public festivity so soon after her husband's death. An entirely different set of mores and customs prevailed among settlers and homesteaders, it seemed. What might be considered scandalous at home in Missouri caused hardly a ripple in raw frontier towns like Guthrie and Enid.

"Are you ready for more dancing?" Nat asked as he led Storm out on the crowded dance floor. She slipped easily into his arms, following his lead smoothly as he guided her through the steps.

Soon other men clamored for a dance, and she didn't see Nat again until quite late in the evening, when he appeared with more punch and claimed her for a slow dance. Storm didn't object when he pulled her closer than she thought proper. By now she felt quite giddy and was flushed with the success of her first night out in months. Nat Turner had been a perfect gentleman and she didn't know when she'd have another chance to enjoy herself so thoroughly. Relaxing in Nat's arms, she surrendered to the enjoyment of the dance. A prickling sensation at the back of her neck was Storm's first indication that she was being stared at. She swiveled her head to search the crowded room.

He was propped against the wall near the open door, arms folded over his broad chest, one moccasin-clad foot crossed over the other at the ankle. He wore his hat pulled low over his forehead, shadowing the vibrant blue of his eyes. He had donned his buckskins for the occasion, in open defiance of the white society he spurned, and wore a fringed jacket she had never seen before. Every splendid inch of him exuded an aura of mystery, danger, and excitement, of lean, hard strength and fierce arrogance. He looked thoroughly, utterly Indian, and he was magnificent.

To Storm's chagrin, Grady Stryker was creating quite a stir among the single women at the dance—and a few that were quite happily married.

Grady's intense blue gaze made a slow, thorough survey of the huge room before coming to rest on Storm and Nat. He usually held frivolous entertainments like this in total contempt, but some perverse demon inside him had made him attend the celebration tonight. The moment he learned Nat Turner was going to escort Storm to the dance he knew he was going to be there to keep an eye on them. Storm was far too gullible to butt heads with a persuasive man like Turner, he thought as he watched Turner twirl Storm around the dance floor in perfect harmony with the music.

Turner's fancy maneuvers whirled Storm toward the opposite end of the dance floor, and she momentarily lost sight of Grady. When she stretched her neck to look for him, he was gone. Her relief was enormous as she allowed herself to relax once again in Nat's arms and enjoy the intricacies of the dance.

"May I cut in?"

Storm was stunned to see Grady standing behind them, tapping Nat on the shoulder. But Nat was even more surprised as he cursed beneath his breath. "Dammit, Stryker, you're not wanted here. Neither Storm nor I appreciate your intrusion." He swung her away, leaving Grady standing in the middle of the dance floor, looking foolish.

Then suddenly the music stopped and the dance ended. Turner reluctantly moved away as Storm was besieged by men clamoring for a dance with her. When the music started up again, Storm was about to choose her next partner when Grady stepped out of nowhere and claimed her. One or two of the men started to protest, but Grady's fierce expression soon changed their minds. When Grady swept her into his arms, Storm's face showed her displeasure. But when she noted the curious way in which people were staring at them, she reluctantly followed his lead.

"I didn't know Indians could dance," she hissed venomously.

"And I didn't know white women could be so damn stubborn," he tossed back. "I warned you about attending the dance tonight with Turner."

"So you did," she said sweetly. "But as I told you, I make my own decisions."

Suddenly the music grew lively and Grady swung her around and around, until she grew dizzy and her head spun. When she stumbled against him, he was quick to offer assistance.

"Perhaps you need some air," he suggested blandly. "The punch is spiked, you know."

With an efficiency of motion he maneuvered her toward the door, and they were outside before Storm knew what was happening. Truth to tell, she was too fuzzy-brained to think clearly. He took off his fringed buckskin jacket and placed it over her shoulders. "Feel better now?"

"There's nothing wrong with me," Storm protested. "If you hadn't whirled me around so fast I wouldn't have gotten dizzy. I must get back inside. Nat will be looking for me."

"I think I should take you home now," Grady said.

Storm bristled indignantly. "I didn't come with you, Mr. Stryker."

"No, but—dammit, Storm, you can't trust Turner."

"Nat Turner has been a perfect gentleman in all our dealings, which is more than I can say for you."

"If you're talking about that night we—"

"That's exactly what I'm talking about. I must have been crazy to let you take advantage of me." She turned to walk away, stumbled slightly, and found herself surrounded by the hard strength of Grady's arms.

"Oh."

"How many glasses of punch did you have? Are you tipsy, Mrs. Kennedy?"

"Certainly not!" Her short sentence ended in a hiccup.

"Did you know that you have the most kissable lips I've ever seen?" Grady surprised himself by saying. Now where in the hell did that come from? He surprised himself further when he brushed his mouth against hers in a most provocative way. When that didn't seem to satisfy him his tongue traced the soft fullness of her lips with slow, tantalizing thoroughness.

The touch of his lips on hers sent a shock wave spiraling through Storm's entire body. She jerked violently, but before she could twist from his embrace, he boldly thrust his tongue into her mouth in a fiery display of possession. It was a challenging kiss, one that probed deeply into the secret chambers of her heart. When his hands slid down to cup the firm roundness of her bottom and pull her closer still, she felt the hard strength of his desire branding her through the layers of her clothing. His kiss deepened, stunning her with its ferocity as his demanding tongue stroked and explored until she was helplessly ensnared.

Then, abruptly, he released her, holding her at arm's length and staring at her as if she had bitten him. "Damnation! What in the hell are you doing to me? When I'm with you I lose all restraint. All I can think about is making love to you. You're a witch, created specifically to make me miserable."

Giddy from Grady's tormenting kisses, Storm could only stare at him and stammer, "I—I—don't—"

"There you are, Storm. I've been everywhere looking for you. It's nearly time to leave and you promised me the last dance."

Nat Turner stood a few feet away, having come from the barn in search of Storm. He had had an inkling that he would find her with the renegade, and when his suspicions proved correct he struggled to conceal his rage. It was to his advantage to control himself until he had what he wanted from Storm Kennedy. Afterward the half-breed was welcome to her.

"Of course," Storm said, stepping around Grady to join Nat. "I just stepped out for a breath of air. I—I felt a little dizzy."

He looked at her shrewdly. "Are you all right?"

"Just fine." She took Nat's arm, blatantly ignoring Grady and the fact that he was glaring daggers at her.

"Storm." Grady's abrasive voice brought her to a skidding halt, though she didn't give him the satisfaction of turning to face him. "My jacket."

Turner took one look at the fringed jacket around Storm's shoulders, plucked it from her body, and tossed it to Grady, who caught it quite handily. Then, without another word, Turner guided Storm inside. But before he led her out onto the dance floor, he poured her another glass of punch, which she downed in one gulp just to spite Grady. Then he gave her another, which she sipped more slowly, but nonetheless eagerly.

It was after midnight when the dance ended. Grady was nowhere in sight when Nat handed her into the buggy and settled a blanket over her knees. Her head was reeling and the urge to sleep was a pressing need inside her. She hadn't wanted to believe the punch was spiked, certain Nat wouldn't have let her drink so much if it were. Except for an occasional glass of wine she'd had little experience with hard liquor. It was unfortunate her farm was ten miles away from Guthrie, she thought sleepily. When Turner hoisted himself into the buggy beside her, she tilted crazily against him.

"Are you feeling ill?" he asked solicitously.

"A little dizzy. Was the punch spiked? I'm not accustomed to drinking."

"Spiked?" Nat repeated in feigned surprise. "Wherever did you get such a preposterous idea? Perhaps the dancing tired you more than you know."

"Yes, I'm sure that's it," Storm agreed with alacrity. The idea of her being tipsy didn't set well with her.

"It's a long ride home," Nat said slyly, "and bitter cold. Perhaps you should take a room at the Guthrie Hotel tonight and return home tomorrow."

When Storm tried to think of a valid reason to object her muddled brain refused to work. Besides, it sounded like a wonderful idea. And defying the brash half-breed appealed to her. Let him think what he wanted when she didn't return home tonight.

"The idea of postponing the ride back to my farm does sound appealing," Storm said. She tried to stifle a hiccup, but it came bursting from her throat despite her best efforts. "Oh, excuse me."

Nat smiled in mute satisfaction. He was inordinately pleased with himself for manipulating Storm into doing what he wanted. She was already quite taken with him, and the spiked punch he had plied her with was working with devastating effect. If all went according to plan, when Storm Kennedy awoke with a hangover tomorrow morning her homestead would be his. He felt confident that a hotel room was the last place the half-breed would think to look for her. He turned the buggy toward the hotel.

"You've made a wise decision, my dear. You'll be snug in your bed at the hotel in no time at all. Leave everything to me."

A lopsided smile stretched Storm's lips as she thought of Grady's reaction when he learned she had stayed in town tonight. He needn't know where she stayed, or the fact that Nat wouldn't be sharing her bed, as long as it showed Grady he had absolutely no power over her.

Once inside the Guthrie Hotel, Storm swayed on her feet as Nat and the desk clerk spoke in low tones. She didn't notice the sly look the clerk sent her or the knowing smile Nat received when the room key was placed in his hand.

"Come, my dear, you'll be tucked in bed in no time." He grasped her arm and led her upstairs to the second floor. He stopped before Room 205, inserted the key in the lock, and held the door open so she could enter. When Storm turned around to bid him good night, she was surprised to see that Nat had entered behind her and shut the door.

"I'll be just fine now, Nat. You can go. Thank you for your concern."

"I thought I'd wait around to see if you have any more dizzy spells."

Before Storm could form a reply there was a discreet knock on the door. Nat hastened to answer, and when he returned he had a bottle and two glasses in his hand. "A sip of bourbon is just what the doctor ordered to help you sleep. Perhaps you took a chill on the ride into town. If so, this will dispel any illness you may have contracted. In the morning you'll feel fit as a fiddle."

"Oh, I don't think—that is—I'm not much of a drinker."

"Just a sip, Storm, to please me. Then I'll be on my way." He was already pouring the tumbler half full of the aromatic spirits.

"Very well," Storm said, accepting the glass he offered. If it meant being left in peace, she'd take just one tiny sip. She held the glass to her lips, intending to drink sparingly, but Turner had other ideas. Grasping the bottom of the glass, he tilted it upward, forcing her to take a huge gulp of the potent liquor. It ran down her throat in a hot, burning gush of molten fire.

Gasping for breath and sputtering indignantly, Storm flung his hand away. "Why did you do that?"

"A small drink never hurt anyone, my dear. You'll sleep all the better for it."

Suddenly Storm's face grew slack and the room spun around in dizzying circles. She clutched at the air in desperate need, finding it appallingly empty. She began a slow downward spiral. Nat caught her before she hit the floor, placing her carefully on the bed.

"Are you ill, Storm?"

"I—I don't know. I feel so dizzy. And I can't think straight."

A slow, enigmatic smile curved Nat's lips as he pulled a chair up beside the bed and sat down. "You work too hard, my dear. You should have listened to me when I told you homesteading was too difficult for a woman. I have a client who is quite anxious to purchase large tracts of land in the Cherokee Strip. You can leave town tomorrow with enough money to start out someplace new. You should let your family take care of you until you find another husband."

His words hardly registered in Storm's muddled brain, yet she knew she shouldn't be here alone with him in a hotel room. She tried to rise, to tell him to leave, but nothing worked. Her body refused her commands and her mind had shut down completely.

"If you'll sign this bill of sale, Storm," Nat said, whipping a document out of his pocket, "you'll receive a fair price for your land. I have sufficient cash with me to pay you immediately."

Though Storm couldn't quite grasp the meaning of Nat's words, his low, soothing voice was relaxing, and she closed her eyes.

"No, dammit, don't go to sleep!"

Somewhere in the deep recesses of her brain Storm heard the rustle of paper and felt something hard being placed between her fingers. "The bill of sale, Storm, sign the bill of sale! All you need do is sign your name and I'll let you go to sleep." Grasping her shoulders, Nat shook her awake. Her eyes flew open.

She muttered crossly when Nat lifted her into a sitting position and spread a sheet of paper across her knees. Why wouldn't he let her sleep? "Sign your name, Storm. If you want to be left in peace, just sign your name. Here," he said, grasping her hand and placing it in position.

Sign my name? Storm thought distractedly. If it meant that Nat would go away and let her sleep, she'd do it gladly. But she'd made no more than one downward stroke with the inked pen when the flimsy door gave way beneath a set of massive shoulders.

# Chapter Eight

"What the hell!" The chair toppled over as Nat leaped to his feet and spun around. "You!"

The pen slipped from Storm's fingers and she stared blankly from Grady to Turner, too dazed to realize what was happening.

"Your vile scheme won't work this time, Turner," Grady growled as he stalked into the room. He took one look at Storm's glazed eyes and another at the document still spread across her knees and turned on Turner with a vicious snarl. "What in the hell have you done to her?"

"Nothing. I haven't touched her," Turner said, backing slowly toward the door. He had no intention of messing with a man whose reputation with a gun was legend.

"Are you all right, Storm?" Grady asked. His words were directed at Storm, but his hard blue gaze pinned Turner to the wall.

"I'm tired," Storm said petulantly "I want you both to go away so I can sleep."

Grady was beside Storm in two strides. Without removing his eyes from Turner, he snatched the bill of sale from her lap, briefly scanned its contents, then tore it into tiny pieces. "If you attempt anything like this again, Turner, I'll make you sorry you were ever born. If you doubt me, remember that I'm knowledgeable in all the subtle methods of torture used by the Sioux."

"See here, Stryker, who appointed you Mrs. Kennedy's keeper?" Turner asked in an unaccustomed show of bravado.

"No one tells me what to do," Grady said with quiet menace. "Now I suggest you leave before I do something you won't find very pleasant."

Turner opened his mouth to protest, then thought better of it. He hesitated a moment too long for Grady's liking. Moving with the speed and stealth of a panther, Grady seized Turner by the collar of his stylish jacket and the seat of his pants and threw him out the open door. Then he slammed what was left of the shattered panel hard enough to rattle the wall. When he finally turned back to Storm, she was still sitting on the side of the bed, weaving from side to side, glassy-eyed and disoriented. He spit out an epitaph and bore her down on the soft surface of the mattress.

"Gra-dy," Storm complained when Grady pulled the covers over her, clothes and all.

"What are you doing here? What's going on?"

Anger boiled up inside Grady, and his voice was roughened by it. "Do you realize what you almost did, you little fool? Are you aware of nothing that happened tonight?"

Storm frowned in concentration, but all it did was give her a headache. "I went to the barn dance with Nat Turner and had a wonderful time." She wanted to giggle, but Grady's fierce expression stopped her.

"Was it your idea to stay in town tonight instead of returning home? Did Nat suggest you rent a hotel room?"

"I—I—For heaven's sake, Grady, will you please stop badgering me? If you must know, I stayed in town because—because I knew it would make you angry."

Grady looked thunderstruck. "You almost lost your homestead. Was making me mad worth it? Women!" He shook his head in exasperation.

"Lost my homestead? That's not possible. I don't understand what you're talking about."

"No, I don't suppose you do," Grady said with an impatient growl. "You're too drunk to understand anything."

"I am not drunk!" Her eyes grew round when a hiccup slipped past her lips.

"I'm not going to argue with you tonight, Storm. You're in no condition to comprehend what took place in this room even if I spell it out for you. You're tired. Go to sleep. I'll take you home tomorrow and we can talk then."

Storm's face wore such a woebegone expression, Grady almost felt sorry for her. Almost, but not quite. She should have known better than to drink so freely of the punch after he'd warned her it was spiked.

Storm struggled to put a meaning to Grady's strange words and came up lacking. There was an odd buzzing in her head and the room was spinning. Perhaps she was coming down with a strange malady. Or maybe she was just too weary to think coherently. In any event, Grady's advice was too tempting to resist. After a good night's sleep she'd feel better prepared to face his anger. Was the man perpetually angry? she wondered dully as she closed her eyes and drifted off to sleep.

The steady rise and fall of Storm's breast told Grady that she was slumbering peacefully, unaware of the danger in which she had placed herself tonight. He'd show her no mercy tomorrow when he regaled her with all the lurid facts about her "friend" Nat Turner and how he'd tried to cheat her out of her homestead. But there was tonight to consider. What was he going to do about Storm tonight? True, she was sleeping quite peacefully now, but the door was all but ruined, and anyone could barge in and do her harm. He solved the problem neatly by renting a room for himself across the hall and tucking her into his bed.

Then he lowered himself into a chair and sat beside her the rest of the night, staring at her as if trying to make up his mind about something.

What made Storm Kennedy different from any other woman he had ever known? he wondered curiously. Was she really the Storm that Wakantanka had referred to in his vision, or was he being fanciful and imagining things because her name happened to be Storm? In his heart Grady knew he wasn't responsible for the death of Storm's husband. So why had he appointed himself her protector? Why did he want her with a fierceness that was more pain than pleasure? And why, after he had loved her only once, did he resent any other man who had ever touched her?

Nat Turner rushed past the dozing hotel clerk as if the devil was on his heels. He went directly to the saloon where both Fork and Purdy were known to hang out and found them playing cards at one of the gambling tables. He snarled out a command and they quickly joined him at a table in the far corner of the room. He motioned for a bottle and three glasses and, when they were delivered, quickly filled them to overflowing and tossed his down, hoping to settle his nerves enough to think clearly. Fork and Purdy drank theirs more slowly, waiting for Turner to speak. They could tell he was upset and figured he would spit it out in good time.

"That's it!" Turner finally blurted out. "I'm through playing good guy. From now on it's all-out war. The first to feel the brunt of my anger is Storm Kennedy. Next is that half-breed bastard who seems to know what's going on every minute of every day. It's uncanny, that's what it is."

"What happened, boss?" Fork asked. He had a good idea what had sparked Turner's anger, but wisely waited for Turner to tell him himself. Fork knew that somehow or other Turner's plans had been foiled again by the renegade. The rich Texas client wanted grazing land in the Cherokee Strip, and Turner hadn't succeeded in buying up one damn acre. Homesteaders were a stubborn lot, Fork thought glumly. They hung on to their land till the bitter end, even if it meant starving to death.

"I was so close," Turner hissed. "So damn close, she had already started to sign the bill of sale."

Purdy whistled softly. "How in the hell did you manage that?"

"I got the woman drunk, that's how. Everything was going according to plan until the breed showed up. Hell, a dance was the last place in the world I expected to see the Injun. When I took Storm to the hotel for the night I thought I'd seen the last of him, but he came bursting into the room scant seconds before Storm signed the bill of sale."

"Damn!" Fork spat disgustedly. "I told ya the man ain't human. "What ya gonna do now?"

"It's not what I'm going to do but what you two are going to do," Turner said, his eyes gleaming maliciously. "Listen carefully and do exactly as I tell you."

Turner spoke in low tones as both men leaned close in order to catch every word. After a few minutes, Purdy said, "Tonight?"

"Hell, yes, tonight! The timing is perfect. Do as I say and you'll be amply compensated."

"We're on our way, boss," Fork said as he surged to his feet, dragging Purdy with him.

"Report to me when you get back."

Turner was still sitting in the saloon when Fork and Purdy returned shortly before dawn. The only thing that had changed was the level of whiskey in the bottle sitting on the table before him. It was empty.

"Well?" Turner asked anxiously.

"It's done, boss," Fork boasted as he plopped wearily into the chair across from Turner. Purdy slouched into the remaining seat at the table. "Everything went as smooth as silk."

"What about the breed?"

"He wasn't nowhere in sight. Neither was the woman."

Turner smiled with slow relish. "Good work, boys. There will be a generous bonus in your next paychecks. Now we just sit back and wait. It won't be long before Storm Kennedy comes begging me to buy her land."

Drops of water bathed her face. Gently at first, then in a raging torrent. Storm sputtered and came awake. Grady was standing above her, pouring the contents of a glass of water over her face. When mere sprinkles failed to awaken her, he upended the entire glass.

"Damn you, what are you doing?" Storm struggled to sit up, then flopped back down when the grinding pain in her temples made even the slightest movement excruciating. But Grady showed no pity as he continued pouring until the glass was empty and her face drenched.

"Wake up, Storm. It's time to start for home."

"Home?" Storm said, trying to remember where she was and failing miserably. "Where am I?"

"In a hotel room."

"What!" This time she managed to struggle to her feet. "With you?"

Grady's grating laughter made her stiffen with indignation. "I spent the entire night in a chair watching you sleep. Do you recall nothing of what happened last night?"

"Of course I remember. I went to a barn dance with Nat Turner. But—how did I end up in a hotel room with you?"

"I'll leave you a few minutes so you can freshen up," Grady said. "Then I'll explain everything over breakfast."

"Damn it, Grady Stryker," Storm said, stomping her foot, "don't you dare leave this room until you tell me if we—if you and I—"

"Relax, Storm, I didn't touch you. When we make love again I want you fully awake and aware of everything I do to you."

"You—"

Whatever she was going to say was lost on Grady, for he was already out the door.

Breakfast was the last thing Storm wanted. Her stomach was churning wildly and she knew if she put anything inside it she would promptly lose it. And her head was pounding with a hundred hammers. She did manage to keep down a cup of tea, but kept her face carefully averted from the huge plate of greasy eggs, steak, and potatoes Grady was shoveling down with such disgusting gusto. Once he had taken the edge off his hunger he began relating the events of the previous night. Storm listened in wide-eyed horror to the tale of how that skunk Nat Turner had very nearly succeeded in tricking her into selling her land.

Once Grady had finished with all the nasty details, Storm stared at him a full minute before speaking. "How did you know where to find me?"

"I followed you."

"Why didn't Nat see you?"

Grady smiled obliquely. "No one sees me if I don't want him to."

"Would I really have signed a bill of sale for my homestead if you hadn't arrived when you did?"

"You already had the pen on paper when I burst into the room. I lost precious time when that blasted hotel clerk refused to tell me which room you were in. Seems Turner paid him to keep quiet. He wouldn't have told me at all if I hadn't offered him something even more valuable."

"More valuable? Did you offer him more money?"

"I offered him his life," Grady said with quiet menace. His tone of voice sent a shiver down Storm's spine.

"I can't believe Nat would get me drunk. He told me the punch wasn't spiked. I was so thirsty from dancing, I must have drunk a gallon of the stuff."

"I tried to tell you what the man was like."

"You also kept interfering in my life when you had no right."

"Where would you be today if I hadn't interfered?" His intense gaze pinned her to the wall.

"I—don't know, and I thank you for last night, but that doesn't make you my keeper. From now on I'll know what to expect and be prepared."

Grady sent her an oblique look as he scraped back his chair and rose to his feet. "If you're able to ride, I'll take you home. We'll have to ride double, but the extra weight will be no burden for Lightning."

Though Storm didn't relish the idea of being so close to Grady for the ten-mile ride home, she wanted to return to her snug little cabin as quickly as possible. "I'll manage."

A weak sun broke through the clouds as Storm and Grady rode home. Though Grady kept their pace deliberately slow and easy, each jolt made Storm aware of his muscular form pressed in intimate contact with hers. Her hips rested snugly in the cradle of his loins, her back was warmed from contact with his chest, and everywhere they touched felt like a burning brand against her flesh. She stiffened her spine in a futile attempt to hold herself upright, but the position soon became impossible to maintain. In the end she grit her teeth and let herself absorb the comfort his huge body provided.

Storm even managed to doze in the saddle a time or two, barely aware when Grady eased an arm around her waist and pressed her more snugly against him. But Grady was more than aware of how perfectly she fit his arms and how small and vulnerable she seemed against his hardness. A surge of protectiveness such as he hadn't felt since Summer Sky's untimely death gave him an unsettling sensation in the pit of his stomach. He didn't need another woman in his life, he cautioned himself sternly. He especially didn't need a white woman whose independence and stubbornness were completely at odds with the qualities he admired in a woman.

A groan left Grady's lips as Storm shifted in her sleep, fitting her bottom more snugly against his loins. Was there no end to the torture he must suffer on Storm Kennedy's account? In his village, when he wanted a woman—usually one of the accommodating widows—he merely made his choice and took her with little fanfare or discussion. But it was different here in the white world, where a man must satisfy himself with prostitutes or take a wife. And Storm was the last woman in the world he would take to wife. She'd probably make Little Buffalo a terrible mother. Or would she? Conflicting emotions were still waging a battle inside his brain when he reached the outer boundaries of Storm's homestead, never anticipating the total devastation that awaited them.

The first inkling Storm had of impending disaster came when Grady reined in Lightning so violently, the poor animal reared and nearly unseated them. She came awake with a jerk, startled to hear a string of vile curses rush past Grady's lips.

"Wha—what's wrong?" she asked groggily as she tried to shake off the bonds of sleep.

His face was taut with simmering rage, his lips drawn back to expose his teeth in a fierce scowl. At first Storm thought Grady's anger was directed at her, until she followed the direction of his gaze. "You've had visitors during the night," he said tightly. The hollowness of his voice frightened her.

"Dear God, no!" The words were ripped from Storm's throat in a tormented shriek. Grady had reined in a hundred feet or so from where the cabin once stood. Nothing remained of the snug little dwelling she had left the night before except charred wood and smoldering ashes. Only the scorched, wood-burning stove she had been so proud of remained, virtually unscathed by the inferno that had destroyed her home.

Without waiting for Grady to dismount, Storm slid from Lightning's back, running, stumbling, falling, picking herself up, then running again. Cursing violently, Grady leaped to the ground and gave chase. Storm was within a few feet from the burnt-out hulk when Grady caught her.

"There's nothing you can do now, sweetheart," he said as she sobbed against his chest.

"Everything I held dear is gone," she choked out. "All my memories of Buddy, things my parents gave me to set up housekeeping, our wedding presents—everything. How? Why? I don't understand. What did you mean by 'visitors'?"

"Perhaps I spoke prematurely. Did you leave an unbanked fire in the hearth?" Instinct told him the fire hadn't started on its own, but he didn't want to alarm Storm until he was absolutely certain.

Still in shock, Storm shook her head.

"What about the stove? Could you have forgotten to douse the flame?"

"No, I distinctly remember banking the fire in the hearth, and the stove was cold when I left home. What am I going to do?" she wailed disconsolately. "There's not enough money left to rebuild."

The air was pungent with the acrid odor of charred wood, and thin wisps of blue mist hung in the cold air above the ruins, suggesting to Grady that the fire had started in the early hours after midnight and had burned quickly. It was suspicious, damn suspicious, Grady thought as his keen eyes made a thorough search of the area. Even the smallest clue could tell him what had happened during the night.

"Stay here," Grady said as he set Storm aside and approached the remains of the cabin.

"Where are you going?"

"To look for signs," Grady tossed over his shoulder. "I don't think the fire was an accident. I believe it was set deliberately."

Only one wall was left standing, charred beyond redemption and ready to topple at the slightest provocation. The other walls had collapsed into a heap of blackened rubble. Nothing remained of the cabin's contents save for the stove and a few scorched pots and broken pieces of pottery. After a cursory glance at the rubble, Grady turned his attention to the immediate vicinity surrounding the cabin. Dropping to his knees, he examined a set of hoofprints in the soft ground, grunting in satisfaction when he located another set, neither of which belonged to him or Storm. From the depth of the print in the damp soil, Grady established that the riders were much heavier than Storm. And he knew with certainty that they weren't Lightning's prints; his mount wore shoes with distinctive markings.

Then he found a telling piece of evidence that proved conclusively that the fire had been deliberately set. He discovered the remains of a crude torch that had been used to set the cabin ablaze. He carried it back to where Storm stood, intending to put it in his saddlebag and show it to the sheriff.

"What did you find?" Storm asked anxiously. She was still in a daze, unable to fully comprehend the disaster that had befallen her. Everything of value she owned had been destroyed in one night's evil doings.

Grady held up the charred torch. "Hoofprints that belong to neither one of us, for one thing," Grady said, "and a torch that was probably used to set the fire."

"Oh, God," Storm said, sinking to her knees. She had never felt so alone or bereft in her life. Though her parents had many children and were barely able to scrape a living from the rocky Missouri soil, she had always felt loved and protected. And Buddy had always been there to lend her support. "Who would do this to me?"

"Someone who wants your homestead," Grady said grimly. "The damn shame of it is, we can't prove Nat Turner is the culprit." He turned pensive. "I could always beat the truth out of him."

"If you do, you'll be thrown in jail for assault," Storm advised. "What am I going to do?" she repeated in such a forlorn voice, Grady experienced an emotion that was utterly foreign to him.

"First I'm going to take you to my place and get some hot coffee into you. After that I'm going back into town to talk to the sheriff."

"Is there nothing salvageable?" Storm asked in a small voice.

"Nothing, Storm. I'm sorry."

Hoisting her into the saddle, Grady swung in place behind her and turned Lightning toward his homestead. Though outwardly calm, he feared he'd find his own cabin destroyed. He knew a man who committed so vile a deed once would have no qualms about attempting it a second time. Grady knew Nat Turner hated him for having spoiled his plans on more than one occasion, and if he found his cabin still intact it was only because Turner feared Grady's retribution.

Grady's worst fears were realized when he was close enough to see tendrils of smoke rising from the vicinity of his cabin. Storm saw them also.

"Oh, no! Not your cabin too!" Tears that were still so close to the surface flowed without restraint down her cheeks. Grady dug his heels into Lightning's flanks, and Storm clung to the pummel to keep from falling as the stallion shot forward.

Grady uttered a cry of relief when he saw that the smoke they had seen from the distance came from one charred wall, not from the burnt wreckage of his cabin, as he had expected. The other walls were virtually untouched. By some miracle the torch had been carelessly thrown and lay beside the charred wall, half submerged in a puddle left from a recent rain. Evidently the arsonists hadn't waited around long enough to watch the conflagration. The torch had been quenched before it did more than scorch one wall and destroy a few shingles. When Grady saw that the smoldering flame threatened to burst into a blazing inferno at any moment, he reacted swiftly.

Leaping to the ground, he found two empty buckets he had left in the yard, grasped one in each hand, and raced to the river. He was back in minutes, dousing the charred side of the cabin. Then back to the river again for more water. Storm saw what he was attempting and hurried to join him, using a large kettle she found nearby. After several trips Grady was satisfied that the smoldering fire couldn't be rekindled into a full-blown blaze and called a halt.

"Another hour and it would have been too late," Grady said as he surveyed the damage to his cabin. In addition to the charred wall, parts of the roof had been destroyed. Fortunately the damage was minimal compared to the devastating loss Storm had suffered. "The wind could have fanned the smoldering embers to life and then we'd both be without a roof over our heads. Our 'friends,' whoever they may be, play rough."

The cabin smelled strongly of smoke as Storm stood just inside the door. Her weary eyes swept Grady's home with a desultory glance. It wasn't nearly as fine as hers and there was no cookstove or comfortable bed, but at least it was still standing, she thought dully. The charred wall was a grim reminder of her own loss and she turned from it with a brave show of defiance. Despite the grievous loss she'd suffered, she would survive somehow.

The bone-chilling cold had penetrated the room, and she shivered as she hugged her wrap closer around her. Grady noted her discomfort and squatted beside the hearth to light a fire. He waited until the blaze took hold before turning back to Storm, who stood suspended in the center of the room, still in a state of shock.

"I'll make some coffee," he offered. "Sit down, Storm. Worrying will serve no purpose.

She moved woodenly toward the chair, perching gingerly on the edge. When the coffee was boiled, Grady poured her a cup and sat across from her, sipping the dark, rich brew and watching her. She hadn't moved since she sat down, or even appeared to know where she was. Her head was lowered and she appeared to be studying the tips of her fingers. Grady assumed the shock of finding her home destroyed had sent her deep into depression.

"Are you all right?" he asked. The obvious concern in his voice brought her head up. She nodded. "Do you want to talk?"

"What can I say? My home is gone; there's not enough money left to rebuild or put in crops. What little cash remains from Buddy's inheritance is earmarked for the purchase of cattle."

"Do you have enough money to get you back to Missouri? If not, I can offer you a small loan."

"And give up my homestead?" Storm shot back, startled that he would suggest such a thing. "You expect me to surrender meekly after what Turner did to me? The land is mine! Do you hear me? No one is going to take that away from me." Her voice rose in fierce defense of what she and Buddy had worked so hard for. Owning land was her dream, and she had won the coveted homestead despite the obstacles she had been forced to overcome.

"What do you intend to do?" Grady asked, amazed by her fierce determination to see her dream through. Most women would be too stricken to continue on alone after suffering losses such as Storm had known. But then, he knew of no other woman who had the gumption to join the rush for land and homestead without a man beside her. Storm Kennedy seemed to thrive on adversity.

"I—don't know. Get a job, maybe, until I can earn enough money to rebuild my cabin."

"That will take years. I'm sure there will be no problem with keeping the homestead, for you did fulfill the necessary requirements. It's not your fault it was destroyed by fire. You probably wouldn't be required to rebuild till spring, but you couldn't possibly earn enough by then to start a new cabin. Then there are taxes. Have you considered that?"

The thought of paying taxes on her homestead nearly defeated Storm. If she was a coward, she could give up everything and go home, but she hated to burden her parents with another mouth to feed. Buddy's parents weren't any better off than her own family, though they only had two children left at home. Besides, she feared the Kennedys would blame her for Buddy's death and hate her for keeping what remained of Buddy's small inheritance from his grandmother instead of returning it to them. She had always gotten along with the Kennedys, but they had never fully forgiven them for taking off for Oklahoma to claim land when he could remain in Missouri and eke out a meager living on the farm.

*I'm homeless and virtually penniless,* Storm thought with humbling insight. The only money available to her lay in the sale of her homestead. But failure didn't sit well with Storm. She was a pioneer in the true sense of the word, and claiming a homestead had been the ultimate experience of her life. It had been a proud day when she drove her stakes into the ground. To sell it now would utterly devastate her.

"I'll think of something."

Grady grew pensive as he watched Storm fight back tears. She appeared on the edge of collapse, and he wondered what had held her together this long. He had thought her white blood made her different from the People, but he was learning that she possessed as strong a spirit as any Sioux warrior. And though he hated to admit it, responsibility for her husband's death weighed heavily on him. He fervently wished he could turn his back on her and let her solve her seemingly insurmountable problems on her own, but he could not.

Then, somewhere from the inner chambers of his brain came the thought that Storm actually did possess qualities that would make her a good mother for Little Buffalo. He loved his son and missed him fiercely. It was time he and Little Buffalo were reunited. It suddenly occurred to him that he could discharge his responsibility to Storm Kennedy and make a home for his son at the same time. He smiled at the simplicity of the solution to all their problems. Storm would have a home, he could have his son with him as he'd always intended, and have a passionate woman to share his bed.

"I have come to a decision, Storm Kennedy."

Storm's eyelashes flew up as she regarded him with mild curiosity. His gaze was so intense, she felt herself drowning in the deep blue pools of his eyes. A thrill of apprehension shot down her spine and she instinctively knew something of tremendous import was about to be revealed. Something that could change her life forever.

"We will marry," Grady said with quiet authority. "I miss my son a great deal and he is at an age where he needs a father. You will have a home, our land holdings will double, and my son will have someone to care for him."

Intense astonishment touched Storm's pale face. Grady Stryker was an ever-changing mystery. She knew he had been married before, but this new revelation stunned her.

"You have a son?"

# *Chapter Nine*

Grady's eyes wore a shuttered expression as he gazed at some distant specter above Storm's head. "His name is Little Buffalo. He is nearly six years old."

"Why didn't you mention him before? Where is he now?"

"Little Buffalo is living on the Sioux reservation with Summer Sky's parents. Summer Sky's younger sister, Laughing Brook, is caring for him. He is very fond of her."

"Do you think it's wise to bring your son here to live with you? Won't he miss Laughing Brook and his grandparents?"

"He is my son," Grady said. His voice was uncompromising yet oddly gentle. "I want him with me now that I have land of my own and a home."

"Let me get this straight. You expect me to marry you and raise your son," Storm said in a voice she hardly recognized. Was there no end to the man's audacity?

"It's the perfect solution," Grady said matter-of-factly. His response was only a buzz in Storm's ears as slow anger began to build inside her head. "You need a home, my son needs a woman's touch, and you won't have to sell your homestead."

Tossing her head, Storm eyed him with cold fury. "Go to hell! I'm not marrying you and I'm definitely not raising another woman's child." Had Grady mentioned love or commitment Storm might have considered his proposal. But her heart told her Grady Stryker was incapable of the kind of love she wanted.

Grady's blue eyes grew stormy as his own volatile temper threatened to explode. "What choice do you have? You know damn well you'll have to build another cabin in order to fulfill homesteading rules. If we combine our homesteads one cabin will suffice. Besides, for some confounding reason I feel responsible for you."

"I couldn't live with the kind of violence that comes looking for you. The fact that you are a renegade half-breed makes marriage between us impossible. Besides, you don't love me and—"

"What in the hell does love have to do with anything?" Grady asked harshly. "I married Summer Sky because I loved her and she was taken from me in a single act of violence. Loving someone and losing them hurts too damn much to do it more than once in a lifetime. I want you, and if you are honest with yourself you'll admit that I made you feel like a woman for the first time."

Storm flushed, recalling all those wonderful, arousing things Grady did to her and how wantonly she responded. The profound depths of passion Grady had plumbed within her body had stunned her. But all it really proved, her mind argued, was that she was capable of experiencing passion. Besides, she wanted more than pity from the man she married—if she ever decided to marry again.

"We've both been married before, we've both experienced love," Storm began slowly. "Even you can see this won't work. We come from different backgrounds. You're Indian. I've not heard you say one kind thing about the white race since I've known you. Why do you hold all whites in contempt? Wouldn't you be happier living on the reservation with your son?"

Grady glowered at her and turned away. "You know nothing about me. My father is a half-breed Lakota Sioux. His mother was the daughter of a chief. My mother is the daughter of a southern planter. That makes me only one-quarter Indian. I'm proud of my Indian heritage and the fact that I so closely resemble my father. As for the white race, except for my mother and her family, I know few of them who are worth one hair on Summer Sky's head, yet they killed her."

His words left her confused. Exactly how had Summer Sky died? "I'm white," Storm reminded him.

"I'm fully aware of that," Grady commented dryly. Suddenly he was on his feet, dragging her from her chair and pulling her against the hard wall of his chest. "But it doesn't make the inexplicable pleasure I feel when you're in my arms any less. I never wanted it to be like this between us, but it is. At least something can be gained from this marriage if you agree to it. A lot can be said for sexual gratification."

He lowered his head and tasted the pulsing hollow at the base of her throat, sliding slowly, tantalizingly upward to brush a lingering kiss against her lips. Raising his mouth from hers, he gazed into her eyes. "The choice is yours, sweetheart. Will we marry or do you need more persuasion?"

Storm's thoughts scattered like leaves before the wind. With Grady's hard body in intimate contact with hers, coherent speech was impossible. Grady chuckled indulgently as he nuzzled her ear. She smelled so good. The scent she used to rinse her hair lingered like the odor of dried crushed flowers after their summer blossoms were gone. And she tasted just as sweet, Grady thought as he placed gentle, nibbling kisses along her cheekbone.

Then, sudden, urgent need made the game seem like innocent child's play. He was no longer satisfied to merely kiss and taste; he wanted more, much more. Through the confusion of her thoughts, Storm knew the exact moment Grady's teasing kisses turned into raw, grinding need. His hands grew bold, seeking her breasts, kneading the tender mounds and massaging her nipples through the material of her dress. When they tired of that sport they drifted downward over her hips to grasp her buttocks, pulling her against the swollen hardness of his groin. Storm gasped and squirmed, trying to escape. She realized her mistake too late.

"Oh, lady, you do know how to drive a man crazy."

"No, I didn't mean—You must let me go. I don't want this. I want—"

"I know exactly what you want, lady, and I'm going to give it to you. When we marry you can have it every day."

"Marrying you would be sheer madness," Storm managed to say between the kisses he was pressing against her lips.

With practiced ease her coat was stripped from her and tossed to the floor. When his nimble fingers undid the fastenings on the front of her dress, loosened the strings of her corset and stroked her naked breasts, Storm began to tremble. "Your body doesn't lie," Grady said with a note of triumph when her nipples tautened beneath his caresses. Then his mouth closed over a rosy peak and suckled roughly. Storm jerked convulsively, the hot warmth of his mouth creating a sweet melting inside her.

Storm wanted to cry out in protest, wanted to make Grady stop. She knew from her past experience with the magnificent savage that his loving was too soul-destroying, too intense for it to be lasting. Lust, pure and simple. When the unaccountable attraction between them cooled nothing would remain. Grady didn't love her; he felt pity and a certain responsibility for her— and he needed a mother for his son.

"No!"

"Yes."

He eased her down on the makeshift bed of furs and blankets and sat back on his haunches, staring at her through narrowed lids. The fire in the hearth was blazing brightly; the room had grown quite warm, but it paled in comparison to the white-hot flame devouring Grady.

He slid her dress over her shoulders and down her arms. The corset quickly followed, then her shift. "Never will I understand why white women wear so many clothes," Grady said as he slid the stockings down her legs and removed her shoes. "Indian women are too practical to force their bodies into instruments of torture."

"I'm not an Indian," Storm managed to say.

"No, you're not. Your skin is too soft and pale."

A thick brown finger stretched out to draw a shaky line down one breast to its pink nipple. Gently, his hand outlined the circle of her breast. The gentle massage sent currents of electricity through her body. Broadening his scope, his hands slid over her silken belly to her thighs, spreading and lifting them to press moist kisses on the smooth insides. Then his mouth grew bold, sliding upward to nuzzle the nest of blonde curls nestled between her legs. When his tongue darted into the moist crevice of her womanhood Storm cried out in dismay.

"You can't! No, please!"

Grady lifted his head. "Did your husband never love you in this manner?"

"Buddy would never do such a perverted thing like that. It isn't right. It isn't . . . Oh . . ."

Ignoring her protest, Grady lowered his head, grasping her hips and holding her in place while he continued pressing warm, wet kisses on that most intimate part of her. Though every nerve in her body fought against this ultimate intimacy, Storm arched against his caress, seeking more of those heady sensations he was creating within her.

"Please stop, I can't stand it!"

"You're close, sweetheart," Grady murmured hoarsely. "Don't hold back. I'll stay with you until the end."

The tender torment of his relentless mouth drove Storm to the very brink of madness, and the delicious agony of his lashing tongue turned madness into ecstasy. She dangled at the edge of eternity for several breathless moments, until Grady's finger found a place so sensitive Storm screamed out in sweet surrender.

When Storm's heart slowed to a dull pounding, she opened her eyes and saw Grady towering above her, removing the last of his clothing. Tossing his breechclout aside, he stood poised beside her, magnificently nude, gloriously male, every splendid inch of him cast in bronze.

*My God, I want him!* she thought with fearful clarity. The undeniable and dreadful fact that no other man had the power to move her in the same earth-shattering way as Grady frightened her. She stared at him with her astonishing level gaze. His manhood was large and heavy, thrusting aggressively out of a nest of curling black hair, and a languid, drugging warmth uncoiled inside her. His face was strained with the harsh fever of desire, dark and striking.

"Do I please you, Storm?" His question startled her.

"I—yes," she said, forcing the words past the lump in her throat. She knew it was useless to lie when her eyes gave her away.

"You please me very much. When I put my body inside yours I am as close to Paradise as I will ever come in this life."

She moaned softly as he lowered himself full length atop her. Instinctively, her body arched toward him. "Now it's my turn, sweetheart," he whispered against her neck. "Spread your legs."

Storm let her legs fall open, amazed that she had obeyed Grady's command without the slightest protest. He didn't enter her immediately, wringing an agonized groan from Storm. Didn't he know how she ached to feel the hard thrust of his strength inside her? Instead he inserted his hand between their bodies, locating the tender bud nestled between her thighs, and massaged in slow, erotic circles. At the same time his lips toyed with her sensitive, swollen nipples. He suckled her breasts as his fingers grew bolder, searching for the pleasure points he seemed to know by instinct.

Suddenly he reversed their positions, bringing Storm atop him. For a moment Storm looked confused. Grady chuckled, delighted that he was the first to teach her new ways to love.

"What are you doing?"

"I told you there are many ways to love. You and your husband must have been innocent babes when it came to loving. It will give me enormous pleasure to teach you all I know. It will probably take me a very long time." Storm's eyes grew round as saucers as she considered his mind-boggling statement.

"Put me inside you." His voice was harsh. By now his control was hanging by a thin thread.

"No." Storm had no idea why she was fighting the issue. She knew he'd soon have her begging him to take her. The man was a devil. He showed no mercy, demanding more than she was prepared to surrender. He wanted her soul.

Grady gave her an enigmatic smile as he raised his head and began suckling her nipple, while with the soft pad of his thumb he manipulated the tiny bud of her desire until it was swollen and throbbing.

"Put me inside you," Grady repeated in a strangled voice. This time she obeyed instantly.

A groan of unholy torment erupted from his lips as she grasped his swollen staff and brought it against her moist crevice. Erupting in a frenzy of unrestrained passion, he grasped her hips and raised her slightly above him, thrusting upward as he brought her down to meet the rigid length of his manhood. His hardness electrified her and the sweet agony of impalement exploded upon her like a thousand tiny bursts of pleasure.

"Grady! Oh, Grady!"

"Do you like it this way, sweet? Ride me, Storm, ride me."

Grady's strokes grew harder, stronger. It was magnificent. It was sweet agony. It was mind-numbing bliss, yet so profound an experience she wasn't certain she'd survive. While he was merely enjoying a moment of physical desire, her soul was being ripped apart.

And then the involuntary tremors of fulfillment began, making her oblivious to all but the searing need Grady had built inside her. A moan of ecstasy slipped through her lips, and hearing her, Grady's thrusts grew more frenzied, freeing her in a bursting of raw sensation. Before the last cries left her throat, his own climax sent him spinning after her. It was several minutes before Storm could move or speak. Her words brought Grady abruptly from a state of euphoria to a rude awakening.

"You bastard!"

"What!"

"You heard me. Let me go!" She tried to slide off him, but Grady held her so tightly his male appendage was still wedged deeply inside her.

"Why are you so angry?"

"Because you took unfair advantage of me. I can't think straight when you—you—"

"—Make love to you?"

Her chin rose several notches in the air. "Seduce me."

"What's wrong with that? It's what we both wanted."

"It's what *you* wanted. I had no choice in the matter." She began pounding her fists against his chest, making no impression at all.

"Dammit, Storm, stop that. Do you intend to beat me every time we make love?"

"There won't be another time. I can't think straight when you—when you're—"

"—Making love to you?"

"Forcing yourself on me."

He laughed harshly. "Are you trying to say you didn't enjoy what we just did?"

"Yes." Her lids fluttered downward to conceal the blatant untruth of her statement.

"You're a terrible liar. Do you think I'm so inexperienced that I don't recognize real pleasure?"

"That's the trouble," Storm said sullenly. "You're *too* experienced. You know just where to touch me to make me feel things I never felt with Buddy. It's not right. Buddy was my legal husband. I loved him."

"Is that why you're angry with me? Because you resent how I make you feel when we make love?"

"That's part of it."

Abruptly he lifted her off of him, setting her down beside him. She scrambled for a blanket to cover her nakedness. "You're a coward, Storm Kennedy. You're afraid of your own sexuality. It's too powerful to cope with so you compensate by accusing me of seducing you. If it salves your conscience, then by all means think of me as a ravisher of innocent women."

Storm flushed, realizing Grady had come too close to the truth for comfort. "It isn't right to feel so—so—"

"—Wonderful?"

"Shameful," she contradicted. "It shouldn't happen like this. Buddy hasn't been dead very long. What kind of woman am I to allow myself to be seduced so easily?"

"A passionate woman who has never been fulfilled until now. I'm not tarnishing your husband's memory. He was obviously young and inexperienced, but dammit, Storm, he's dead. You're a true pioneer. Not many women could accomplish what you did on your own. You can remain stubborn and lose everything you've won or accept my proposal of marriage and lose nothing."

"Except my soul." Grady recognized the pain in her voice and was puzzled by it.

"I don't want your soul, Storm Kennedy. What I want from you is much simpler." Even as he spoke the words he realized he wasn't being truthful. Was it really pity or responsibility he felt for the young widow? Or was it another, more complicated reason that had nothing to do with her husband's death? "I want my son with me. He's still young and impressionable and needs a woman's influence. That's where you come in."

Storm's thoughts raced in every direction, finally returning to one inescapable fact. Grady didn't want her for herself and she damn sure didn't want a man who had no room in his barren heart for love. He gave her too much of everything but himself. Yet, what choice did she have? Losing her homestead would devastate her. But being a wife to Grady in every sense of the word would be even more devastating. He'd proved his mastery over her twice and was likely to do so again, stripping her of her pride, her identity—her soul. Was there no way to keep their relationship less intense without surrendering everything to him? she wondered dismally. When it came the answer was a stroke of genius, and she smiled at the simple solution.

"You want me to make a home for your son," Storm repeated, making certain she knew exactly where she stood with Grady. "And at the same time you'll be giving me a home and salving your conscience where I'm concerned."

"Yes," Grady said.

"Then I see no reason to share a bed if we marry."

"What!"

"I said—"

"I heard what you said, dammit! Are you crazy? How can you ask that of me after what we just experienced together?"

"Easy. I don't want to be forced into something I'm not ready for. I'm newly widowed. Let me mourn my husband for a decent interval before accepting another man in my bed."

"It's a little late for that, isn't it?" Grady said with mocking arrogance.

"It's never too late to mend one's ways. Have you never been assailed by guilt, or felt the crushing weight of having done something you're not exactly proud of?"

Grady sent her a sharp look, wondering if she was trying to make him feel as guilt-ridden as she was. What man or woman alive hasn't done things they're not proud of? He thought about his parents and how he had hurt them by taking himself and Little Buffalo from their home and not writing or communicating with them in over five years. Since he'd been separated from his son he'd had a glimpse of the pain and distress he had caused his own parents. And they certainly must have heard about

Thunder, the renegade Sioux who led daring raids against those who did harm to the People.

"Each of us must atone for his sins in his own way," he said cryptically. "If you do not wish to share my bed, then so be it. There are any number of women willing to lie with me. I do not need you for that purpose. All I ask is that you be a mother to my son."

Grady's easy acquiescence stunned Storm. She had expected an argument, or at least a few bitter accusations. What she hadn't expected was his bold statement that he would find another woman to accommodate him in bed. What was she getting herself into? she wondered dismally. But it was too late to back down now. She had made her bed and she must lie in it.

"I love children, so caring for Little Buffalo will prove no hardship."

Satisfied, Grady nodded, the harsh lines of his face softening into a reluctant smile. "We will marry when you are rested and over the shock of your loss. I won't have a hollow-eyed bride by my side when we say the words. Go to sleep, Storm. It's nearly dawn and you've earned your rest."

"You won't—"

"You have my word. A Lakota warrior does not lie. I will not make love to you until you ask it of me."

He lay down, wondering how he could survive living in the same house with Storm yet not touching her. He was strong, but not that strong. He had practiced celibacy in his life and not been harmed by it, but Storm was so great a temptation his strength would be tested to the limits. Even now, after just having loved Storm, his loins ached with need for her. He could always ease himself with another woman, he reasoned, but somehow that thought appalled him. How could another woman satisfy him when it was Storm he wanted?

Thunder and Storm.

The day would come, he predicted, when Thunder and Storm would make the heavens ring with the fury of their dueling souls.

The next day was Sunday, and Storm slept late. When she awoke Grady was gone. She busied herself around the house, mentally listing all the things that were needed to make his cabin more homey. He returned at dusk with the wagon and horses, which had survived the fire, and a few odds and ends rescued from the ashes. One was a framed wedding picture of her and Buddy taken from a twisted metal trunk. It was a memento Storm would treasure forever. Unfortunately, none of Storm's clothing survived the fire, and she was forced to wear the same dress for her wedding that she had worn at the dance.

They drove the wagon to Guthrie Monday morning. Storm was solemn-faced and stiff, Grady pensive as they huddled against the biting wind. December had swept across the land with a vengeance. The skies were gray and a light dusting of snow covered the hard-packed earth. They rode in a silence broken by an occasional comment, each contemplating an uncertain future with a barely known partner. Yet both were willing to admit, at least to themselves, that an attraction existed between them that was hot enough to singe the air around them.

They found a preacher easily, and though the good man was somewhat startled by their request—the same preacher had officiated at Buddy's burial—he married them willingly enough. They were married in the preacher's home with his wife as witness. When they left he shook his head in consternation, certain the young widow had lost her sanity. What woman in her right mind would marry a man whose skill with a gun had marked him for a violent end? And besides, the man was obviously a savage who knew little of white ways.

"That marriage is doomed to failure, Martha," he remarked to his wife as they watched the newlyweds drive away in the wagon.

The twinkle in Martha's eyes was unmistakable as she replied, "I wouldn't be too sure about that, dear."

"Harumph. Then you saw something I didn't."

Martha merely smiled in the secretive way of women and left her husband to wonder at the complexity of the female mind.

Storm was still too numb from the swiftness of events during the past two days to feel anything. She was married, married for the rest of her life to a man who thought and acted like an Indian. She was still pondering the rationality of her decision when Grady stopped the wagon in front of the general store.

"You'll need clothes for yourself and things to make the cabin more homey. I know women appreciate such things. Summer Sky took great pride in her home during the short time we had together. Charge anything you need to my account."

Storm swiveled her head to look at him. She hoped she wasn't always going to be compared to Summer Sky, the love of Grady's life. "Do you have money?"

"Enough that you can robe yourself decently and fix up the cabin to suit your tastes. I know my cabin isn't as nice as yours was, but I wasn't planning on marrying again."

Storm let that pass. It sounded as if he was sorry they were wed.

"There are things I need to do before we head back home. Take your time. When I return we'll go to the land office. You'll need to change your name on the deed. You're Storm Stryker now, not the Widow Kennedy."

As if he needed to remind her, Storm thought glumly as Grady assisted her from the wagon. How could she forget being married to a man who was too thoroughly male, too physically disturbing, and much too tempting to ignore?

Grady watched her enter the store, then turned resolutely away. He had business, all right, and he didn't want Storm in the way when he conducted it. His first stop was the sheriff's office, where he reported the acts of arson and presented the evidence to corroborate his claim.

"Have you any idea who did this, Mr. Stryker?" the sheriff asked.

"Obviously someone who wanted Mrs. Kennedy's homestead," Grady said, "and hoped to scare her into selling. Since I have no proof I'm not naming anyone, but we both know who's been trying to buy up homesteads in the Cherokee Strip, don't we?"

Sheriff Danville stroked his chin, staring pensively at Grady. "I'll ask around and keep my eyes and ears open. But if we're both thinking of the same man, I doubt we'll find anything to connect him to the fires. The man is slick, I can say that for him. Did you know he opened an office in town?"

"What kind of office?" Grady couldn't imagine Turner engaged in anything legal.

"Don't rightly know, but he calls himself an investments broker."

"Maybe I should pay our friend a little visit."

"I won't stand for no trouble, Stryker," Danville warned. "Let the law take care of it. The town hasn't forgotten that last bit of commotion you caused a while back. I'll bet Widow Kennedy hasn't forgotten it, either. Does trouble always come looking for you?"

"I'd like to forget the past and look to the future, Sheriff. I'm a genuine homesteader now. And a married man. I'll be bringing my son to live with me come spring."

"Married? When did all this happen."

"This morning."

"Where is the little woman? Is she one of the squaws from the reservation?" His voice held a hint of mockery, making Grady want to knock the smirk off the man's face.

"For your information, I married Storm Kennedy." He waited for the sheriff's gasp of shock and wasn't disappointed. "You could spread the word that anyone who messes with Storm now has me to contend with, and I'll show no mercy for the bastard who harms what belongs to me." He nodded, then turned and walked briskly toward the door. Suddenly he stopped and spun around. "On second thought, sheriff, I'll tell the bastard myself."

"Stryker, don't go breaking the law," Danville called after him. Grady gave no indication that he had heard Danville's parting shot.

Nat Turner's office wasn't difficult to find. It was located in a prominent place on the main street between the hardware store and the bank. The outer office was deserted when Grady entered a few minutes later, but the buzz of voices coming from behind a closed door brought a slow smile to his lips. His fingers flexed convulsively above his holster as he kicked open the door. Splintered wood flew in every direction as the three occupants of the room, their faces frozen in shock, turned to face the unwelcome intruder.

"Are these the scum you hired to do your dirty work?" Grady growled in a voice cold enough to freeze the ears off a brass monkey. "Say your prayers, Turner."

# Chapter Ten

"It's the renegade!" Fork gasped, reaching for his gun.

"I wouldn't do that if I were you," Grady warned ominously. "Your friend knows how foolish it is to try to outdraw me."

"What do you want?" Turner asked, finally finding his voice.

"I want all three of you out of town by midnight," Grady said. "You succeeded in burning down Storm's cabin, but you'll not get another chance to terrorize her. If any of you make one move to harm her I'll strip the skin from you piece by piece. When I finish you'll beg me to kill you."

"Sweet Jesus!" Fork turned pale, and cold sweat popped out on his forehead as he envisioned his bloody corpse after Grady finished with him. "He means it, too."

"Don't believe him," Turner sneered. "The law knows how to deal with men like him."

Quick as a flash, Grady whipped the knife from his waistband with his left hand. It was a wicked-looking weapon, honed to razor sharpness. The stench of raw fear enveloped Grady as Turner backed away.

"Wait, Stryker. What am I being accused of?"

"I should have known you three would find each other and form an unholy alliance. You and your henchmen burned down Storm Kennedy's cabin and tried to do the same to mine."

"Ya mean yours didn't burn down?" Purdy blurted out. Turner spat out a curse and Fork groaned and rolled his eyes after hearing his partner's revealing statement.

"Fortunately, no. But it doesn't take a genius to know who's behind the fires."

"You misjudge me, Stryker. I wouldn't harm Mrs. Kennedy," Turner said with exaggerated innocence. "What will the dear lady do now? Perhaps I can help her. My offer to buy her land still stands."

"The lady is now my wife. We were married this morning and she has no desire to sell her land. I'm perfectly capable of handling both homesteads. I'm giving you fair warning, Turner. If you or your henchmen are still in town tomorrow, you'll find the air dangerous to your health."

Having flung down his challenge, he carefully backed out the door, leaving the three men shaking in their boots.

"What do ya think?" Purdy asked. He made no attempt to conceal the tremor in his voice.

"I think I'm gonna light outta town this afternoon," Fork said. "Guthrie is gettin' a mite crowded fer my liking. I heard stories about the renegade that would curl your hair. No siree, I'm outta here."

"Cowards!" Turner spat.

"Damn right," Purdy agreed. "If yer lookin' fer company, Fork, I'll join ya. The half-breed scares the shit outta me."

"Glad to have ya, Purdy, but ya gotta hurry. I aim to shake the dust of Guthrie from my boots long before midnight."

They both turned toward Turner, waiting to hear what he intended to do. He had called them cowards, but they knew him to be even more cowardly than themselves. Turner seemed deep in thought. The odds most definitely weren't in his favor, and Turner wasn't one to buck the odds.

"Well, boys, the way I see it, this town hasn't much to offer an enterprising man like myself. I hear Texas is the place to be right now. They're prospecting for oil, and when that first gusher comes in it will open up a whole world of opportunities. I want to be in on it when that happens."

"I didn't think you'd stick around to test the renegade's mettle," Fork chuckled knowingly. "See ya around, Turner." Then he was gone,

Purdy following in his wake. No one noticed or cared when the two desperadoes rode out of town a few hours later. Nor was Nat Turner's absence noted when he boarded the first train to Fort Worth that same evening.

Storm was waiting when Grady returned to the general store to pick her up. He appeared grim and somewhat distracted when he loaded her bundles into the wagon, convincing Storm that not all of his business had been pleasant. She was surprised, though, to find the wagon already loaded with a bedstead, a feather mattress, and several other functional pieces of furniture.

"You've been busy."

For a moment Grady looked startled, then a slow smile spread over his features. "You have no idea. Are you ready to go to the land office and then have something to eat?"

"I—there is one stop I'd like to make before we leave town." Grady looked at her expectantly. "I'd like to visit the cemetery. I haven't bid Buddy a proper good-bye."

The thought that Storm felt more for her dead husband than she did her living one gave him a sinking feeling in the pit of his stomach. But what did he expect? There was no great love between them, only a mutual need that made marriage appear attractive and the right thing to do at this particular time. My God, they weren't even going to share the same bed, so why should he be upset by Storm's need to remain true to her dead husband's memory?

"I'll drop you off and wait in the wagon," Grady said tightly.

It was snowing quite heavily by the time they left the land office, had a rather subdued lunch, and drove to the cemetery. Grim-faced, Grady watched as Storm made her way slowly to Buddy's grave. It was still unmarked, but Storm had ordered a modest gravestone to mark his final resting place. Grady frowned when she knelt in the mushy snow and bowed her head. He could see her mouth moving and realized she was either speaking or praying, but he was too far away to hear her words.

The silence was deafening as Storm knelt beside Buddy's grave. The world seemed wrapped in a chilling blanket of snow that muffled all sound, including her soft sobs. She knew it was time to let Buddy go, that he would want it that way, but it was hard to part with him. Time stood still while she spoke to him, telling him her hopes and dreams for the future, explaining about Grady and her reason for marrying him. She remained on her knees for so long a time, the cold and her grief had numbed her to everything but the fact that she'd never see Buddy's smiling face again.

When snow began piling up around Storm and she seemed to be unconcerned that she was in danger of freezing to death if she didn't move, Grady took matters into his own hands. Leaping from the driver's box, he rummaged in the wagon bed until he found one of the new blankets he had purchased and walked resolutely to where Storm still knelt in the snow. She looked so small and vulnerable that Grady's heart went out to her. She must have loved her husband a great deal to mourn him so deeply, he thought, feeling a pang of regret for the way he had insisted upon a quick wedding without allowing her sufficient time to mourn. He could sympathize with her, for he had mourned Summer Sky just as deeply.

Storm started violently when she felt Grady wrap the blanket around her shoulders. When he swept her into his arms, she cried out in dismay. "What are you doing?" He looked into her face, not too surprised to see icy tears frosting her pale cheeks.

"Taking you home, lady. Nursing you through pneumonia is hardly my idea of a honeymoon."

"But Buddy . . ."

"You've said your good-byes. Buddy wouldn't want you freezing to death at the foot of his grave." He lifted her onto the seat, tucking the blanket around her. "I just hope we reach home before the snow gets too deep. I bought a set of runners for the wagon, but I don't exactly relish the idea of attaching them in the middle of a snowstorm."

The ride home was slow and bitterly cold. By the time they reached the cabin Storm felt like a solid chunk of ice. The fire had gone out, and Grady saw to it immediately. While Storm huddled before the kindling blaze trying to thaw out, Grady carried their purchases inside.

"When you're sufficiently warm perhaps you can start supper while I set up the bed," Grady said, sliding her a sidelong glance. He couldn't help but wonder if she would insist on enforcing her silly rule that they not share a bed. Her forlorn figure bending over her dead husband's grave had touched him deeply. He wanted to comfort her, to help her forget the past and look toward the future. Making love to Storm would be a healing rite, and pleasurable for both of them. If she would allow it, mutual gratification had much to commend it.

If she would allow it . . .

The supper dishes were done and Grady was outside seeing to the animals. Storm used his absence to wash herself and slip into her nightgown. When he returned, stomping snow from his feet and blowing on his hands to warm them, Storm was already curled up in the new bedstead he had set up in the far corner of the room. He spent agonizing minutes shedding his jacket and shirt and washing up at the washstand before moving toward the bed. The mattress sagged beneath his weight when he sat down. Instantly wary, Storm jerked upright.

"What are you doing?"

"Going to bed."

"You promised . . ."

"Dammit, Storm, do you still insist that I honor that silly condition you set? This will be a damn cold marriage unless you give a little."

209

"It's the way it has to be," Storm said stubbornly. "I'm not ready yet to surrender myself completely to a man like you."

"A man like me?" Grady repeated angrily. "What is that supposed to mean?"

"I—nothing. Just go to sleep. We're both tired, and there's still much to be done tomorrow before we're snowed in." What Storm didn't say was that Grady was the kind of man who would demand total surrender yet give nothing of himself in return.

"One day you'll beg me to love you, lady," Grady predicted. "I hope for your sake I'm around when that day arrives." His words left Storm with an ominous feeling of impending disaster.

The next days passed quickly enough. Storm was constantly busy as she sewed curtains and fixed up the cabin to suit her tastes. It was quite homey by the time she finished, and even Grady remarked on the changes she had wrought. Each night Grady insisted on sleeping beside her, torturing her with the seductive warmth of his body. The nights were bitter cold and many a morning she awoke nestled against him, seeking the comfort of his big body. But to his credit, Grady did not attempt to make love to her.

Though Grady suffered the agonies of Hell, he made no move to seek other sleeping arrangements. He wanted Storm to become accustomed to having him sleep beside her.

Often during the night he would awaken to find her cuddling into the curve of his body, seeking his warmth. Then his arms would automatically close around her, bringing her even closer against him. If his hand accidentally found a tempting breast or brushed a rounded hip, he merely groaned and persevered. His honor as a Lakota warrior was a vital part of his character. He would not make love to Storm unless she asked him.

Was there no end to the suffering he must endure on Storm's account?

The sizzling tension between Storm and Grady was nearly unbearable. Each time Grady began the nightly ritual of undressing, Storm quickly looked away or was occupied elsewhere with some pressing duty. Just looking at Grady made her legs weak and her head spin. It wasn't supposed to be like that. She had loved Buddy but had never felt the overwhelming need or suffocating desire she experienced in Grady's presence. The guilt over her response to a man the complete opposite of Buddy made her more determined than ever to resist his devil's lure.

Christmas approached, and one fine morning Grady drove into town, returning late in the day. He stunned Storm by producing a Christmas tree he had cut on his way home. It wasn't nearly so fine as those Storm knew as a child in Missouri, but the gesture was heartwarming as well as surprising. She didn't think Grady had a sentimental bone in his body.

During the times Grady was away from the house Storm worked on his Christmas gift. She was sewing him a white shirt made of the finest linen. She was proud of her small neat stitches and hoped Grady would like it. She had to admit that he was being exceptionally understanding of her demand that they not make love and she wanted to show her appreciation with a gift worthy of the sacrifice.

On Christmas day, besides cooking a fat turkey Grady had shot, Storm presented Grady with her gift. The gesture left him speechless. He'd had no idea she was making him a gift and exclaimed over the fine workmanship. Then he rummaged in his pocket and with a flourish presented Storm with a small, elegantly wrapped box. She stared at it for several minutes before daring to open it.

"For me?"

"Yes. Go ahead and open it."

Storm's hands shook as she ripped off the paper and snapped open the lid. Her lungs emptied of air when she saw the delicately wrought gold wedding band nestled on a bed of velvet.

"Oh."

"There wasn't time to buy a ring when we were married. Besides, I ordered this one specially made and the jeweler needed time to complete it."

Storm turned the ring over and over in her fingers, studying the design, which consisted of strange symbols and signs. "What does it mean?"

"Those engravings are Indian symbols. They hold a special meaning." She was rendered immoble by the intensity of his incredible blue eyes. "One day I'll tell you what they mean."

Storm looked at him squarely. "Aren't you going to tell me now?"

"No. Someday, maybe, when the time is right. Here, let me slip it on you." He grasped her hand, sliding Buddy's ring off her finger and replacing it with his. He hadn't said anything before about her wearing the wedding band given to her by a dead man, but now that he'd given her a replacement, he felt as if a great weight had been lifted from him.

"It—it's lovely," Storm said, admiring the golden circlet that banded her finger. For the first time since their marriage she felt truly and irrevocably wed to Grady Stryker. Before he had placed his ring on her finger she had felt like an actress merely playing out a role. "Thank you."

"Is that the best you can do?" Grady asked in such a solemn tone, Storm thought she had offended him.

"I don't understand."

"You will," Grady said cryptically.

When he dragged her into his arms Storm finally understood what he wanted from her, and was angered by it. Was he trying to bribe her?

"I want you, Storm. A day doesn't go by that I don't long to make love to you like a real husband."

His arms tightened and his mouth swooped down to claim hers. His lips were hard and searching, leaving her mouth burning with fire. The unspoken demand of his kiss left little doubt what he wanted, what he was determined to take. But guilt over her wanton response to Grady made her unwilling to surrender again to his seduction.

"I—can't."

"You want me."

"I don't deny it. I'm a brazen hussy to feel the way I do. I'm afraid of the powerful emotions you rouse in me, and it hurts to know that I never felt this way with Buddy."

"Let me love you."

"No. You promised."

"Storm, look at me."

Her head came up slowly, her honey brown eyes hazy with the heat of passion. When she met the electrifying cobalt of his gaze, a shudder passed through her body.

"Why should we both suffer because of your stubbornness?" Grady asked. His control hung by a fragile thread. "This marriage doesn't have to be a sterile one. Two people who want each other like we do shouldn't deny themselves. We are husband and wife."

He kissed her again, his lips hard and demanding. Her emotions whirled and skidded, her thoughts spun. He forced her lips open with his thrusting tongue, demanding a response. Her stubborn refusal angered him, and the more she protested, the more forceful and hungry his kisses became. Why was she resisting something as fundamental and basic as making love? Grady wondered as his hands joined his lips in convincing Storm that their loving was as natural as eating and breathing. Why should it distress her if he made her feel the kind of pleasure and emotion she had never experienced with her dead husband? What Grady desired above all else was to love Storm so thoroughly she couldn't recall her dead husband's name.

Buddy. The name filled him with rage. Why should a dead man hold Storm's affection when he, Grady, was alive and capable of giving her pleasure in a way Buddy never could? All Storm's resolve was swept away as Grady swept her into his arms and carried her to their bed. Her lips were parted and he could feel her breath fan his cheek. It came in short staccato bursts of air that conveyed her passion—and her fear.

"You promised."

"Damn you!" He dropped her onto the mattress and turned away. His fists were clenched, and the stark planes of his proud features wore a look of anguish. "Go to sleep. I won't touch you." Then he grabbed his heavy jacket from the hook beside the door and stormed out into the bitter cold.

When he returned hours later, chilled to the bone, Storm had donned her nightgown and was sound asleep, wrapped in a coccoon of furs and blankets. Giving her a look of utter disgust, Grady tossed off his clothes and joined her, careful not to touch her until his body had warmed. It didn't take long. Lying beside Storm turned his body into a blazing inferno.

The longer Grady lay there, the more aroused he became. He didn't even need to touch Storm to maintain an erection. Just thinking about her and how loving her made his body burst into flame made him painfully aware that his legal wife was just a touch away.

Just when Grady began to feel the fuzzy edges of sleep overtake him, Storm turned in her sleep, molding her softness against his back and buttocks. His body reacted instantly, his member becoming fully distended and throbbing. It was more than a human could bear. Even a Lakota warrior had his breaking point, and Grady had reached his.

Storm sighed in her sleep, instinctively seeking the warmth of Grady's body. Curling herself around him and squirming into a comfortable position, she began dreaming. As it so often happened these past weeks of enforced abstinence, her dreams became erotic in nature. The logic behind her dreams escaped her the next day when she recalled them, but she supposed it had something to do with the dormant passion Grady had discovered and unleashed in her. A passion that filled her with shame. But since her dreams had no bearing on reality, Storm usually succumbed fully to her dream lover.

Grady turned to face Storm, bringing her fully against him. When she made no protest his hands slowly hiked up her nightgown, raising it above her hips. When his member prodded her boldly, she arched her back and opened her thighs so that his hardness could slip between her legs. He lay still for a breathless moment, savoring the warmth, hardly daring to breathe as he waited for Storm to awaken and voice her usual protests. Nothing left her lips but a soft burst of air and a sound that could only be described as mewling.

His hands slid down her back to her buttocks, gently squeezing the soft mounds as he brought one of her legs over his hips. But still he didn't enter her, waiting—hoping for the words of acceptance that would end his misery. One hand slid down her taut stomach to the moist crevice between her legs. He found her wet and ready for him. Still he hesitated, recalling his vow not to make love to her until she invited him. When his fingers grew bold, exploring the tender petals of her womanhood, Storm began whimpering words that made little sense. Assuming she was awake and that her whimpers were her way of granting permission, Grady flexed his hips and thrust into her.

Storm's body burned with desire and she whimpered in her sleep. Her dream lover was making love to her and she welcomed it, aware that she would awaken in the morning and find it all a fantasy. But, God, it felt so wonderful, so right—so good! She hoped she wouldn't awaken this time until it was all over. Usually her dreams only went so far, then stopped before that final burst of ecstasy she knew herself capable of. She felt him prodding between her legs, felt his hands kneading her buttocks and stroking her nipples. Felt him thrust into her.

"Oh, God!" She jerked violently awake. It wasn't a dream after all. They were lying on their sides facing one another, and she felt herself stretch and fill as he thrust into her. "What are you doing? You promised."

Grady went still, forcing his body into a calmness that nearly killed him. "What are you talking about? It's too late now. You should have stopped me before."

"I was sleeping. I thought it was all a dream. I didn't want this to happen."

"Oh, lady, it's happening," Grady groaned, probing ruthlessly as he held her hips in place. "It's too late to stop now."

"What about your honor? Does it mean nothing to you?"

"My honor means everything to me and I know I'll regret this in the morning, but as God is my witness, I can't stop now."

Then he was thrusting wildly, making Storm forgot her reason for denying him in the first place, driving everything from her mind but the urgent need he was creating inside her. Waves of ecstasy throbbed through her, and she cried out for release. It exploded upon her in a downpour of fiery sensations.

"Grady!"

"Oh, lady, that's what I want to hear. I want you to know who's making love to you. It's *my* name I want to hear on your lips when you cry out in ecstasy. I want to hear it again, sweet, do you think it's possible?"

It wasn't only possible. By the time Grady had finally allowed his own climax, he had taken Storm a second time to that lofty place where only lovers dwell.

When Grady floated back to reality Storm had deliberately turned her back on him. Her shoulders were rigid, her spine stiff, and Grady felt the heavy weight of her rejection. He also felt the suffocating disappointment of having broken his promise. How in the hell did he know Storm was sleeping and wasn't aware that he was making love to her? To make matters worse, he knew he would break his word again and again, until he could no longer bear Storm's hatred. Remaining in the same house with her was impossible.

"Storm, I thought it was what you wanted." His words, meant to be an apology, sounded cold and unfeeling to her. Once again he had succeeded in dominating her with his strength and sensuality. "I had no idea you were sleeping." He touched her shoulder and she jerked violently.

"You're a damn liar, Grady Stryker."

Since Grady had no answer to her bitter accusation, he remained mute. He had many things to think about, many decisions to make. Storm had fallen asleep before he reached a compromise that he thought would make Storm happy and keep him from breaking his word again. He arose from bed and dressed in his warmest clothes, packed his saddlebags and bedroll, took his guns and bullets, and quietly left the house.

He returned just before dawn, found a pencil and paper, and scribbled a hasty note, leaving it on his pillow, where Storm was sure to find it. He paused at the door before stepping outside, gazing at Storm's sleeping form with such longing it plumbed the very depths of his heart. His eyes were as bleak as the Oklahoma winter. The last thing he did before closing the door behind him was to pick up the snowshoes he had purchased in town and tuck them under his arm.

Storm awoke late the next morning. The fire had gone out during the night and the cabin was freezing. It was the first time since marrying Grady that she could recall waking up to a cold room. He was always so good about doing all those little chores that added comfort to her life. Then she remembered last night and how he had made love to her against her will and all the anger and resentment returned.

Grady was making it extremely difficult for her to remain true to Buddy's memory, and she didn't know how much longer she could go on like this. She had asked for time to bring herself to accept marriage to another man and Grady's answer was to seduce her time after time. The man was a savage who trampled her feelings beneath his masculinity. If he loved her—Dear Lord, what was she thinking? Storm wondered, surprised that she'd even want the love of a man like Grady Stryker.

The cabin appeared deserted; usually she could sense Grady's presence, but this morning there was nothing to indicate that he was nearby. Peering cautiously over the edge of the blanket, Storm realized that she was indeed alone. Where had Grady gone, she wondered. There was enough wood piled against the house to last the winter and it was too cold outside to do much else. Unless he had gone hunting. Finding no excuse to lie abed, she dressed hurriedly and built a fire in the hearth. She didn't find the note until she returned to make the bed.

Grady was gone. He had left her to go to the reservation for his son. He would return in time for spring planting. The cold, carefully worded note went on to say that he had put the runners on the wagon so she could travel to town for supplies and that she could draw money from his bank account, for he had put her name on the account the day they were married. There were no words of affection, no apology or good-bye, no explanation for his sudden departure in the middle of winter. Did he miss his son so much or did he merely want to escape from a marriage he found distasteful?

"I hate you, Grady Stryker," Storm shouted into the emptiness of the cabin. "I hate you . . ." Suddenly seized by panic, she realized she was alone, living in as near a wilderness as she had ever seen in her life. Yet not too many weeks ago, after Buddy's tragic death, she had been perfectly content to homestead alone. Had marriage to Grady changed her so much? she wondered bleakly. The next words that came rushing out of her mouth left her stunned. "My God, Grady, what am I going to do without you?"

# *Chapter Eleven*

The winter of 1894 in Oklahoma Territory was a mild one compared to previous years. After the bitter cold of December 1893, the rest of the winter lost its bite. The river continued to flow, and Storm was able to draw water with little difficulty. The wood Grady had cut before he left was more than adequate for her needs during January and February. By March green tufts of grass began pushing through the melting snow and rain nourished the earth with its life-giving abundance. It was the beginning of a new cycle, but to Storm, January and February were the longest two months of her life.

She never realized how much she had come to depend on Grady until he left and she was faced with empty days and desolate nights. He had always appeared to her as bigger than life, a man who feared nothing, except perhaps his own private demons, and faced the challenges of life with fierce purpose. As the first week of March slid by, Storm began to fear that Grady never intended to return, that her impossible demands had forced him to flee. Being made a widow had been a painful shock, but being abandoned brought another kind of pain—that of rejection.

If he came back to her, she'd lie with him willingly, she silently vowed, gladly, sharing her life with him and caring for his child as if he were her own.

She'd make Grady love her.

They would forge a living out of this raw land and learn to live together and love one another. One day Buddy and Summer Sky would become pleasant memories from their pasts.

*Foolish dreamer,* her mind taunted. *Grady is gone and you'll never see him again. You have the land; be satisfied with that.*

The land offered little comfort on cold nights when she yearned to feel Grady beside her, willing and eager to share his warmth with her. Why couldn't she be satisfied with the small part of him he gave her instead of wanting all those things he didn't offer?

On one of her trips into Guthrie, Storm learned that Nat Turner had mysteriously left town in December, and she wondered if Grady had had anything to do with his going. Knowing him, she supposed he had. She was grateful she no longer had to deal with the scoundrel.

# A Special Offer For Leisure Historical Romance Readers Only!

## Get Four FREE* Romance Novels

### A $21.96 Value!

Travel to exotic worlds filled with passion and adventure—without leaving your home!

Plus, you'll save at least $5.00 every time you buy!

# Thrill to the most sensual, adventure-filled Historical Romances on the market today…

## FROM 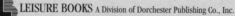 LEISURE BOOKS

As a home subscriber to the Leisure Historical Romance Book Club, you'll enjoy the best in today's BRAND-NEW Historical Romance fiction. For over twenty-five years, Leisure Books has brought you the award-winning, high-quality authors you know and love to read. Each Leisure Historical Romance will sweep you away to a world of high adventure…and intimate romance. Discover for yourself all the passion and excitement millions of readers thrill to each and every month.

## SAVE AT LEAST *$5.00* EACH TIME YOU BUY!

Each month, the Leisure Historical Romance Book Club brings you four brand-new titles from Leisure Books, America's foremost publisher of Historical Romances. EACH PACKAGE WILL SAVE YOU AT LEAST $5.00 FROM THE BOOKSTORE PRICE! And you'll never miss a new title with our convenient home delivery service.

Here's how we do it. Each package will carry a 10-DAY EXAMINATION privilege. At the end of that time, if you decide to keep your books, simply pay the low invoice price of $16.96 ($17.75 US in Canada), no shipping or handling charges added*. HOME DELIVERY IS ALWAYS FREE*. With today's top Historical Romance novels selling for $5.99 and higher, our price SAVES YOU AT LEAST $5.00 with each shipment.

## AND YOUR FIRST FOUR-BOOK SHIPMENT IS TOTALLY FREE!*

*IT'S A BARGAIN YOU CAN'T BEAT! A Super $21.96 Value!*

**LEISURE BOOKS** A Division of Dorchester Publishing Co., Inc.

# GET YOUR 4 FREE* BOOKS NOW—
## A $21.96 VALUE!

Mail the Free* Book
Certificate
Today!

## 4 FREE* BOOKS 🌸 A $21.96 VALUE

*Free Books Certificate*

**YES!** I want to subscribe to the Leisure Historical Romance Book Club. Please send me my 4 FREE* BOOKS. Then each month I'll receive the four newest Leisure Historical Romance selections to Preview for 10 days. If I decide to keep them, I will pay the Special Member's Only discounted price of just $4.24 each, a total of $16.96 ($17.75 US in Canada). This is a SAVINGS OF AT LEAST $5.00 off the bookstore price. There are no shipping, handling, or other charges*. There is no minimum number of books I must buy and I may cancel the program at any time. In any case, the 4 FREE* BOOKS are mine to keep—A BIG $21.96 Value!

*In Canada, add $5.00 shipping and handling per order for first shipment. For all subsequent shipments to Canada, the cost of membership is $17.75 US, which includes $7.75 shipping and handling per month.[All payments must be made in US dollars]

*Name* _____

*Address* _____

*City* _____

*State* _____ *Country* _____ *Zip* _____

*Telephone* _____

*Signature* _____

If under 18, Parent or Guardian must sign. Terms, prices and conditions subject to change. Subscription subject to acceptance. Leisure Books reserves the right to reject any order or cancel any subscription.

(Tear Here and Mail Your FREE* Book Card Today!)

# Get Four Books Totally
# F R E E\* —
# A $21.96 Value!

(Tear Here and Mail Your FREE\* Book Card Today!)

PLEASE RUSH
MY FOUR FREE\*
BOOKS TO ME
RIGHT AWAY!

Leisure Historical Romance Book Club
P.O. Box 6613
Edison, NJ 08818-6613

AFFIX
STAMP
HERE

She would thank Grady, if she ever saw him again.

Grady returned unexpectantly one exceptionally warm day in early March. Storm was turning over clods of dirt with a shovel in preparation for planting a backyard vegetable garden when she looked up and saw him standing so close she could reach out and touch him. Never would she become accustomed to the silent way in which he moved. His massive frame was clad in buckskins and moccasins; his ebony hair was longer than ever and his face more gaunt. His high cheekbones had hollows beneath them she hadn't noticed before, and the dark circles beneath his eyes made them appear more vivid a blue than she remembered. His intense gaze searched her face, then roamed over her figure. What he saw must have disappointed him for he scowled.

"You came back," she murmured.

For a moment he looked bewildered. "Did you think I wouldn't?"

"I—didn't know."

Suddenly, from the corner of her eye, Storm caught a movement. A small body came hurtling toward them, running as fast as his small legs could carry him. "Papa, Papa, is this my new home?"

Grady's expression softened as he gazed down at his exuberant son. Little Buffalo was the picture of his father, but without the blue eyes. His skin was golden brown, his eyes dark, his hair blacker even than Grady's. There was a nobleness about the child that proclaimed his proud Indian heritage. One day he would be every bit as handsome and imposing as his father. Storm looked for signs of Summer Sky in the boy and found it in the softness around his chin, the midnight darkness of his eyes.

"This is our homestead, Little Buffalo, and this is your new mother. From now on you will speak only English so that she can understand you. Greet Storm properly, son. She will be caring for you in future."

Little Buffalo's face grew hostile as he regarded Storm in an insulting manner. "I don't want a new mother, Papa. I am perfectly happy with Laughing Brook. Why can't she be my mother?"

"Because Laughing Brook belongs on the reservation with her family," Grady explained patiently, "and Storm is my wife. Therefore, she will be your mother."

Little Buffalo kicked viciously at a clod of dirt with his moccasined toe, then peered up at Storm resentfully. "Why did you marry *her*? Laughing Brook is much prettier."

"Little Buffalo!"

"It's all right, Grady," Storm said, realizing that winning over Grady's son wasn't going to be easy. She dropped to her knees, until she was on the same level with the child. "I don't want to take your real mother's place, Little Buffalo, or take away any of the love you feel for Laughing Brook, but I hope we can become good friends."

"I don't remember my real mama," Little Buffalo retorted sullenly. "I only remember Laughing Brook. I don't need a mother as long as I have her."

"But Laughing Brook isn't here," Storm explained gently.

"Yes, she is," the boy said with an enthusiastic nod. "Papa brought her along."

A probing query came into her eyes as her gaze flew up to search Grady's face. His eyes were shuttered, his expression dark and unreadable. At the moment only one thought raced through Storm's mind. Grady had told her that if she wasn't willing to fill his needs, he'd find someone who would. Had he brought his dead wife's sister here to be his mistress? Storm's first glimpse of the lovely Indian maiden rounding the corner of the cabin sent her heart plummeting. The young woman was so beautiful, it hurt to look at her.

Her sleek black hair danced around her waist as if it had a life of its own and her huge dark eyes appeared enormous in her small golden face. Her lips were generously curved and lush in a way that could only be described as sultry. The ornately beaded deerskin dress and moccasins she wore revealed rather than concealed her tall, voluptuous figure. If Summer Sky had been as lovely as her sister, Storm reasoned, it was no wonder Grady would accept no substitutes.

Laughing Brook was laughing happily as she ran to Grady and flung her arms around his

227

neck, babbling in a language Storm assumed was Sioux.

"We will speak English for Storm's benefit," Grady said, unwinding her arms from around his neck. "Little Buffalo must become proficient in that language if he is to survive in the white world." Then he turned to Storm, saying, "Storm, this is Laughing Brook, my sister-in-law. She has been caring for my son since my wife's—since Summer Sky's death. Laughing Brook, this is my wife, Storm. You must help her become acquainted with Little Buffalo, for she is now his mother."

Laughing Brook's smile dissipated into a pout. Her lower lip jutted out belligerently and her eyes glowed with a savage inner fire as they raked over Storm in an insolent manner. "She isn't much to look at," she said with a disdainful toss of her head. "Why is she so pale, Thunder?"

With her face and hands smudged with dirt and her hem dragging in the wet earth, Storm felt and looked like a bedraggled beggar woman compared to the resplendent Indian maiden. But Grady thought she was beautiful and would have said so if Storm hadn't spoken up in her own defense.

"My skin has always been naturally pale. And," she paused and shot Grady a fulminating look, "had I known when to expect *my husband* I would have made myself more presentable."

Grady groaned inwardly. He could sense a storm brewing. "Take Little Buffalo inside the cabin, Laughing Brook. I wish to speak with Storm privately."

Little Buffalo looked from Laughing Brook to Storm and then to his father. Astute for one so young, he recognized Laughing Brook's scorn for the white woman his father had married and came to a decision. During the long trip from the reservation, Laughing Brook had filled his head with horror stories about the terrible things white women did to small Indian children, until he hated and feared Storm long before he met her. And now, following Laughing Brook's example of icy disdain, he squinted up at Storm and said, "I don't like you. I'll never forgive you for marrying Papa. He should have married Laughing Brook. It is the custom of the People."

Smirking spitefully, Laughing Brook grasped Little Buffalo's hand and led him away, pleased by her small charge's lack of respect toward the white woman she had hated on sight. She was unaware of Storm's dismay and Grady's dark scowl, but had she been it wouldn't have mattered in the least. One thing Laughing Brook felt secure in was the love of Little Buffalo. And Little Buffalo was the most important person in the world to Thunder. It wouldn't be long, Laughing Brook thought gleefully, before Thunder's white wife was sent packing and she, Laughing Brook, would take her place. It was the way it should have been in the beginning, and would have been if Thunder had followed tribal custom.

Grady's scowl darkened as he watched Laughing Brook and Little Buffalo disappear around the corner of the cabin. When he turned back to Storm, her scowl was nearly as ferocious as his.

"Why did you bring her?" Storm asked, still in a state of shock over Grady's arrival with another woman in tow.

"I had no choice," Grady said. "Little Buffalo resisted leaving the reservation and I thought it would make his leaving less painful if I brought along Laughing Brook. She is like a mother to the boy and separating them would have been cruel. When he is fully adjusted to his new home and to you I will send Laughing Brook back to her people."

"How long do you suppose that will be?" Her sarcasm was not lost on Grady.

Grady shrugged. "I don't know."

"Weeks? Months? Years? My God, Grady, can't you see Laughing Brook doesn't like me? She'll poison your son against me if she remains. He already resents me."

"How can you say that?" Grady challenged. "You just met her. And Little Buffalo will come around. He just turned six years old and is still a child in mind and body."

"Little Buffalo will do as Laughing Brook says. He obviously loves her."

"Perhaps," Grady said cryptically, "but I have every confidence you will win him over. Meanwhile, separating him from Laughing Brook now will only confuse and upset him. Besides, I've always found Laughing Brook a warm and generous woman. First meetings are often deceptive. Given time she'll adjust to the fact that you're my wife."

"There isn't enough time in the world for that," Storm muttered sourly. *Lord help us all,* she thought as she turned away.

"Storm." He touched her shoulder and she swung around to face him, her eyebrows raised. "Aren't you glad to see me?"

"I hated you after you left me the way you did."

The harsh planes of his face softened and his blue eyes grew luminous. "I had to. I thought you understood. It was the only way I could retain my honor. If I remained in that cabin with you the entire winter, not even my solemn vow could have kept me from loving you as my body demanded."

Storm flushed and looked away, unable to face the stark reality of his words. "What—what now? You've come back. Does that mean you no longer want me in that way? Has Laughing Brook given you what you want? I don't understand why you didn't marry Laughing Brook. Obviously your son loves her, and it was more or less expected of you."

"If I wanted Laughing Brook, I would have taken her long ago," Grady said with quiet emphasis. "Dammit, Storm, didn't you miss me at all?"

"Did you miss me?" Storm shot back.

If she could have looked into his heart, she would have heard his silent cry. *I missed you like the morning misses the sunrise and the night misses the dawn.* But he was a Lakota warrior and flowery phrases did not come easily to his lips. "You are my wife."

"I'm surprised you remembered it."

"Oh, lady, I remember. I remember more, much more. Like how wonderful you feel in my arms and how hotly you burn when my hands and mouth release the fire in you."

"Grady . . ."

Suddenly she was in his arms, crushed tightly against the hard wall of his chest, crying out with the wonder of having every inch of his magnificent body pressed intimately against hers. It had been so long . . . so damn long.

Then he was claiming her mouth, shattering her thoughts with the hunger of his kisses, oblivious to the world around them. She savored the taste of him, of his tongue as it thrust into her mouth, and with sudden, painful insight she realized she would always want this man.

"Thunder, Little Buffalo is hungry. Shouldn't your wife be fixing a meal for us?"

Grady's frustrated groan brought Storm abruptly to her senses as she shot out of his arms. Laughing Brook had definitely picked the wrong time to intrude upon their privacy. Or had it been the right time? Obviously the Indian maiden knew exactly what she was doing.

"Laughing Brook is right," Storm said, flushing. "You must all be hungry as well as tired. I'll clean up at the river and be right in to fix you a meal." She turned and hurried off before Grady could stop her.

"I don't think your white wife likes me," Laughing Brook said, bringing her full lips together in a sensual pout. "Obviously you didn't learn your lesson after what the White Eyes did to my sister."

"Storm had nothing to do with Summer Sky's death."

"She's white."

"I brought you here for Little Buffalo's sake," Grady said sternly, "and I won't abide trouble from either you or Storm. I have made my choice. Storm is my wife; please treat her with the respect and courtesy due her."

"Bah, a husband does not leave his wife so soon after marriage unless he is not pleased with her. My eyes do not deceive me, Thunder. My heart tells me you are not pleased with your white wife. But I am not greedy. I will be your second wife. I will give you what she does not."

"I have chosen to live in the white world, Laughing Brook, and am allowed only one wife by law." He glanced toward the river, where Storm had fled, his blue eyes hazy with unquenchable heat. When he spoke again there was a gentle softness in his voice that Laughing Brook had never heard before. "Storm is the only wife I want."

Her dark eyes flashing defiantly, Laughing Brook turned on her heel and marched back to the cabin. Though Thunder seemed to be obsessed with his wife, she sensed things weren't as they should be between them. No new bridegroom would leave his bride for two months if he wasn't desperate to escape an unpleasant marriage. She had no idea what had prompted Thunder to take a white bride, for he was a taciturn man not given to divulging the secrets of his private life, but Laughing Brook wasn't discouraged. Thunder had brought her to his homestead, hadn't he?

Having the love of Little Buffalo gave her a hold on Thunder that his pale wife couldn't duplicate, Laughing Brook reasoned. And as long as she was in a position to control the child's mind, she would make certain Little Buffalo and Storm never became close. Already the boy disliked his stepmother because of the seeds of discontent she had planted in his mind.

The evening meal was a solemn one. Little Buffalo fell asleep at the table and Grady carried him to the pallet of furs and blankets he had fixed on the floor. The boy was to share it with Laughing Brook until Grady could build a separate bedroom for him and Storm. He had voiced his intention earlier to go to Guthrie the next day and buy lumber. Storm wondered if Grady intended to share the bed with her that night with his son and Laughing Brook in the same room. Although they were married, she knew she'd be embarrassed. But knowing Grady she figured it would make little difference who slept in the room.

She had heard somewhere that Indian families shared the same tepee.

After slanting Storm a furious look, Laughing Brook settled down on the pallet beside Little Buffalo. Grady blew out the light and Storm undressed, feeling more nervous than she had the first time Grady had crawled into bed beside her. At least that time they hadn't had an audience. She didn't know what she'd do if Grady wanted to make love. Before he returned from the reservation she had decided to be a wife to Grady in every way, but bringing Laughing Brook back with him had made a mockery of that decision.

The bed sagged beneath Grady's weight, and Storm tensed when his naked thigh touched hers. When he turned to take her into his arms she went rigid.

"Are you still determined to keep us apart?" Grady whispered against her ear. "When I kissed you I could have sworn . . ."

"We're not alone," she hissed.

"What goes on in the marriage bed is private no matter who is present. When a Lakota warrior makes love to his woman no one else hears. It is the custom."

"It may be all right for savages, but it's not all right with me."

Grady went still. So she still thought him a savage, his mind raged. He wanted to show her how much a savage he could be and ravish her until he'd had his fill. But he knew he'd never have his fill of Storm. He could have had his pick of women on the reservation, including Laughing Brook, but he wanted none of them. His one consuming thought was to return with his son to his homestead as quickly as possible and taste Storm's sweetness once again.

"Is that your final word?"

"That's how it must be as long as Laughing Brook and Little Buffalo are sleeping in the same room with us."

Rising from the bed, Grady pulled on his pants and ordered Laughing Brook into bed with Storm. Then he slid down beside Little Buffalo and spent the rest of the night trying to quell his raging hunger for a woman who had no intention of ever being a wife to him. Did she still hold him responsible for her husband's death?

Laughing Brook was delighted when Thunder left his wife's bed. She realized she had been right in assuming all was not well with the newlyweds, and she slyly planned other ways to drive a wedge between husband and wife. If for some reason Thunder didn't want to divorce his wife according to white law, they could return to the reservation. It was where Thunder and Little Buffalo belonged anyway. Despite his white blood, Thunder was the bravest, fiercest warrior she had ever known.

After her sister's brutal accident Laughing Brook had assumed she'd take Summer Sky's place in Thunder's heart. She already had the love of Thunder's son, so it was only natural that Thunder should love her too. The marriage must already be in desperate straits or Thunder would be sleeping beside his wife, demanding his rights, Laughing Brook reasoned. A sly smile curved her lips, thinking that half the battle for Thunder's affection was already won.

Early the next day, Grady went to town and returned with lumber and seed. Since planting could wait a few more weeks, he began building the extra room immediately. Meanwhile Storm set about winning over Little Buffalo. It didn't help any when Storm suggested that they begin calling the boy by his white name. Little Buffalo was adamantly opposed to the change, as was Laughing Brook, but Grady had the last word and henceforth Little Buffalo was to answer to the name Tim. Storm also gave the boy a haircut, and earned another slice of Tim's contempt.

Tim's animosity, Laughing Brook's jealousy, Grady's smoldering passion, and the crowded cabin made for a volatile combination. The looks Grady sent Storm were hot enough to fry eggs, while Laughing Brook literally threw herself at the handsome half-breed, blatantly offering Grady what Storm refused to give him. While the bedroom was being built, sleeping arrangements remained the same as on the first night. Each night Laughing Brook crawled into bed beside Storm while Grady shared the pallet with Tim. But one night the arrangement differed slightly.

Tim woke up from a nightmare and cried out for Laughing Brook. The Indian girl took the boy into bed with her and Storm in order to comfort him. At length he fell asleep between Storm and Laughing Brook, seemingly appeased. Storm drifted off to sleep a few minutes later. She was sleeping soundly when Laughing Brook quietly left the bed.

Grady was stung that his son preferred Laughing Brook to his own father. But what could he expect? he chided himself, when he had virtually abandoned the boy to Laughing Brook's care while he rode with renegades, seeking revenge for Summer Sky's death. Sighing regretfully, he closed his eyes, trying to forget how desperately he wanted to make love to Storm.

When he first felt the warm body snuggling against him, he merely thought Tim had crawled back into bed with him. The thought pleased him and he gathered the warm body in his arms. His hand closed over a soft breast, and before he could draw it away, a much smaller hand pressed it tightly against the swelling mound. Grady felt the nipple pucker and harden against his palm, and for a brief moment he was too mesmerized to move. Then his hand was drawn between her legs to the moistness of her woman's flesh and the breath left his chest in a soft explosion of air.

"Storm . . . Oh, God, lady, I hope I'm not dreaming."

"Do you think Storm is the only woman who can make you pant with desire?" Laughing Brook laughed into his ear. Boldly she molded her fingers around his throbbing erection. "You are magnificent, Thunder, just as I always knew you'd be. I ache for you. Let me ease your body. Let me give you comfort."

Tim's restless tossing and flailing limbs brought Storm instantly awake. He had inadvertently jabbed her in the ribs, and she awoke with a grunt of pain. She became aware that Laughing Brook had left the bed when she raised up to suggest that the Indian maiden carry Tim back to the pallet with his father. It was much too dark in the cabin to see where Laughing Brook had gone, but the agonized groan coming from the opposite side of the room told Storm exactly what Laughing Brook was up to. Obviously Laughing Brook and Grady were deep in the throes of passion.

Tears flooded her eyes and she felt a crushing weight squeezing the breath from her. She must have been naive to think Grady had brought the beautiful squaw home with him for his son's sake. He should have been truthful and told her Laughing Brook was here for his pleasure—the kind of pleasure Storm had refused him. He had warned her that he would take another woman if she refused to share his bed, and at the time it hadn't seemed to matter. How could she willingly sleep with the man responsible for Buddy's death? But that was before. Before . . .

Before he had made her need him.

Before she had grown to love him.

"Laughing Brook, what the hell are you doing in my bed?" Grady's harsh whisper hissed through his clenched teeth.

"I want you, Thunder. Little Buffalo loves me. Why did you marry *her*? She is no good for you. I can make you happy. My parents expected us to marry after my sister's death. Why did you disappoint them?"

"Get back to your bed immediately," Grady said in a low growl. "Do you want Storm to hear us?"

"I don't care." She sounded like a spoiled child denied a sweet.

"Now, Laughing Brook. I will send you back to the reservation immediately if you ever attempt anything like this again."

"You are a warrior. How can you live without a woman's comfort?"

"Go, Laughing Brook." Laughing Brook knew when she was defeated. The threat in Grady's stern voice finally made an impression on her. Reluctantly she crawled from under the covers and back into Storm's bed.

Storm knew the moment Laughing Brook returned to bed. She had no idea how long Laughing Brook had been with Grady on his pallet before she awoke and noted her absence, but it must have been long enough to—to—God, she couldn't even say it.

In the space of a week Grady had built the addition to the cabin and moved the double bed he and Storm shared into it, placing two cots, one for Tim and one for Laughing Brook, in the main room of the cabin.

He had worked at a frantic pace so he and Storm could be assured of the privacy they so desperately needed. Now all they needed to do when they wanted to be alone was close the door to their bedroom. During that week he had been puzzled, then angered by Storm's coldness. It seemed as if they hadn't a moment alone to discuss their differences. With either Tim or Laughing Brook making demands upon his time any privacy he and Storm might have found was forever being interrupted.

And the state of affairs between Storm and Tim hadn't improved any. The boy seemed to hate Storm and still looked to Laughing Brook for direction. Grady stopped just short of punishing his son for his defiance. He wanted Storm to win Tim's love through her wit and ingenuity. He believed that once Tim lost his belligerence they would form a close relationship. In the meantime he hated to send Laughing Brook away for fear of traumatizing Tim, who seemed unable to function without his surrogate mother.

Grady felt as if a great weight had been lifted from him as he put the finishing touches on the roof of the new room he had built. Tonight, he thought gleefully, he and Storm would be alone in the new bedroom, where they could talk and make love. Being in the same room with her these past days and unable to love her had been the sweetest agony he had ever suffered. So close yet so damn far. If he were on

241

the reservation he'd be the brunt of many jokes once his friends learned that a Lakota warrior couldn't control his woman.

Grady walked around to the back of the cabin, hoping to find Storm alone in the vegetable garden she had planted so he could tell her they would be moving into their new bedroom tonight. He found Storm and Tim deep in conversation. His small son was standing before Storm, hands on hips, his lower lip protruding at a stubborn angle and his black eyes defiant. He stopped short when he heard Tim say, "You're a white witch. I don't have to listen to you. Laughing Brook says you must be a witch to get Papa to marry you." Suddenly he stared up at her curiously, as if trying to make up his mind. "Are you? Are you really a witch?"

Grady waited, unwilling to interfere until he heard Storm's reply. He knew his son was being deliberately cruel, but he was also aware that Tim came by his stubbornness naturally, and the boy was angry at having been uprooted from the reservation, the only home he remembered.

"If I was a witch I'd wave my magic wand and make Laughing Brook disappear," Storm replied, more sharply than she intended. She was at her wit's end trying to make Tim accept her. "I don't want to take Laughing Brook's place in your heart, I just want us to be friends."

"Laughing Brook is my friend. Papa should have married her."

"But he didn't, Tim. Shouldn't you accept the fact that your father did what is best for him? If he wanted Laughing Brook, he would have married her. Have you forgotten that your father has more white blood in him than Indian blood?" How does one communicate with a stubborn six-year-old? Storm wondered desperately. Her heart went out to the small boy, and she would have given anything to have him love her.

Tim appeared to be mulling over Storm's words, unable to equate what Laughing Brook had told him with Storm's plea for friendship. Storm had also raised an issue Tim hadn't considered before. His own father, though he looked and acted like a fierce Lakota warrior, was more white than Indian. Deep in his heart Tim wanted to like Storm, yet the thought of losing Laughing Brook was too much for the little fellow.

Screwing his face up tightly, he bellowed, "Papa is a Lakota warrior. He doesn't like White Eyes. You *are* a witch, otherwise he wouldn't have married you."

"Tim!" Grady decided it was time to make his presence known. "You will apologize to your stepmother."

Tim's face grew mottled as he turned and flung a challenging question at Grady. "Why did you marry her, Papa?"

For the first time in his life Grady was at a loss for words. Many reasons came into his mind as he searched Storm's lovely face,

243

foremost of which was the fact that she had touched his heart in a way that no other woman had, not even Summer Sky. He and Summer Sky had been children when they had married, but now he was a man. A man who needed a strong woman with the same values and matching passion. Summer Sky would have been an obedient, loving mate had she lived, but her sweet, giving nature would have made her incapable of being the kind of woman Grady needed now. She was perfect for the naive boy of eighteen he once was. What he needed now was a woman with the strength necessary to endure both good times and bad, a woman he could . . . Love . . .

# *Chapter Twelve*

Storm hadn't realized she was holding her breath until her lungs began to ache and her heart to pound. She had no idea how Grady would answer his son's question, for she knew their marriage was merely one of convenience. She needed a home and he needed a mother for his son. The raging passion that existed between them was something Storm hadn't counted on.

Grady remained silent so long Storm felt like turning and fleeing from the hot glare of Tim's accusing dark eyes. Obviously Grady couldn't come up with a plausible explanation for their marriage, one that would satisfy his son, and it hurt. Then he said something so outrageous, so utterly untruthful that Storm wanted to scream out that he lied.

"I married Storm because I wanted to."

Storm felt singed by the heat and hunger of Grady's gaze, but she resisted looking up into his eyes, fearing the mockery she'd find in their cobalt depths. She knew he wanted her—no one could mistake that devouring look—but since Laughing Brook's arrival Grady had no need for his wife. True, she hadn't been aware of Laughing Brook sharing Grady's pallet since that time she awoke and heard them making love, but that didn't mean they hadn't found other times to be intimate.

"Why can't Laughing Brook be your second wife?" Tim wanted to know. "Flies-Like-A-Hawk has three wives."

"White law allows for only one wife," Grady explained. Though he spoke to his son his eyes never left Storm's face. "And besides, I don't want a second wife, or a third. I'm perfectly satisfied with one wife. I have learned much since I rode with renegades and left the reservation," he continued, dropping to his knees before his small son. "The time when Indians walked the earth as free men, proud of their heritage and secure in their future, is long past."

"But I am an Indian, Papa, and so was Mama. How can I forget what I am?"

"You must never forget your proud heritage, son," Grady said passionately. "We both come from noble stock, and our dark skins will never allow us to forget who or what we are. Nor should we. But I want a better life for you than the reservation offers. My father, your grandfather, served the President of the United States and fought for the freedom of all people regardless of race and color. Don't ever forget that. I feel strongly that our future, yours and mine, lies here in Oklahoma, on our own land."

"But you always hated the White Eyes, Papa," Tim said, puzzled by Grady's turnabout.

"I've since learned there are good White Eyes and bad White Eyes, just as there are good Indians and bad Indians." He rose to his feet. Suddenly he reached out, took Storm's chin between thumb and forefinger, and lifted her face so she was forced to look into his eyes. "Storm is a good White Eyes. She has never done anything to hurt the People. She is not meek, gentle, or obedient like your mother was, but I have learned that the qualities Storm possesses are more desirable in the world we live in." His eyes sparkled with mirth and one corner of his mouth tilted upward in the parody of a smile. "Though there are times Storm sorely tries my temper, she is my wife for better or for worse and will remain my wife. Once you realize that, Tim, you'll be able to accept Storm and we'll all be happier for it."

Storm was truly stunned by Grady's words. When he released her chin the tips of his fingers caressed the hollow at the base of her throat in a gesture so intimate her flesh tingled long after he removed his hand. She wanted to believe Grady had married her because it was what he truly desired, but she found it difficult to swallow. Before they were wed he had admitted that there was no room in his heart for love, that having loved once he had no intention of doing so again. Obviously no woman alive could take the place of his dead wife. But that had been perfectly agreeable with her, for she had loved Buddy and wanted no other man replacing him in her heart.

But that was before . . . Before she learned about passion and being loved in ways she never dreamed possible and experiencing the kind of bliss she never attained with Buddy. If it was possible to love twice, Storm reasoned, then Grady was truly her soulmate in ways she had never imagined with Buddy. But it was difficult giving your heart to a man whose loving inspired guilt and shame, Storm thought contritely.

Storm wasn't the only one dazed by Grady's words. For the first time since leaving the reservation, Tim realized that Storm would always be a part of his life. And that he could never look backward to the life he had once known with Laughing Brook. His father had chosen to live in the white world and he must conform to those rules if he was to attain a modicum of happiness.

"Do I have to call her mama?" Tim asked sullenly.

Grady seemed at a loss for words, but Storm quickly jumped into the void. "Not if you don't want to. Just call me Storm until we feel more comfortable with one another."

Tim thought about that for awhile, then nodded slowly. "If it's all right with Papa, then I shall call you Storm."

"I think it's a fine idea, son," Grady said solemnly. "And if you'd like, later you can help me build a chicken coop. Having chicken and fresh eggs whenever we want will be a treat."

Satisfied, Tim ran off, leaving Storm and Grady staring after him. When Grady turned to face her the tension loomed between them like a heavy mist. She waited for him to speak, but he seemed as reluctant as she to break the silence. It was as if this moment had been building from the moment Grady had returned home; he was like a volcano on the verge of erupting. Grady touched her cheek, and the breath seemed to solidify in her throat.

"Storm . . ."

"Thunder, where is Little Buffalo? I can't find him."

Once again Laughing Brook had intruded upon a private moment. It seemed to Storm as if the Indian maiden deliberately spied on them and knew exactly when to interrupt. Never had she felt so close to Grady or so ready to admit that she had forgiven him for Buddy's death. For the first time since their hasty wedding, Storm truly felt they could make something of this marriage.

Muttering an oath, Grady swung around to glare at Laughing Brook. He sincerely hoped Tim would learn to cope without her soon so he could return her to the reservation. It was time she chose a husband from among the warriors vying for her hand.

"Tim can't be far, Laughing Brook," Grady said tightly. "Perhaps he went down to the river."

"Then I shall help Storm dig in the garden," she offered sweetly, knowing full well that she had interrupted a special moment between husband and wife.

Storm smiled ruefully. "Since you have offered, I welcome your help." She handed Laughing Brook the shovel.

Seething with frustration, Grady turned and stomped off. But the look he gave Storm before he departed was more potent than a glass of fine brandy.

After supper that night Laughing Brook managed to corner Grady alone when he went to the river to fetch water for Storm's bath. She had sneaked out of the cabin while Storm was busy putting things in place in the new bedroom. Tim had wandered into the bedroom after Storm, leaving Laughing Brook free to pursue Grady. She found him standing knee deep in the river, bathing. His bronze skin shimmered with iridescent drops of water, and his hair was dripping. His back was to her and despite the coolness of the March night he was splashing icy water over his entire body.

Laughing Brook stared greedily at the taut mounds of his bare buttocks, reluctantly moving her eyes upward to the thickly bunched muscles of his arms and torso, flexing involuntarily from the shock of icy water against his heated flesh. She licked her lips, feeling her need for Grady in every crevice and curve of her body. Then, in one fluid motion, she removed her dress and kicked off her moccasins. She stepped into the water, shivering violently but warmed by the vision of Grady's hard body pressed intimately against her own lush curves.

She had nearly reached him when Grady heard her. He whirled, stunned by the sight of Laughing Brook, naked, her supple skin gilded a tawny gold by the moonlight. He stood motionless, staring at her as if mesmerized, until she was close enough for the heat of her body to reach out and scorch him.

"Isn't it a little cold for you to be bathing in the river?" he asked, striving to keep his voice level. It was difficult with the full ripeness of her breasts so close to his chest.

"It's not too cold for you."

"I'm a man."

"I know. Not just a man but a mighty warrior." She looked pointedly downward. "Your loins are full and heavy. I would ease you if you'd allow it. I know your wife hasn't been a true wife to you. I would comfort you in your need." She moved closer, until the diamond-hard tips of her breasts stabbed against his chest.

"You shouldn't be here. If I'd known you wanted to bathe, I would have given you privacy," Grady said in a strangled voice.

Laughing Brook's answer was to wind her arms around Grady's neck and rub her body against his. "You know what I want, Thunder."

Grady started violently when she pressed her mouth to his. He felt the flick of her hot tongue against his lips and tried to step backward, but Laughing Brook refused to be dislodged. They stood suspended in the knee-deep water for the space of a heartbeat before the sand beneath his feet suddenly gave way and Grady lost his balance. He fell into the water, taking Laughing Brook with him. The shock of the cold water relaxed her grip on him as she came up sputtering. Grady seized the opportunity. He turned abruptly and waded back to shore, leaving Laughing Brook sitting in the cold water, sputtering in indignation.

Storm was tucking Tim into bed when Grady entered the cabin. Drops of water beaded his hair, and his shirt clung wetly to his back and shoulders. He carried a bucket of water in each hand, and she assumed he had bathed in the river when he went to fetch water. Bathing in the cold river was a habit she couldn't accustom herself to, though Grady did it nearly every day except for the coldest days of winter. He set the buckets on the stove to heat before speaking.

"The water will be hot shortly. I know how you appreciate a hot bath. Take your time; I'll see to the animals."

"Thank you," Storm said, declining to look at

him. She knew they would be alone tonight for the first time in months, and she wasn't certain what she would do or how she would act. But from all indications, Grady knew exactly what he wanted.

Laughing Brook entered the cabin a few minutes later, looking enormously pleased with herself. Storm frowned when she noted that the Indian girl looked sensuously bedraggled. Her hair was dripping wet and her buckskin dress damp. Had she been with Grady at the river? Had they bathed together? Had they . . . Storm's lips turned down into a frown when she envisioned Grady and Laughing Brook making love in the water. The pain of it nearly doubled her over.

Laughing Brook's bubbling laughter floated to her from across the room. "Thunder was magnificent tonight. Have you ever made love in the water? No," she said, forestalling Storm's answer, "I doubt that you have. Thunder says you are a cold woman. Did you know he is thinking of making me his second wife?"

Her face flaming, Storm withheld comment. What could she say? With studied indifference she tested the water in one bucket, found it comfortably warm, and carried it into the bedroom she would be sharing with Grady. She had to admit that being able to close the door on Laughing Brook gave her enormous pleasure. Too bad she couldn't do the same with Grady and banish him from their bedroom.

Earlier, Grady had placed the large brass tub

Storm had purchased in town in the center of the room. All Storm had to do was fill it with the buckets of warm water. Undressing quickly, she eased into the tub and let the heady warmth envelop her. Aware that Grady would return at any moment, she picked up the soap and began to wash. She gave a squeak of dismay when Grady entered the room a few minutes later and quietly shut the door behind him.

His breath caught in his throat when he saw her, and he leaned against the door, looking his fill. Storm felt the effect of his potent stare in the way her body warmed and tingled wherever his gaze touched.

"I've waited forever for this night." His voice had a certain gravel roughness that Storm recognized immediately. Her knees jerked upright to her chest and she hugged them tightly, exposing as little of herself as possible. Grady grinned in wry amusement. "If that's meant to discourage me, it's not working, lady."

"I—I'm not through bathing yet."

"I'd hoped you wouldn't be. Let me scrub your back."

She offered a feeble protest when he took the washcloth from her hand and moved behind her. When she felt the cloth touch her back and the gentle motion of his hand against her sensitive skin, a shudder raced down her spine. The musky, masculine scent of him filled her nostrils and she gave a breathless murmur of pleasure. When Grady bent to touch his lips to her bare shoulder, she nearly jumped out of her skin. Suddenly the washcloth hit the water and Grady leaped to his feet, a growl of impatience rumbling from his throat.

"Bath time is over, lady," he said harshly. His chest was heaving, as if each breath was raw agony, and his face was stark with raw need.

When Storm failed to move he scooped her out of the water and carried her dripping to the bed. "Grady!"

"Tonight I'm going to love you the way I've wanted to, the way I've dreamed of since the day I arrived home."

When she tried to jump from the bed, he pinned her down with his body. "You're not going anywhere, lady."

"Isn't one woman a night enough for you?" Storm hissed from between clenched teeth.

"What in the hell are you talking about?"

"Weren't you at the river with Laughing Brook tonight?"

Grady went still. "How did you know that?"

Storm snorted derisively. "It wasn't difficult to guess what went on when you both came in dripping wet."

"I admit Laughing Brook found me at the river tonight, but nothing happened."

"Ha! You expect me to believe that? I know she's served as your mistress since you brought her here, and probably before that. You warned me you'd find another woman to take my place in your bed and you did. All you wanted me for was to raise your son. What I don't understand is why you didn't let Laughing Brook raise Tim.

Things were fine before I came into the picture. Tim will always resent me and love Laughing Brook."

Grady's expression hardened as he raised himself on his elbows and stared down at Storm. "Is that what you think? That Laughing Brook is my mistress? I told you my reasons for bringing her home with me. Didn't you believe me?"

"How could I believe you when I saw and heard Laughing Brook in your bed?" Storm said with brutal honesty. "She told me herself that you—you made love to her tonight. Do you think I'm a fool? Laughing Brook is smitten with you and obviously you like what she gives you. Wouldn't it be better if I left the three of you alone?"

"Lakota warriors do not lie," Grady said gravely. "If I say Laughing Brook is not my mistress, it is the truth. If I tell you I have *never* bedded her, you must accept my word."

Storm stared at him. His expression was harsh in the flickering lamplight. Though his blue eyes blazed hotly, she saw nothing in their azure depths to indicate he was lying or attempting to deceive her.

"But I know for a fact Laughing Brook was in your pallet that night Tim had a bad dream and awoke crying for her."

"In my pallet, perhaps, but that was all. I sent her back to bed the moment I realized who it was. For one crazy moment, I thought you had crawled into bed with me," he said ruefully.

"Lord, I wanted it to be you, but the moment I realized it was Laughing Brook I ordered her back to bed."

"And tonight, at the river? Laughing Brook told me . . ."

"She lied. She told you what she had hoped would happen but didn't. I may be many things, Storm, but I am not a liar."

Storm's heart soared and fragile hope took root in that sacred place where love dwells. "You've not had a woman since—since the day you left our homestead? Why, that seems incredible!"

Grady looked affronted. "I have practiced restraint many times in the past. A Lakota warrior must learn to control his passions before he goes into battle against the enemy. It was no great hardship for me."

"But your note said you left me because you *couldn't* control yourself around me. I don't understand. Why am I different from any other woman?"

"Oh, lady, if I knew the answer to that I'd know the secrets only Grandfather knows. My pride, my honor, they mean nothing to me when I am with you. I would gladly forsake them for one sweet kiss from your lips. I want you as I've never wanted another woman."

"What about Summer Sky?" Storm asked breathlessly.

"We were childhood friends and marriage to her was a confirmation of the love and respect we felt for one another. When we married we were still children who needed to grow both emotionally and physically. Unfortunately, Summer Sky didn't live to realize her full potential. You are her complete opposite in nature."

"Tell me about Summer Sky. How did she die?"

"No, not now. I need you too much. The time for talking will come later. Much later. For the first time in months I have my wife in bed with me, lying naked in my arms."

He was still resting atop her and he suddenly realized that the dampness from her wet skin was seeping through his clothing. "You're wet, sweet, let me dry you."

Before Storm realized exactly how he intended to dry her, he lowered his head and began licking the beads of moisture from her breasts. The pad of his thumb caressed her nipple, and Storm felt her breast swell and harden in response to his touch. Threads of fire spiraled outward, bringing a gasp from her lips. Then he took each nipple in turn in his mouth and gently laved the hardening buds with his tongue. After what seemed like an eon to Storm, his lips shifted lower, lapping the moisture from her belly and sipping from her navel. Her body trembled as his mouth drifted across her skin, his tongue flicking and soothing by turn, until his lips shifted lower and the tiny bud of her pleasure was captured by the hot sucking of his mouth.

"Grady!" Storm expelled his name on a

breathless murmur of pleasure.

Abruptly Grady raised his head, his lopsided grin sending her heart spinning. "You're right, sweetheart, it's too soon." Then he rose to his feet and began removing his clothes. Storm stared in mute admiration when he stood in all his naked glory before her. She doubted there was a man dead or alive to compare with him. Wide of shoulder, broad of chest, narrow of waist, legs like twin oaks, skin the color of tawny bronze. Taut-fleshed, thickly muscled, supple, every splendid inch of him exuding raw power and masculinity. Just looking at him gave her goosebumps.

This time Storm needed no urging to reach out and touch him, for her hands moved with a will of her own. He groaned in sweet agony when the fingers of both hands closed around his powerful erection, stroking in the way he had taught her.

"Oh, lady, you do know how to drive a man crazy."

"Just the way you do me," Storm whispered in a voice made raspy with need.

"Are you ready for another lesson?"

"You mean there is more to learn than you've already taught me?" Storm asked with wonder. The thought boggled her mind.

"You have no idea." Then he grasped her wrists and pulled her from the bed, leaving a damp spot where she had lain.

Storm waited with baited breath to see what Grady would do next. She was somewhat startled when he sat down on the bed and lifted her over his lap until she straddled him and her knees rested on either side of him. "Are you comfortable, sweet?" Unable to speak, Storm merely nodded. "Kiss me."

She did, covering his mouth just as his lips opened and he thrust his tongue into her mouth. His tongue tasted her deeply, joined hers, battled hers, demanding that she yield to him all that he required. Just when Storm despaired of ever breathing again, Grady allowed her a brief respite. But her breathlessness returned when he took her swollen nipples into his mouth, laving them with the rough, wet edge of his tongue. First one, then the other. A startled cry left Storm's throat when she felt Grady's hands slip between her spread thighs. He heard her soft intake of breath as he began stroking her. When his finger slid inside her she nearly jumped off his lap. Then all thought skidded to a halt as her mind expelled everything but what Grady was doing to her and how he made her feel.

She wanted to touch him everywhere, kiss him everywhere as his sweet torment drove her high and higher. Her kisses fell wherever they could touch, his face, his neck, his shoulders, while her hands slid over the firm flesh of his back and buttocks, glorying in his virile, masculine strength and magnificent control.

"Oh, lady, hurry, I can't wait much longer. I want to be inside you so bad I ache." His teeth were tightly clenched, his eyes closed, his face stark with anguish.

His words came to her as if from a great distance. But she understood enough of them to know that Grady needed her as much as she needed him, that he was deliberately withholding himself in order to bring her pleasure. Lifting herself slightly, she shoved aside his hands and slowly impaled herself on his rock-hard erection. He groaned so loudly Storm was certain Laughing Brook could hear him in the next room.

Gritting his teeth, Grady let her set the pace, watching her passion-glazed face as she grasped his shoulders for leverage and moved slowly up and down his hardened length. Trying to concentrate on anything but the profound need to explode inside Storm's receptive body, Grady took a nipple into his mouth and began suckling. Then, suddenly, he could wait no longer. The time for delay was long past; his body demanded satisfaction. Grasping Storm's hips, he worked her up and down furiously, his breath harsh as it exploded from his lungs.

"Oh, Grady!"

"Now, Storm, now!"

He could feel it coming from his toes and working upward, traveling through his entire body in wave after wave of incredible sensation. The moment Storm felt the hot stream of fluid spurt against the walls of her womb her own tremors began, so violent she screamed out once, twice, then collapsed in a boneless heap on Grady's lap. After several minutes Grady eased her down on the bed, lying beside her and pulling the coverlet over them. It was a full five minutes before either of them could speak.

"Allow me a few minutes and I'll teach you another way in which to love," Grady whispered into her ear. He chuckled when her honey brown eyes grew round and her mouth flew open.

"How can you? *Again*, I mean. Buddy never . . ." Her face flushed and she looked away, suddenly recalling one of the reasons she had resisted making love with Grady. Buddy had never made her feel the way Grady did.

"Storm, look at me." His commanding tone brought her head swiveling around. "I'm not Buddy. Buddy is dead, just as Summer Sky is dead. But we're alive and life goes on."

"I loved Buddy."

"And I loved Summer Sky. But she was the love of my youth. I realize that now and I will treasure that love always, just as I will treasure the son she gave me."

"And I will treasure Buddy's love," Storm said slowly. It suddenly dawned on her that she and Grady were much alike. That they had both loved and lost mates dear to them. And Grady had been right about their mates being the loves of their youths. She had never felt the wild, abiding passion for Buddy that she did for Grady or experienced pleasure such as Grady gave her. But a voice inside her whispered that she'd be foolish to believe Grady's words meant he loved her.

"I—I don't want to take Summer Sky's place," Storm said hesitantly.

"No one can ever take Summer Sky's place," Grady said fiercely. "She was the mother of my son." His words were like a knife thrust to her heart and as close to a denial of love as any Storm had ever heard.

"I hope this passion we share will be enough to build a marriage," she said wistfully.

Grady looked at her sharply. In her own way, was Storm trying to tell him she could never love him? he wondered bleakly. It didn't matter, he tried to tell himself. She would make a wonderful mother for his son, and obviously she cared for him a little or she wouldn't respond with such passion to his loving. Better to accept what Storm freely offered, he reasoned, than to long for what could never be.

"If passion is all we will ever have, then I will settle for that," Grady finally said, "as long as you are content."

Content? Storm thought bitterly. Hardly that. Why couldn't Grady love her as deeply as he had loved Summer Sky? It would be so easy to love Grady if only he wanted her love, she reflected sadly. Though he gave every appearance of accepting the white man's life, she knew that deep in his heart he still harbored bitterness and resentment for the white race. Until he learned that violence begat violence and that a heart filled with hate soon withered and died, there was little hope of their finding love.

"For the time being I am content," Storm said. "But the first time you go courting violence or allow another woman to come between us, I will leave you and Tim."

"I am done with violence. Avenging Summer Sky's death has turned me from my family and friends. I pray someday they will forgive me for the abrupt way in which I left six years ago."

"Have you ever thought of returning for a visit?"

Grady remained silent so long Storm thought he hadn't heard the question. She started to repeat it, but his soft words forestalled her. "Many times, but I am afraid."

"Afraid," Storm scoffed. "I didn't think you were afraid of anything."

"Sometimes the bitterness in my heart frightens me." His strangled words sounded as if they were torn from his soul, but Storm heard them and was stunned by the anguish he was suffering. It was also the first time he had truly opened up to her about his past.

"Perhaps if you told me about Summer Sky's death it might help," Storm suggested hopefully.

Silence.

"Grady? I truly want to help you."

Silence.

"I'm sorry, I didn't mean to pry."

"No, I will tell you. It happened six years ago . . ."

# *Chapter Thirteen*

Storm turned in Grady's arms until she could see the harsh outline of his face in the lamp's dull glow. The flickering light danced provocatively on his stark features, revealing all the misery and anguish he was suffering.

"I take it Summer Sky's death was unexpected."

Grady snorted bitterly. "Not only was it unexpected but an act of depraved cruelty by despicable men."

Storm held her breath, waiting for him to continue without being prodded. She truly believed that by opening up to her some of the hurt and bitterness he harbored in his heart would heal.

Grady's mind traveled backward in time, reliving again that terrifying day when his whole world fell apart. He had been barely twenty-two years old and Summer Sky a few months younger. Tim wasn't quite a year old, and Summer Sky was already swelling with his second child.

When he spoke again his voice was devoid of all emotion.

"I was with Father the day it happened, helping round up horses for the army, and Mother was visiting a sick neighbor. Summer Sky took the wagon to town to purchase material for baby clothes. She left Tim at home with Sweet Grass, Summer Sky's mother. Summer Sky's parents lived on the ranch, where Jumping Buffalo worked for Father. That's why Summer Sky and I were raised together. Laughing Brook was three years younger than we were. A boy, born later, died at birth; only the girls survived."

He paused, dragging in a ragged breath that seemed to sear his lungs. Storm didn't know if he would continue, but he cleared his throat and proceeded in a toneless voice, as if reciting something that had been indelibly etched upon his brain.

"Somewhere between the ranch and town, Summer Sky was attacked by three desperadoes. We learned what happened from Summer Sky before she died. She said that three thugs stopped the wagon and began tormenting her, calling her 'Indian squaw' and 'white man's whore.' They noticed her pregnancy and taunted her about carrying a white man's bastard.

"Oh, Grady, how terrible," Storm said, genuinely appalled.

"Summer Sky was the gentlest, most giving creature alive," Grady replied bitterly. "She wouldn't have hurt a living soul. Her entire life was devoted to making me happy and raising our children in a peaceful atmosphere."

"What happened then?" Storm prodded.

"One of the men lunged for her, pulling her down from the wagon. He held her while his friends began tearing off her clothes. She feared they would rape her and harm her unborn child. She reacted violently, fighting desperately for her life, but the men easily subdued her. They bore her to the ground and she screamed. Her screams must have frightened the horse hitched to the wagon, for she said it reared and began stomping the ground in a wild frenzy.

"The three men leaped out of the way, but Summer Sky did not react swiftly enough. She tried to protect her child, but the badly frightened animal stomped her viciously, injuring her gravely. The men fled when they saw how badly Summer Sky had been hurt. They might have saved her had they sought help for her immediately. Instead, they rode away and left her to abort her child in the dirt. Father and I found her hours later when we returned from the pasture. She lived long enough to tell me what happened before dying in my arms."

Storm was horrified. No wonder Grady was so bitter. "What happened to the men who caused Summer Sky's death?" Storm asked softly. "Did they go to jail for their vicious act?"

Suddenly Grady seemed to come out of his lethargy. His expression grew fierce, his voice heated as he spat out his answer. "They could never be found. Since Summer Sky was merely an Indian, little effort was made to bring them to justice. From that day on I despised that part of me that was white. I hated the men responsible for the death of an innocent woman and I blamed the law for failing to find Summer Sky's killers."

Storm's eyes grew misty, feeling compassion for the confused youth who had lost his wife and abandoned his family because of man's inhumanity to his fellow man. The men responsible for Summer Sky's death were cruel, vicious animals.

"So you left your parent's ranch," she whispered.

"They begged me not to go, pleaded with me to leave Tim in their care," Grady recalled, "but my hate even extended to them. If Father hadn't needed my help that day and if Mother hadn't allowed Summer Sky to go into town alone, my wife might still be alive today. I'm afraid I said things I didn't really mean before I left. My God, I'm appalled at how deeply I've hurt them," he agonized.

"I'm sure they've forgiven you."

"Perhaps they have forgiven me my hasty words, but they will never be able to forget what I became after I left the ranch. After Summer Sky's death, her parents and sister no longer felt safe at Peaceful Valley, and I escorted them to the reservation in the Black Hills. I felt such a kinship with the People that I became one of them. I learned all there was to know about their ways, forgetting all the values I was taught by my mother and father. Eventually I became a fierce warrior, bent on destroying the White Eyes responsible for the death of my wife. As a final act of defiance, I rode with renegades who raided and stole food and guns. I even fought against the army in which my own father served.

"I'm sure it must have hurt my father deeply when he learned what I was doing. He's devoted his life to fighting discrimination, and so has Mother. It never occurred to me that what I was doing was as much an act of prejudice as what those drifters did to Summer Sky."

"I think you're too hard on yourself, Grady."

"No harder than I deserve. It wasn't until I realized my son was more important to me than vengeance that I tried to escape the violence that followed me wherever I went."

"Is that why you left the reservation?"

"I left because Wakantanka came to me in a vision and told me it was time to go," Grady explained. "Even then I refused to give up my violent ways and drifted for six months, searching for a place where I felt as if I belonged. I lived by the gun. I accepted all challenges and made a name for myself as a gunslinger. As you have good reason to know, men came looking for me, hoping to make a name for themselves by outshooting the Renegade, the name given to me by those who knew of my past."

"Do you know the men who caused Summer Sky's death?"

"I have never seen them, but Summer Sky gave me their descriptions before she died, and the sheriff found their names on wanted posters. I will never forget them."

"What if you run across them one day? Will you take the law into your own hands? You have a son to think about, Grady, and a wife."

For the first time since Buddy's death Storm saw things clearly. She was wrong to hold Grady responsible for Buddy's death. Poor Buddy just happened to be in the wrong place at the wrong time. The truth of the matter was that Grady had been challenged, and if he hadn't reacted swiftly he would have been cut down in the street. The bullet that killed Buddy did not come from Grady's gun. Living with vengeance had changed Grady from a happy youth to a hardened renegade called Thunder and made him a bitter and remorseless man. The same thing could happen to her if she didn't forgive Grady for his part in Buddy's death.

"I truthfully don't know what I would do if that happened," Grady said slowly.

"I forgive you, Grady."

"What?"

"I shouldn't have held you responsible for Buddy's death. It was an accident—a tragic one, but an accident nevertheless."

"What about the other?" Grady asked solemnly.

"Other? What do you mean?"

"What about the guilt you feel when I make love to you? Do you still regret that it is me bringing you pleasure instead of your dead husband? Do you still feel shame that I can make you feel things that Buddy never did?"

Storm flushed, embarrassed that he read her mind so effortlessly. "I can't help it. I knew Buddy all my life, just as you knew Summer Sky. It frightens me that you have touched my life so profoundly in such a short time. What kind of woman am I?"

"A passionate woman, Storm Stryker, who never knew the joy of sexual fulfillment until I gave it to you. It pleases me more than you'll ever know to think that you gave me much more than your virginity, which rightfully belonged to Buddy. I'd much rather have your fire, your passion, your soul."

Storm went still. "You said you didn't want my soul," she said quietly. "You didn't even want my love."

"Do I have it?"

"Do I have yours?"

How like Storm to answer a question with a question, Grady thought, suppressing a grin.

"You have the only emotion I am capable of at the moment."

"What is that?"

"I care for you. I wouldn't have married you if I didn't. My body wants you, more than it's ever wanted another woman. You have my passion, my care, my consideration. As for love, let's take one step at a time. Now it's your turn."

"I could love you so easily, Grady," Storm confessed, "but I'm afraid."

"What do you fear?"

"I fear the hatred that still exists in your heart, the violence that comes searching for you, and the lust for vengeance that fills your life. I fear losing you as I lost Buddy—and I fear surrendering my soul and receiving nothing in return."

"Don't ever fear me," Grady said, raining gentle kisses on her lips. "I won't ever hurt you. Loving you with my body cleanses my soul of all its hatred. You're good for me, Storm. I need you. Tim needs you."

"Oh, Grady, I want to believe you."

"If you can't believe me, then believe in the way I make you feel and trust your emotions. I'm going to love you again, sweet, and when your body is burning and you're panting with rapture, remember that few couples ever experience anything so profound. Then tell me whether or not you believe what I have just told you."

His kisses fell like gentle summer rain on her face and throat, and she felt his hand slide over her abdomen, her skin shivering beneath his touch. When his fingers moved lower, seeking the center of her desire, Storm opened her legs and allowed him free access.

"Oh, God, this is what I want," Grady gasped as his hands sought the moistness between her legs. Storm felt helpless, but instead of being shamed by it, a blossoming excitement built within her and her body grew taut as a stretched canvas. His lips silenced her soft cries and his tongue danced against hers in desperate need. Then suddenly he was on her, in her, thrusting, retreating, thrusting again.

The force of Grady's fervor rocked her to her very core, and Storm gasped as she was flung over the edge of pleasure's peak. Her body shuddered as she watched Grady strive toward his own climax. In the throes of passion he looked more fierce and threatening than the renegade savage she had originally thought him to be. Yet she knew him to be more vulnerable at this moment than at any other time in his life. Suddenly he threw back his head and roared. His seed spilled against her womb as he held her fiercely, possessively. Unwilling to be privy to so intimate a moment, Storm closed her eyes.

"Open your eyes, sweetheart," he whispered, stroking the silky strands of her blonde hair.

She did as she was told and found her eyes straying to the curving sweep of his lips. Flushing, she recalled what those lips could do to her, how they could drive her wild with need. Her next thought was that his lips were the only soft part of him.

"Are you ready to answer my question now, lady?" His voice held a note she'd never heard before.

Storm thought a long time before recalling what he had asked. "I believe your body wants me, and I believe you *want* to live without violence and the need for vengeance, but I don't believe you are ready yet to forget the past and look only to the future. Your old life is too deeply ingrained in you. But I'm willing to give you the benefit of the doubt and trust that our life together will be serene."

"Serene? Ha!" Grady laughed. "You don't have a serene bone in your body. I suspect we'll disagree often, and you'll win more times than you'll lose. With you I won't know one day to the next what to expect, until we go to bed. Then I will make you purr like a contented kitten."

"Grady Stryker!" She punched him playfully.

"Go to sleep, sweet, before I exhaust you so thoroughly you'll not be able to rise from bed tomorrow."

"Grady."

"Ummmm." His eyes were closed, his breathing even. Storm could tell he was on the edge of sleep.

"About Laughing Brook. Isn't it time she returned to the reservation?"

Silence.

"Dammit, Grady, answer me, I don't think . . ."

His soft rumbling snore told her he hadn't heard a word she'd said. So much for demanding answers from a strong-willed man like Grady Stryker.

274

\*   \*   \*

During the weeks that followed Storm found a happiness she had despaired of ever finding again after Buddy's death. Even Laughing Brook ceased to annoy her, and to her joy Tim began to accept her into his life. The child no longer ran to Laughing Brook for comfort or advice, and little by little his resentment of Storm began to wane. Storm knew that the time had arrived to send Laughing Brook back to the reservation, and Grady concurred wholeheartedly.

Grady had already tilled a large section of their land and planted wheat, a backbreaking job, but an immensely rewarding one. One day Storm received word that the cattle she'd ordered had arrived and were in the holding pen in Guthrie. She and Grady rode to town, and she spent nearly all the money left in her bank account to pay for the cattle. When Grady tried to pay for the animals with his money, Storm adamantly refused. Since it was something she had planned before they married, she felt she should be the one to pay. Grady didn't feel right about it, but decided to let her have her way. The cattle were driven home and turned loose on Storm's 160 acres.

While in town Grady arranged to have a well drilled on his land and water piped into the house so it could be pumped from the sink. Once it was completed Storm was thrilled that she no longer had to draw water from the river. When Storm asked if Grady could afford it, he

275

merely laughed, telling her they weren't as dirt poor as she suspected.

But the best part of those weeks were the nights. Lying in Grady's arms was pure heaven—and sometimes the most tormenting hell. No matter how hard Storm tried, she couldn't shut out the lingering guilt over the wanton way in which she responded to Grady's love-making. But she was astute enough not to let it interfere with her budding relationship with her husband and assumed that in time those feelings would disappear altogether.

When Laughing Brook was told to prepare for her return trip to the reservation she begged to be allowed to remain, and even enlisted Tim to plead in her behalf. But Grady was adamant. He had promised Jumping Buffalo, Laughing Brook's father, that he would return his daughter when Tim no longer needed her, and he sensed that the time had arrived when Tim could dispense with Laughing Brook's company. Grady felt he had indulged his son long enough. Tim was old enough to realize that he must grow up. Storm was ecstatic when Grady told her Laughing Brook would be leaving in a few days. Then something happened that shattered Storm's newfound happiness.

One day Storm accompanied Grady to Guthrie to buy supplies. While driving through town she saw someone she had hoped never to see again. Nat Turner had returned to Guthrie. He was standing in front of the bank, talking to a man neither she nor Grady had ever seen before.

"Grady, look!" Storm said as they passed the bank. "Isn't that Nat Turner?"

"What the hell!" Grady spat disgustedly. "I thought I told him never to show his face in Guthrie again."

"Do you know the man he's talking to?"

The man in question was big; big and ugly and nearly as broad as he was tall. His barrel chest and thick arms gave mute testimony to his massive strength. He wore his guns in the style of gunfighters, shoved into a leather holster riding low on his hips and tied down at his thigh. Suddenly Turner spotted them and said something to the man beside him. Then they both turned and stared pointedly at Grady and Storm. The gunman's beady eyes narrowed until they were mere slits in his florid face. His considering gaze rested on Storm for a brief moment before continuing on to Grady, where they stopped abruptly and remained.

An unexpected shudder traveled down Storm's spine. "Why is that man staring at you?"

Grady gave a careless shrug. He knew exactly what the man wanted, but deliberately kept that information from Storm. He'd seen that look too many times in the past not to recognize it. The man represented the kind of violence Grady had once relished but had been hoping to avoid since his marriage to Storm. They all had the same look about them; the cocky attitude, the guarded expression. Grady knew what to expect but tried to deny it. He had promised Storm he wouldn't seek violence and he intended to keep his promise.

Grady's body tensed, his eyes narrowed and watchful. Years of training and experience had taught him to trust no one, especially those men who came looking for a fight. He had hoped that in the months he'd settled in Oklahoma his reputation for mayhem would have slowly died. But unless he was mistaken, he was about to receive another challenge. This time the challenger wouldn't find him so eager to defend his reputation. That reputation just wasn't worth losing Storm.

The wagon turned the corner and Grady reined in before the seed store. The general store, where Storm intended to shop, was across the street.

"What do you suppose Nat Turner is doing back in town?" Storm asked worriedly as Grady swung her to the ground.

"It doesn't matter," Grady said. "He can do nothing to hurt you. He knows I'll kill him if he so much as touches you."

"Did you recognize the man he was talking to?"

"I never saw him before," Grady said guardedly. But he had seen men just like him in every town along the western frontier.

"He looked at you as if he knew you."

Grady shrugged. "Forget him, sweet. There are countless men like him in the territory.

They'll never amount to anything. They drift from place to place making a living by whatever dishonest means they can."

"I don't like the idea of him being with Turner."

"Don't worry, Storm, I promise those men won't harm you. It's getting late. I suggest you get your shopping done."

"It's not me I'm worried about," Storm muttered as she crossed the street to the general store.

When Storm returned to the wagon a short time later Grady hadn't returned yet from the seed store, but Nat Turner and his cold-eyed friend were leaning against the wagon waiting for them.

"Well, Mrs. Stryker, how nice to see you again," Turner said, tipping his hat cordially.

"The feeling is not mutual," Storm said. She swished her skirt haughtily as she deliberately avoided both men.

"That's no way to act," Turner said, affronted. "We were good friends once."

"That was before you tried to steal my homestead."

"That's your opinion." Turner grunted as all pretense of cordiality disappeared. "My friend and I were just discussing your husband."

"If you have questions, ask me, not my wife." Grady's voice was deep and menacing, giving the gunman enough reason to whirl and reach for his gun. "I wouldn't if I were you." Grady had left the store only moments before and his temper nearly exploded when he saw Turner and the gunman talking to Storm.

The gunman's hand dropped to his side and Turner held open his coat, showing that he wasn't armed. "Now, what was it you wanted to know?" Grady asked with icy disdain.

"My friend here wants to meet you," Turner said, gesturing toward the gunman. "You both have a lot in common." Grady's glacial glance flicked contemptuously over the gunman. "His name is Bull. Just Bull," Turner repeated when Grady stiffened suddenly and turned the potent fury of his blue eyes back to the gunman.

"Bull," Grady repeated tersely. "Ever been to Cheyenne, Bull?"

"Maybe," Bull said testily. "What's it to ya?"

"Just curious. If that's all you wanted, I'll bid you good-bye. It's time I was getting home."

"Not so fast, Renegade," Bull said, placing a hamlike hand on Grady's arm. "I know who you are. My friend Turner's been tellin' me about you, about how fast you are with a gun, and how you and your band of renegades attacked wagon trains and killed innocent women and children and all."

Grady went still, every nerve in his body demanding that he respond violently to Bull's words. A nudge from Storm calmed him down. "You're mistaken. I've never attacked wagon trains carrying women and children. You're confusing me with someone else. I'm a respectable farmer."

"I ain't confusin' you with no one," Bull said slyly. "Every man in the territory has heard stories about the renegade Injun and how fast he was with a gun. When Turner here told me he knew ya personally, I persuaded him to come to Guthrie with me so he could introduce us."

Grady stared at Bull through shuttered lids. He tried to ignore the voices in his head, but he knew who Bull was. Summer Sky had described him accurately before she died in his arms, and the descriptions of him and his friends were etched upon his brain forever. He glanced at Storm, wondering how she would react if he followed his intuition. For years he had been searching for the three men responsible for Summer Sky's death and now one of them stood before him, bigger than life and twice as ugly.

"Say what you've come to say," Grady ground out.

"I'm saying that ya ain't as good with a gun as people say ya are. I'm willin' to put my life on the line and tell ya I'm better."

Storm stifled a gasp and tugged at Grady's arm, urging him away from the violence she knew was inevitable. He shrugged her aside, for a moment forgetting she even existed. His thinking process shut down the moment he realized Bull was one of the men responsible for Summer Sky's death. "Are you challenging me to a gun duel?"

Bull grinned evilly. "I'll be a hero when it's known that I drew against the renegade and won."

"Sure of yourself, aren't you?"

"Yeah, damn sure. You ain't had much practice out there on your farm. What do ya say, Renegade, are ya willin' to meet me fair and square?"

"Grady, no!"

Storm's plea fell on deaf ears. "When was the last time you were in Cheyenne, Bull?"

Bull spat out an oath. "What's so damn important about Cheyenne?"

"Where are your friends Cox and Bickley?"

"Huh? How do you know about them? They were both killed robbin' a bank in Fort Worth."

"Too bad you weren't with them," Grady spat. "Do you remember a day five years ago when all three of you were in Cheyenne together?"

"Oh . . ." Storm felt as if she had been struck in the stomach with a fist. She knew exactly what Grady was talking about.

"Maybe," Bull said guardedly. "What's it to ya?"

"Do you recall an Indian girl that day? She was driving a wagon to town. You and your friends stopped her and pulled her from the wagon. You tormented her, calling her a squaw, and then you tore off her clothes."

Turner looked from Bull to Grady, realizing he had placed himself squarely in the middle of a potentially explosive situation that had nothing to do with him. It was something he hadn't counted on. But it was too late now to back out. He was in this with Bull and had every confidence in the gunman's ability. He had seen for himself how fast Bull was on the draw and knew for a fact that Stryker hadn't had much practice defending himself lately. Turner's object, of course, was land. He'd be on hand to buy poor Widow Stryker's double claim after her second husband's funeral.

"I don't remember nothin' like that," Bull said sullenly.

"Think hard, Bull. I have a very reliable description of you and your friends. That girl was my wife. She was carrying my child. You and your friends were going to rape her, but she fought you and spooked the horse. She was stomped and gravely hurt. But that's not the worst part. The worst part is that you left her lying in the dirt, badly injured and about to lose her child. She died, Bull. Died from her injuries and loss of blood."

"Think what ya want, Renegade, that don't change nothin'. Will ya take me up on my challenge?"

"When and where?" Grady's face was stark, his expression fierce. His lips were drawn so tightly against his teeth, he appeared to be snarling.

"Sundown tomorrow, behind the livery at the edge of town."

"I'll be there, of course," Turner threw in. "Just to see that no one interferes, you understand."

"Say your prayers, Bull. At sundown you'll meet your maker," Grady vowed tersely.

"Didn't think you'd reformed." Bull laughed nastily as he turned away. "You don't look like no farm boy to me. Tomorrow at sundown, Renegade."

Storm stared at their departing backs with something akin to horror. She couldn't believe Grady had accepted the challenge so calmly. Did his promise to her mean nothing? She had thought he'd given up his violent ways, yet here he was preparing for a shootout with a desperado. That the man was one of those responsible for Summer Sky's death made little difference to Storm. A promise was a promise.

"Why, Grady, why did you do it?" Her voice cracked with emotion.

"Weren't you listening?" Grady asked as he searched her face for some sign of understanding. "Bull is one of the men who accosted Summer Sky the day of her death. I knew their names and had their descriptions, but little else. But I prayed that one day I would meet up with them. Killing Bull will be a pleasure."

"Killing him will land you in jail," Storm said bitterly.

Grady withheld comment. Killing Bull could very well land him in jail, but it was a chance he had to take.

"What about your promise, Grady? You said you wouldn't knowingly court violence again, that you'd given up that kind of life for good. Think about your son. Do you want Tim to remember his father as a killer?"

"Perhaps Bull *will* kill me," Grady admitted softly. Storm paled visibly. Not once had she considered that possibility. "It's better than having Tim remember me as a coward. I'm doing this for his sake as well as for mine. I can't let his mother's death go unavenged when one of the men responsible has handed me the opportunity I've been praying for."

"Is that your final word?" Storm asked, giving him every opportunity to recant.

"That's my final word."

"Then obviously I mean nothing to you. I thought—Never mind what I thought. It no longer matters. If you insist on this madness, then I won't be here when you return—if you return."

A white line around his taut mouth was the only indication that Grady had heard her.

"I'm not returning to the homestead with you, Grady. I'm moving to town. I'll be at the Guthrie Hotel if you change your mind. I've lived through this once; I can't bear it a second time."

"Storm, you don't understand."

"No, Grady, *you* don't understand."

# *Chapter Fourteen*

"You're going home with me and that's final," Grady said as he swept Storm off her feet and lifted her onto the seat of the wagon with enough force to jar her teeth.

"Dammit, Grady, I don't want to be made a widow again."

"You won't be." He swung onto the seat beside her and picked up the reins. Storm's face was mutinous as they left Guthrie. By the time they reached their homestead she was so angry she could neither speak nor look at him.

Laughing Brook knew something was amiss the moment Storm jumped from the wagon and stomped into the cabin. She lingered outside while Grady unhitched the horses. The muscles of his face twitched and his motions were short and jerky as he struggled to keep his rage under tight rein.

"What happened in town, Thunder?" Grady sent her an oblique look, then turned back to his task.

"Why is Storm so angry?"

"Dammit, Laughing Brook, it's between me and Storm."

"I sense it goes beyond that," Laughing Brook said quietly.

Defeated, Grady turned to face her. "In a way it does concern you."

"Storm does not want me here."

"This has nothing to do with your presence in our home. It concerns your sister."

"Summer Sky?" Laughing Brook's lovely features wore a bewildered look.

"I encountered one of the men responsible for your sister's death in town."

Laughing Brook went still. "Are you certain?"

"As certain as I can be."

"Did you kill him? Is that why Storm is angry?"

"I didn't kill him—yet. But I will when I meet him tomorrow at sundown behind the livery. Storm begged me not to accept the challenge, but once I realized who he was there was no turning back."

"Your wife should never have asked such a thing of you," Laughing Brook said spitefully.

"It is your right to avenge Summer Sky's death."

"Storm doesn't see it that way," Grady replied. "Her first husband's death occurred as a result of a gunfight and she made me promise to avoid violence."

"Surely you didn't promise such a thing!" Summer Sky said, aghast. "You are Thunder, a man admired by the People for your courage. Your enemies fear you because you are cunning and fearless. You were not meant to be a farmer. Farming is women's work, unfit for a Lakota warrior."

"Times have changed, Laughing Brook. Indians no long reign supreme in the west. They have been herded like animals to reservations that can't support half their numbers. I am doing what I deem best for myself and my family."

"But you didn't keep your promise, Thunder," Laughing Brook reminded him. "Tomorrow at sundown Summer Sky's death will finally be avenged."

"And I will have lost my wife," Grady said bleakly.

"Storm isn't the woman for you. She never was."

"That's for me to decide," Grady said as he stared toward the cabin with a look of utter hopelessness. "Go help Storm with supper. My marriage isn't up for discussion."

Supper that night was a grim affair. Storm waited until everyone had eaten before sitting down to her own supper. Then she

closed herself in the bedroom and for the
first time since their marriage, latched the
door. When Grady found himself locked out
of his own bedroom he seethed with anger
and humiliation. He felt Tim's eyes on him
and knew that if he failed to command
proper respect from his wife, his son would
hold him in contempt. The certain knowledge
that Laughing Brook already thought him a
fool made him react violently to Storm's
deliberate snub. Raising a booted foot, he
broke the flimsy door open with one well-
aimed kick.

The door flew inward and Storm whirled,
her face a mask of astonishment. And fear.
Grady's fierce expression sent her stumbling
backward, one hand clutching her throat. She'd
always known he was a violent man, but thus
far his anger had never been directed at her.
She watched in trepidation as Grady calmly set
the door straight, then pulled it shut. When he
turned back to glare at her she swallowed her
fear, lifted her chin, and glared back at him
with all the bravado she could muster.

"Don't ever try to lock me out of our bedroom," he gritted out. "I won't be made a fool
of before my son."

"You should have thought of that before you
accepted a challenge from that gunman."

"I had no choice," he bit out harshly.

"You had two choices. You could have walked
away."

"You know why I agreed to meet Bull."

"I know, but it makes no difference. You broke your promise."

"I never thought I'd find one of the men responsible for Summer Sky's death. It's been several years."

"Think, Grady, think what this will do to your son," Storm pleaded. "If you don't care about my feelings think about Tim."

"It's too late for logic, Storm. I'm meeting Bull tomorrow at sundown and nothing you can say will dissuade me. Go to bed, lady."

"I'm not sleeping with you."

"I said go to bed. I won't touch you, if that's what you're concerned about. You'll feel differently about this tomorrow after you've had time to think about it."

"Never!"

Sleep did not come easily for Storm. She was more frightened than at any time in her life. The thought of losing Grady was terrifying. How many times must she mourn someone she loved? She had told him she'd leave if he went through with this insanity and she wouldn't back down now. She could be just as stubborn as Grady. If he insisted on facing Bull in a shootout, she wouldn't be here when he returned. She'd been stupid to think Grady was ready to give up violence. If he broke his promise once, doing so the next time—and the next—would come easier, until Storm would be afraid to go into town for fear some drifter looking to make a name for himself would challenge Grady.

Grady was up at dawn and gone from the house shortly afterward. When Storm heard the distinct sound of gunfire she knew Grady was practicing for tonight. Bull had been correct in assuming that Grady had lost some of his skill during the months he'd been inactive, Storm reflected, else he wouldn't be out there right now practicing. The thought was not comforting.

Grady didn't return at noon, and Laughing Brook carried lunch to him. When she returned she marched up to Storm and asked, "Why are you doing this to him?" Her voice was ripe with condemnation.

"I'm doing nothing that I'm aware of."

"You don't deserve a man like Thunder. If you loved him you'd stand by him and support him. It's what Summer Sky would have done. Thunder could do no wrong in my sister's eyes."

"I am not Summer Sky, nor will I ever be. Grady knew that when we married. Had he wanted a replica of Summer Sky he would have married you."

Laughing Brook bristled with silent indignation. "Today may be the last day he walks the earth."

A terrible pain knifed through Storm. "I'm aware of that. I begged him not to do this, but he refused to listen to me."

"As well he should," Laughing Brook said huffily. "My sister's spirit will not rest until her death is avenged."

"You're as bloodthirsty as Grady," Storm said with disgust. "I can't live with violence, not the kind Grady seems to enjoy, so I've decided to leave if he goes through with this madness."

Laughing Brook's pleased smile told Storm exactly how the Indian maiden felt about that. "It will be for the best."

It was mid-afternoon before Grady returned to the house. His mouth was grim, his eyes bleak but determined. The tensing of his jaw betrayed his deeply troubled thoughts. He didn't want to lose Storm, but he'd despise himself the rest of his life if he refused Bull's challenge. His son would think him gutless and his own conscience would plague him until the day he died. Stripped of his pride, a man is no good to himself or to his family. Why couldn't Storm realize that?

Grady went directly to the bedroom, where he changed into his buckskins and strapped on his gunbelt. He adjusted the height carefully, then tied it down at his thigh. The last thing he did before he left the bedroom was write a will leaving everything to Storm with the condition that she would care for his son until he reached his majority. After her death the homestead would be Tim's. He placed it on the nightstand where Storm would be most apt to find it and went in search of Tim. After patiently explaining to the lad what was happening and why, Grady looked for Storm. He found her in the garden, pulling weeds with such fierceness that clods of dirt were flying in every direction.

"It's time," he said simply.

Silence. A clod of dirt came hurtling his way and he sidestepped it neatly.

"Will you be waiting for me?"

She glared up at him. "Is there nothing I can say that will change your mind?"

"You've already said it."

"Then I won't be here when you return."

Grady frowned. "This is your home."

"I can't live like this. If Bull doesn't kill you, other men will come looking for you sooner or later."

"You're not thinking clearly, Storm. After Bull there will be no others. I promise."

"Just like you promised before? Good-bye, Grady. I—I wish you luck."

"I'll be back." He stared at her, memorizing her features. His eyes lingered on her lips. Lord, he loved her lips! Their lush sweetness drove him wild. He could kiss them forever and never tire. Right now he wanted to taste them so desperately he could feel the pressure building inside him.

Storm raised her head and met Grady's eyes, the tension so thick it could be sliced with a knife. When her eyes slid over him his skin felt too tight for him, and he deliberately looked away. One more look like that, he thought with a jolt of awareness, and he'd scoop her up in his arms, take her in the house, and make love to her. And that was something he couldn't let happen right now. He had an appointment at sundown and nothing short of his own death would stop him from appearing at the appointed time.

Without another word, Grady turned abruptly and left. Storm collapsed in a heap on the ground, shivering with cold despite the warm April day. She wanted to run after Grady, to throw herself at him, beg him one last time not to meet Bull, but she did none of those things. When she heard the thunder of hoofbeats pounding against the ground she knew it was too late. Hardening her resolve, she wiped her eyes and walked into the cabin and into the bedroom.

Storm decided not to pack everything she owned, hoping against hope that Grady would change his mind before sundown. After stuffing several items of clothing inside an old carpetbag she spent a few extra minutes gathering her keepsakes, which she packed in the carpetbag with her clothes. She experienced one terrible moment when she found Grady's will, but it served only to strengthen her resolve to leave. Then she stood in the center of the room, staring at the bed and remembering how wonderful it was between her and Grady. But it was too late now—too late. Obviously Grady didn't care enough for her to give up the violence she abhorred.

"So you are really leaving," Laughing Brook said when Storm came out of the bedroom carrying the valise. Tim was standing nearby, listening to every word. When he heard that Storm was leaving his face screwed up into a frown.

"Are you going away, Storm? Are you going to watch Papa kill that bad man?"

"I can no longer live here, Tim." Storm decided not to lie to the boy. He was too astute not to realize the truth.

"But I thought you were Papa's wife."

"I am, but your father seems to have forgotten it. He is more concerned with revenge than he is with his family. But this is my choice, Tim, you mustn't blame your father."

"Don't you like me?" Tim asked soulfully.

"Oh, Tim, don't ever think that. I've come to love you a great deal."

"Then why are you leaving?"

"It's something I must do for my own peace of mind. You have Laughing Brook and your father. You don't need me."

"But I do, Storm, I do need you. Laughing Brook is leaving soon, Papa has said so."

"I will stay as long as you need me, Little Buffalo," Laughing Brook assured him. "Let her go; we don't need her. You are more Indian than white. Once she leaves, your father will realize his place is with the People."

Storm turned away, unable to respond to Laughing Brook's logic. Leaving Grady would be difficult, but she couldn't live with the knowledge that other nameless men from his past could show up in Guthrie one day and challenge him. It would be like living with a bomb ready to explode. She had lost one husband because of a senseless gunfight and couldn't survive losing another loved one in the same way. She should have known better than to think Grady could give up his violent ways.

"Good-bye, Tim," Storm said as she walked out of the cabin. Determination alone kept her chin high and her eyes dry. After renting a hotel room in town Storm had no idea what she would do. Divorce was a possibility and would bear some thinking about. If she and Grady eventually did divorce, she wanted her homestead back.

Since she considered the wagon hers, Storm hitched the horse and drove to Guthrie. She arrived an hour before sundown, the time set for the shootout between Grady and Bull. She checked into the hotel immediately, trying to keep her eyes from straying in the direction of the livery where Grady was to meet Bull. She was given a room on the second floor and deliberately avoided looking out the window of the small room, but she couldn't stop her hands from shaking as she placed her meager belongings in the drawers and hung her dresses in the wardrobe provided. Only when her small chore was done did she walk to the window and note the position of the sinking sun in the sky.

Sundown.

Suddenly she was propelled by a nameless terror she had never known before. She found herself rushing out the door and down the hallway. Racing down the stairs and through the lobby, skirts held high so she wouldn't trip. Into the street, where her legs churned vigorously; gasping for breath, her face flushed, Grady's name became a litany on her tongue. People turned to stare at her, at her flashing ankles, at her blonde hair streaming in disarray down her back, but their curiosity went unheeded. Storm was beyond caring. All that mattered was that she reach Grady before the shooting began. If he was wounded, or God forbid, killed, he'd go to his death thinking she didn't care about him.

The livery was just yards away, and she reached it not a minute too soon. Storm's face was red, her lungs burned from lack of air, and she was on the verge of collapse. Abruptly the ominous sound of gunfire reverberated across the distance. One shot, then another, then nothing but sinister silence. Storm's legs turned to rubber as she skidded to an abrupt halt. The searing agony of breathing stopped completely as she went still.

Too late. Oh God, too late.

People began running in the direction of the shots, leaving her behind, unable to walk, unable to talk, her breath struggling to emerge from her throat. Finally one word came spewing out on a scream of terror.

"Grady!"

Her legs pumping furiously, Storm picked up her skirts again and took off at a run. Following the crowd to the open field behind the livery, Storm came upon the scene abruptly. Two men lay sprawled on the ground. Neither moved; both looked dead. A circle of people began forming around them. Someone bent down to feel for a pulse. It was at this point that Storm found the courage to move forward. She gave Bull a cursory glance before concentrating on the other man. She could see the slow spread of blood beneath Grady and feared she was too late.

She pushed her way through the crowd and people cleared a path for her, some shaking their heads, others clucking their tongues in obvious disapproval of the gunfight. Storm had just dropped to her knees beside Grady when the doctor approached, huffing and puffing from having been hastily summoned from his office. Reluctantly, Storm gave way to his expertise, watching anxiously as he used his stethoscope to find a heartbeat.

"Is he—is he—"

"Are you his wife?" the doctor asked brusquely.

"Yes, I'm Storm Stryker."

"Your husband's alive, Mrs. Stryker, barely. If I can get this bleeding stopped, he should make it. He's a strong specimen and, unless I miss my guess, in excellent shape."

"Take your time, Doc," a bystander said, "the other man's dead. You can't do him any good now."

"Where was Grady shot?" Storm wanted to know.

"Left side, just below the heart. Another inch and he'd be a goner. Soon as I stop the bleeding, I'll have him carried to my surgery, where I will remove the bullet."

"Are you sure he'll be all right?" Storm asked anxiously.

"He'll be fine if you let me do my work and stop asking questions."

Storm bit her tongue while the doctor worked over Grady. From the corner of her eye she saw that the sheriff had arrived and was talking to several bystanders, then to Nat Turner, who she had just noticed for the first time. When she saw Bull being carried away she turned her attention back to Grady and what the doctor was doing.

"Mrs. Stryker." Storm looked up to see the sheriff looming above her. "I'd like to ask you a few questions."

"Please, Sheriff, not now. Can't you see my husband is hurt?"

"This will only take a moment."

Reluctantly, Storm rose to her feet, keeping her eyes on Grady's still form while trying to concentrate on what the sheriff was saying.

"What do you know about this, Mrs. Stryker? This sort of thing is illegal in Guthrie. I warned your husband once about making trouble."

"This isn't Grady's fault, Sheriff," Storm said indignantly. "I was with my husband when Mr. Turner and Bull—the dead man—came up and challenged him."

"Why did your husband feel it necessary to accept? This whole unsavory mess could have been avoided if he had refused. Stryker was involved in one killing already, as you well know. He should have walked away from this one."

"Are you going to arrest him?" Storm asked, aghast.

"Mr. Turner seems to think it was your husband's fault."

"He's a liar! I was there when Bull challenged Grady."

"Rumor has it your husband once rode with a band of renegades. Some say he's a gunslinger called Renegade. Frankly, I'm confused. Who is he?"

Storm hesitated, unwilling to divulge anything that might hurt Grady. "Gossip is unreliable. Don't believe everything you hear. My husband is a family man."

"Turner insists the rumor is true, but Captain Starke says Stryker came from good stock, that his father was a hero. I decided to give your husband the benefit of the doubt as long as he caused no trouble."

"What happened today isn't Grady's fault, Sheriff, I swear it. Turner wants our land and will go to any lengths to get it. You've got to believe me."

"Frankly, I don't know who to believe. Personally, I like your husband. That's why I haven't pursued the rumors. But I don't relish having drifters come looking for trouble in Guthrie. This town doesn't need men who live by the gun.

"Guthrie is still a raw, new town. The law is just being established here, and I don't want Guthrie to be known as a lawless place. Captain Starke is a powerful man in the territory, and if he says your husband is a law-abiding citizen, then I'll take his word for it, until he's proven otherwise."

Just then two men arrived with a litter, and the doctor directed them as they lifted Grady onto the stretched canvas.

"I'm sorry, Sheriff," Storm said distractedly, "but I must go now. They're taking Grady away." Without waiting for a reply, she hurried after Grady and the men carrying him away.

Grady's face was white as a sheet, and he was so still, Storm could barely detect the slow rise and fall of his chest. The stench of her own fear filled her nostrils. She couldn't lose Grady, not now, not after she had learned to love him in a way she had never loved even Buddy.

The operation went well. When Dr. Finney came out of his surgery two hours after the operation began, he was grinning from ear to ear. "I told you your husband was a strong man, Mrs. Stryker. He's going to be just fine. It was a little tricky removing the bullet, but he came through it with amazing fortitude."

Storm had spent the two hours it took to remove the bullet pacing the waiting room, her mind in turmoil. Hearing the doctor's words now brought such a rush of gratitude, it was all she could do to keep from falling on the doctor's neck. "Can I see him now?"

"You can peek in on him, but he won't know you're there. He's heavily sedated. I suggest you go home and rest. By tomorrow he'll be able to speak to you, though he won't be up to carrying on a long conversation."

"Go home?" Storm asked, dismay coloring her words. "I want to stay with Grady."

"I don't think—"

"Please, Doctor, I must. What if he wakes up in the night and wants something?"

The doctor sighed wearily. "Very well, young lady. You certainly are persistent. I'll see that a comfortable chair is available so you can rest."

"When can I take Grady home?"

"Not for several days. It's best he remain here in case infection develops."

Grady awoke several times during the night, asking for water. He didn't appear to know her or recognize his surroundings or recall the circumstances that brought him to such a pass. Toward dawn Storm managed to snatch a few hours of uninterrupted sleep. She didn't awaken until the doctor came in to see his patient the next morning, before he opened his office.

"How long before Grady regains consciousness?" Storm asked as the doctor inspected Grady's wound and changed his bandage.

"He should awaken soon," the doctor predicted. "See that he stays calm and does nothing to dislodge the bandage or reopen the wound. I'll be in my office seeing patients. Call me if you need me." He started out the door, then turned back to Storm. "I'll have my wife carry you up some breakfast."

303

It was nearly noon when Grady began showing signs of coming out of his stupor. When he began thrashing around in the bed Storm had to literally hold him down. He opened his eyes, looked at her without comprehension, then drifted off again. He was still in a state of semi-awareness when the door to the room burst open and Laughing Brook stepped inside.

Storm whirled, shocked by the wild look in the Indian girl's black eyes. "Is he dead?" Laughing Brook asked. She was in a state of near panic. "It is your fault! If Thunder wasn't thinking about you and your decision to leave him, this wouldn't have happened to him. He's faster with a gun and more cunning than any man alive."

"Laughing Brook! What are you doing here? How did you know?"

"When Thunder didn't return home last night I knew something terrible had happened. I went to the sheriff's office and he told me what happened and where to find Thunder. Is he dead?"

"No, don't even think it. The doctor operated and he's going to be just fine. He should be coming around any moment now. Where is Tim? You didn't leave him alone, did you?"

"No, Little Buffalo is outside." She walked to the bed, her eyes filled with tears as she searched Grady's face. "Why is he so white?"

"He's lost a great deal of blood."

Just then Grady opened his eyes, searching the room restlessly until his gaze settled on Storm, standing at the foot of the bed. His first attempt to speak failed, but he was finally able to ask, "Where—am I?"

"In Dr. Finney's surgery," Storm said, moving closer. "You were shot yesterday. Do you remember?

For a moment Grady looked confused. "I—"

"Don't try to speak. Rest now; you're going to be all right. Would you like some water?"

He nodded, and Storm offered him a sip from the glass sitting on the stand beside the bed. Suddenly his eyes narrowed and he looked at her strangely. His penetrating gaze sent a prickle of apprehension down her spine. He opened his mouth, but nothing came out. "Grady, what is it?"

"Storm—don't want you—go away."

"What!" Storm's heart was pounding so loudly it drowned out everything but his startling words. Was Grady trying to tell her he didn't want her anywhere near him? Was he still angry at her decision to leave him?

His eyes glittering like two brittle diamonds, Grady struggled to speak again. "Don't want you—go away."

"Oh." Storm's hands flew to her face. Grady's rejection was like a knife thrust to her heart. Abruptly, she whirled and fled from the room, unable to bear Laughing Brook's gloating look.

Had she remained one moment longer she would have heard Grady say, "Storm, I—don't want you—to go away." Only Laughing Brook heard Grady's plea, and nothing short of death would drag it from her. When she saw that Grady had fallen back to sleep she quietly left the room. She found Storm standing just outside the door, weeping into her hands. Laughing Brook taunted her cruelly. "You abandoned him when he needed you. You have no reason to stay with him now; you heard what he said."

"He didn't know what he was saying," Storm said defensively. "Who will raise his son?"

"I will continue to do what I have done since Summer Sky's death. Little Buffalo is like my own child, and Thunder belongs to me. It is the way of the People. What further proof do you need?"

What proof indeed? Storm thought bleakly. Grady had spoken his mind and obviously couldn't bear the sight of her. She had hurt and angered him by leaving when he needed her and now he truly wished her gone. In her absence Laughing Brook would gladly care for his son and warm his bed.

Laughing Brook searched Storm's expressive face, gleefully anticipating her reaction. It was everything she could have hoped for. "I won't stay where I'm not wanted," Storm said. "I will honor Grady wishes."

"Where will you go?"

"I don't know, but I'll think of something. I have a room at the hotel. You and Tim are welcome to it. It's paid for until the end of the week. By then Grady should be ready to go home. Tell him—tell him—" Her words fell off. What could she say to a man who didn't want her? That she loved him? That she had never really wanted to leave him? That she had only wanted him to understand how much she deplored violence?

"I think it best that you do not see Thunder again," Laughing Brook said. "It will only upset him. I will care for him quite diligently."

"I'm sure you will," Storm said dryly.

# *Chapter Fifteen*

The heavy weight of rejection rested heavily on Storm's shoulders as she walked away from Grady. During those few moments before sundown when she had rushed out of the hotel, she began to realize just how much Grady meant to her. Hearing him tell her to go away had been a shattering experience. She'd expected him to be angry at her for leaving, but she had hoped he'd realize she was forced to act as she had because she had as much pride as he. How foolish she had been to think she could persuade Grady to mend his ways or be reasonable about her request. But Grady Stryker was a man with little patience or forgiveness in his barren heart.

Rushing out the door of the doctor's surgery, Storm nearly stumbled over Tim's small form crouched on the porch steps. When the boy saw her he jumped to his feet and hugged her fiercely, his little arms barely reaching around her legs.

"Is Papa all right, Storm?" he asked anxiously. "May I please see him? Laughing Brook told me to stay outside until she sent for me."

Smiling through her tears, Storm knelt and gathered the child in her arms. "Your papa is going to be fine, Tim. He is beginning to wake up. I'm sure he'll be pleased to see you."

Tim's face was radiant. "I was so afraid," he choked out as he tried so hard to be brave. "Where are you going? You're not going to leave Papa while he's sick, are you?"

Bitter anguish clouded Storm's face. "It's what your father wants, Tim. But perhaps I won't go far and we can still see one another occasionally."

"It's not what Papa wants!" Tim denied fiercely. "He told me he married you because he wanted to, and Papa doesn't lie."

The child's words added fuel to Storm's distress. Grady was ordinarily a very truthful man. She knew he wasn't lying when he told her he wanted her to leave.

"I know how anxious you are. Why don't you go inside and see your father now. Tell Laughing Brook—tell her I'll trade the wagon for the horse she rode to town. She'll find it at the livery. She'll need it to carry your father back home." Without waiting for a reply, she turned abruptly, mounted the horse hitched to the railing, and rode away. It was the most difficult thing she'd ever done.

Storm stopped at the hotel first, where she informed the clerk that Laughing Brook and Tim would be occupying her room. Then she quickly packed her clothes and left the room. Once in the street she attached the valise to the saddle and stood beside the horse, deep in thought. She hadn't the slightest notion where she was going or what she should do. It came to her suddenly that the cattle feeding on the lush grass growing on their land belonged to her. She had purchased them with the remainder of Buddy's money, and Grady had insisted that they be treated as her property alone.

If she sold half the herd, she might have enough money to rebuild her cabin on the land she had homesteaded. The deed had been changed to show that her name was now Storm Stryker, but legally the land was still hers. Something else Grady had insisted upon. As long as they were married, it wasn't necessary to divide the land into what belonged to her and what was Grady's, but since Grady no longer wanted her as his wife she felt justified in taking what was hers. Her mind settled, Storm mounted and reined the horse toward the homestead. Since no one would be occupying the cabin while Grady mended in town, she felt safe in staying there.

Storm's mind went in many directions during the ride to the cabin, but her decision never wavered concerning her reluctance to return to

Missouri. She had nothing to look forward to in Missouri but a bleak existence. Buddy's parents would certainly blame her for his untimely death, and her own parents, though they loved her dearly, didn't need another child to shelter or feed. She had much to think about, Storm decided as the cabin came into view. She and Grady were as separate as two humans could be, and her future depended on her ability to survive through adversity.

Briefly, she considered selling her quarter section of land to Nat Turner and settling farther west, in Wyoming or Montana. But the thought of Turner making a profit off the land she had won was abhorrent to her. And Grady would be livid.

It was dusk when Storm dismounted and unfastened her valise from the saddle. She spent a few minutes unsaddling the horse and rubbing him down before carrying her valise into the house. Lengthening shadows created dancing specters in the corners of the dark room as she opened the door and stepped inside. Dropping the valise beside the door, she went directly to the table to light the lamp. Suddenly she froze, feeling the hackles rise on the back of her neck. Her senses told her she wasn't alone, and every nerve recoiled at the thought.

"Who's there?" she called out, whirling to face the unseen foe.

"I will not hurt you, wife of Thunder."

Storm sucked in a shaky breath. "Who are you?"

312

A man stepped out of the shadows. Dressed in buckskins, his tall, muscular form was painfully thin, creating an illusion of fragile strength. His moccasined feet were noiseless on the wooden floor as he moved to where Storm could see him clearly. His braided hair was no longer black but generously streaked with gray. His dark face was creased, his brow deeply furrowed, his eyes sharp and assessing. Storm recognized a commanding strength in his aging body; the same unyielding strength she found in Grady. At first she thought the man was Grady's father, but she had assumed that Blade Stryker no longer dressed like an Indian or followed their customs.

"I am Jumping Buffalo, father of Laughing Brook. I have come for my daughter. Her mother has great need of her."

Storm allowed herself to relax, realizing this man would not hurt her. "Laughing Brook is not here. She and Tim are in Guthrie with Grady. Grady has been shot."

Jumping Buffalo turned his dark gaze on her. "Why are you not with your husband? Are my daughter and grandson all right?"

"They're fine, Jumping Buffalo. Laughing Brook stayed in town to care for Grady until he can be brought home. He was shot defending himself against one of the men who—who— caused Summer Sky's death."

Jumping Buffalo's stoic features gave away nothing of what he was feeling, yet Storm could tell her words gave him enormous satisfaction.

"It is not like Thunder to allow himself to become careless. Am I to assume the other man is dead?"

Storm nodded. "Not only is Bull dead, but so are the other two men who were with him that day in Cheyenne. They were killed in a bank robbery."

Jumping Buffalo's nostrils flared and his eyes glowed darkly with pleasure. "It is as it should be. Summer Sky's spirit is at peace now and Thunder's soul will no longer be troubled. I will take my daughter home with me. It is not her place to care for your husband."

Suddenly Storm became very busy as she struck a match and lit the lamp, flooding the room with light. Then, because she intuitively knew Jumping Buffalo would see through her lie, she faced him squarely and said, "Grady prefers Laughing Brook. He doesn't need me."

Jumping Buffalo searched Storm's face, her expression revealing all the anguish she was suffering. "I am sorry that my daughter has interfered in your life. It is good that I have come for her. Times are hard and food is scarce on the reservation, but her mother is ill and needs her."

"Do not blame your daughter, Jumping Buffalo. Oh, I'll not deny that jealousy wasn't involved, but Laughing Brook is not the cause of the trouble between me and Grady. Our problem is much more complex. I cannot abide the violent life Grady lives. My first husband died because of a senseless act of violence, and I cannot bear to see Grady killed in the same way. I told him I'd leave him if he engaged in a gunfight with Bull, and he chose vengeance over me. I can't live that way."

"Thunder did what his pride demanded. He is wounded. Would you leave him when he is helpless?"

"I was given no choice," Storm said stonily. "It's what Grady wants. I'll abide by his wishes."

"I am sorry for both you and Thunder," Jumping Buffalo said slowly, "but it doesn't change my decision to take Laughing Brook back to the reservation with me. Sweet Grass needs Laughing Brook to care for her, and I will not return without my daughter."

"Laughing Brook must care for Tim while Grady is recovering," Storm said.

"I will take my grandson back to the reservation with me," Jumping Buffalo decided.

"No! You can't do that. Grady needs Tim here with him."

"I will do what must be done," Jumping Buffalo said philosophically. "I will leave now."

"No, wait!" Storm cried in sudden inspiration. Jumping Buffalo stared at her curiously, waiting for her to continue. "Let me go with you in Laughing Brook's place. I will care for Sweet Grass so Laughing Brook can remain here to care for Grady and Tim."

It seemed perfectly logical, Storm thought, since Grady didn't want her and she really had no place to go for the time being. If she quietly disappeared from his life for a short time, he might come to his senses about her. And if she left a note telling him where to find her, perhaps he would come after her.

Jumping Buffalo wore a stunned look. "You would do that? You must love Thunder a great deal. The reservation is not a pleasant place. It offers little luxury for a white woman unaccustomed to hardship. If not for the beeves and food my good friend Blade Stryker sends me, we would have starved long ago. He is aware that I have been caring for our grandson these many years and did not wish for him to starve."

"Grady's father knew that Grady and Tim were living on the reservation?" Storm said, more than a little surprised.

"Blade and Shannon both know and were deeply hurt by Thunder's refusal to see them. But they have abided by his wishes in hopes that he will relent one day and bring their grandson to visit them."

"Grady is deeply ashamed of his association with renegades," Storm said defensively. "He fears his parents won't find it in their hearts to forgive him."

"He is wrong. But who can tell a hotheaded young man what is right and what is wrong? It is something he must learn himself. He also must learn what is important in his life."

Storm shifted restlessly as Jumping Buffalo's keen eyes seemed to probe into her very soul.

"Will you take me with you?" she asked, suddenly apprehensive. "If your wife is very ill, we shouldn't waste time."

"I think Thunder has made an unwise decision. I love my daughter, but I know her faults. You must love Thunder and Little Buffalo deeply to be willing to sacrifice your own happiness because of Thunder's stubbornness. Yes, Storm, wife of Thunder, I will take you with me. But only because you wish it and Thunder needs time to come to his senses. We will leave at dawn." He turned to leave.

"Wait! You may sleep in Tim's bed if you'd like."

"I will sleep on the ground. My bones may be growing old, but they are unaccustomed to the softness of a mattress. Thank you, wife of Thunder. I will return at dawn."

Storm was up long before dawn, packing food and other essentials for their lengthy journey. When Jumping Buffalo arrived she was writing a note to Grady, telling him where to find her should he so desire. Jumping Buffalo nodded his approval as she placed the note on the pillow in their bedroom, where Grady was sure to find it. She glanced back only once as she rode away with Jumping Buffalo, to take one last look at the cabin where she and Grady had been happy together for such a brief time.

Grady felt as if his body was on fire. Fingers of stinging heat radiated from his left side, where he was heavily bandaged. A groan of pain slipped past his lips as he tried to move.

"No, don't move." The voice was sweet, low and female. Storm? he wondered groggily. He recalled waking up during the night, asking for water and seeing Storm, her eyes clouded with concern, bending over him. He spoke her name aloud.

"No, it is Laughing Brook. I will care for you, just like it was always meant to be."

Grady frowned as the haze slowly lifted from his eyes and he saw Laughing Brook bending over him. Shifting his gaze, he searched the room. Tim stood slightly behind Laughing Brook, looking anxious. Grady tried to smile at the boy, but his lips twisted into a grimace of pain. Searching restlessly, he saw that except for him the room held only two other people. He knew he hadn't been dreaming when he saw Storm earlier. Had she stepped out for a moment?

Suddenly Laughing Brook's puzzling words penetrated the fuzziness of his brain and his eyes shifted back to the Indian maiden. "What do you mean? Where is Storm? I saw her here earlier. Has something happened to her?"

"Now is not the time to speak of your white wife."

"Now is a perfect time," Grady said weakly. "Tell me, I want to know."

"Storm is gone," Laughing Brook crowed delightedly.

"Gone? Gone where?"

Laughing Brook shrugged expansively. "Does it matter? She no longer wishes to be your wife. She packed her clothes and left."

Grady's brow furrowed in painful concentration. "But I distinctly recall her being here with me."

"She was here for a short time only," Laughing Brook admitted with marked reluctance. "She stayed with you briefly, until I arrived in Guthrie to take care of you. She abandoned you, Thunder. You need a woman who will bow to your wishes and be submissive to you in all things. I am that woman, Thunder. I will not leave you and Little Buffalo."

A pain far greater than that caused by his wound brought a groan to Grady's lips. Storm's desertion brought him a new kind of anguish. How could she abandon him when he needed her? he wondered, clearly distraught. How could she leave him and Tim without telling them where she was going or what she intended to do? Suddenly a thought came to him, and he motioned Tim forward.

"Did you speak to Storm before she left, son?"

"Yes, Papa," Tim acknowledged.

"Tell me what she said."

"She said she had to leave."

"Did Storm say where she was going?"

Tim shook his head. "I asked her to stay, but she wouldn't."

Laughing Brook watched hope die in Grady's eyes and was jubilant. Now Thunder couldn't send her home, she thought gleefully. He needed her, not just to care for his son but for his own sake. It wouldn't be long, she told herself, before she'd become a permanent part of his life. She'd loved Thunder even before he married her sister, but at the time she was too young to do more than look at him with yearning. Now she was a woman, with a woman's needs and a woman's cunning. She would nurse Thunder back to health with all the tenderness in her woman's heart and he would come to love her as he once loved her sister. It was meant to be.

After that Grady refused to speak of Storm, not even to the doctor, who questioned him about his wife's absence. In a week he was strong enough to return to the homestead. Before he left he visited the bank and learned that Storm hadn't withdrawn any funds from their account, nor did she have any money of her own. That bit of knowledge not only worried but puzzled him. Where could she have gone without funds? A visit to the hotel drew a blank when he learned Storm hadn't been seen in a week. He found it difficult to believe she'd leave her homestead without demanding some sort of payment for her half.

But then he'd never thought Storm would actually leave him. By the time Laughing Brook picked him up in the wagon, Grady was exhausted and ready to go home to the cabin. He even consented to lie in the wagon bed, cushioned by blankets and pillows the doctor had generously offered for the jarring ten-mile ride home.

Laughing Brook couldn't recall when she'd been so happy. Life with Thunder would be good, she reflected. Much better than living on the reservation, ravaged by sickness and hunger. Remaining at the homestead with Thunder was a much better solution than trying to persuade him to return to the reservation with her, she decided. To Laughing Brook Thunder would always be a mighty warrior, and though she preferred that Thunder live with the People, perhaps his way was the best after all. Her father had told her that the days when the People roamed free were gone forever and that she should adapt to the white man's ways. Once Thunder become a prosperous farmer her life would be good. Yes, she decided happily. Everything she'd ever wanted was finally within her grasp.

Both Tim and Grady were dozing in the wagon when they reached the cabin. Deciding not to awaken them, she jumped lightly to the ground and entered the cabin, going directly to the bedroom, where she turned the bed down in preparation for Grady. She spied the note Storm left immediately. Since she could neither read nor write English, she slipped it under the mattress, intending to get rid of it later. She had no inkling what Storm had written to Grady, but decided that any kind of correspondence from Storm meant trouble for her. She had just turned away from the bed when Grady and Tim, refreshed from their nap, entered the bedroom.

"What are you doing?" Grady asked curiously.

"Turning down the bed," Laughing Brook informed him. "You'll want to rest before dinner."

"I've had sufficient rest," Grady returned shortly. "There's no time for dawdling on a productive farm. I have crops to see to and animals to tend."

"But you're not well enough yet!" Laughing Brook cried. "I will do what needs to be done."

"Don't coddle me, Laughing Brook. See to Tim. I can take care of myself. Leave me, I wish to change clothes."

Giving him a sulky glance, Laughing Brook sidled from the room. Once she was gone Grady immediately went to the wardrobe he had purchased for Storm. The doors stood slightly ajar and he pushed them open. It was empty. The drawers in the bureau were similarly bereft of clothing, and for the first time since being wounded the full impact of Storm's leaving hit him sqarely. He had already suffered the pain of rejection but wasn't prepared for the explosion of raw anger that surged through him.

Why had he made a fool of himself by letting Storm become indispensable to him? There was a tremendous war of emotions raging inside Grady. He could no longer deny his feelings. What he felt for Storm went beyond the youthful love he once felt for Summer Sky. When he was with Storm, making love to her, holding her, something deep inside him reached out and touched something deep inside her. He remembered every sweet, lush curve of her body and how perfectly the two of them fit together.

Yet even as he admitted in his heart that love might be involved in his feelings for Storm, he hated her for what she had done to him. Leaving him when he was weak and vulnerable filled him with frustrated fury, and he knew he could never forgive her. She had callously abandoned him when he was hurt, unconcerned whether or not he would recover.

Why couldn't things be like they were during those halcyon days of his youth, when he and Summer Sky, the companion of his heart, had been happy at Peaceful Valley? he wondered despondently. Then, as he had done so many times in the past, Grady's thoughts turned to his parents, Blade and Shannon, and how deeply he had hurt them by leaving so abruptly and taking his son with him, and remaining out of touch for years. Then and there he made a silent vow to visit Peaceful Valley soon and reacquaint his son with his parents.

Resolving to banish Storm from his mind, Grady hardened his heart and focused on Tim and the life they would build together in Oklahoma.

Storm had no idea it would take so long to reach the reservation deep in the Black Hills.

So far Dakota Territory was unlike anything she'd ever seen. Its stark beauty was awesome, and she couldn't help but gawk at the treeless hills, high plateaus, and deep gullies spread out before her. Jumping Buffalo told her the hills were composed of flint, which attracted lightning during fierce storms. Though she was duly impressed by the naked emptiness and raw splendor, she couldn't help but wonder why the government had banished great numbers of Indians to a barren land so obviously bereft of the necessities to sustain life. It was clearly evident, even to her inexperienced eyes, that the land was hostile to humans. There were no lush grasslands to feed livestock, no rich soil to grow crops, and no small game or buffalo to support life.

They came upon the reservation abruptly, tucked between two hills. Tepees dotted the ground for as far as Storm could see. Barking dogs heralded their arrival, and the raised voices of children at play drifted to them on the breeze. As they drew closer she could see old men seated cross-legged before the entrances of their tepees, smoking pipes and talking. Though the day was warm, most of those aging warriors were shrouded in blankets, their proud, copper faces deeply lined, their eyes empty. They wore defeat uneasily, and Storm sensed their anger and loss of pride the moment she rode into their midst.

Storm was appalled by the squalid conditions of the village and silently deplored them.

No wonder Grady had turned renegade, she reflected angrily. His father's People were a dying race, and rather than accept it he had tried to change it, even though he knew it was a lost cause. What truly amazed her was that most white men believed Indians were being adequately cared for by the government, provided with homes, food, and clothes. But Storm could see at a glance that all those suppositions were false. These poor, downtrodden people were thin, gaunt, and sickly beyond belief. Thank God Grady had taken Tim to Oklahoma, where he would grow strong and healthy.

Jumping Buffalo reined in before a large tepee, dismounted, and helped Storm from her horse. The journey had taken over a week, and her legs were so sore Jumping Buffalo had to steady her before she was able to stand alone. Though the pace Jumping Buffalo set hadn't been grueling, it was nevertheless brisk and steady. He feared that Sweet Grass would die before he returned.

"This is my home," Jumping Buffalo said simply. "Welcome, Storm Stryker. Allow me to greet my wife first. I will summon you when I have prepared her for your arrival." Turning abruptly, he lifted the flap and entered the tepee.

Storm watched helplessly as Jumping Buffalo disappeared inside the dark interior. She felt completely alien in this foreign place and wondered what had made her volunteer to come to the reservation to nurse Jumping Buffalo's wife in Laughing Brook's stead. Storm felt as if everyone in the entire camp was staring at her, and she forced herself to remain calm. She knew Jumping Buffalo would protect her, but she couldn't help feeling more than a little uneasy.

"You are not Laughing Brook." The words were delivered in halting English.

Storm started violently. She hadn't heard the young warrior approach and was immediately reminded of Grady, who moved as silently as a cat. The young man was tall and slim—too slim, perhaps—with shiny black hair, dark fathomless eyes, and a muscular build. He wore stained buckskins that had seen better days.

"I—who are you?"

"I am called Soars-Like-An-Eagle. Who are you?"

"I am Storm Stryker."

"Storm Stryker," the young brave repeated. Suddenly his face lit up. "You are Storm, wife of Thunder. Where is my friend Thunder? I would like to greet him."

"He didn't come."

Soars-Like-An-Eagle looked puzzled. "Jumping Buffalo was supposed to bring Laughing Brook back with him. Where is she?"

"Laughing Brook couldn't come. I came in her stead."

"White customs are strange indeed," Soars-Like-An-Eagle said, shaking his head. "Why would you leave Laughing Brook with Thunder and travel to the reservation in her place?"

"It's a long story. I have come to care for Sweet Grass."

"I was expecting Laughing Brook," Soars-Like-An-Eagle said sourly. "It is time she returned to her people. I have offered many horses for the honor of marrying Laughing Brook, and her father has promised to intercede for me."

"You want to marry Laughing Brook?" Storm asked, surprised that Laughing Brook would refuse this handsome young man.

"Many men want Laughing Brook, but she is stubborn and refuses to marry any of us. I suspect she is waiting for Thunder to claim her. That's why I was overjoyed when Thunder returned for Little Buffalo and told us he had married. But I was not pleased that Laughing Brook went to Oklahoma with Thunder. I expected her to return long before now."

Before Storm could form an answer, the tepee flap opened and a grim-faced Jumping Buffalo stepped out, followed by an ancient crone whose lined face dissolved into deeply plowed furrows.

"I have explained to Sweet Grass that Storm, wife of Thunder, will be caring for her. Though she doesn't understand why Laughing Brook could not come, she welcomes you. Come, I will take you inside now so that Crooked Nose can go home and rest."

Both Crooked Nose and Soars-Like-An-Eagle melted away as Storm bent low to enter the tepee, uncertain what she would find.

Sweet Grass's wasted form lay on a bed of furs. Despite the stifling heat inside the tepee, she was covered with a blanket. Her eyes were open, and despite the woman's debilitating illness Storm thought she had never seen eyes so gentle or uncomplaining. The thought struck her that Summer Sky must have taken after her mother if she was as sweet and compliant as Grady indicated.

"Welcome, wife of Thunder," Sweet Grass rasped. "It is good of you to come."

"Since Laughing Brook is unable to come I thought it fitting that I should take her place," Storm said. "Besides, I wanted to come." It came as a shock to Storm that she actually meant what she said. She *did* want to come with Jumping Buffalo, and she was glad to be of some service to Sweet Grass, for Grady held both Sweet Grass and Jumping Buffalo in high esteem.

Sweet Grass smiled sweetly, then closed her eyes. She slept a great deal during her illness, which worried Jumping Buffalo.

Taking Jumping Buffalo aside, Storm asked, "What is wrong with her? Has the doctor seen her?"

"Sweet Grass took a fever during the winter, seemed to get better with the coming of warm weather, then suddenly grew worse. As for the doctor, I cannot abide the man the government sends to treat our sick. He is dirty and nearly always drunk. Crooked Nose has been treating Sweet Grass with medicine concocted

328

from herbs and bark. It is better than anything the doctor can give her."

"I know nothing of medicine," Storm said.

"I ask only that you follow Crooked Nose's instructions. She is old and cannot be here all the time, for there are others who need her services. Everyone on the reservation has sick family members; that is why I had great need of Laughing Brook. It is a daughter's place to care for her mother."

"I will do my utmost to care for Sweet Grass," Storm said earnestly. "I pray it will be enough."

"It will be enough, wife of Thunder," Jumping Buffalo said solemnly.

# *Chapter Sixteen*

"Thunder, it is late. Please come inside. I've kept your supper warm."

Grady paused in his work, reluctant to go inside the cabin, where memories of Storm were so strong. The curtains she had hung at the windows, the furnishings they had purchased together, even the scent that lingered on the air in their bedroom combined to make his life empty and unbearable. How could she leave him without so much as a good-bye? He wondered for the thousandth time during the past weeks. Missing Storm proved to be an agony surpassed only by the death of Summer Sky. And even that sad event had dimmed in his memory when Storm had filled the void left by the death of his young wife.

"Thunder, do you hear me? Why must you

work so long and so hard?"

Grady expelled an exasperated breath. Work was his salvation and his solace. From the moment he had returned home after being wounded by Bull he had plunged recklessly into work, disregarding the pain caused by his healing injury and the distinct probability that he could do himself more harm than good by pursuing so active a life after being recently hurt.

The thought that he had allowed himself to become careless still stung. It never would have happened if he hadn't been thinking of Storm's threat to leave him if he dueled with Bull. And not having used his skill with a gun in several months had no doubt contributed to his lack of speed. Of course, learning that his bullet had struck and killed Bull almost instantly had helped relieve his feelings of inadequacy, but did little to ease his anguish over Storm's leaving.

"Thunder, please."

"I'm coming," Grady grumbled once he realized Laughing Brook wasn't going to give him a moment's peace until he returned to the house.

It was becoming much too dark to work anyway. In the weeks since Storm had left he had plunged deeply into backbreaking work. He had built a stable to shelter the horses and store the wagon and was now hard at work on a barn. Not only was hard physical labor good for the soul, but it helped keep haunting memories of Storm at bay.

Grady paused at the back door to wash up in the bucket of water placed there for his convenience before entering the cabin. A small whirlwind hurtled into Grady's arms and he hugged his son tightly.

"Why do you work so hard, Papa?" the little boy asked. "Laughing Brook says you will sicken if you don't rest more."

Grady shot Laughing Brook a quelling look. "Hard work never hurt anyone, son."

"It's late. Laughing Brook and I have already eaten.

"There is plenty left over for your father," Laughing Brook was quick to add. "Sit, Thunder."

Grady bolted down his meal, neither tasting nor savoring the food set before him, though it was tasty enough. These days he ate to nourish his body, finding little enjoyment in the act. Tim sat beside him, chatting about his day while Laughing Brook hovered nearby, ready to cater to Grady's every whim. The moment he was finished he rose abruptly and disappeared into his bedroom. He returned a few minutes later with soap and towel.

"Put Tim to bed, Laughing Brook," he said brusquely. "I'm going to the river to bathe."

Laughing Brook watched Grady leave, her eyes dark with intense longing. Nothing was turning out the way she'd planned. Weeks had slipped by since Storm walked out of Thunder's life, yet he hadn't turned to her in desire as she had hoped. She knew he was aware of her wish to please him in every way, yet he had deliberately kept his distance. He was remote, untouchable and cold. Only to his son did he display the soft side of his nature, and then only fleetingly.

Laughing Brook was at her wit's end. She no longer knew if what she had done was right, for it had made Grady sink deeper into a world of bitterness and silence. If only she could get through to him, she thought desperately. If only she could convince him to accept her into his life. Grady needed the kind of comfort that could only be obtained from a warm, loving woman eager to ease his suffering.

Intuitively Laughing Brook realized that she must take the initiative if she wanted Grady, and an arrested look came over her features. She had waited patiently for Grady to make the first move, but since he continued to ignore her she was forced to take matters into her own hands.

Grady lingered as long as possible at the river. The night was exceptionally warm and the water refreshing after his hard day's labor. His body was sore and stiff, a feeling he had grown accustomed to of late, as his muscles protested being worked without respite. But his muscles weren't the only part of his body that ached. His loins ached with the memory of how wonderful it had felt to thrust himself deep inside Storm's softness. He wanted to be inside her, filling her, moving in and against her, feeling

the delicious heat curl through him, burst into
flame and consume their bodies. He had been
celibate for a long time after Summer Sky's
death and had managed to control his urges
without undue discomfort. But somehow wanting and needing Storm far surpassed anything
in his experience or memory.

Bitter regret sighed through Grady as he
waded from the river, gathered up his soiled
clothes, and returned to the cabin wearing only
his breechclout. He hoped Laughing Brook
had already retired, for he felt too emotionally drained to spar with her. His heart was
heavy with the burden he had accepted when
he had denied Storm's request to ignore Bull's
challenge. He knew then he could lose Storm,
but never in his wildest dreams had he imagined she would callously walk away from their
relationship without a backward glance. She
had too much to lose if she left.

Yet in the end it hadn't mattered. Storm obviously didn't care enough about him or their
homestead to work out their differences.

The cabin was dark when he entered. Both
beds at the far end seemed occupied, so Grady
gave them little more than a cursory glance.
When he entered the bedroom he didn't bother
lighting a lamp, for the moon was at its full-
est and illuminated the room quite adequately.
Slipping off his breechclout, he slid between
the cool sheets. A curse left his lips when he
realized he wasn't alone.

"Dammit, Laughing Brook, what does it take

to convince you I am not interested in having you in my bed?"

"I do not believe you, Thunder," Laughing Brook said softly. "You have not had a woman in many weeks. Don't I please you?"

She leaned up on her elbow, and Grady felt the soft flesh of her bare breasts brush against his chest. He groaned in genuine agony and tried to reach for anger in his weary soul, but could find none. Not for Laughing Brook, who cared for his son without complaint. His anger was directed in another direction, toward a woman who cared so little for him that she had abandoned him when he was sick and helpless.

"I do like you, and you are very pleasing, Laughing Brook. That's why I won't take you to my bed. You are more like a little sister to me than a lover. You played with my own sisters when they were growing up. I feel no special bond with you outside of friendship."

Laughing Brook frowned, trying to make sense of his words. "You need a woman." Her hand slid boldly down his stomach, feeling the muscles jump beneath her fingertips, then lower into the wiry thatch of black between his legs. When her fingers curled around him, he jerked violently. A delighted gurgle bubbled past her lips. "See? I do not lie. You are ready and I am willing. Thunder, why do you resist?"

Why, indeed, Grady thought harshly as his whole body began to tremble beneath her touch. With more restraint than he thought possible, he flung her hand aside. "I already have a wife and I refuse to ruin you. Jumping Buffalo is my friend. I will not violate his trust. I assume you are still a maiden. Your virginity rightfully belongs to your husband."

"I will be your second wife," Laughing Brook offered. She was growing desperate now, realizing her seduction wasn't working.

"As I have said, a man is allowed only one wife in the white world," Grady explained patiently.

"Storm is no wife to you!" Laughing Brook contended. "She left willingly enough. Is there no white man's law that deals with such things?"

"If Storm wants a divorce, she will have to pursue it," Grady said stubbornly. "Leave me, Laughing Brook, before I do something I will regret."

"You are no warrior," Laughing Brook spat derisively. "A warrior takes what he wants."

"What I want is for you to leave my bed. Now. Your action tonight tells me that it is time you returned to the reservation. I'm sure there are men aplenty waiting for your return. You are very beautiful, Laughing Brook. Any man would be proud to have you for his wife. You deserve better than serving as second wife to a man who would only use you for one purpose."

"If you are the man, then you can use me in any way you please. I love you. I have always loved you."

She slid atop him, rubbing against him like a cat in heat, bringing every part of her body into intimate contact with every part his. Grady grit his teeth and nearly lost the ability to think. He *did* need a woman. His body burned and ached with that need, so why should he deny himself the gratification Laughing Brook generously offered? The answer was simple. Because he had given his word to Jumping Buffalo to keep his daughter safe, and to break that trust would be to lose his honor. But more importantly, he couldn't make love to Laughing Brook because his need for Storm was so strong it rendered him incapable of bedding another woman.

"Stop that!" Grady grit out, grasping her about the waist and plucking her from atop him. Her flesh was firm, satiny smooth, and warm to his touch, and Grady nearly lost his resolve. "Go back to your bed. Tomorrow I will make provisions for your return to the reservation. And there is something I have been considering for a long time, something to ease my own peace of mind. I want to visit my parents at Peaceful Valley. It is time I made my peace with them and reacquainted them with their grandchild. Perhaps they will find it in their hearts to forgive me for alienating myself from them and seeking a life different from the one they wanted for me."

"Let me go with you, Thunder, please," Laughing Brook pleaded. "It has been many years since I have seen your parents and they were as dear to me as my own. Your sisters were my only playmates."

"I suppose both Dawn and Spring are married now and living with their husbands," Grady said with aching sadness, "and my mother and father are alone at the ranch. I can be there and back before harvest if I start immediately."

"You need me to care for Little Buffalo on the trip," Laughing Brook persisted. "And I would love to see the ranch again." Her voice held a wistful note that tugged at Grady's heart. "I will return willingly to the reservation if you allow me to visit your family first."

"I will take you to Peaceful Valley only if you promise nothing like this will ever happen again," Grady warned sternly. "Another day I might not be in so generous a mood and do something we will both regret."

Laughing Brook swallowed her delighted smile, hoping Grady meant what he said. One day, she vowed, she'd catch Grady at a vulnerable moment, and afterward his conscience would force him to make her his second wife. White man's laws meant nothing to the People, who followed their own rules.

"I will try not to tempt you, Thunder," she promised in a contrite voice. Grady chose to read more into her words than she intended.

"Very well. You may accompany me to Peaceful Valley," Grady said, heaving a sigh of resignation. "We will take the train to Cheyenne and shorten the trip by many days. Go to your bed, Laughing Brook."

He deliberately turned his head as Laughing Brook slipped nude from the bed and padded from the room. Though his mind rejected her utterly, his body wasn't as easily appeased.

When Grady went to town the next day he heard some startling news. He had gone to Guthrie hoping to hire a couple of men to protect his homestead in his absence against predators and speculators like Nat Turner. He was shocked to learn that Nat Turner had been killed by an irate gambler who had caught him cheating in a poker game the previous night. Though it did not solve his immediate need to hire someone to watch the farm in his absence, knowing that Turner was dead eased Grady's fear over leaving his homestead until harvest. He expected a good crop of wheat from the acres he had planted and looked forward to a profitable first year.

Not every homesteader had the same advantage he did, Grady reflected. Some folks were so dirt poor, and wood so scarce, that they were forced to live in caves dug from hillsides that were dark and dirty, though relatively dry. Or they erected houses from clumps of sod cut into brick size. Since sod houses were built above ground they provided more light and ventilation than dugouts, but they always leaked, and rain and windstorms caused great damage. Grady considered himself damn lucky to have money available to purchase wood to build a cabin and seed to grow crops.

In the best of times even the elements conspired against the homesteaders. Oklahoma seemed cursed with the worst of all weathers. In the summer rain was infrequent, and the blazing sun scorched and parched crops while grasshoppers and other pesky insects descended and stripped young farms clean of greenery. Plagued alternately by long droughts and sudden gully-washing floods, violent hailstorms and tornadoes, settlers in Oklahoma Territory had to learn to survive hardships of all descriptions. What made the land attractive was the fact that it was free to those with grit and determination, those with hope and dreams, and those who had nothing to which to return.

Grady's luck held when he found a widow and her strapping seventeen-year-old son to stay at the homestead in his absence. Since he no longer needed to worry about Nat Turner causing trouble, Grady felt secure in leaving the farm in the Martins' capable hands. They had been forced to sell their own homestead after the death of Mr. Martin and were hoping to buy a small business in town with the proceeds from the sale of their land. Grady bought train tickets to Cheyenne for the following week and returned home to tell Laughing Brook and Tim of his arrangements.

Grady regretted being unable to take Storm to meet his parents. He knew instinctively that they would like and approve of Storm, but he had no idea where to find her. He had questioned the ticket agent at the train station, but the man swore he hadn't sold a ticket to her. And the owner of the livery had no idea where she had gone after she left the wagon in his care. Grady suspected she had gone back to her family in Missouri and had to forcibly stop himself from going after her. But he had too many responsibilities to go traipsing after a woman who didn't care enough about him to stay long enough to learn if he had survived his bullet wound. Obviously Storm didn't want him and he'd damn well better find a way to keep himself from wanting her. But it wasn't going to be easy.

For the third morning in a row Storm rushed from the tepee and spewed the meager contents of her stomach onto the ground a short distance from the village. When she returned Sweet Grass took her aside and offered her a drink of cool water.

"What is wrong with me, Sweet Grass?" Storm asked worriedly. "Have I caught your illness?"

Sweet Grass smiled shyly. After many days and nights of being tenderly cared for by Storm she had come to love Thunder's wife as dearly as she did her own daughter. It was mainly through Storm's efforts that she was recovering from her debilitating illness, and both she and Jumping Buffalo greatly appreciated Storm's dedicated nursing.

"Crooked Nose says my fever isn't catching," Sweet Grass said, putting Storm's fears to rest.

Have you had this sickness before?"

"No, I've rarely been ill in the past," Storm said after careful thought.

Just then Crooked Nose entered the tepee, took one look at Storm's pasty complexion, and smiled broadly. Then she started babbling to Sweet Grass in the Sioux language. Storm tried to understand, but they spoke too fast for her to decipher from the smattering of the language she had picked up in the weeks she had been living on the reservation.

"What did she say?" Storm asked Sweet Grass. "Does Crooked Nose know what's wrong with me?"

As if in answer to Storm's query, Crooked Nose nodded sagely.

"Crooked Nose says your ailment is a natural and expected condition in young married women," Sweet Grass said, stifling a giggle. Her mirth puzzled Storm. Since when was being ill a cause for levity?

"Is it serious?"

"It can be, but it runs its course in nine months."

"Nine months? Why that's—oh no, it can't be! I can't be having a baby. Not now."

"Both Jumping Buffalo and I have noticed changes in you. Crooked Nose says it is so, and she is wise in such matters. Thunder will be pleased to add another child to his family."

Storm gnawed worriedly on her lower lip, aware that having Grady's baby wouldn't change the way he felt about her. He hadn't wanted her before she was going to have his child, and she definitely wouldn't go back to him knowing he'd only want her for the sake of their baby. On the heels of that thought came another. Now that Sweet Grass was well and Storm's usefulness ended, where would she go? Grady hadn't cared enough about her to come for her and she was determined not to intrude where she was not wanted. On the other hand, there was her land and cattle to consider. She had much to think about during the next days, she concluded, for her own future and that of her unborn child was at stake.

"Jumping Buffalo will escort you back home," Sweet Grass declared. "I am well enough to manage on my own until he returns with our daughter. I do not know what is wrong between you and Thunder, but the child will heal your troubled souls."

"I fear it will take more than a baby to cure what is wrong between me and Grady," Storm said sadly. "In all these weeks I have heard nothing from him. Perhaps all he ever wanted from me was my homestead. But he can't have it," Storm said fiercely. "I'd sell it before I'd leave it to him."

"Has my daughter caused this conflict between you and Thunder?" Sweet Grass asked in a concerned voice. "Jumping Buffalo had little to say about your reason for coming here in Laughing Brook's place."

"I won't deny that Laughing Brook is part of the problem, but she isn't what ultimately caused the rift between Grady and me," Storm confided. "I can't live with Grady unless he gives up his violent ways. I begged him not to participate in that gunfight. I even told him I'd leave him if he did, but he chose to ignore my plea. After he was wounded I changed my mind and would have stayed with him, but he—he didn't want me. He told me to leave."

"That doesn't sound like Thunder," Sweet Grass observed with a frown. "Perhaps you were mistaken."

"There was no mistake," Storm said bitterly. "If a mistake was made, he would have come to the reservation and told me so. I left a note telling him where I could be found."

Sweet Grass grew thoughtful. "What will you do? You are welcome to stay here with us for as long as you like, but the reservation is no place for a white woman unaccustomed to our ways. Winters are hard, and many of us do not survive. It is especially difficult for babies and small children. If not for Thunder's father, we would have starved long ago. Each winter and summer he sends us food, blankets, and clothing."

"I'll think of something," Storm said dispiritedly as she turned away to busy herself with a task that would take her mind away from Grady and the dilemma that faced her.

Jumping Buffalo looked up from the tedious chore of attaching steel tips to his arrows and stared into the distance, an arrested look on his rugged features. A man driving a wagon was just entering the village. Shading his eyes against the glare of the sun, Jumping Buffalo stared at the man with an increasing sense of familiarity. Something in the set of his massive shoulders and the way he held his head gave Jumping Buffalo his first clue to the man's identity. Suddenly a broad smile creased his weathered features and he began to walk briskly out to meet the visitor.

Strong, capable hands the color of burnished bronze drew the team of horses to a halt beside Jumping Buffalo. The two men looked at each other for the space of a heartbeat before the man in the wagon jumped to the ground and warmly embraced Jumping Buffalo.

"It has been a long time, old friend."

"I have missed you, Swift Blade," Jumping Buffalo said, thumping Grady's father on the back in exuberant welcome. "If you have come for your grandson, he is not here."

Blade Stryker's dark eyes betrayed the anguish in his heart. "I didn't think he would be, but I had to find out for myself. Shannon is beside herself with grief over the boy. If not for you, we would have no word at all about Tim. Nothing has been the same since Grady left the ranch and took Tim with him. Where is my grandson?"

"Little Buffalo is with Thunder."

"Thunder," Blade repeated, swelling with pride. "He is also called 'Renegade,' is he not? Thunder is a fit name for my son, but Renegade brings him no honor. Even in Cheyenne we have heard of the Sioux renegade who is sometimes called Thunder. Shannon and I are deeply saddened by Grady's pursuit of violence since Summer Sky's death. Lord knows, the boy wasn't brought up like that. Living with the People and learning their customs has been a fine experience for him. What saddens me is the way he has chosen to conduct his life."

"Living with anger changes a man," Jumping Buffalo said cryptically. "Especially a very young man. Thunder was a green youth when he lost Summer Sky. He has changed much from the boy you once knew, Swift Blade."

"Shannon and I feared we had lost our only son forever until we recently heard a bit of news that gave us hope where none existed before. I pray it is true. That's why I've come in person this time to deliver food and clothing to the People. I deliberately stayed away before because it was what Grady wanted."

"What is it you learned?"

"When Captain Starke came to Peaceful Valley recently to purchase horses for the army he told me he saw my son in Guthrie, Oklahoma. He said Grady had taken part in the race for land in the newly opened Cherokee Strip. Is that true, old friend? Has Grady finally decided to abandon his violent life and become a farmer? And if it is true, why hasn't he contacted me or his mother? Doesn't he know he is still our son no matter what he has done?"

"It is true, Swift Blade. Thunder—it is difficult to think of him as Grady—won a quarter section of prime land that he is homesteading. I saw him last when he came to collect his son. Laughing Brook accompanied him to care for the child until he felt comfortable with his new surroundings. The reservation is the only home Little Buffalo remembers."

"Has Grady married Laughing Brook?" Blade asked, surprised. "It would please me if he has, but I was under the impression that he thought of Laughing Brook as one of his younger sisters."

"There was no marriage, yet after many moons Laughing Brook is still with Thunder in Oklahoma."

Blade frowned, displeased by Jumping Buffalo's answer. "Has Grady changed so much? Has he dishonored your daughter?"

Jumping Buffalo remained thoughtful for a long interval before answering. "I do not think so. Thunder is an honorable man, and he swore to protect my daughter. I trust him. But there is something else you should know. Thunder is married."

"Grady is married?" The news was startling indeed. "If he is married, why is Laughing Brook still with him? I don't understand."

"Thunder's wife is no longer with him. I will tell you all I know." Then Jumping Buffalo proceeded to tell Blade everything, from the time he encountered Storm at the cabin until the present. When he finished Blade was more bewildered than ever.

"It appears as if Grady has married an extraordinary woman," Blade mused thoughtfully. "I'm anxious to meet Storm and judge her for myself. My son must be a fool to let someone like her go. Her decision to come to the reservation to care for Sweet Grass was a selfless act of charity."

"Sweet Grass and I have come to love the girl and think of her as our daughter. But there is another thing I must tell you about Storm."

"What is it? Have you found some flaw in her character?"

"If she has a flaw, we have not found it," Jumping Buffalo said with a smile. "Since Storm's arrival a change has occurred. And these past few days has strengthened our belief that Storm is carrying Thunder's child. She probably did not realize it at first, but now she cannot deny the truth."

"My God! Have you any idea what caused the rift between Storm and Grady? If she is to bear his child, she must go back to him."

"Storm says she cannot live with the violent way of life Thunder has chosen. He has killed two men in Guthrie, one of them Storm's first husband."

"Then he hasn't changed," Blade said sadly. "I had hoped . . ."

"It would be remiss of me if I didn't tell you that I suspect Laughing Brook of contributing to the dissension between Thunder and Storm. My daughter is one of the reasons Storm refuses to return to Thunder. And Storm insists that

Thunder ordered her to leave him."

"If that is true, then I don't know my son anymore," Blade lamented.

"Only Thunder can tell you if it is true," Jumping Buffalo said. "But it does not sound like the brave Sioux warrior I have always loved like a son."

"What will Storm do now that Sweet Grass has recovered and no longer needs her?"

"I do not know. She may stay here as long as she likes, but conditions on the reservation are deplorable and she would be miserable raising her child here."

"Grady's wife has a home," Blade said with quiet authority. "Her home is at Peaceful Valley with me and Shannon."

Inside Jumping Buffalo's tepee Storm sat beside Sweet Grass, brushing her long blonde hair and thinking of Grady and the child she carried. She looked up as two men entered through the open flap, their bulk blotting out the sun. Storm paused, resting the brush in her lap as she tried to see the men's faces through the filtered light. When Jumping Buffalo greeted Sweet Grass, the identity of one of the men was solved, but it wasn't until the other man moved more fully into the tepee that recognition came to her.

The incredible width of his shoulders and massive chest, the narrow hips and muscular thighs; everything she'd ever loved and admired about Grady Stryker was standing before her.

At long last Grady had come for her. Leaping to her feet, she threw herself into his arms, repeating his name over and over.

Stunned, Blade opened his arms wide to receive his son's wife. If Storm didn't love Grady, then she was a wonderful actress, he thought as he held her close for a moment until she gained her composure.

Storm realized her mistake the moment Blade's arms closed around her and she lifted her head to stare into the darkest eyes she'd ever seen. Black and quickly intelligent, with a touch of humor, she decided, as she carefully studied this older version of Grady. His father was every bit as handsome and a bit more rugged, with jet black hair liberally sprinkled with silver and a commanding strength so impressive in a man his age that it nearly took her breath away.

"I wish I *were* Grady," Blade said with a hint of amusement. "But since I'm not, I'll settle for being your father-in-law. I'm very happy to meet you, Storm. I can't wait to introduce you to Shannon."

# Chapter Seventeen

Blade Stryker used the kind of logic Storm found difficult to argue with. When he invited her for a walk so they might have a private conversation his questions about Grady and Tim and the kind of life they were living in Oklahoma were filled with concern and yearning. But when he suggested that Storm come to Peaceful Valley she had a million excuses why she couldn't.

"I don't know what has happened between you and Grady and I don't want to interfere, but Shannon and I would love to have you visit, if only for a short time. Or do you have something else in mind? I feel sure Grady would be happy to have you with him on the homestead."

Storm's teeth sank into her lower lip as she searched for an answer. How could she tell

Grady's father that his son didn't want her? Their marriage had been a mistake from the very beginning. Grady had felt a misguided sense of responsibility toward her and she had needed a home. It was as simple as that.

"I—can't return to Grady," Storm said in a strained voice. "He's made it abundantly clear that he doesn't want me. Please, I don't want to say things about your son that will hurt you."

"I have no illusions about Grady," Blade said bluntly. "I know what he has become and how he's conducted his life since Summer Sky's death. I also understand what drove him to turn renegade. Grady's life until that time had been storybook perfect. He wanted for nothing. The family was respected in Cheyenne and he had all the advantages money could buy.

"Summer Sky was his childhood love, his soul mate. They married very young, had a son after only nine months of marriage, and another on the way a few months after that. The incident in Cheyenne was such a shock, it changed Grady's entire outlook on life. His hatred for whites extended not just to the despicable men who had caused Summer Sky's accident that day but to all people of the white race."

"Grady told me he took Tim and went to live on the reservation," Storm said.

"We didn't know he had turned renegade until rumors reached us in Cheyenne. I worried about Tim, but Jumping Buffalo sent a message saying the boy was living with him and his family. I wanted to go after him immediately, but Shannon stopped me. She feared Grady would resent us for interfering. We prayed that our son would come to his senses one day and bring Tim home. Then Captain Starke showed up and told me he'd met Grady in Guthrie, and I had to come to the reservation to find out for myself what had happened to my son and grandson."

"Tim is fine," Storm assured him. "Grady would never let anything happen to his son."

"I'm glad to hear that," Blade said. "I was afraid Grady had turned into someone I no longer knew. Shannon is grief-stricken over the way Grady left and the violence that has become a part of his life. But just knowing that he has married someone like you has given me renewed hope."

A dull red crept up Storm's neck. "Our marriage was—not a love match. I needed a home and Grady wanted someone to care for Tim. It's a very long story."

They were walking toward the stream when suddenly Blade clasped Storm's hands and led her to a fallen log. "I have plenty of time." He sat down, pulling her down beside him. "Jumping Buffalo tells me you were a widow before you and Grady married. He also intimated that Grady was partly to blame for your first husband's death."

"It wasn't really Grady's fault," Storm said, absolving Grady of all blame. "It was an accident, a horrible accident."

355

"Yet despite this 'accident' you married."

"I really don't want to talk about the reasons behind our marriage, Mr. Stryker," Storm said. "They are no longer valid. Grady no longer needs me, and I refuse to stay where I'm not wanted."

"I'd feel honored if you'd call me Blade. What will you do? Where will you go?"

"I don't know," Storm said truthfully. "I could sell my quarter section of land or the cattle I purchased with my own money."

"But you really don't want to do that, do you?" Blade said astutely. Storm shook her head. "You love my son, don't you?"

Storm lifted her head in surprise. How could Blade know that after speaking with her for such a short time? "I . . ."

"It's all right, Storm, I understand. You remind me of Shannon many years ago, when she tried desperately not to love me but couldn't deny what was in her heart. You and my wife are alike in many ways. Life was not easy for us in the beginning. Even now there are people who despise me because I am a half-breed."

"Nothing is guaranteed in life," Storm said bitterly. "I thought Buddy and I would live happily forever-after when we were married. I must have been terribly naive."

"Are you carrying my son's baby?" Blade asked, stunning Storm with his bluntness.

"I—yes, both Sweet Grass and Crooked Nose have told me it is so."

"Then you must come to Peaceful Valley, where Shannon and I can care for you. Unless you wish to return to Grady. I'm sure that would be the best solution."

"No! I mean," she said more calmly, "I don't want to go back to Grady. I couldn't live with a man who doesn't want me."

"Are you absolutely certain Grady doesn't want you?"

"Yes," Storm said with quiet conviction. "He has Laughing Brook to look after Tim. He doesn't need me. But I don't want to burden you and your wife with my problems."

"Burden us?" Blade laughed. "My dear girl, it would be a pleasure. Our daughter Dawn has married and moved to San Francisco. And Spring is in Boise visiting her Branigan relatives. Her last letter indicated that she has met a young lawyer whom she intends to marry. With Grady and Tim gone, our lives are quite empty. We would welcome you and your child with open arms. I won't take no for an answer. I'll wire Grady so he'll know where to find you when he comes to his senses."

"No! You mustn't! I'll come to Peaceful Valley, at least until my baby is born, but you must promise not to tell Grady where I am."

"Storm, be reasonable," Blade argued. "Grady has a right to know about his child."

"If you don't promise, I won't come." Her jaw was set, her mouth tight with resolution. She was even more stubborn than Shannon,

Blade decided, realizing that if he didn't agree she would leave and he would lose another grandchild. Later, once she was settled at the ranch, he and Shannon could try to change her mind.

"Very well. I promise. How soon can you leave? We'll travel overland to the nearest railhead and take the train to Cheyenne."

"I can leave whenever you like," Storm said. "Now that Sweet Grass is well she no longer needs me. Perhaps they will accompany us. Life on the reservation is very difficult for them."

"I've already asked," Blade said. "Jumping Buffalo wishes to remain on the reservation with the People. But one of the young braves expressed a desire to work on the ranch. He is unhappy with the slim opportunities that exist on the reservation for an ambitious young man, and I have promised to teach him the art of raising horses. His name is Soars-Like-An-Eagle."

"I know him," Storm said. "He is a fine young man. We have spoken many times. He wishes to marry Laughing Brook."

"It's settled then. We'll leave in two days," Blade decided. "I don't like leaving Shannon alone any longer than necessary."

"You must love her very much," Storm said wistfully.

"Little Firebird is my life and my salvation," he said with such feeling it brought tears to Storm's eyes. To be loved like that by Grady would be all that she could ever ask for in life.

Blade reined in at the crest of one of the hills surrounding Peaceful Valley, his dark eyes gleaming with pride. Storm drew her mare up beside him, and Soars-Like-An-Eagle joined her. The large, rambling ranch house was set on a level piece of ground next to a bubbling stream surrounded by numerous outbuildings and paddocks. Horses of all sizes and description grazed on the hillsides and valley for as far as the eye could see. A carefully tended garden surrounded by a white fence spread out behind the house, basking in the afternoon sun.

"There it is," Blade said expansively. "Peaceful Valley. Shannon and I moved here before Grady was born, and it's been our home for nearly thirty years."

Storm was visibly impressed by the prosperous ranch that Grady had given up to become a renegade. "You have a right to be proud, Blade," she said sincerely. "I don't know how Grady could have left all this behind."

"Come along. Shannon is expecting us. I wired her from the train station before we boarded." Blade led the way, anxious to greet his wife. He hated being parted from Shannon for more than a few hours. But one good thing had come of his trip to the reservation: He was returning with Grady's wife, and soon there would be a child in the house again. Shannon would be ecstatic.

The three riders had just entered the yard when the door to the house burst open and Shannon came hurtling toward them. Bending low, Blade scooped her onto his lap and kissed her soundly. Peals of delighted laughter floated past her lips as Blade kissed and nuzzled her neck.

"Put me down, Blade," Shannon scolded when it became apparent her bold husband wasn't about to let her go. "What will our guests think?"

"They'll think that I love my wife and haven't seen her in a long time." Blade laughed as he carefully set Shannon on her feet. He quickly dismounted and joined her, one arm draped possessively around her waist.

Storm could feel Shannon Stryker's inquisitive blue eyes on her as Soars-Like-An-Eagle helped her dismount. Her first glimpse of Grady's mother gave her quite a start. Shannon Stryker looked young enough to be Grady's sister. There wasn't one strand of gray in her gleaming chestnut hair. Her skin was smooth and unlined and her figure was as slim and supple as a girl's. But it was to Shannon's eyes that Storm was drawn. Her eyes were the same incredible shade of blue as Grady's.

Shannon's smile was warm and welcoming as she held out her hand to Storm. "Welcome, my dear. I'm so pleased you could come. Blade's telegram gave me quite a shock. I had no idea Grady had remarried, but I couldn't be more pleased. Later you must tell me all about my son and grandson. It's been so long." The wistful note in her voice tugged at Storm's heart.

"I'm sure Storm will tell us all about Grady and Tim once she's had time to rest," Blade said. "Why don't you take our daughter-in-law upstairs to her room, Little Firebird, so she can rest before dinner."

"Forgive me," Shannon said, "you must be exhausted. Come along, Storm, you can have Grady's old room." Blade followed with Storm's bags as Shannon led the way up the stairs.

Grady's room was filled with childhood mementos, but Storm saw nothing that reminded her of the proud, ruthless man Grady had become after he left the ranch. The possessions in the room belonged to a youth with dreams untarnished by reality. The man Storm loved displayed no youthful softness and had no fanciful dreams to nurture. Grady Stryker was a man who battled personal demons, a man who had found no room in his heart for love.

Storm was silent so long, Shannon asked, "Would you prefer another room, Storm?"

"Oh, no, this is fine," Storm assured her. "I was just trying to picture Grady in this room. He's changed, you know."

Shannon's face fell. "I expected as much. Do you think he'll ever return home?"

"I believe he will," Storm said with such heartfelt conviction, Shannon felt her heart constrict with the first stirrings of hope.

\*     \*     \*

If not for missing Grady so desperately, Storm would have been truly happy at Peaceful Valley. Shannon and Blade were wonderful. Storm wondered if Grady knew how badly he had hurt his parents by refusing to communicate with them. He had spoken often about his parents, and deep in her heart Storm felt that Grady intended to reconcile with them one day. Both Shannon and Blade were eager to hear everything she could tell them about Grady and Tim and hung on her every word. She told them about the land rush, their homestead, and mentioned how much Grady doted on Tim. She tried not to dwell on the code of violence by which Grady lived, or the men he had killed in Guthrie. She also saw no reason to tell them that Grady didn't love her, that their marriage was strictly one of convenience. And she damn sure wasn't going to admit just how desperately she had come to love her husband.

Storm still hadn't found the courage to talk to Shannon about the baby she carried, though she realized Blade had surely imparted that bit of information to his wife. Since she was nearly three months pregnant, the baby would soon make its appearance known in the most basic way. Though still slim as a reed, Storm knew it wouldn't be long before her body would expand. Already her clothes were becoming snug at the waist and bust, but if one didn't know her well it would be difficult to tell that she was increasing. The one thing Storm continued to insist upon was that neither Shannon nor Blade inform Grady of her presence at the ranch. Though they gave their reluctant consent, Storm knew that one day they would refuse to honor her request.

At the end of two weeks Storm felt extremely comfortable with Blade and Shannon. Their love for one another was so tangible it reached out and touched her. She had never known two people so profoundly in love after nearly thirty years of marriage.

It was a blistering hot afternoon in July when Storm wandered out to the porch to catch a breath of air. She had tried to nap in her room, but it was too stifling inside for sleep. Finally she rose and wandered downstairs to see what Shannon was up to. She knew Blade was out on the south range branding horses, and at this time of day Shannon could usually be found in the office, working on the books. Blade hated confining book work, but Shannon found it stimulating. Deciding not to disturb Shannon at her work, Storm had stepped outside to the porch.

Pausing at the rail, she saw Soars-Like-An-Eagle working in the paddock with one of the horses and was quite impressed with the young man's patience with the animals. He was working out well on the ranch, and not for the first time Storm wondered why Laughing Brook had spurned his offer of marriage. Then, in her mind's eye, she saw Grady, so handsome, so strong and virile, that Soars-Like-An-Eagle paled in comparison. She, too, would be reluctant to accept a substitute.

Why did every waking hour of every day have to be filled with memories of Grady? Storm wondered bleakly. Why did each night become a reservoir of painful reminders of how wonderfully he made love to her and how hotly her body burned for his touch? In her dreams his strong arms held her, his mouth kissed and teased every inch of her body, and when he thrust inside her his flesh felt like the softest velvet stretched taut over a pillar of tempered steel.

"Storm, I thought you were upstairs napping."

"Oh," Storm said, startled from her erotic daydreams. "I didn't hear you, Shannon. I couldn't sleep; it's too hot. I hoped to catch a breeze out here on the porch."

"I'll get us a pitcher of lemonade and join you," Shannon said. She started to turn away when she spotted riders approaching the house. "I think we have guests. I didn't know Blade was expecting anyone."

Storm scanned the hillside and saw a cloud of dust trailing behind two riders. A thrill of anticipation danced along her spine as she watched the riders approach. Though they were still too far away to identify, her senses leaped in joyful recognition.

When the riders entered through the gate, Shannon started trembling and her mouth dropped open in wordless shock.

"Grady." Storm was the first to speak his name.

He had come for her.

Entertaining similar thoughts, Shannon and Storm started forward at the same time. When Shannon broke into a run, Storm deliberately held back, allowing mother and son a moment of privacy for their first meeting in several years. Tears came unbidden to her eyes and she looked away when Grady slid from his mount and opened his arms wide. Then Shannon was swept into his embrace, weeping and laughing at the same time. Several minutes later, when Storm dared to look again, they were still embracing and Grady was whispering into Shannon's ear. Then he set her aside and moved away so that she could greet her grandson, who still sat astride Grady's horse, smiling shyly. Shannon held out her arms and Tim slipped happily into them.

Storm had been so swept up in the tender reunion that she had failed to notice the second rider. It wasn't until Laughing Brook dismounted and sidled up beside Grady that Storm realized the Indian girl was still with Grady. Her loud gasp ended in a sob, making her presence known as surely as if she had called out. Slowly Grady turned and saw Storm. Visibly shaken at finding his wife at Peaceful Valley, his face turned white. His shock at seeing her was so obvious, Storm realized he couldn't have come to Peaceful Valley on her account. His mouth formed her name, but no sound emerged.

She could feel the searing heat of his piercing gaze as it settled upon her, and a shudder of primitive yearning shook her to the very depths of her soul. Grady had grown so still, Shannon turned to look askance at him. It was Tim who finally spoke her name.

"Storm! What are you doing here? Papa said we'd never see you again."

The excitement and unexpectedness of the moment was too much for Storm. Turning abruptly, she fled into the house and up the stairs to her room, where she slammed the door behind her and threw herself on the bed in a tearful rage. Nothing had changed. Grady and Laughing Brook were still together. He *hadn't* come for her as she'd first supposed. Finding her here had been a complete shock to Grady. Sending Laughing Brook home to the reservation had never been Grady's intention.

Storm's furious tears flowed freely while Grady fought for composure. Not in his wildest dreams had he expected to find Storm at Peaceful Valley. He had so many questions to ask he didn't know where to begin.

Shannon solved the problem handily by asking, "Why have you waited so long to come for Storm? Your father and I don't care what brought you here, we're just grateful you've come. Go to her, son, your wife needs you."

Grady lifted one shoulder in a dispirited shrug and looked away. "I had no idea Storm was here, Mother. If I had, I might not have come. She made it perfectly clear that she wanted nothing more to do with me."

Shannon looked bewildered. "But her note. I assumed you traveled to the reservation first and Jumping Buffalo told you where to find Storm."

"The reservation? What are you talking about, Mother? What in the hell would Storm be doing at the reservation? She left no note."

Shannon glanced purposely at Laughing Brook, who refused to meet her eyes. "I think I understand. What do you know about Storm's note, Laughing Brook?"

Grady's face turned stony as he rounded on Laughing Brook. "Answer my mother, Laughing Brook. Did Storm leave a message for me?"

"I saw nothing," Laughing Brook said sullenly.

"I can't abide liars."

"I didn't think it was important," Laughing Brook whined.

"Where is it?"

"I put it under your mattress and forgot about it until your mother mentioned it just now. I'm sorry, Thunder. I meant no harm."

"Take Tim to the kitchen, Laughing Brook," Shannon said, diffusing a volatile situation. "I imagine he's hungry after the ride from town." Sending Shannon a grateful look, Laughing Brook took Tim's hand and hurried off.

367

"Don't be too hard on her," Shannon said. "She's young and fancies herself in love with you. You're here now, and so is Storm."

"Why did Storm go to the reservation? How did she get there? This is all so confusing."

"I can only tell you what I know," Shannon said as she gave a brief explanation of why and how Storm went first to the reservation and then came to Peaceful Valley. She concluded by saying, "You have chosen wisely, son. Both your father and I have grown to love Storm. She will make a wonderful wife and mother. You must reconcile with her."

Grady's expression hardened and his eyes grew cold. "I don't think reconciliation is possible, Mother. Storm left me, I didn't leave her."

His words gave Shannon hope. Grady thought Storm had left him, yet Storm said that Grady had asked her to leave. Something was very wrong somewhere. "You're as stubborn as your father," Shannon said with a hint of exasperation. "When your face is set like that you look just like him. Go to Storm, son, while I reacquainted myself with my grandson. Blade will be ecstatic when he returns and finds you've come home at last. We have so much to talk about, Grady, so many wasted years to make up for."

"And I've much to atone for, Mother. I hope you and Dad can forgive me for hurting you. My life these past six years has been a far cry from what you and Dad wanted for me. If you knew how I conducted my life, you'd order me from your house at once."

"I doubt that," Shannon said succinctly. "We'll talk later. Go to your Storm."

When Storm had first fled to her room her tears were those of pity, hurt, and shock. But her tears had ceased and her self-pity had changed to raging anger. How dare Grady flaunt his mistress before his parents? Had he no respect for the wonderful couple whom she had grown to love? Rising from bed, she began to pace.

When Grady opened the door and stepped into the room Storm whirled to face him, her cheeks blazing, her eyes glowing like twin flames. Her expression was so hostile, Grady recoiled in shock. But that didn't stop him from admiring her. Storm looked absolutely magnificent. Not at all like a wife who had been pining for her husband. He snorted derisively. Why would Storm miss him when it had been her choice to leave him?

He opened his mouth to spit out a scathing retort, but what came out was the complete opposite of what he intended. "I've never seen you looking more beautiful." Where did that come from? he wondered distractedly.

Storm bristled indignantly. "I know you didn't come here for my sake, so there's no need for pretty words. You have some nerve bringing your mistress with you. Have you no feelings at all for your parents?"

369

Her words sliced cleanly through his confusion, bringing him to a rigid state of awareness. "I had no idea you were here. Mother told me you were with Jumping Buffalo and the People. She explained why you went to the reservation and I'm grateful for what you did for Sweet Grass, but that doesn't excuse you for abandoning me when I needed you."

"My note explained everything," Storm said succinctly.

"I saw no note."

Storm made a derisive sound deep in her throat. "I placed it in plain sight. How could you not have seen it?"

"Let's forget the note for a moment. Let's discuss the fact that you left without so much as a good-bye."

"I told you I would leave if you met Bull that day. It was something I had to do. Living with violence and fear would kill my lo—would make staying with you a virtual hell on earth. I'd never know when someone would sneak up behind you and challenge you. Or blow you to kingdom come without warning."

"You could have trusted me. I told you I was finished with violence. Taking on Bull was something I had to do for Summer Sky and my own peace of mind."

"You told me to leave. You said you didn't want me."

"I what?" He was beside her in two steps, grasping her shoulders, giving her a little shake. "I said no such thing. I begged you not to leave.

When I came to my senses Laughing Brook told me you had already left. Even Tim begged you to stay."

"I heard you, Grady. I distinctly heard you say you didn't want me. You told me to go away."

"I realize I wasn't in full control of my mind, but I certainly don't recall saying that. In fact, just the opposite is true."

"I thought you hated me for not being the kind of wife you wanted. I just wanted you to understand that I couldn't live with a man who openly courts danger and violence.

"I did understand, but facing Bull was something I had to do. I had hoped *you* would understand *my* need."

"Then we're still at an impasse," Storm said bitterly. "If you cared for me, why didn't you come to the reservation? My note told you exactly where to find me."

"I told you before, I saw no note. I suspect Laughing Brook made sure I never saw it."

"Laughing Brook," Storm repeated with scathing sarcasm. "Why did you bring your mistress here?"

Grady sighed in exasperation as he explained with commendable patience, "Laughing Brook never was my mistress. She's like a little sister to me. I'd never bed her."

"But . . ."

"Laughing Brook was born on the ranch. It was her home until her father took her away six years ago. She loved my parents and expressed

371

a wish to see them again before returning to the reservation. You've been to the reservation. You've seen how difficult life is for the People. Can you blame her for wanting to visit Peaceful Valley?"

"Are you denying that Laughing Brook wants you? She wants to be your wife. She expects it."

"Why can't you accept the fact that I don't desire Laughing Brook in that way? It was wrong of her to deliberately hide your note, but I can't find it in my heart to hate her. She's been like a mother to Tim since Summer Sky's death."

"How do you feel about me, Grady?" Storm asked bluntly. "Do you love me?"

Grady opened his mouth to say the words Storm yearned to hear, then closed it abruptly. He had loved Summer Sky and she had been taken from him. If he bared his soul, what assurances did he have that loving Storm wouldn't destroy her just as it had Summer Sky? What he feared most was losing Storm. He had tempted the Gods these past years by living on the fringes of the law, and now that he had a second chance at happiness he feared his love would harm Storm just as it had destroyed Summer Sky.

For the first time in years he was frightened of the evil forces that had controlled his life. Frightened for Storm's sake.

Besides, Storm had never expressed love for him; quite the contrary. She despised him for the kind of life he had led and for the violence that followed him. The passion they shared was something neither of them had counted on. If he never had anything else from Storm, he would have her passion.

"My God, Grady, don't you feel anything for me?" Storm cried, turning away. "I'll pack my things and leave. I won't hurt your parents by remaining where I'm not wanted."

"Not wanted?" Grady repeated, swinging her around to face him. "I've always wanted you. I've never wanted anyone like I've wanted you." His blue eyes glowed with a savage inner fire and his expression was fiercely possessive. "I've always prided myself on my ability to control my needs and emotions. But with you all my resolve and willpower flees like leaves before the wind. I have no need for pretty words and vows. My actions demonstrate what I feel for you."

"Your actions merely tell me you are a virile animal whose lust cannot be controlled," Storm said. Grady winced but did not contradict her.

"I don't deny it, sweetheart," Grady said. The intensity of his lowered voice sent a thrill of apprehension down her spine. "I cannot control myself where you're concerned. Call it lust or whatever you like, lady, just know that you're mine and you're going to return with me to the homestead when I leave Cheyenne."

She answered quickly, over her choking, beating heart. "You'll have to be more convincing than that."

## Connie Mason

Grady's face went slack with disbelief then
flushed with pleasure when he realized what
her words implied. Without further hesitation
he swept her into his arms.

# Chapter Eighteen

Storm experienced the same hot breathlessness she felt every time Grady touched her. The air around them seemed to be thickening, vibrating, turning dark with emotion. With an efficiency of movement Grady released the fastenings on her dress and bared her breasts. His lips lowered slowly until they were hovering over the exposed flesh swelling in avid anticipation of his next move. His breath was so warm she could feel her skin sizzling from the contact. Though he hadn't actually touched her breasts they felt heavy and full, the nipples engorged by the sweet abrasion of his breath.

"You're trembling; are you cold?" The smile in his voice told her he knew exactly what made her tremble.

His lips touched her flesh.

She made a strangled sound and involuntarily arched upward.

His warm wet tongue slashed over her right nipple. Made ultrasensitive by her pregnancy, the sensation was exquisite. When he shifted to caress the other nipple, Storm groaned in sheer delight.

Grady raised his head and looked deeply into her eyes. "Your body has missed me."

"I have no control over the response you force from my body." No matter how much or how often Storm tried to deny her feelings, her body betrayed her.

"Am I convincing enough yet?"

"I'd rather you told me how you felt."

"And I'd rather show you. I've missed you too." His head lowered and his mouth closed on her left breast.

Storm gasped as the strong suction of his mouth created a fire in her blood she hadn't known since she left Oklahoma—pulling, drawing, his teeth gnashing on the engorged nipple. The heat he was creating became a tingling ache between her thighs. Commanding the last of her dwindling strength, she tried to rise from the bed. She could see the pulse beating wildly in Grady's temple and his breath coming faster, harsher, as he shifted his weight off her. For a moment she thought he meant to let her go, but he merely pushed her back down and began to strip off his clothes.

In moments he stood before her naked, proud, magnificently aroused, and she stared at him in utter fascination. She could see Grady like this every day of her life until she grew old and never tire of the sight of him. He stood over her, all bronze masculinity, the powerful sinews cording his thighs, the smooth, tight musculature of his stomach, the taut roundness of his buttocks. His blue eyes glowed with dark fire, his mouth heavy with sensuality. His eyes intent upon her face, he bent and stripped her bare.

She tensed, exposed, burning, as his gaze slowly slid down the length of her body. She clenched her legs tightly, but he merely smiled and shoved them apart, moving between them. His fingers began caressing her, massaging, then plunging into the center of her.

Her body arched up from the bed and she gave a tormented cry.

"Are you becoming more convinced?" He was breathing harshly, his muscles taut with tension, his face fierce as his long, hard fingers moved rhythmically in and out of her.

By now Storm was beyond speech as her head wagged from side to side. She begged him to end her torture, but Grady was just warming to his pleasurable task. Lowering his head, he touched his tongue where his fingers had been moments before.

"Grady!"

She tried to close her legs against this unorthodox intrusion, but Grady shoved them farther apart, settling more deeply into the cradle of her thighs as his mouth and tongue delved deeply into the sensitive core of her womanhood. He lashed her relentlessly until pleasure so intense it stole her breath shuddered through her. Allowing her no time to recover from the volatile release he had forced from her, Grady slid upward and thrust into her. His fullness stretched her, filled the emptiness of the past months without him—made her complete.

Wildness seized Grady as he plunged and thrust, long, hard, short, gentle, losing all control now as he felt Storm's moist heat surround and enfold him. She was just becoming accustomed to one tempo when he changed it to another, each stroke bringing her once again to the brink of madness.

Just when Storm thought she could stand no more, Grady added a new dimension to their loving when he kissed her deeply, his tongue moving wildly in her mouth to the same tempo as his thrusting below. He reached around and cupped her buttocks, bringing her up hard to his every thrust.

"Hurry," he breathed, raising his head. "I can't wait much longer." His expression was blissful agony, his nostrils flared as his thrusting hips grew more forceful with every movement.

Suddenly the tension broke and she surged upward convulsively.

Grady cried out and clutched her against him.

Spent and limp, Storm lay unmoving as Grady lifted himself from her and sank down on the bed beside her. His breath was still coming harsh and quick, his black hair tousled, making him appear amazingly young and vulnerable.

Storm's hand slid across her belly where her baby lay sheltered in her womb. The slight bulge beneath her fingertips reminded her that she hadn't told Grady yet about their child. She wasn't quite ready for that, she decided as she deliberately reached down and pulled the sheet over her nakedness. Grady still hadn't proved to her that he was finished with violence. For all she knew he would still participate in gunfights with men who came to Guthrie to challenge him. Once he learned she was carrying his child she would be forced to return with him to Oklahoma. Both Blade and Shannon had promised they wouldn't tell Grady about her pregnancy until she was ready, and she hoped they intended to keep their word.

"Have I convinced you to return with me to the homestead? We need each other, Storm."

"Will Laughing Brook accompany us back to Oklahoma?"

"I've given my word. I will personally return her to the reservation. I thought we'd take Laughing Brook to the reservation first before returning home. I wouldn't feel right sending her alone."

"Can't one of your father's men take her home? Or Soars-Like-An-Eagle?"

379

"Laughing Brook is my problem, not my father's. She'll go with us."

"Then I'm not going with you," Storm said.

Grady took one look at her stubborn, jutting chin and sighed in exasperation. Though he was weary of Laughing Brook's constant attempts at seduction, he was determined to resist Storm's unreasonable jealousy and demands. He felt strongly that Storm should be the one to make amends, for she was the one who had left him, not the other way around.

"When Tim and I leave Peaceful Valley both you and Laughing Brook will accompany us. We'll travel by wagon this time. The trails are safe enough for overland travel and the weather at this time of the year is good."

Storm deliberately turned her back on Grady, refusing to give him the satisfaction of seeing how hurt she was by his stubborn refusal to bow to her wishes.

"How do I know you won't meet someone along the way who's out to prove he's a better gunman than the infamous Renegade? What assurance do I have that a gunman isn't waiting for you in Guthrie, itching to prove he's a faster draw than you are?"

"You have no assurance," Grady said quietly. "Neither do I. You'll just have to accept my word that I will only draw to defend myself. Look at me, Storm." He turned her around to face him. "A man who refuses to defend himself winds up dead. What am I supposed to do when a man challenges me?"

Storm stared at him for the space of a heartbeat, her eyes as bleak as her heart. "I don't want to go through life wondering when someone from your past will show up and disrupt our lives. I deserve better. Your son deserves better."

"Sooner or later someone faster on the draw than I will emerge to take my place and I'll be forgotten. Meanwhile, we go on as before, living our lives on our homestead with our children. You do want children, don't you?"

Storm hesitated, trying to decide whether she should tell Grady about the baby. She was silent so long, Grady thought she couldn't bear the thought of having his child. Anger overrode his better judgment as he flung himself from the bed.

"Perhaps Laughing Brook would like to have my child," he flung out carelessly. "Most wives are overjoyed to bear their husband's children."

Storm sucked in a scalding breath. "I'm not a brood mare. And furthermore, I'm not like other women."

"Damn you, Storm! Damn you to hell! Wouldn't it be ironic if I just planted a baby in you? You'd have little to say in the matter if a baby was growing in you right now." Suddenly a devious smile curved his lips and Storm shuddered at the coldness of the gesture. "If you *are* carrying my child, you'll have to return with me to Oklahoma."

By the time Storm found her voice Grady had flung on his clothes and stormed from the room. She lay there in silence, mulling over his words and what they implied. Since they had never talked about children, she had no idea how strongly he felt on the matter. Obviously he didn't want Tim to be an only child. She knew Summer Sky had been pregnant with their second child when she was killed, but she certainly didn't intend to breed year after year until she was a worn-out shell of a woman. Grady's mother obviously hadn't been overburdened with children, and Blade didn't seem to mind.

Grady went in search of his father immediately after he left Storm. When he had arrived earlier Blade had been out on the range. He found Blade in his study, waiting for him. When he entered the small room that smelled of leather and tobacco, poignant childhood memories came rushing back to him. He had spent many a happy hour with his father in this room, learning how to balance the ledgers and run the ranch. Blade stood up the moment Grady entered.

Father and son started at one another, neither moving, each aware of the differences that separated them. Both men were tall, both thickly muscled and broad shouldered. Grady was as darkly handsome as Blade, possessing the same bronze skin, midnight black hair, and proud bearing. Of the two, Grady more closely resembled their Indian forebears, with his fierce expression and stark features. Blade was the first to speak.

"Welcome home, son. I've waited a long time for this day." He held out his arms in open welcome.

Grady hesitated a moment, then rushed forward, returning his father's bear hug and pounding him on the back. He was so choked with emotion all he could say was, "I'm sorry."

"We've missed you."

Grady held Blade at arm's length, staring into his eyes. "I had to leave, Dad. I was bitter, disillusioned, and too immature to accept the terrible blow fate had dealt me."

"You were a youth when you left, Grady, and now you're a man. The years may not have been kind to you, but you've learned lessons I couldn't have taught you had you remained at Peaceful Valley."

"Can you and Mother forgive me for my neglect? And—I've done things you might not want to forgive me for. The kind of life I've led since leaving the ranch would shame you and Mother."

"I know everything—or nearly everything," Blade said quietly. "We're not so isolated out here that we didn't hear about the renegade Indian who fought against oppression on the western plains."

"The People call me Thunder."

"Jumping Buffalo has already told me. Returning to the People and learning their ways was a bold and brave thing to do. It made a man of you. We won't speak of the other

383

because I hope you've given up that kind of life now that you have a wife and home of your own."

"I suspected you've kept in touch with Jumping Buffalo. I shouldn't have hurt you and Mother by taking Tim away."

"He's back now," Blade said simply. "I'm proud of you for the way you've taken hold of your life once again. Storm has told me so much about your homestead. It pleases me, though it would please me more if you came back to the ranch and took your rightful place here at my side. This will all be yours one day, you know. Dawn's husband has no desire to live away from San Francisco, and Spring writes that her future husband has a thriving law practice in Boise. What will happen to Peaceful Valley if you return to Oklahoma?"

"You'll be here many years yet, Dad, keeping tight rein on the ranch. Though I love the place, it isn't mine as the Oklahoma homestead is mine. I won that piece of land in a grueling race and earned the right to settle there. It's all mine, just like this ranch is yours and Mother's. If you must leave it to someone, leave it to Tim. He'll appreciate it when he's older. The homestead will be my legacy to any children Storm and I have together. If there are children," he added darkly.

Blade searched Grady's face, suddenly aware that Storm hadn't told Grady that she was carrying his child. He knew there had been ample time for Storm to tell him while they were alone upstairs, for Shannon had told him Grady had gone to Storm's room immediately. He speculated a moment on Storm's reluctance to reveal her pregnancy to Grady, but shrugged off his inclination to tell Grady himself. It was best, he decided, to let them work out their problems in their own way.

"I'm sure there will be children," Blade offered. "Your mother mentioned that Laughing Brook destroyed the note that Storm wrote to you before she left. Has that all been settled between you?"

"Storm is too stubborn to listen to reason." Grady's voice was harsh with exasperation.

"Your mother and I have become very fond of Storm. She has a deathly fear of violence, and with good reason."

"What has Storm told you about her first husband?" Grady asked curiously.

"Only that he was killed accidentally. You and Storm have a lot in common."

Grady made a harsh sound deep in his throat. "I don't think Storm will ever forgive me for the death of her husband. You see, I was involved in a gunfight and a stray bullet hit him. Buddy was the great love of her life. She married me because she needed a home, and I needed a home for Tim."

Blade knew differently, but wisely kept his counsel. "What about Laughing Brook? Why is she still with you?"

"She was ready to return to the reservation

when I was wounded. When Storm left so abruptly Laughing Brook stayed to care for Tim."

"You didn't ask Storm to leave?" Blade asked sharply.

Grady looked disgruntled. "Is that what she told you? I certainly would recall if I asked her to leave. No, Dad, just the opposite is true. I begged her to stay."

"Perhaps neither of you recall what was said," Blade suggested. "It was a very trying time. If I were you, I'd concentrate on finding a way to make your marriage work. A good start would be sending Laughing Brook back to the reservation."

"Laughing Brook is my responsibility." The tautening of his jaw gave Blade an indication of Grady's stubbornness on the subject of Laughing Brook. "I'll do as I see fit. Storm left me; she is in no position to make demands."

Blade wanted to shake his stubborn son until his teeth rattled. Grady reminded him of himself when he was that age. But thank God he had more good sense than his hotheaded son displayed. "Don't be too hard on Storm, Grady. Do you love her?"

"I—love is a strong emotion. After losing Summer Sky I didn't think I was capable of loving again. Storm is Summer Sky's complete opposite.

"Either you love Storm or you don't. If you don't, then I see little hope for your marriage."

\*     \*     \*

Grady decided to occupy another room that night—and the night after that. He knew Storm was still angry, her feelings confused where he was concerned. He also knew that if he slept in the same bed with her nothing could keep him from making love to her. Blade's words had been prophetic. Without love on both sides there was little hope for their marriage. Did Storm love him as much as he loved her or did Buddy's ghost intrude upon their happiness? Did Storm love him enough to have his children?

Grady knew that Laughing Brook had deliberately hidden Storm's letter. Had she done other things to cause trouble? Why was he being so damn unreasonable about Laughing Brook? he wondered. He supposed he really should send her back to the reservation with one of his father's men, but he had promised Jumping Buffalo he would bring his only surviving child safely back home when Tim no longer needed her. Why couldn't Storm understand that his honor would be damaged if he failed to keep his word?

Storm had much to think about during those days. Seeing Grady again, making love with him, had proved indisputably that she couldn't live without him. Besides, she knew now that Grady was telling the truth about the letter she wrote and left for him, that Laughing Brook had hidden it to keep him from following her. After careful thought she decided that he had a right to know she was carrying his child. Perhaps she had misunderstood him when he told her to leave. He was still groggy from surgery and could scarcely speak coherently.

But now that she was prepared to tell Grady about the baby and admit that a misunderstanding had occurred, Grady seemed to be avoiding her. He must be using another bedroom in the sprawling house, she thought wistfully, for he certainly wasn't sleeping with her.

One day Shannon found Storm alone in the parlor, looking as if she'd lost her best friend. "Is something wrong, Storm?" Her concern gave Storm a warm feeling. She had come to care deeply for Blade and Shannon. "You're not ill, are you?"

Storm shook her head. "No, not ill, just confused. Grady and I seem to be growing farther apart. When he isn't avoiding me he is out with Blade somewhere on your endless acres. I haven't had a conversation with him since—since the day he arrived."

"I take it, then, that you haven't told him about the baby."

"No, but I intended to before he made himself scarce. I don't think he wants me anymore. I'm not even sure he ever did."

Shannon smiled warmly. "Believe me, dear, Grady wants you. I'm his mother and I should know. Expectant mothers often feel neglected. Are you still ill in the mornings?"

"No, that passed before Grady arrived."

"Would you like to help me in the kitchen

today? I thought I'd make Grady's favorite meal and Tim's favorite dessert."

"I'd love to." They went off arm in arm, unaware of Laughing Brook, who stood out of sight in the passageway between kitchen and parlor. She had arrived just in time to hear Shannon's words about Storm being an expectant mother.

Seething angrily, Laughing Brook stormed from the house. She saw Grady entering the stable and hurried after him. She had to know exactly how he felt about becoming a father again. Knowing Grady as she did, she assumed he would be pleased, but she wanted to hear for herself that he and Storm had reconciled. If he wasn't pleased about the coming child, then there was still hope for her.

Grady was at the end of his tether. He was ready to shout to the world that he loved Storm, but he wasn't sure she was ready to hear it. For the past several days he had all but ignored her, allowing her time to sort through her feelings. The simple truth was that he loved Storm and couldn't live without her. He intended to do all in his power to make her love him as much as she had loved Buddy. He was so engrossed in his thoughts, he didn't hear Laughing Brook enter the stable. The crunch of her moccasins on the fresh hay was his first indication that he wasn't alone. Laughing Brook touched his elbow and he whirled to face her.

"Laughing Brook! What are you doing here? Are you looking for Soars-Like-An-Eagle?"

Grady was aware of Soars-Like-An-Eagle's tender feelings for Laughing Brook and wondered why the young brave wasn't more forceful with her. She needed a strong hand to tame her.

"It is you I wish to speak to, Thunder. We have not been alone since we reached Peaceful Valley."

Grady sucked in a quick breath. He sincerely hoped Laughing Brook wasn't going to attempt another seduction. He was getting damn tired of it. "I'm busy, Laughing Brook. What is it you wanted?"

Her eyes luminous, she clutched desperately at his arm. "I don't want to go back to the reservation. I want to stay with you and Tim."

"That's not possible," Grady said. "There is room for only one woman in my house and that woman is Storm. She's my wife."

Laughing Brook was growing desperate. "I will be your second wife."

"I only need one wife." Perhaps if he repeated it often enough she would get the message.

"Is it because Storm is carrying your child? Is that why you are willing to take her back?"

Grady went still. "What did you say?"

"Storm will give you weak children. I can give you strong children; sons and daughters like Little Buffalo, with the blood of the People flowing through their veins."

Grady gave her an exasperated shake. "What did you say about Storm? What makes you think she is carrying my child?"

Laughing Brook saw her mistake instantly.

She suddenly realized that Grady hadn't been told about the child. He gripped her arms so tightly she winced, fearing he wouldn't let her go until she answered his question.

"Do you hear me, Laughing Brook? Who told you Storm was pregnant?"

"I heard her talking with your mother," Storm said with marked reluctance.

"Are you certain? Absolutely certain?" His fingers bit cruelly into the soft flesh of her upper arms.

"Yes! I know what I heard."

A string of curses spewed from Grady's mouth. Without another word he flung her away and strode out the door. The taut set of jaw and brusque, jerky steps gave a hint of his great anger. Laughing Brook breathed a sigh of relief and sank down on a bale of hay when she realized that his anger wasn't directed at her, as she had assumed.

Laughing Brook started violently as Soars-Like-An-Eagle stepped from the shadows. "Why do you shame yourself with Thunder? Offering yourself to a man who does not want you brings you no honor."

"Where did you come from? Were you spying on me?"

"I was not spying. My work often takes me to the stable."

"I suppose you heard everything."

"Enough to know that Thunder cannot be seduced. A fool can see that Thunder loves his wife. Why do you continue to badger him?

When we are joined I will be the only man in your life."

"I will marry no one but Thunder."

"Storm carries his child." A dull red crept up Laughing Brook's face. "It is time you learned that I will be your husband. I have allowed you to have your own way in hope that you would get over your infatuation with Thunder. Your father has already given me permission to join with you. I will take you back to the reservation myself, where we will be joined according to the rites of the People."

"You spout foolishness," Laughing Brook scoffed, turning away.

Soar-Like-An-Eagle's face grew dark as he swung her around to face him. "I speak the truth. You have been spoiled shamelessly by your family and need a strong hand to rule you. Swift Blade has offered me a permanent position on the ranch and I have accepted. He is pleased with my way with horses and my hard work. We will have a good life, Laughing Brook. Peaceful Valley is a healthy place in which to raise our children."

"I will have no children by you."

She peered timidly at Soars-Like-An-Eagle through a curtain of long sooty lashes. His forceful manner both surprised and thrilled her. It was true he was handsome, perhaps every bit as handsome as Thunder, but he had never been particularly aggressive or forceful before. Suddenly she saw him in a new light. Tall and solidly built, his hawkish features and high cheekbones bore evidence of his proud heritage. He was a fierce warrior even though he had chosen a different path from Thunder.

"I have been too lenient," Soars-Like-An-Eagle said as he planted his feet solidly before Laughing Brook. Grasping her arms, he pulled her roughly to her feet. "You are mine," he said fiercely. "If I didn't know Thunder was an honorable man, I would never have allowed you to accompany him to his homestead."

His black eyes glittered as he lowered his head and with slow relish placed his lips on the exact spot where her shoulder met her neck.

She tried to pull away. Soars-Like-An-Eagle could feel her tension, the flutter of her pulse beneath his lips, the feverish warmth of her skin, and his heart soared. It pleased him to know that Laughing Brook wasn't as immune to him as she'd like him to believe.

"Do you like that, little one?"

"No! Not from you," Laughing Brook denied in a voice not quite believable.

Soars-Like-An-Eagle laughed. "What about this?" His lips roamed upward, dancing across her throat, her cheek, before pressing against her mouth with firm insistence.

It was Laughing Brook's first real kiss, and she groaned in response to the magic touch of his warm lips against hers. Liquid fire surged through her veins, and Laughing Brook forgot for a moment that it was Soars-Like-An-Eagle and not Thunder who was kissing her. The kiss seemed to go on forever, until Laughing Brook felt dizzy and her head began to whirl. When he released her she fell back against him, staring up at him with an arrested look on her face, making no effort to move away.

"Laughing Brook," Soars-Like-An-Eagle groaned, "you don't know how long I've waited for this moment. I have loved you for many years. It's been agony waiting for you to grow up."

Laughing Brook swallowed convulsively as she felt his hands on her breasts, touching her where no man had touched her before, and when they slid down to cup her buttocks and pull her close, she felt the hard thrust of his manhood nudge the soft roundness of her stomach.

"You belong to me, little one. From now on you will leave Thunder alone. If you make a fool of yourself over another man again I will beat you. Do you hear me!"

Mutely, Laughing Brook nodded, shocked and enthralled by the change in Soars-Like-An-Eagle. Her eyes grew round as saucers as he swept her up in his arms and carried her to an empty stall, where they would be hidden from view. She gasped aloud when he lowered her to the mound of sweet-smelling hay he had placed there just this morning and dropped to his knees beside her.

# *Chapter Nineteen*

Grady left the stable in a rage, his expression thunderous. How dare Storm keep something as important as having a child from him! he fumed angrily. She'd had plenty of time to tell him he was going to be a father since his arrival. What made his anger even more profound was the fact that she had said nothing when he asked her pointedly if she wanted children. Her silence had led him to believe she didn't want his children. He tried to bring his temper under control before he entered the house, but his jerky steps and murderous expression gave him away.

Shannon took one look at him as he strode through the parlor and felt a sinking sensation in the pit of her stomach. She hurried after him.

"Grady, wait! Has something upset you?"

"Where's Storm, Mother?"

"I sent her upstairs to rest a few minutes ago. Can't it wait?"

"I think not." His face was set in grim lines, his mouth taut.

"Has Storm done something to displease you?"

"You could say that, Mother. Why am I the last to know my wife is carrying my child? You did know, did you not? And I imagine Father knows too."

Shannon blanched. She knew it was wrong of Storm to keep her state of impending motherhood from Grady, but she had expected Storm to inform Grady in her own good time. Obviously Grady had stumbled across the information on his own and was in a rage over being kept deliberately uninformed.

"We knew, son, and Storm would have told you very soon, I'm sure of it. Don't go to her now. Give yourself time to calm down before confronting her."

"I'm sorry, Mother. This can't wait." Turning on his heel, he mounted the stairs.

"If you hurt Storm, I'll never forgive you," Shannon called after him.

Suddenly Grady went still. He turned slowly and faced his mother. "I've given you little reason to be proud of me these last few years, Mother, but I would never stoop to abusing a woman." Then he turned and continued up the stairs.

Alone in her room, Storm had taken off her dress and petticoat and stretched out on the bed. She did seem to tire more easily these days, and the afternoon heat was oppressive. The sheets were cool against her cheek and she closed her eyes. But no matter how hard she tried to drift off to sleep, thoughts of Grady kept intruding. If he continued to avoid her, she would have to track him down and tell him about their child. Soon no one would be able to mistake her condition.

Her stomach was no longer flat. A little bulge protruded where once she had been slightly concave. Her breasts were larger than she could ever remember them being, and somewhat tender to the touch. But it was her narrow waist where the most noticeable difference lay. It was at least two inches thicker than it had been before her pregnancy, and she had already let out the seams in her dresses. She knew if she and Grady had been on intimate terms these past days he would have noticed the changes immediately.

As if just thinking of him had conjured him up, the door flew open and Grady stepped into the room. She didn't notice his glowering expression as she cried out his name in joyful welcome. It wasn't until he slammed the door behind him and stomped toward the bed that she knew something was amiss.

"What is it, Grady? Are you angry about something?"

"You could say that."

"Do you want to tell me about it?"

"Oh, I'll tell you, all right. But first, take off your clothes."

"What?"

"You heard me. Take off your clothes—all of them."

Storm's mouth went dry. "If you want to make love, you have only to ask. What's wrong? I've never seen you like this before."

"I've never been this angry before. Are you going to take off your clothes or must I do it for you?"

A tremor of fear snaked down Storm's spine. She had a good idea what had angered Grady. She took her time removing her underwear, stockings, and shift. When she lay naked and vulnerable to his penetrating gaze she glanced up at Grady, taking heart when she saw something flicker in his eyes. But it quickly passed, replaced by simmering anger. She started violently when he bent down and placed a large callused hand on the swelling beneath her ribcage.

"Why didn't you tell me? Hearing that I'm to become a father in a roundabout way makes me furious."

"I wanted to tell you. I truly intended to tell you."

"When? After I discovered it for myself?"

"If you hadn't been avoiding me, I would have told you days ago." Her voice was rising steadily. How dare he direct his anger at her when she was guilty of nothing. She would have told him in her own good time.

"When am I to be a father?" he asked in a voice far too calm for her liking. She feared his icy contempt more than she feared his anger.

"In six months."

"I see. And what would you have done if I had gone back to Oklahoma alone as you insisted?"

Storm's chin jutted out at a stubborn angle. "I would have survived." Suddenly she flung his hand aside and jerked upright. "And get your hands off me. I won't let you intimidate me. You might frighten big bad gunslingers, but you don't frighten me."

Grady rocked back on his heels, shaken by Storm's words. Good Lord, had he sunken so low that he resorted to intimidating pregnant women? "I'm not trying to frighten you, Storm," he said more reasonably. "I just want to know why you saw fit to keep your pregnancy a secret from me. Did you think I wouldn't want our child?"

"I didn't know what to think," Storm admitted shakily. "I told you before, I thought you no longer wanted me in your life. When you showed up at Peaceful Valley with Laughing Brook I assumed you preferred her to me. Telling you about our baby would have only complicated matters."

"For the last time, I never told you to leave. What you thought you heard wasn't what I said. I was wounded and helpless when you left. Laughing Brook stayed to care for me and

Tim. I've always wanted you, Storm. Grandfather Spirit predicted long before I knew you that I must meet and conquer the Storm before I would find peace. I believe the Storm he spoke of was you. He also said Thunder can exist only in the bosom of Storm."

"I don't understand," Storm said softly. A glimmer of hope soared in her heart, but she desperately wanted to hear Grady say the words. She had waited so long.

"I think you do, lady," Grady admitted in a rare moment of confidence. He dropped to the bed beside her, his voice harsh with emotion. "I know I can never take the place of Buddy, but dammit, Storm, I love you. I know your first husband was special to you, just as Summer Sky was special to me. But since I met you I've come to realize that Summer Sky was the love of my youth. You're the love of my life."

Storm was so shocked by Grady's admission, her voice froze in her throat. Grady loved her! Truly loved her.

"You don't know how sorry I am that I had a hand in Buddy's death. If I could bring him back I would."

"Stop!" Getting to her knees, Storm threw herself at Grady. He opened his arms and brought her against his heart. "What's done is done. Of course I loved Buddy. He was the only man I ever really knew, the friend and companion of my childhood. But we had such a short time together as man and wife that I never really had a chance to know him as a lover."

"I want to be everything to you, lady. Husband, friend, lover."

"Are you sure, Grady, absolutely certain it's me you want and not the baby I carry?"

"I've never been more certain of anything in my life."

"What about the violence? Can you give up the violence you've lived with these past years? I couldn't bear to lose you, Grady. I love you too much."

Grady's heart nearly burst with happiness. It was the first time Storm had admitted she loved him. "If I wanted a life filled with violence, I wouldn't have made the run for land in Guthrie. I can't help what other men do, but I promise I'll not instigate another violent act. Just tell me you're happy about the baby."

Looping her arms around his neck, she kissed his nose, his chin, his mouth, anyplace her lips could reach. "I love the babe you put inside me, almost as much as I love his father—or her father." Storm giggled. "I hope you're planning on a daughter or two."

Grady grinned in genuine pleasure. "At least. And I want to get you home before travel becomes difficult for you. But don't think I'm letting you off the hook. From now on there will be only truth between us. I'm still unhappy about finding out about your pregnancy from someone other than my own wife." He tried to sound stern, but it was extremely difficult with Storm sitting on his lap naked as the day she was born.

"Grady, about Laughing Brook—"

"I don't want to talk about Laughing Brook. I'm taking her back to the reservation where she can't interfere in our lives again. But most of all, lady, I want to make love to you. I've been living in hell these past few days."

"The door to my room wasn't locked," Storm argued. "You could have come in any time you pleased."

"I had some decisions to make that weren't easy. After Summer Sky's death I was afraid of loving again. Losing someone you love is too painful; it was easier to harden my heart against every emotion except rage and revenge. After searching my soul I discovered I *could* love again, if the woman was you. For the first time in years my soul is truly at peace. Wakantanka was right. You are my peace."

Storm's eyes grew misty and the lump in her throat prevented her from coherent speech. Instead, she burrowed deeper into his arms and sighed in utter contentment.

Grady groaned deeply as the tension of passion swept through him. Storm's body was warm and flushed and so damn tempting that the need to make love to her was like a fire in his blood. His mouth ground against hers as he pressed her onto her back. His tongue trust deeply, tasting her, demanding that she return his hunger in kind. His lips brushed her closed lids, the curve of her cheekbones, the tender arch of her neck. He lowered his head and suckled her breasts, lashing the dusky nipples with the rough, wet edge of his tongue until he wrung a cry of pleasure from her lips.

She moved against him in sinuous response as she tugged his shirt from his pants, urging him out of his clothes. He complied instantly, tossing them aside while she watched through heavy lids. When he was naked she pulled him down and ran her hands across the hard planes of his back, tracing the knobby ridges of his spine, then up again to smooth the taut cords of his neck.

"Oh, lady, I love it when you touch me. God, your hands . . ." The heel of her hand came down to rest against his stomach, and her fingers caressed his rigid member. He sucked in a ragged breath.

Fearing he would lose control, Grady reluctantly stilled her, but she continued to explore his flesh. Wherever the tips of her fingers touched, his skin seemed to jump in response. In self-defense he nudged her legs apart and slipped his hand between her thighs. He heard her soft intake of breath as he began to stroke her. When his fingers penetrated her she knew a moment of raw pleasure. When his mouth replaced his hand, Storm simply ceased breathing. She made a feeble protest, but it went unheeded as Grady's tongue lashed deliciously at the dewy petals opening to him like a flower to the morning sun.

Intense rapture simmered through her, making her lightheaded as she floated on a fluffy cloud of incredible sensation. She was no longer flesh and blood but a spirit with no substance, existing on a high plane of physical awareness. When Grady's first thrust filled her, her body responded, tightening around him, memorizing the shape and size of him. She raised her eyes and found him staring at her. His face was stark and intense, his eyes dark with fierce passion. Tension pulled his cheeks taut, making the hallows beneath more pronounced, his mouth nearly grim with purpose. She closed her eyes.

"No," he said fiercely. "Look at me. I want you to know what you do to me." His thrusts grew more rapid.

Storm was panting now, nearly senseless with the need to reach completion as she tilted her hips and thrust against him, meeting his frantic strokes with the frenzy of her own. Her eyes remained open. Not just because Grady had asked her to look at him, but because the stark beauty of his face and the raw passion in his expression held her enthralled. She wanted to savor the moment as her climax began, rising up from somewhere deep inside her. Grady's mouth slanted across hers, swallowing her cry as his seed flooded her.

Flushed and perspiring, Grady remained embedded in Storm as the last shiver of pleasure coursed through him. His skin was so sensitive, he could have sworn white-hot sparks were dancing along his nerve endings. After several long minutes of silence their breathing eased and their heartbeats slowed to a dull pounding. Grady shifted his weight and lay beside her. "I didn't hurt you, did I?"

"I didn't notice." Storm sighed dreamily. "I never knew loving could be so wonderful."

"With the right person it is."

"I loved Buddy, but—well, I never felt such profound rapture with him as I do with you. I used to feel guilty about it, but no longer. I loved Buddy in a completely different way."

"Storm."

"Ummm?"

Grady turned on his back, pulling Storm atop him. Her hair fell like a bright curtain about her face and shoulders. His hands grazed her breasts. "Are you tired?"

Storm grinned impishly. "What do you have in mind?"

"I want you again. This time you ride me." He grasped her hips, urging her upward with the firm pressure of his hands. "Take me and put me inside you." He almost exploded when she held him, guiding him into her. "Do whatever you want."

She moved experimentally, and Grady followed. She leaned over, offering him her breasts. He took one nipple into his mouth, suckling with tortuous urgency. The exquisite pleasure mounted as he kneaded her breasts and thrust against her. His mouth whispered against hers, repeating her name as hot, sweet passion built inside him. His hands glided over her breasts and down her stomach until they rested at the place of their joining. When he

405

massaged the tiny, sensitive button nestled at the juncture of her thighs, Storm arched her spine, threw back her head, and cried out in sheer joy. Grady bucked beneath her and found his own release.

Still panting, Storm raised herself and fell down beside him. If she wasn't tired before, she was utterly exhausted now.

"I need a bath," she said, wrinkling her nose. "I smell like I've been—"

"—Making love. You smell wonderful."

"You're incorrigible. I don't know how I'm going to put up with you for the next hundred years or so."

"Oh, lady," Grady groaned, pulling her close. "If we keep this up, I'll be worn out after the first fifty years. Go to sleep, sweetheart. I'll wake you in time for supper."

Grady was surprised to see Shannon pacing at the bottom of the stairs when he left the bedroom a short time later. "Mother, are you still here?"

"I couldn't leave," Shannon said, searching Grady's face for a hint of what had happened upstairs. "I thought—that is—what if Storm needed me?"

Grady smiled, placing an arm around his mother's narrow shoulders. "I told you I wouldn't hurt Storm. I love her too much to harm her."

Shannon clapped her hands together. "Oh, Grady, do you mean it? I was so worried. I know you were angry, but I feel certain Storm would have told you about the baby soon. Are you happy? It's time Tim had a brother or sister."

"Yes, Mother, I'm happy. And since you've waited you may as well know that Storm and I have settled our differences. We'll be leaving soon, before travel becomes dangerous for her in her condition. I also have wheat fields waiting to be harvested and a farm to run."

"You know your father and I would love for you to stay on at Peaceful Valley." Grady opened his mouth to speak. "No, don't say anything. I know how you feel about your homestead. Blade and I felt the same about Peaceful Valley when we first settled here. As long as we keep in touch, I'll be content."

"I'll never shut you or Dad out of my life again," Grady vowed sincerely. "And I want you to visit us when the baby is born. Storm will need you."

"I'll be there, son, you can count on it."


Grady made plans for their departure. Though Storm would miss Shannon and Blade, she was ecstatic about returning to the homestead to await the birth of her child. The one discordant note was Laughing Brook. Storm still hated the thought of the beautiful Indian maiden traveling with them, even if it was for a short time. Fortunately that problem was resolved when Soars-Like-An-Eagle and Laughing Brook approached Grady two days before their departure.

Soars-Like-An-Eagle's handsome face wore a smug smile when he announced, "Laughing Brook will not join you when you leave Peaceful Valley."

Grady slanted him a startled look. "Of course she will. I'm taking her back to the reservation."

"No, you do not understand, Thunder. Laughing Brook is no longer your responsibility. It is my duty to see that she gets home safely."

Grady's puzzled glance shifted to Laughing Brook, who stood slightly behind Soars-Like-An-Eagle, her eyes downcast. "What's this all about, Laughing Brook? What is Soars-Like-An-Eagle talking about?"

"Laughing Brook has promised to join with me," Soars-Like-An-Eagle said before Laughing Brook could reply. "When we reach the reservation we will be joined according to the rites of the People. When I return to Peaceful Valley she will accompany me. Swift Blade has promised to hold my job for me until my return and has offered us the house Jumping Buffalo and Sweet Grass once occupied. I am most pleased with his generous offer."

"Well, I'll be damned," Grady said wonderingly. He speculated on what Soars-Like-An-Eagle had done to wrought such a change in Laughing Brook. Then he looked into Soars-Like-An-Eagle's eyes and recognized the proud gleam of possession, and the mystery was solved. He would have advised Soars-Like-An-Eagle to bed the little hellion long ago if it meant getting her off his back. "Is this what you want, Laughing Brook?"

Laughing Brook looked up at Soars-Like-An-Eagle with a sensuality Grady had never noticed in her before. Her lids were heavy, her lips slightly swollen, her face flushed. Having been awakened to sexual pleasure, she couldn't keep the look of contentment from her eyes or turn her gaze from the man who had satisfied her so completely. Since that first time in the stable they had made love as often as they dared, and each time was better than the last. Laughing Brook had no idea Soars-Like-An-Eagle was a man of such fire and passion. So masterful, so powerful a lover! Why hadn't she noticed it before?

"It is what I desire above all things, Thunder," Laughing Brook said shyly.

"Then so be it," Grady said, relieved to be spared the burden of returning the girl to the reservation. "I trust Soars-Like-An-Eagle to return you home safely."

"I will guard her with my life." Soars-Like-An-Eagle's promise was pronounced with such passion Grady knew he had nothing to worry about. "She may already be with child."

If Soars-Like-An-Eagle's words shocked Grady, he gave no sign of it. Despite all the problems the girl had caused him and Storm, Grady felt that Laughing Brook would make a wonderful wife and mother to Soars-Like-An-Eagle's children. He was glad they would live at Peaceful Valley instead of on the reservation, where survival was a constant struggle.

Storm was ecstatic when she heard about Laughing Brook and Soars-Like-An-Eagle. Nothing stood in the way now of attaining the kind of happiness she had always dreamed about. She wasn't going to delve into the method Soars-Like-An-Eagle used to convince Laughing Brook that he was the man for her, but she'd be forever grateful to the young brave. And since they no longer had to make a detour to the reservation they could ride in comfort to Guthrie on the train.

Shannon and Blade accompanied them to the train station two days later. It was a sad parting, but one filled with renewed hope for the future. Grady was no longer a renegade Indian obsessed with revenge. Nor was he the mysterious drifter who hated white men and used his guns to prove it. He was Grady Stryker. Husband, father, farmer.

Tim was excited as the train approached Guthrie. But not as excited as Storm. Since their marriage she and Grady hadn't been alone more than a few days. She looked forward with relish to her own household, with just Grady and Tim to occupy her days and nights. And the new baby, when it came, would make their life complete.

The train traveled through land lush with ripening wheat, and Grady hoped his own acres were faring half as well. The golden stalks appeared to be reaching out to the sun, their heads bobbing in the breeze. In a very short time he could begin harvesting. If this year's crop was as good as expected, he'd soon be able to build Storm the kind of house she deserved. Grady couldn't recall when he'd been so happy.

"We're here!" Tim cried as the train pulled into the station in Guthrie only an hour behind schedule. Grady had been gone but two weeks, but Storm had been away over two months, and in that short time things had changed. There were several new businesses in town, a new church, and three new saloons.

"I left the wagon at the livery," Grady said as they joined the passengers leaving the train. "We'll stop for supplies first, then head out to the homestead. I hope the Martins fared well in my absence."

"They're the people you left in charge, aren't they?" Storm asked curiously. Grady had told her how lucky he considered himself to find someone trustworthy to take care of things in his absence.

"Yes, Mabel and her son Clem. They were forced to sell their own homestead when the elder Martin died. I'd like to ask them to stay on and help out, but our house is too small to shelter two more people. They spoke of opening a business in town, but I got the feeling their hearts were set on farming."

"Perhaps something can be worked out," Storm mused thoughtfully.

After two stops, one at the general store and the other at the bank, Grady aimed the wagon toward the homestead. When they reached the outer borders of their land his heart swelled with pride at the sight of tall stalks of wheat bending in the gentle breeze. He hadn't been able to plant all his and Storm's combined acres, but enough had been cultivated to assure them a good yield. And as added protection for their investment, there were still Storm's cattle to fall back on if the crop, for some unforeseen reason, failed. But from the looks of the healthy plants there would be no reason for failure.

Grady had sent a telegram ahead giving the date and approximate time they could be expected, and Mabel Martin had cooked a veritable feast in honor of their return. While Grady, Tim, and Storm devoured the meal, Clem and Mabel packed their belongings. Storm thought she saw a lingering sadness when Mabel looked around the snug cabin one last time.

"You've done a wonderful job looking after the farm, Mrs. Martin," Storm said sincerely. "Grady was lucky to have found you and your son."

"Please call me Mabel. It was a pleasure, Mrs. Stryker. Farming is really all we know, but when Hal died we had no money to support our farm. Clem worked hard, but our land isn't as good as yours, and he wasn't able to cultivate enough acres to make us a living. We sold out to a speculator for half what the land was worth. I'd give anything if we had a place like this," Mabel added wistfully.

"I have a suggestion," Grady offered. "As you know, Storm homesteaded the quarter section of land adjacent to mine before we were married. Her cabin was burned down by hired gunmen, but the well is still intact. I could rent part of the acreage to you and Clem, and as payment Clem could work for me part time and you could help out Storm, since she's expecting our first child. The only drawback is the lack of living quarters."

Mabel's brown eyes glowed with excitement as she mulled over Grady's offer. "What do you think, son?" she asked as Clem came up to stand beside her. Clem was a big, strong lad of seventeen who had plenty of brawn but lacked direction. That was one of the reasons they'd had to sell their farm. The boy needed someone to tell him what to do.

"It's better than living in town, Ma," Clem said. "I don't think I'd make a good shopkeeper. I'm not even sure we could afford to start a business with the money we got for the homestead. But we do have enough money to build a cabin if we rent land from Grady," Clem added, warming to the subject.

"It would be wonderful having another woman close by," Storm said, her eyes shining. Leave it to Grady to come up with a solution that served everyone concerned.

"Then it's settled," Mabel said, offering her hand to Grady to seal the deal.

"Take the wagon back to town," Grady offered. "I'll help build your cabin when you

413

return with the material. Your help on the farm will be welcome, Clem. From the looks of the wheat, it will be ready for harvesting in a few days."

Storm couldn't recall when she'd been so content. Grady and Clem had worked tirelessly to erect the large, one-room cabin that would shelter the Martins. When it was completed Clem drove the wagon to town to pick up their furnishings, which had been stored in an empty warehouse after they moved from their homestead. Storm helped Mabel sew curtains. Mabel was thrilled with the results and expressed her gratitude for being given the opportunity to live where she and Clem would be happy doing the kind of work they enjoyed.

A couple of days later Grady went to town and returned the proud owner of a combine. Storm was dismayed, realizing that such a machine must be terribly expensive.

"Grady, where did you get the money to purchase such a machine," Storm asked, eyeing the contraption with a hint of misgiving. "Did you borrow the money from your father?"

"I didn't pay for it yet, sweetheart. I borrowed the money from the bank on the strength of our crop. It's done all the time. I'll pay for it when I sell our wheat."

"What if something happens to the crop?" Storm asked worriedly.

"Nothing is going to happen, sweetheart," Grady said, pulling her into his arms. "How is the baby today?" His hand rested on the bulge of her stomach, then slid upward to graze her breast.

"Grady Stryker, don't change the subject!" Storm said, slapping his hand aside. "The baby is getting bigger every day, as you well know."

"Where is Tim?" Grady asked, looking around for his son.

"He's helping Clem today. Mabel promised to bake him some cookies."

"Are we alone? If we are, I have a wonderful suggestion on how to spend our afternoon." His caress grew more insistent.

Storm laughed. "Grady—" Suddenly she went still, cocking her ear toward a sound she couldn't identify. "What is that?"

Grady heard it too. The sound was distinctive, like a steady drone that grew louder and louder. Then the sun seemed to disappear as the sky darkened. The noise was deafening now, and an enormous cloud blotted out the sun. Only it wasn't a cloud. It was—

"My God! Locusts!"

# Chapter Twenty

Storm stared at the ominous sky with growing apprehension. She had heard of locusts, but she wasn't aware that they appeared in great hordes of tens of thousands, winging across the sky like a harbinger of disaster. When the solid mass of destruction swooped down from the sky toward the ripe stalks of wheat, Storm realized why Grady had become so distraught. Abruptly the droning buzz of insects on the wing changed to a chomping sound produced by scores of insects feasting on their crops.

"Grady, can't we do something? They're eating our wheat!"

Racing to the shed, Grady snatched a wide shovel and ran toward the fields. "I don't know if it will help, but I'm going to kill as many of the bastards as I can."

Feeling helpless, Storm grabbed a broom from the doorstep and followed. She recoiled in horror when she suddenly stood amid thousands of insects relentlessly advancing from stalk to stalk, methodically devouring every grain of wheat in their path. When Grady started wielding the shovel, Storm followed suit. Soon Clem, Mabel, and Tim joined them, using whatever was handy to swat at the voracious insects. But the more they swatted and stomped, the faster they came, until Storm's arms felt like lead, her legs wooden.

She cried out in horror when she felt the grayish-green insects crawling up her dress and clinging to her limbs. They gathered in her hair, skin, and clothing until Storm felt a suffocating blackness steal over her. The breath squeezed from her lungs and she swayed drunkenly. From the corner of his eye Grady saw Storm stagger, and he let out a cry as he flung down the shovel and leaped to her aid. Brushing the insects from her face and clothing, he scooped her up in his arms and raced toward the house.

"Mabel!" he called over his shoulders. "Take Tim inside!" Tim's small body was covered with so many locusts he was barely recognizable.

"Stay inside," Grady said gruffly as he deposited Storm just inside the door. "There's nothing more we can do. When they've destroyed the crops they'll move on to neighboring fields."

"Oh, Grady, I can't bear it!" Storm wailed. "All our crops, everything we've worked so hard for. What will we do?"

"Don't worry, sweetheart, we'll survive somehow," Grady said grimly. Then Mabel arrived with Tim, and Grady left to continue his losing battle with the locusts.

Storm watched from the window, wringing her hands and fretting. How were they to survive with their crop destroyed? It didn't even help to know that all the homesteaders in the area were suffering the same fate. Before the scourge was over not a field for miles around would be left unscathed. No wonder so many homesteaders gave up, selling their land to speculators or losing it outright when taxes came due and no money was available to pay them.

By nightfall the destruction was complete. Around dusk Grady and Clem returned to the house. All they had managed to save was the vegetable garden. Grady's face was grim, his eyes bleak. They sat down to a silent, dismal meal. After the dishes were done the Martins returned home. Storm put Tim to bed while Grady stood in the open doorway, his eyes sweeping across the golden stubble that had once been abundant fields of grain. After she tucked Tim in, Storm joined him.

"How will we survive?" She was thinking of their new baby and the burden another mouth to feed would place on Grady.

"We could sell your land," Grady suggested. "Speculators are buying up large tracts. There is talk that rich deposits of oil lie beneath the surface. Drillers are already predicting success in Texas."

"You can't sell the land—you've just rented part of it to the Martins. They'll be devastated if they have to leave. They've spent the last of their money building their cabin."

"With no crop to harvest, there will be little work for Clem. Thank God for the cattle. I've already been out to check on them and they're prospering. Tomorrow Clem and I will round them up and count the calves. Fortunately, there have been many new births this year. We can sell the older cows to the army and keep the calves and bull. We'll get by, sweetheart, and if we're careful there will be enough left over for seed next year." He turned to smile at her. "If you hadn't insisted on those cattle we'd be in a hell of a mess right now."

"What about the Martins?"

"I'll start paying Clem a small salary in addition to the free rent. I was going to offer him a share of the profits from the wheat, but now he'll have to make do with a salary. There's always the vegetable garden for our immediate needs."

"You could ask your father for help," Storm said. "I know he'd be glad to lend you enough money to get by on until another crop can be planted."

"This is something I have to do myself," Grady said stiffly. "I'd feel less of a man if I couldn't support my family through my own efforts. I'll turn to Dad for help only as a last resort. I'd never let my family starve. Come to bed, sweetheart. I need you tonight. I don't think I've ever needed you more."

Turning into his embrace, they kissed with a need born of desperation. With their mouths still joined, Grady picked her up and carried her into their bedroom. He undressed her slowly and made love to her with such loving tenderness that when he finished there were tears in her eyes.

"I love you so much, Grady," she said on a shaky sigh.

"Oh, lady, you make me feel ten feet tall. I know I'll never measure up to Buddy, but I don't ever want you to have regrets about marrying me."

"Buddy is just a dim memory from my past. You're my life, my love, my future."

Grady hugged her tightly. "I hope I never give you reason to change your mind."

The combine was returned two days later. With the crop destroyed they would have no need of such a machine. Storm knew Grady hated to part with it, but if they had a crop next year they could think about purchasing one then. When Grady returned from Guthrie he was full of news.

"There isn't a field left intact anywhere in the Cherokee Strip. Speculators in town are doing a booming business buying up homesteads from destitute owners. Nat Turner may no longer be around, but other men like him have arrived to take his place. It's a damn shame that good farmers are placed at the mercy of unscrupulous men because of a swarm of locusts. Next year it could be a drought, or excessive rain, or any one of a dozen natural disasters. I tell you, sweetheart, it's a damn miracle any homesteaders survive."

Grady and Clem began the tedious job of rounding up the cattle from the surrounding hills and driving them down to graze on the stubble left behind by the locusts. Grady was overjoyed to find that the herd had nearly doubled in size due to the large number of calves born during the spring and summer. Days later, when he heard that the army was in Guthrie buying cattle for the surrounding forts, he informed Storm that he was going to town to contract with the quartermaster for the sale of their cows. When Storm expressed the need to purchase material for baby clothes, Grady suggested that she accompany him. She eagerly agreed, and they dropped off Tim to spend the day with Mabel and Clem. Before they left Tim begged to spend the night with the Martins, and they gave their permission.

As usual Guthrie was teeming with people. After dropping off Storm at the general store, Grady headed directly to the small office where the army quartermaster was buying cattle for nearby forts. Grady waited in line until it was his turn, and when he finally spoke to Lieutenant Murphy, a deal was struck without too much haggling. Murphy set a time for him to come out to inspect his purchase two days hence, and Grady left feeling he'd accomplished something. Thank God they would have money to see them through the winter. By the time the new baby arrived next spring the fields would be replanted and the cattle thriving.

Storm hadn't finished shopping when Grady arrived at the general store to pick her up so he headed to the nearest saloon. It had been a long time since he'd been in a saloon, and longer still since he'd shared a drink with male companions. He and Storm needed to meet some of the nearby homesteaders, he decided as he entered the smoky interior of the Whistle Stop Saloon, across the street from the general store. He ordered a beer and lounged against the bar while he looked the place over. It didn't look much different from any other saloon he'd visited in frontier towns across the west.

The man standing to his right was deep in conversation with the bartender, so he turned his attention to the man on his left. He was startled to find the man staring intently at him. He looked like a drifter, no different from any of the other nameless, faceless drifters Grady had encountered in saloons just like the Whistle Stop. The drifter was dressed in dusty, rumpled clothes that reeked of the trail. A dark stubble shadowed the lower half of his face and a battered, wide-brimmed hat covered a head of dark, shaggy hair.

"Don't I know you from someplace, mister?" The man's small eyes narrowed thoughtfully as he searched Grady's face.

Grady shrugged, uninterested in continuing the conversation. He'd met scores of men like him before and wanted nothing more to do with them. "Could be." He turned away.

The man wasn't about to be brushed off so easily. "I ain't through talkin' to ya, mister." He placed a hand on Grady's shoulder and turned him around.

Grady stiffened, sensing immediately that the drifter spelled trouble. Would he never be free of his violent past?

"What's yer name, mister? Mine is Darnell. Slade Darnell. I know I seen ya someplace."

"The name's Grady Stryker, and I seriously doubt we've met before. I own a homestead ten miles west of town."

"Homesteader, huh. That's damn interestin'. Didn't know they let half-breeds homestead. Ya sure look like someone I should know."

"Sorry, Darnell, you've got the wrong man. We've never met." He finished his beer in one gulp. "Well, better get going. My wife is waiting for me at the general store. See you around, Darnell."

"Yah, see ya around, Stryker." Grady left the saloon as quickly as possible without seeming to be in a hurry. While Darnell had been talking he had suddenly recalled where they had met.

It was at the Long Branch Saloon in Dodge City, Kansas.

Grady had just paid for the services of a young whore and was accompanying her upstairs when Darnell, drunk and looking for a fight, insisted that he had already engaged her services. Though the whore had said otherwise, Darnell had persisted, until Grady had been forced to throw the man from the saloon. Darnell had picked himself up from the dirt and drawn on Grady. Because Darnell had been drinking, Grady hadn't wanted to kill him, so he had merely winged him in the left arm. When Grady returned downstairs after his romp with the whore, Darnell was gone. Afterward Grady had forgotten all about it. But apparently Darnell had not.

Grady hurried across the street to the general store, where he had left the wagon. He waved and grinned when he saw Storm waiting for him. Her pregnancy was quite noticeable now, and a warm, melting feeling spread upward through his body whenever he looked at her. Which was quite often. He couldn't believe that Wakantanka had given him such happiness. He took the packages from Storm's hands and placed them in the wagon bed. Then he lifted her onto the seat.

"Are you ready to go home, sweetheart?"

"All set. Did you get a good price for the cattle?"

"The army is desperate for cattle to feed the troops through the winter months. The price I received is slightly more than I expected. Some-one will be out to inspect them in a couple of days."

Grady waited until Storm settled comfort-ably on the seat, then started to walk around to the driver's side. He had managed only a few steps when he saw Darnell hurrying across the street toward him. He let loose a few choice words beneath his breath. He wanted to leap onto the wagon and whip the horses into a fine froth, but it was too late. Even as the thought came to him, Darnell was standing before him.

"I recollect who ya are now, Renegade. Yer the hombre what winged me a few months back. I was laid up fer two weeks and had ta pay a doc ta patch me up. I swore I'd make ya pay if we ever crossed paths. Pick yer time and place, Renegade. Right now would suit me jest fine."

"Grady!" Storm's voice rose on a note of panic. This couldn't be happening again. How many times would Grady be forced to defend himself before he'd be left in peace? "Please, tell the man to go away."

Grady's face was stark as he fought his natu-ral inclination to oblige Darnell. But he had promised Storm, and he had every intention of holding to that vow. "You heard my wife, Darnell. Go away. I'm not interested in draw-ing against you."

"Well ain't that too bad." Darnell raked Storm's swollen belly with contempt. "Has the little woman stolen yer guts?"

"Get out of here, Darnell, before I forget I've sworn off violence."

"Sounds ta me like ya turned yellow," Darnell said slyly, seeming to know exactly the right words to goad Grady.

Grady's hands balled into fists and his face grew so red Storm feared he would explode. Slowly his hands inched upward, pausing scant inches above his holstered gun.

"Go ahead, Renegade, I'll even let ya draw first. I ain't drunk this time, and I've been practicin' some. I rode with the Dalton gang fer a spell."

"Grady!" Storm's voice brought Grady abruptly to his senses. It wasn't easy to let a miserable, worthless skunk like Darnell call him a coward and get away with it. He slanted Storm a look filled with regret and apology, then turned back to Darnell.

"This is neither the time nor the place, Darnell. My wife is pregnant and doesn't need the aggravation of seeing me gun you down."

Grady's words brought Storm's world tumbling down around her feet. Did Grady's word mean nothing to him? Why couldn't he just turn and walk away? So what if the man called him a coward? They both knew Grady was no coward and that was all that mattered. Darnell didn't dare shoot Grady in cold blood; the sheriff of Guthrie was a scrupulous peacekeeper and Darnell would surely hang for murder.

"So yer gonna be a papa, ain't that touchin'," Darnell sneered, obviously unmoved by Grady's words. "Name the time and place, Renegade."

Grady thought a moment, then said, "Sundown, behind the saloon. I want to take my wife home first."

"Oh, God." Storm clutched her stomach as the baby lurched inside her. Why did this have to happen now, when they had come so far to attain happiness?

"Sundown," Darnell agreed. "Don't be late or I'll come lookin' fer ya." He flashed Storm a leering grin, then walked away.

Grady scrambled into the driver's seat. "Are you all right, sweetheart?"

"How could you?" Storm screamed, clearly distraught. "Does your word mean nothing? You promised! I hate you, Grady Stryker! I hate you for what you're doing to me and Tim and your unborn baby."

Grady picked up the reins and set the horses into motion before replying to Storm's angry outburst. "I don't intend to break my promise."

"How can you say that when you've just agreed to meet a gunslinger behind the saloon? I never should have returned to Oklahoma with you. It would have been best for all concerned if I had just disappeared from your life. I don't know if I can go through the terrible anguish of losing you."

"You're not going to lose me, sweetheart."

"You're not God, you don't know that."

"As soon as we get home I'll explain what I have in mind. You're too distraught now to think coherently."

Storm lapsed into sullen silence, wondering how many times she would go through this same kind of torture if she stayed with Grady. When they reached the homestead she jumped down from the seat without waiting for Grady to assist her and stomped into the house. She was waiting for him when he returned a short time later after unhitching the team and carrying their supplies inside.

"I'm ready to hear what you have to say now," she challenged hotly.

"Sit down, sweetheart," he said, taking her by the hand and leading her to the couch. "There isn't much time left before I have to return to town, but I'll try to explain what I intend to do. I'm definitely not going to draw against Darnell."

"But you agreed to meet him."

"I had to say something. If I didn't he probably would have forced the issue, and I would have had to kill him. I didn't want you witnessing anything like that. Not in your condition, anyway."

"But—I don't understand. Are you going to meet him and then refuse to draw against him? Or are you not going to show up at all?"

"I'm going to meet him all right, but I'm not going to wear my guns," Grady said quietly.

Storm gasped aloud. "You'd do that for me?"

"For us, and for our children."

"What if it makes no difference to him? What if he kills you anyway? Darnell doesn't strike me as a particularly fair man. He holds some kind of grudge against you."

"I'll just have to take my chances and trust in God. I'm counting on Darnell leaving town and spreading the word once he realizes I mean what I said about no longer being interested in violence."

"He called you a coward," Storm said softly. She knew Grady wasn't the sort to take the insult lightly.

"I've been called worse."

"I love you, Grady Stryker." She slid easily into his arms and he hugged her close. His head lowered and he kissed her fiercely. When he lifted her onto his lap she snuggled happily against him.

"I wish I had time to love you, sweetheart."

"We'll have the rest of our lives," Storm whispered against his lips. Her breath was warm and fragrant and so arousing Grady felt himself harden.

"Wife of my heart," he murmured thickly. "Did you know that's what those Lakota symbols engraved on your wedding band stand for? They say, 'Wife of My Heart.' I knew even then how special you were."

Storm's eyes grew round. "How could that be? You didn't even like me very well when we met."

"I've always loved you, sweetheart."

He cupped the back of her neck and brought her close so he could kiss her again and again, her lips, her cheeks, her chin, before unbuttoning her dress and kissing the tops of her breasts.

"I love your breasts," Grady said as he bared the ripe fruits and drew an engorged nipple into his mouth. "Oh, lady, I want to be inside you." A little moan escaped Storm's lips.

His hand slid under her dress, into the slit in the crotch of her pantaloons, finding that tender, moist place that gave him so much pleasure. He massaged gently while Storm writhed and squirmed in his lap. When he slipped two fingers inside her she jerked wildly. "Grady," she gasped, "I thought you said there wasn't time for this!"

"There is just enough time for what I have in mind," Grady said hoarsely. "Relax, sweetheart, I want to make you happy. When I return tonight you can return the favor." Then he was kissing her again, licking at the corners of her provocative mouth before thrusting his tongue between her lush lips. His fingers plunged deeper, stroking in and out as his thumb worked the sensitive nub of flesh where pleasure began.

"Oh, lady, you feel like silk inside," Grady panted as his talented fingers drove Storm higher and higher.

She arched against his hand, the sweet agony of his deep caress building inside her until she was rocking against him, clutching him desperately and calling his name. When he sucked her nipple into his mouth and nipped it gently with his teeth, then laved it with the wet roughness of his tongue, she exploded in exquisite climax.

Connie Mason

"Keep that thought, sweetheart," Grady said as he lifted Storm and set her gently aside. "When I return tonight we'll continue where we left off." He rose, unbuckled his gunbelt, and set it on the table.

"Grady, be careful!" Storm called to his departing back. Dragging herself from her lethargy, she stood in the open door and watched him ride away.

Grady hadn't been gone five minutes before a numbing fear seized her. A shattering premonition that Grady was walking into certain death made the baby lurch inside her womb. A man like Darnell wouldn't think twice about shooting an unarmed man. Had she sent him off to be killed? That terrifying notion galvanized her into motion. Resolutely she picked up the shotgun sitting in the corner by the door and left the house. It took several precious minutes to hitch the horses to the wagon, but when she finally headed the team toward town she was a scant fifteen minutes behind Grady, who was riding Lightning and able to make better time than she.

Storm arrived in Guthrie at sundown. She halted the wagon in front of the saloon, set the brake, and climbed clumsily to the ground. She looked around fearfully, panting with anxiety. The absence of a crowd and the lack of commotion gave her a brief glimmer of hope. Perhaps she was worrying unnecessarily and everything was going as Grady hoped. Taking up the shotgun, she slipped into the alley between the saloon and the bank, the quickest route to the area behind the saloon where Grady and Darnell were to meet.

The sound of voices made her pause cautiously and listen before rushing out into the open. Barging recklessly into a potentially dangerous situation would do Grady little good. Despite her fear for Grady's safety, she still had her child to protect.

"I'll say one thing fer ya, Renegade, ya got more guts than I gave ya credit fer," Storm heard Darnell say. "Showin' up without yer guns took guts, but it ain't gonna work. I owe ya and ya ain't gonna leave here alive."

"You'll have to shoot me in cold blood," Grady said with amazing calm.

"I've done that before. Besides, ya ain't stupid. Ya wouldn't come here unarmed. Ya got a gun on ya somewhere."

"I told you before, Darnell, I'm through with violence. I won't draw against you. I have nothing to prove, no reputation to uphold. Besides, it's against the law."

"I've broken the law before," Darnell sneered. He gripped the handle of his gun, slowly withdrawing it from his holster. "Say yer prayers, Renegade."

"Listen to me, Darnell," Grady said earnestly. His voice was calm, but inside he was cursing himself for being dumb enough to think Darnell would go on his merry way when he refused to draw against him. "Shooting an unarmed man will gain you nothing but a pack of trouble.

I could have just stayed home and refused to show up, but I wanted to show you and your friends that defending my title as a fast gun and engaging in violence no longer interests me. I'm through with all that. What I hoped you'd do is spread the word that the man known as Renegade no longer exists. He's a peaceful farmer now, with a family to support."

Darnell hesitated for a brief moment while he mulled over Grady's words. Then his features hardened and the gun in his hand steadied and took aim. Still hidden in the crevice of the alleyway, Storm drew in a ragged breath. She loved Grady too much to see him gunned down by a man with no scruples and even less conscience. She could see Darnell's finger slowly squeeze upon the trigger, and in that instant she reacted out of pure instinct and an all-consuming love that knew no right or wrong. After all, it was her fault Grady had gone out unarmed to face a desperate man like Darnell. If she hadn't pried that stupid promise from him, he wouldn't be facing certain death now.

Resolutely, the shotgun came up to her shoulder and she took careful aim, fearing that if she merely shouted a warning Darnell would still have time to squeeze off a shot. Though the light was fading, she saw clearly enough to fix her target and jerk on the trigger. The shot reverberated in her ears, deafening her to Darnell's shot, which was loosed almost at the same instant. Grady lurched sideways in time to avoid all but a grazing wound as the

"I don't think it will any more, sweetheart. I feel certain Darnell will spread the word and I'll be left in peace. Let's go home. If I remember correctly we have some unfinished business there."

"That's what I love about you, Grady. You are most diligent about taking care of unfinished business," Storm said, her eyes twinkling.

"When the unfinished business involves you, lady, it's pure pleasure." He wagged his eyebrows and flashed an impudent grin that made her heart beat faster. "And sweetheart, it's always a pleasure doing business with you."

"Take me home, Grady," Storm sighed happily. "It's time to start the rest of our lives."

# *Epilogue*

*Guthrie, Oklaholma*
*1906*

"Hurry, Mama, Papa says Number One is ready to blow!"

Ten-year-old Chad's blue eyes glowed with excitement as he grabbed Storm's hand and dragged her through the kitchen door.

"Chad, I have a pie in the oven. I can't leave now." Storm laughed at the pure exuberance of her son.

"This is more important than a pie, Mama," Chad said as he cast frantic glances toward the people gathered beside one of the four tall oil rigs rising like dark specters above the golden fields of ripening wheat.

"Let me take the pie out of the oven first

439

and I'll join you in a few minutes," Storm said. "Where's your sister?"

"Tim took her down to Number One when Papa told us the drillers expected the well to come in at any time. She's riding Tim's shoulders and I hope he keeps the little pest from getting in the way."

"Chad," Storm chided gently. "Is that any way to talk about your little sister?" Four-year-old Abby, a small, inky-haired, dimpled darling, was the apple of her father's eye and quite spoiled. Even sixteen-year-old Tim seemed to dote on her, for he carried her around on his broad shoulders whenever he wasn't assisting Grady on the farm.

"Well, Abby is a pest," Chad complained. "She follows me and Tim around like a little puppy."

"Nevertheless, I'll not have you calling Abby a pest. Tim doesn't seem to mind. You go along. I'll be there directly, as soon as I remove the pie from the oven."

"Hurry, Mama, Papa wouldn't want you to miss the gusher." Spinning on his heel, he raced off across the fields.

Storm paused a moment to watch Chad's sturdy legs eat up the distance between the house and Number One before turning back into the house. Her first born was an inquisitive, eager lad whose blue eyes were a replica of his handsome father's. He resembled Grady, in other ways, except for his hair, which was a deep russet. But while Grady and Tim could never deny their Indian heritage, Chad's features gave little hint of his Sioux ancestry. Little Abby, on the other hand, held great promise of turning into a dark, sultry beauty, with shining black hair and dark snapping eyes, just like her grandfather, Swift Blade.

Tim was the big brother of the family, so like Grady it was uncanny. At sixteen he was already a man, broad of shoulder, slim of waist, and as dear to her as her own children. In a few months he would leave for Peaceful Valley for an extended stay with his grandparents, Blade and Shannon. Since the ranch would one day belong to Tim, Blade had suggested that the boy spend time with them learning about ranching and horses. Both Storm and Grady would miss him, but not as much as Chad and Abby, who idolized their big brother.

Turning to her task, Storm slid the pie from the oven and set it on the windowsill to cool. Then she removed her apron and hurried out to join the family. She glanced back toward the house once to make certain the pie was in no danger of falling and experienced a tremendous burst of pride. Grady had built her a wonderful house to take the place of the small cabin they had lived in until several years after Chad's birth. Actually, she had been saddened to see the old cabin torn down, but the new house was everything she could have hoped for.

Two stories tall, it boasted four bedrooms, an honest-to-goodness bathroom with plumbing, a dining room, a parlor, and a large, roomy kitchen, with a separate pantry, where all the family took their meals. Grady even had a small study where he could escape when the children became too rowdy. A front porch running the entire length of the house and a back entry to hold boots and winter coats when weather was blustery completed the rambling wooden structure. Grady had built several new outbuildings and hoped to run more cattle when they could afford it. Of course, if the wells came in, they would no longer have to worry about the cash flow.

There had been many lean years since the locusts had devoured their first crop, but undaunted, Grady had replanted and they had prospered. When oil was discovered in Texas, geologists turned their sights on Oklahoma. The very first well came in in 1905, and when Grady was approached by geologists from a large drilling company asking permission to dig exploratory wells on their property, he gave reluctant consent. Results had been so promising, three more wells had been dug. Now, it looked as if their patience was going to be rewarded.

"Storm, the drillers think it's only a matter of minutes before Number One comes in," Grady cried jubilantly as he spied her hurrying across the field. The entire family was assembled by the huge derrick in anticipation of the big moment. "If they're right we'll be rich beyond our wildest dreams. The children can go to the best colleges and have all that money can buy."

He held out his arms, and when she rushed into them he pulled her hard against the taut strength of his lean body.

Breathlessly Storm was drawn into the warmth of his embrace, savoring the closeness she shared with the man who had become the great love of her life. Never would she cease to need this special man, to feel his arms around her, making her feel loved and cherished. In the years since he had retired his guns and promised to avoid violence, he had never given her cause to doubt him.

"The children don't need money to be happy," Storm said, hugging Grady fiercely. "You have instilled courage in them, given them love, and taught them respect."

Grady's eyes were suspiciously moist as he gazed down at her. "And you, wife of my heart, have made our lives special."

The words were no sooner out of his mouth than an ominous rumble emanated from deep in the bowels of the earth, shaking the ground beneath them.

"Here she comes! Get back everyone, it's going to be a gusher!" one of the drillers cried. Men began scattering in all directions as the rumble grew louder. Grady grasped Storm's hand and pulled her back, shouting for the children to stand clear.

With a mighty roar the top of the derrick seemed to explode as a thunderous spray of dark liquid spewed upward. Storm felt the heavy drops pepper her skin and clothing and looked down, expecting to see thick black sludge. Instead, she saw what looked like muddy water.

"Grady, what is it? It looks like dirty water."

"Be patient, sweetheart," Grady cautioned as he kept his eyes glued to the erupting well. Suddenly, he gave a mighty whoop, picked up Storm, and swung her around and around, laughing uproariously. "Look, Storm, look up!"

Storm's eyes shot upward, and her face was immediately covered with a thick, inky film. She glanced at Grady, and saw that his face was so grimy with black sludge that all she could see were his white teeth and the whites of his eyes. A resounding cheer went up as a tremendous pressure from inside the well shot a stream of oil high into the clear Oklahoma sky, as thick and black as the darkest midnight.

# The OUTLAWS: Rafe

## Connie Mason

He is going to hang. Rafe Gentry has committed plenty of sins, but not the robbery and murder that has landed him in jail. Now, with a lynch mob out for his blood, he is staring death in the face . . . until a blond beauty with the voice of an angel steps in to redeem him.

She is going to wed. There is only one way to rescue the dark and dangerous outlaw from the hanging tree—by claiming him as the fictitious fiancé she is to meet in Pueblo. But Sister Angela Abbot never anticipates that she will have to make good on her claim and actually marry the rogue. Railroaded into a hasty wedding, reeling from the raw, seductive power of Rafe's kiss, she wonders whether she has made the biggest mistake of her life, or the most exciting leap of faith.

___4702-0                           $5.99 US/$6.99 CAN

**Dorchester Publishing Co., Inc.**
**P.O. Box 6640**
**Wayne, PA 19087-8640**

Please add $1.75 for shipping and handling for the first book and $.50 for each book thereafter. NY, NYC, and PA residents, please add appropriate sales tax. No cash, stamps, or C.O.D.s. All orders shipped within 6 weeks via postal service book rate. Canadian orders require $2.00 extra postage and must be paid in U.S. dollars through a U.S. banking facility.

Name_____
Address_____
City_____State_____Zip_____
I have enclosed $_____ in payment for the checked book(s).
Payment <u>must</u> accompany all orders. ❑ Please send a free catalog.

... and coming
May 2001
from. . .

# THE OUTLAWS: SAM — CONNIE MASON

Down and out, his face on wanted posters across the West, Sam Gentry needs a job. And the foreman of the B & G ranch is hiring cowhands. But who is the behind-the-scenes owner the ramrod mentioned? Surely this Lacey isn't the same one who has haunted his dreams for the last five years. This Texas rancher can't possibly be the dyed-in-the-wool Yankee whose betrayal sent him to a Northern prison camp. Most unlikely of all, this widowed mother simply cannot be the hot-blooded wife who once warmed his bed. Yet one look in her emerald eyes tells him the impossible has happened. How can he take a paycheck from the golden-haired beauty when what he really wants to do is take her back in his arms?

___4865-5 $5.99 US/$6.99 CAN

**Dorchester Publishing Co., Inc.**
**P.O. Box 6640**
**Wayne, PA 19087-8640**

Please add $1.75 for shipping and handling for the first book and $.50 for each book thereafter. NY, NYC, and PA residents, please add appropriate sales tax. No cash, stamps, or C.O.D.s. All orders shipped within 6 weeks via postal service book rate. Canadian orders require $2.00 extra postage and must be paid in U.S. dollars through a U.S. banking facility.

Name_____
Address_____
City_____ State_____ Zip_____
I have enclosed $ _____ in payment for the checked book(s).
Payment <u>must</u> accompany all orders. ❑ Please send a free catalog.
CHECK OUT OUR WEBSITE! www.dorchesterpub.com

# ATTENTION ROMANCE CUSTOMERS!

## SPECIAL
## TOLL-FREE NUMBER
### 1-800-481-9191

*Call Monday through Friday
10 a.m. to 9 p.m.
Eastern Time
Get a free catalogue,
join the Romance Book Club,
and order books using your
Visa, MasterCard,
or Discover®*

Leisure
Books

Love
Spell

**GO ONLINE WITH US AT DORCHESTERPUB.COM**